A mysterious discovery off the c
Dane Maddock and his intrepi
legendary hero, and in the c
international conspiracy bent on
hidden forever.

PRAISE FOR DAVID WOOD AND THE DANE MADDOCK ADVENTURES!

A great read that provides lots of action, and thoughtful insight as well, into strange realms that are sometimes best left unexplored." Paul Kemprecos, author of Cool Blue Tomb

"Dane and Bones.... Together they're unstoppable. Rip-roaring action from start to finish. Wit and humor throughout. Just one question - how soon until the next one? Because I can't wait." Graham Brown, author of Shadows of the Midnight Sun

"David Wood has done it again. Quest takes you on an expedition that leads down a trail of adventure and thrills!" David L. Golemon, Author of the Event Group series

"Ancient cave paintings? Cities of gold? Secret scrolls? Sign me up! A twisty tale of adventure and intrigue that never lets up and never lets go!" Robert Masello, author of The Medusa Amulet

"A non-stop thrill ride triple threat- smart, funny and mysterious!" Jeremy Robinson, author of Instinct and Threshold

"Let there be no confusion: David Wood is the next Clive Cussler." Edward G. Talbot, author of 2010: The Fifth World

THE ELEMENTALS

A DANE MADDOCK ADVENTURE

DAVID WOOD
SEAN ELLIS

This omnibus edition includes:

OUTPOST
Copyright 2018 by David Wood
All rights reserved

ARCANUM
Copyright 2018 by David Wood
All rights reserved

MAGUS
Copyright 2018 by David Wood
All rights reserved

Published by Adrenaline Press
www.adrenaline.press

Adrenaline Press is an imprint of Gryphonwood Press
www.gryphonwoodpress.com

This is a work of fiction. All characters are products of
the authors' imaginations or are used fictitiously.

ISBN: 978-1-950920-13-6

BOOKS and SERIES by DAVID WOOD

Cavern
Devils' Face
Herald
Brainwash
The Tomb
Shasta

Jade Ihara Adventures (with Sean Ellis)
Oracle
Changeling
Exile

Bones Bonebrake Adventures
Primitive
The Book of Bones
Skin and Bones

Jake Crowley Adventures (with Alan Baxter)
Sanctum
Blood Codex
Anubis Key
Revenant

Brock Stone Adventures
Arena of Souls
Track of the Beast (forthcoming)

Myrmidon Files (with Sean Ellis)
Destiny
Mystic

Sam Aston Investigations (with Alan Baxter)
Primordial
Overlord

Stand-Alone Novels
Into the Woods (with David S. Wood)
Callsign: Queen (with Jeremy Robinson)
Dark Rite (with Alan Baxter)

David Wood writing as David Debord

The Absent Gods Trilogy
The Silver Serpent
Keeper of the Mists
The Gates of Iron

The Impostor Prince (with Ryan A. Span)
Neptune's Key
The Zombie-Driven Life
You Suck

BOOKS and SERIES by SEAN ELLIS

The Nick Kismet Adventures
The Shroud of Heaven
Into the Black
The Devil You Know (Novella)
Fortune Favors

The Adventures of Dodge Dalton
In the Shadow of Falcon's Wings
At the Outpost of Fate
On the High Road to Oblivion
Against the Fall of Eternal Night (with Kerry Frey)

The Mira Raiden Adventures
Ascendant
Descendant

Magic Mirror
The Sea Wraiths and Other Tales
Camp Zero
WarGod (with Steven Savile)

(with Jeremy Robinson)
Prime
Savage
Cannibal
Empire
Herculean
Helios
Flood Rising
Callsign: King (novella)

OUTPOST

Book One of The Elementals

PROLOGUE

The massive aircraft raced across the surface of the dark water, churning up froth and cutting a broad wake as it fought its way through the choppy waves. Dodge Dalton focused on its silver outline, his heart falling even as the plane took off and slowly gained altitude. He let out a whispered curse, watched it shrink from sight in the distance.

We've failed.

Cold wind and salty spray spattered his face, running down his cheeks in rivulets like tears, but the despair he felt was beyond sadness. He fought to suppress the images that flashed through his mind, the evils that would be unleashed. Breath came in gulps, rage ran in tremors through his body. Thousands of miles from civilization, no help coming, and nothing he could do. He felt impotent.

"There's another plane!" Hurley's cry jarred him from his reverie. He pointed at a diminutive craft floating on the swells. "It's the Duck!"

The Grumman JF "Duck" was a single-engine amphibious biplane. Compared to the massive X-314 that was even now drawing farther away, it was like a fly on an elephant's backside. But it was all they had. And though it lacked the larger craft's range, it was every bit as fast.

His heart raced. A scant hope remained.

Molly's on that plane. And the president. We have to try.

They made their way to the floating plane, steadying themselves atop its pontoons as the tiny craft rose and fell along with each cresting swell. They piled in as quickly as they dared. Dodge settled into the pilot's well while the others slid into the observer's compartment. He took a moment to familiarize himself with the controls before starting up the Wright Cyclone engine. All the while he was keenly aware that the X-314 was getting farther away with each second that passed.

The tiny plain surged forward, battered to and fro by the waves until it gained sufficient speed to take to the sky. The craft banked and yawed, the turbulent sea churning just feet beneath the tips of its wings as it teetered its way skyward. Dodge was impressed that his companions chose not to critique or react to his flying as he overcorrected several times before getting the feel of the plane.

He guided the plane upward on a steep trajectory, seeking to climb above the weather and give them a better chance of spotting their quarry. He kept the throttle wide open as he fought to gain ground on their quarry. What did it matter if he burned out the engine? If they didn't catch up with the X-314, so much more would be lost.

Hurley served as navigator, guiding them along the larger plane's path, until they finally spotted it, its running lights twinkling in the distance. For the first time since the chase had begun, he felt a glimmer of hope. Hoping luck was finally on their side, he nudged the engine a little farther into the red, gaining another five knots of speed, then turned the aircraft into a dive, gaining a couple more.

The lights grew larger and brighter. Dodge's heart leaped as the Duck ate up the intervening airspace. He glanced down at the fuel gauge. It had been at half-a-tank when they took off, and now it was down to a quarter. It was going to be a close thing. They had to close the remaining space and make their move before the engines ran dry. He resisted the urge to look down at the dark sea as he contemplated the possibility that it would be his grave.

He glanced over his shoulder toward his companions seated in the rear of the cockpit. . "When we get close enough, try to shoot out the engines. If we can force them to land, maybe we'll have a chance."

Each man replied in the affirmative. They were disciplined soldiers and would not disobey an order from their leader, no matter how mad it might sound.

The enormous flying boat seemed to materialize in front of them, a dark spot growing larger, details becoming visible. Once again he marveled at its size. It was difficult to believe that such a behemoth could even float, much less fly.

Hurley pushed the cowling back and leaned out of one side of the plane, Hobbs the other. Dodge brought the Duck up above the Boeing and then dove, giving his companions the best possible field of fire.

Light flashed and sparks flew as the men scored hits on both starboard engines. The inner propeller continued to spin but smoke poured from the outer. Dodge brought the plane up again to assess the damage before making another attack run, but was forced to roll the plane as the Boeing's weapons returned fire.

"Damn!" He had hoped the Boeing's occupants would have taken a bit longer to register the tiny plane's presence, but no such luck. What was more, the damage they had dealt to its engine was sufficient to draw the crew's attention, but not enough to slow the plane's progress. He rolled again as another burst of fire threatened to knock them from the sky.

The Duck took a glancing hit to the fuselage, forcing Dodge to take it into a dive, and then climb again as the Boeing's gunners adjusted their fire.

"What now?" Hurley shouted.

Dodge had only one answer. The Boeing was too large, could withstand too much damage. He had to do something desperate, crazy. Heart in his throat, he shouted back to his men.

"Hang on! And be ready to move!"

He didn't add that there was a fair chance none of them would be able to move when this was over. But they had certain protections, high-tech exoskeletons, that would keep them safe.

He hoped.

Here goes nothing.

He pushed the stick forward and the tiny craft dove like a bird of prey. Closer, closer…

And then it swooped down onto the tail section of the giant X-314. The Duck's propeller blades sliced through the aluminum skin like hot knives through melted butter. With an ear-splitting shriek and a thunderous boom, the Duck smashed into the Boeing's cabin.

Dodge, he thought as the Duck's wings snapped off and its remaining fuel sprayed out onto the deck and a spark from the smoldering engine set it alight, *you'd better hope you haven't killed us all.*

1

"We got a hit!"

Dane Maddock looked away from the view through the forward windscreen—a vast, limitless expanse of deep sapphire blue water, dazzling in the afternoon sun—and over to the console where his friend Corey Dean sat hunched over the display of a laptop computer. Before Maddock could ask Corey to elaborate, the imposing six-and-a-half-foot tall form of Maddock's partner and soon-to-be brother-in-law, Uriah "Bones" Bonebrake, appeared in the doorway behind him.

"Did we find it?" Bones asked, eagerly.

"Not sure what we found," Corey said, peering at the screen. "It's big."

"That's what she said," Bones quipped.

Corey studied the image a few seconds longer, then leaned back with a disappointed sigh. "But it's not big enough."

"That's what she said to Maddock," Bones said.

Maddock, who had long ago developed an immunity to his friend's off-color put downs, heard the note of disappointment in Bones' voice. "What are we looking at, Corey?"

Corey turned the screen so Maddock could see it from the helm station. The image was orange and grainy, a computer-generated visual interpretation of sound waves bouncing off the sea floor. To an untrained eye, it looked like so much static, but Maddock had seen enough side-scan sonar profiles to recognize the straight lines of a manmade object. Corey however was the expert.

"It's in several pieces. Whatever it was broke up before it reached the bottom. This largest piece is what got my attention. It's long and narrow—"

Maddock leveled a finger at Bones. "Don't say it."

Bones just kept grinning.

"I'd say about a hundred feet in length," Corey said. "The *Waratah* was five hundred feet long. There's not enough debris to indicate a ship that large."

Maddock stared at the image intently. "Judging by the shape, I'd be more inclined to say we're looking at an aircraft. Anything like that on the charts?"

"Let me check." Corey tapped in a few commands, then managed a hopeful grin. "Nope. We're the first to record anything here."

'Here' was the waters of the continental shelf about two hundred miles off the tip of South Africa. Maddock and his treasure-hunting crew—Bones and Corey, along with Willis Sanders and Matt Barnaby—were plying the waters of the southern hemisphere aboard his 80-foot motor yacht *Sea Foam*, halfway around the world from their usual stomping grounds in the Atlantic, to investigate the almost legendary disappearance of the *S.S. Waratah*.

In 1909, the *Waratah*, a five-hundred-foot-long cargo-liner with 211 passengers and crew aboard, had left Durban for Cape Town, on its way to London, and promptly vanished. Subsequent searches for the missing ship had only deepened the mystery.

Early on, it was believed that the *Waratah* was still afloat, abandoned and adrift, but extremely high seas prevented Royal Navy search vessels from entering the area where the ship was thought to be. Ten days later, the

Australian government received a cable notifying them that a ship believed to be the *Waratah* had been spotted, steaming toward Durban, but that ship, whatever it was, never reached port. Three days after that, two different ships reported seeing bodies in the water near the mouth of a river two hundred miles southwest of Durban, but none were positively identified as passengers from the missing vessel. In 1912, a life-preserver with the name of the ship washed up in New Zealand, and thirteen years after that, a pilot flying over the same section of coast reported a wreck that he believed was the *Waratah*. Subsequent attempts to locate the wreck had failed to produce anything remotely definitive, but despite, or perhaps because of those failures, the quest to find the *Waratah* had taken on an almost mythic quality. Some had taken to calling it Australia's Titanic.

Maddock thought it was a fool's errand, but a wealthy action-adventure novelist with a passion for finding lost shipwrecks had come to him with a lucrative contract to conduct yet another search for the legendary vessel, this time in open water rather than along the coast where all previous expeditions had focused their attention. It was an offer Maddock couldn't reasonably refuse. Even if the search yielded no results, which was the most probable outcome, it was a valuable connection that might lead to other, more rewarding expeditions.

Now it seemed, the deal had produced some unexpected, if unrelated fruit.

"Finding the *Waratah* was always a long shot, but maybe we can solve another maritime mystery that slipped through the cracks." He pulled the throttle controls back, reversing the screws. "Might as well get some pictures before we go."

Bones grinned. "I'll get Uma prepped."

Uma was Bones' nickname for their ROV—remotely operated underwater vehicle. Although Maddock and Bones, along with their fellow crewman Willis Sanders, were all former Navy SEALs and experienced divers, there were limits to what they could accomplish with SCUBA equipment. Uma could go places that they simply could not. Places like the ocean floor nearly half-a-mile beneath *Sea Foam*'s hull.

By the time Maddock had the boat positioned above the location Corey had identified, Bones was ready to put Uma in the water. The little submersible was equipped with a high-resolution digital video camera and a powerful searchlight, but there was very little to see during the descent. The screen displaying Uma's video feed remained an unchanging black, so Maddock kept his eye on the horizon. The seas were thankfully calm, but the area they were in, at the boundary between the Indian and Atlantic Oceans, was known for rogue waves, one of which had probably been responsible for sinking the *Waratah*. Conditions under the water would be even more challenging since the collision of oceans created extraordinarily strong submerged currents. Bones was uncharacteristically subdued, focused intently on piloting Uma into the depths.

It took about fifteen minutes for the little submersible to reach the bottom and another five to locate the wreck. Maddock now turned his attention to the video screen, watching as Uma's searchlight and camera revealed the submerged landscape. The sea floor was uniformly flat and everything was a dull beige, the color of sediment. Then, with almost no warning, the wreck appeared.

"As usual, Maddock," Bones announced. "You were half-right,"

Maddock saw immediately what his friend meant. Although lightly dusted by an accretion of sediment, there was no mistaking what they were looking at: not one, but two airplane fuselages, though it was hard to tell where one ended and the other began. The aircraft were entangled like conjoined twins.

Corey shook his head in disbelief. "How did that happen?"

"Probably a mid-air collision," Maddock said. "Looks like the smaller plane almost took the tail off the bigger one."

Bones moved Uma in closer, revealing broken struts and the stubs where the wings had been sheared off. The smaller plane was about one-third the size of the other, and appeared to have been a biplane with an open cockpit. The larger aircraft actually did look more like a ship at first glance, with a wide-body that seemed better suited to riding on the high seas than cruising at high altitude, but part of one wing remained attached, complete with a single engine nacelle, sprouting three twisted propeller blades.

"Talk about a blast from the past," Corey said. "Those are vintage. How old do you think they are?"

Maddock shook his head. "Hard to say. Bones, try blowing some of that silt away. See if you can find any identifying marks."

Bones brought the ROV in even closer, until it was practically sitting in the crumpled cockpit of the smaller biplane, then turned it around and hit the thrusters, sending out a blast of water that stirred up the sediment. Uma shot away, but Bones quickly brought her back around and shone the spotlight into the cloud rising above the wreck. It only took a few minutes for the current to sweep away the sediment, revealing the instrument panel and old-fashioned stick controls. There were actually two seats in the cockpit, but both were empty. Either the crew had bailed out before the crash, or their bones had long since dissolved away.

Seeing nothing distinctive enough to make an identification of the aircraft, Bones pulled Uma back and then cautiously piloted her through the gaping hole in the top of the larger plane's fuselage.

Maddock felt a chill as the bulkheads comprising the plane's interior seemed to close around him. Unlike the cockpit of the smaller biplane, this felt much more like a place where men had died, sealed into a coffin for burial at sea. The interior reminded him a little of the cargo bay of a modern military transport plane, which perhaps contributed to his sense of foreboding. He wasn't claustrophobic, but he felt strangely anxious, and had to resist the urge to tell Bones to back away.

Uma moved down the length of the cargo bay, the camera scanning every shadowy corner for anything that might help identify the aircraft but as with the smaller plane, there were no distinguishing features.

"Might as well wrap it up," Maddock said. "We can get some more exterior shots and send them to Jimmy. Maybe he can do some computer magic and get us a positive ID."

If anyone could identify the wrecked airplanes from photographs, it was Maddock's old pal Jimmy Letson. Jimmy was both an ace investigative reporter and a computer whiz, and frequently helped Maddock out with research into subjects ranging from ancient shipwrecks to diabolical global conspiracies.

"Wait a sec," Bones said, backing Uma up and tilting her down a few degrees. "Look at that."

The image on the screen showed a misshapen triangle, made of what appeared to be black metal, lying on the deck, partly buried in silt.

"What is that?" Corey said. "A piece of the propeller?"

"It looks more like an axe head," Maddock said. "The wooden handle probably rotted away."

"Close." Bones brought the ROV in even closer until the object almost filled up the screen. "It's a tomahawk."

Maddock glanced over at his friend, skeptically. "You're sure?"

"Trust me on this, *kemosabe.*"

Maddock almost regretted having raised the question. Bones, a Cherokee Indian, was not likely to make a mistake about that.

Bones traced the outline of the object on the screen. "You can tell by the curve of the blade, and this spike on the back end. They don't really make 'em like that anymore."

"What I mean is, what's a tomahawk doing on an old airplane off the coast of South Africa?"

"Looks like there's an engraving on it," Corey said, peering at the close-up. "Can't make out what it says. A name maybe? And that looks like a date on the bottom. Nineteen-fifty-eight. Wow. You're right, Bones. That is old."

Maddock stared at the screen for a minute. "That's not a nine. It's a seven. Seventeen-fifty-eight."

Corey looked again, wide-eyed. "Holy crap."

Maddock nodded. "I think we should bring it up."

2

From the comfort of his apartment in the Washington DC metro-area, Jimmy Letson watched the feed from Uma's camera. He allowed the video to play through completely before winding it back to what he thought was the best shot of the wrecked airplanes and froze the playback there. With a couple of mouse-clicks he was easily able to isolate the airframe and create a three-dimensional model, which he then compared against the Jane's aircraft identification database.

"Easy peasy," he announced just thirty seconds later. "Your wreck is a Boeing 314, sometimes called a Clipper."

It took a few seconds for the Skype transmission to bounce through Jimmy's extensive proxy-chain network to reach Maddock's computer on the far side of the world, and then for Maddock's reply to return. "Clipper? One of the old flying boats from the 1930's?"

"Like the plane in *Raiders of the Lost Ark*?" Bones chimed in. "The red line express."

Jimmy grinned. "Right. Although that scene is a bit anachronistic. The 314 wasn't produced until 1938, which was two years after Raiders supposedly took place."

"What can you tell us about this specific plane?" Maddock asked.

"Without tail numbers or some other identifier, not much." Jimmy tapped in a few keystrokes. "Oh. That's strange." He reread the data on the screen, wondering if he had overlooked something.

"What's strange?"

"Well, it turns out that only twelve Clippers were ever produced, which would ordinarily make this a pretty simple process of elimination. But it looks like all twelve are accounted for. Only two of them crashed— neither one anywhere close to where you are—and both were scuttled in place. All the rest were scrapped for parts."

"Could those records be wrong?"

"Possibly," Jimmy admitted. "The Clipper fleet was pressed into war time service. Maybe one of the planes was requisitioned for a secret mission and to cover it up, they listed it as scrapped. I'll have to do a little more digging into that."

"What about the smaller plane?"

"Not enough left of it for me to work my magic. I'm good, but not that good."

"Sounds like he's holding out on us," Bones said after a moment.

"I wish I were," Jimmy said. "But even if I could narrow it down to a specific airframe design, we'd still be looking at hundreds of possibilities, and unlike a big passenger plane, a lot of those old biplanes ended up in private hands. Some are probably still flying today."

"Fair enough," Maddock said. "Okay, switching gears. I'm sending you pics of the tomahawk we found."

While he waited for the image file to arrive, Jimmy played with various search strings that included terms like: Clipper; Africa; crash; missing. One of the crashed 314's had been originally called the *Cape Town Clipper*, but its demise had occurred off the coast of Portugal, thousands of miles from where Maddock had discovered the sunken aircraft. After a few minutes, he tabled the effort. Identifying the wreck was going to take some real digging which oddly pleased him. He liked a challenge.

A chime sounded to alert him to the arrival of a file attachment. He opened it and saw a photograph of an axe head with a sharp spike on the back end. The metal was dark, almost black, without any signs of corrosion. A second photograph was a close-up of the engraving on the flared blade.

Steven Thorne
28, April 1758

"President Monroe was born that day," Maddock supplied. "I doubt that's relevant."

Jimmy knew that Maddock wouldn't have enlisted his help without first trying his own hand at the Google game, but Maddock wasn't a professional researcher. "That would have been smack in the middle of the French and Indian War. Tomahawks were issued to colonial militia. They weren't just used by Indians, you know."

"No kidding," Bones rumbled, with just a hint of sarcasm. "So that Mel Gibson movie wasn't total crap after all?"

Jimmy let the comment slide. "I'd guess this Thorne was a militia officer. There are records of that stuff believe it or not, but most of them haven't been digitized."

"Our working theory is that the tomahawk was a family heirloom that belonged to a member of the plane's crew," Maddock said. "One of Steven Thorne's descendants. If you can trace his genealogy, we might be able to figure out who it was, and from there, figure out what he was doing on that plane."

"Not bad, Maddock. I can definitely try that." Jimmy scrolled through the results of his cursory search. "Thorne was already a very common surname in colonial America. Particularly in New York." He drummed his fingers on the desktop. "I might be able to whittle the list down a bit, but I'm limited to what's actually been put into the online databases, and that may only be a fraction of what's available. Your best bet would be to talk to a historian, someone who specializes in the colonial period. Show them that tomahawk, and they'll probably talk your ear off."

The silence went on too long to merely be the result of signal lag. Maddock had clearly and simply hit the disconnect button, eager to get started on what had the makings of an honest-to-goodness historical mystery.

There were, as he saw it, three possible solutions.

The first, was that his preliminary identification might have been wrong. He had initially rejected that possibility since there were no other planes that matched both the dimensions and shape of the airframe. The closest similar aircraft, the Martin M-130, had a similar profile, but was nearly twenty feet shorter than the Boeing 314. As aviation technology improved during the war years, the need for large aircraft with water-landing abilities diminished, and designers began favoring a more streamlined cylindrical fuselage design, as compared to the Clipper, which was almost square in profile.

The second possible solution—and the likeliest—was what he had suggested to Maddock: an error—intentional or accidental—in the historical record. He started by verifying the accuracy of reports concerning the fate of the twelve Clippers, which he was able to do up to a point. The records did exist, but not in such detail that he could rule out a falsification or cover-up. When he felt he had exhausted that line of research, he turned to the third possibility: the existence of an unrecorded thirteenth Clipper.

Figuring he could kill two birds with one stone, he surreptitiously probed—Maddock would have said 'hacked,' but Jimmy disliked the term—Boeing's archives looking for more detailed records of the 314 aircraft project. He spent a good half-hour browsing the logs of the twelve known aircraft, before expanding the search parameters to look for unlucky number thirteen. He noted that the Clipper tail numbers ranged from NC18601 to NC18612, with three exceptions—the seventh, eighth and tenth planes—had been sold to Great Britain and issued new tail numbers. On a whim, he tried looking for NC18613, and then NC18600, but neither search yielded anything meaningful. He tried several different approaches to no better effect, before deciding to take a break from the search. There were other avenues available to him. If nothing else panned out, he could probably find some answers, or at least some better questions, on an aircraft history forum. He clicked on the X to close the browser window and stood up to stretch his legs.

When he looked down again, he saw that the browser was still open. Frowning, he moved the cursor over the X again, and clicked on it, but the screen refused to wink out. He tried the shortcut keys, and saw a message appear on the header: (Not responding).

Jimmy Letson felt a sudden chill. He quickly entered the shortcut to bring up the task manager, but the computer seemed to be ignoring him.

To an ordinary computer user, that would be an annoyance, but to Jimmy, it felt like staring into the abyss.

Somebody had taken note of his intrusion.

"Not possible," he whispered. But what other explanation could there be?

Without a moment's hesitation, he threw the master power switch, killing the flow of electricity not only to the computer, but also to the network of router-repeaters he used to hide his physical location from the World Wide Web.

The risk of getting caught had long ago ceased to be a source of thrills for Jimmy. He kept his hacks very low profile, and utilized redundant proxy chains to reduce the chances of anyone back-tracing his IP address. The repeater network, which stretched across two suburban Virginia neighborhoods, was his last line of defense—removing him from the physical location associated with the IP address. That system was bombproof, he was sure of it....

Mostly sure of it.

He waited ninety seconds before restoring power and booting up the system, one subroutine at a time, running diagnostics as he went to see if anything had been compromised. Lastly, he started up the repeater network and accessed the Web.

Despite the fact that he kept his apartment a mild sixty-eight degrees, Jimmy was sweating. "It's nothing," he told himself. "You're just jumping at shadows, ace."

He brought up the connection logs for the chain of IP proxy servers, but that was as far as he got. When he tried to edit the logs, he received an error message informing him to contact the system administrator.

"Locked out," he whispered.

He hit the power switch again and stood up quickly, backing away from the computer as if it were red hot.

Hollywood depictions notwithstanding, tracing someone's IP address, particularly when the connection was routed through multiple international proxies, was a challenging and time-consuming process. The fact that someone had blocked his access to the connection logs of servers in six different countries, to effectively prevent him from wiping away his digital fingerprints, indicated that he had just woken up one hell of a big sleeping giant.

He couldn't erase the source IP address, that much was certain. The unknown hunter would trace it back to a trendy coffee shop that Jimmy had never once visited, and that would be the end of that, provided he never tried logging in with that IP address ever again.

At least he hoped that was the case.

What if they find the repeaters?

He shook his head. No. He was a needle in a haystack. As long as he kept his head down, he would be fine.

But maybe it was time for a nice vacation. A road trip.

As he headed out the door, he wondered exactly what it was he had blundered into. He couldn't believe that an eighty-year old plane crash was a secret big enough to necessitate such a swift and decisive response, but what other explanation was there?

He would have to get word to Maddock somehow. Warn him to back off, lay low.

If it wasn't already too late.

3

Maddock glanced over his shoulder, taking one last look at Durban harbor, and then steered *Sea Foam* south, toward the search area. With its sub-tropical climate, palm trees and festive, touristy vibe, Durban, South Africa reminded him a lot of Miami, South Beach, and that made him think about Key West, which in turn made him homesick. It was a new feeling for him, and probably had something to do with the fact that, for the first time in a long time, there was somebody waiting at home for him.

Well, not literally.

Angelica Bonebrake, a professional mixed-martial-arts fighter, was training for an upcoming championship bout, and that left her with little time—or energy—for domestic pursuits. That was fine with Maddock. They were both independent people with careers that meant a great deal to them, and were more than comfortable with the idea that there would be times when they wouldn't see a lot of each other.

Still, he was a bit surprised at how much he missed her, and felt the mildest twinge of jealousy toward Bones and Willis who were probably somewhere over the Atlantic, on their way back to the States to follow up on the tomahawk head, while he was stuck with what he knew in his gut would be a fruitless search for a ship that refused to be found. Normally, that wouldn't have bothered him. He liked being on the water, liked looking for things that had eluded everyone else, but right now, the mystery that was calling to him was not the *Waratah*, but Steven Thorne's pre-Revolutionary War axe and the as-yet-unidentified plane wreck where it had evidently spent the better part of a century. Unfortunately, he was the boss, and that meant he had to stay focused on the job at hand, running grids until he could say with certainty where the *Waratah* wasn't. Besides, Bones was probably better suited to chasing the mystery of the tomahawk than he was, and since they couldn't both leave the operation, Willis was the logical choice to accompany Bones and keep him out of trouble, which even Bones would admit was probably a good idea.

He was also disappointed that Jimmy had not gotten back to him. Usually, he could count on his old friend coming up with answers to the stickiest research questions in a matter of hours, if not mere minutes, but it had been twelve hours since Jimmy ended the Skype call, and in that time Maddock had not heard a peep from the hacker.

Maybe he had finally handed Jimmy a nut that couldn't be cracked.

The answer, whatever it was, would probably have to wait a few more days. While Maddock had a satellite phone, capable of both voice and data transmissions, satellite coverage in the region was iffy at best, which was the primary reason why they had been obliged to make the unscheduled port call.

Quit stalling, he told himself. *Time to get back to work.*

Maddock and his two remaining crew members—Corey and Matt Barnaby—took turns at the helm for the ten-hour cruise back to the search area. It was just after midnight when they reached their destination, but since they didn't need daylight to look for shipwrecks on the sea floor, they immediately deployed the sonar "fish" and started down the next lane on the search grid at a sedate twelve knots. Maddock knew that the lane would eventually bring them close to the spot where they had found the crashed planes and expected to find more debris, but that wouldn't happen for at least a couple hours. What he did not expect however was a radar contact on the surface.

"Where did he come from?" Corey asked.

Maddock eyed the orange blob on the radar display. It had appeared suddenly, blinking into existence seemingly from out of nowhere. The signature was too well-defined to be a cloud and too small to be a rogue wave. It had to be another vessel, and it was coming after them at a speed of about twenty-five knots.

"We're outside the shipping lanes," Corey said. "What's he doing out here?"

Maddock could think of only one answer. "He's looking for us."

He grabbed a pair of binoculars and headed out onto the open deck, but all he could see through the high-powered glasses was inky blackness. The approaching vessel was running dark.

"Corey," he called out, still sweeping the horizon with the binoculars. "Bring in the fish." Then he added, "Matt, prepare to repel boarders."

Corey poked his head out from the bridge. "Seriously?"

"Seriously," Maddock said. "Pull in the fish."

"I meant the other part. Repel boarders?"

"Let's hope it doesn't come to that," Maddock said, but he knew hope alone wouldn't do the trick. While he couldn't begin to guess at their motive, there was little question in his mind that the other vessel had hostile intentions.

While Corey reeled in the towed sonar array, Matt—a former-Army Ranger—broke out their arsenal, which consisted of a single AR-15 and two semi-automatic pistols: a Colt M1911 and Maddock's favorite, a Walther P99. He handed Maddock the latter, and kept the other two weapons for himself.

"So what are we dealing with? Pirates?"

"Your guess is as good as mine, but I'd rather not wait around to ask them in person." Maddock stuffed the gun in his waistband and passed the binoculars to Matt. "They're coming in from our four o'clock. I'll try to outrun them."

Matt took the glasses and started scanning the water to starboard while Maddock returned to the helm station. The radar screen showed the approaching vessel was less than two nautical miles away from them and still closing fast. As soon as Corey gave the signal, Maddock pushed the throttles to full.

They immediately pulled away from the pursuer, but within minutes, the gap was shrinking again. The skipper of the other boat had somehow found a way to wring another five knots out of his craft, which was just a little faster than *Sea Foam*'s maximum cruising speed.

Maddock considered his options. If he redlined *Sea Foam*'s engines, he might be able to squeeze a little more speed from them, but at the risk of doing permanent damage and even then, there was no guarantee that they would be able to elude the hunters. In fact, it was far more likely that they would blow a gasket or throw a screw long before reaching safe harbor, at which point they would be completely at the mercy of the pursuer.

If he didn't, the other ship would overtake them within the hour. Sooner or later, the hunters would catch up to them.

Maddock reached for the throttle, but instead of pushing it forward, he drew it back all the way.

Full stop.

Matt stuck his head in a few seconds later. "What's wrong?"

"You know that old saying about the best defense being a good offense? We're about to put it to the test."

4

As soon as he was out of the cab and standing on the sidewalk, Bones hugged his arms across his chest and grimaced. "Frigging Maddock."

Willis looked back at him. "What are you whining about now?"

"'I should stay with the boat,'" Bones said, in a mocking falsetto. "'Bones, you're the adventurous one. You should go.' You think he didn't know it was below freezing here?"

Willis shook his head. "Man, first of all, it was your idea to come here…" He took out his phone and tapped the screen a couple times to bring up a local weather report. "Where it's actually forty-one degrees, which ain't below freezing. Second…that's about the worst Maddock impersonation I've ever heard."

Bones rolled his eyes. "Kiss ass. Where else were we going to go to do research on an artifact from the French and Indian War? Honolulu?"

"Fine. Let's get inside. I know how sensitive you are to cold temperatures."

"What the hell is that supposed to mean? And don't say a thing about shrinkage."

Willis just grinned and started up the walk to the front doors of Park Hall, where the History Department of University at Buffalo was located.

Despite Bones' comment, they had not come to the upstate New York locale simply because of its proximity to the battlefields of a war that was even older than America. During the long flight from South Africa,

Bones had put in a call to Avery Halsey. Avery was Maddock's half-sister and Bones' ex-girlfriend—one of many—and worked for a special CIA task force, which he and Maddock sometimes moonlighted for, but before she had taken that job, she had been a college history professor. Avery didn't have any particular, but she had recommended a colleague, and arranged a meeting.

As they entered the History Department offices on the fifth floor, Bones spied an attractive red-haired thirty-something woman behind the reception counter. He stepped forward quickly to beat Willis to the introduction. "Hi," he said, leaning one elbow and the counter, bringing him down to her eye-level. "I came here to see Dr. Greer, but it looks like I saw you first."

The woman burst out laughing. "Oh my goodness. Does that line ever work for you?"

Bones grinned. "You tell me. No, wait. How about you tell me tomorrow, after breakfast. I'm from out of town, so…your place?"

The woman was still laughing, but the twinkle in her hazel eyes told Bones that she wasn't laughing at him. Not too much, anyway. "Well, that's quite an offer," she said. "But I think you skipped a couple meals. I haven't even had lunch yet."

"Great. Me either. Let's go."

The woman grinned. "Tempting. I was supposed to be meeting someone here to talk about some boring old history, but hey…why not?"

Willis finally broke his silence. "You wouldn't happen to be Dr. Greer, by any chance?"

"My students call me Dr. Greer," she replied, turning her warm and slightly mischievous smile in his direction. "You can call me Rose." She glanced back at Bones. "If you behave, you can, too."

"When you say behave…?"

Rose shook her head in mock-despair. "My goodness. Avery wasn't kidding about you."

Bones winced. Even though his post-relationship-relationship with Avery Halsey was amicable, she was still an ex. There was no telling what she had done to poison the well.

"All kidding aside…" He slid his backpack off his shoulder and took out a cloth-wrapped bundle. "We should probably get down to business."

Rose's eyes flashed with anticipation, but she shook her head. "Let's do this in my office." She came around the counter and led them down a short hall to a small perfunctory room with an uncluttered desk and a row of utilitarian plastic chairs against one wall.

"This is your office?" Bones remarked. "I would have expected a history professor to have more… stuff."

Rose shrugged. "I keep my stuff elsewhere. This is mostly just a place for advisory meetings." She gestured to the desk. "Well, let's see it."

Bones set down the bundle and unwrapped it to reveal the axe head. Rose's forehead immediately creased into a frown. "Is this a joke?" Her voice had gone several degrees colder than the air outside.

Willis came forward. "If so, the joke's on us, ma'am. Is there a problem?"

"It's widely known that I'm looking for the hatchet that belonged to Captain Steven Thorne. I've seen plenty of decent fakes, but that looks like something you picked up from a hardware store on the drive over."

"I can assure you, it's not," Willis said. "I can't speak to its authenticity, but we found it in a sunken aircraft.

At the very least, it's nearly a century old."

"Sunken aircraft?" Rose looked up suddenly, her eyes widening in surprise for a moment. Then she shook her head again. "No, I'm sorry. I simply don't believe you." She held her hand over the axe head, but seemed reluctant to touch it. "You can't actually expect me to believe that this has been immersed in water for decades."

Bones shrugged. "Believe what you want. If you aren't interested, maybe you can recommend someone who might be."

Willis held up his hands. "Let's all just take a step back, okay? You'll have to pardon us ma'am. We're a bit jet lagged. I promise you, we're not trying to shine you on. This is what we found, but we don't understand what it means. Or how it ended up where it did. We were hoping you could shed some light on that."

The historian drew her hand back, folded her arms across her chest in what might have been a defiant pose, but then just as quickly reached out for the tomahawk blade and picked it up. She tilted it so the overhead light was shining on the engraving. "Steven Thorne was an officer in a colonial militia company. Rogers Rangers."

Bones and Willis exchanged a grin. "Ma'am, we're former military," Willis explained. "We both attended Ranger school. They made us memorize Rogers' Rules. Rule number two: 'Have your musket clean as a whistle, hatchet scoured.' Some Ranger units still carry tomahawks to this day."

Bones added, "My favorite was always: 'Let the enemy come till he's almost close enough to touch, then let him have it and jump out and finish him up with your hatchet.'"

Rose smiled despite herself. "I'm afraid your instructors did you a disservice. Those 'rules' were actually adapted from the novel *Northwest Passage,* written in 1937. I'm afraid Major Robert Rogers' actual Rules of Ranging are quite a bit more prosaic, but you are correct about the importance of the hatchet." She glanced at Bones. "Or tomahawk, if you prefer.

"Captain Thorne fought with the Rangers during the French and Indian War, and probably carried several hatchets over the years, but according to family legend, he passed one down to his son, who carried it during the Revolutionary War. It was handed down through the family for several generations, and through several wars."

Bones and Willis exchanged another look. "One of Thorne's descendants was on that plane," Willis said. "We figured it had to be something like that. What we don't have is a name."

Rose frowned again. "You say you found this in a wrecked plane? Underwater?"

Bones nodded. "A couple hundred miles off the coast of South Africa. The plane was one of the old Clippers from the 1930s but we haven't been able to find a record of a crash."

Rose pursed her lips together as if still trying to make up her mind about her visitors, then took a deep breath. "In 1867, the wife of Colonel Zane Thorne—a veteran of the Civil War—gave birth to a daughter—their only child, whom they named Rosalyn. Rosalyn was a bit of a tomboy, and while she couldn't carry on the family tradition of military service, she did earn quite a name for herself as a war reporter for a New York newspaper. I've always entertained the notion that she carried the old Ranger hatchet with her on her adventures, but if she did, she didn't advertise the fact.

"Rosalyn Thorne eventually married a man named Jack Falcon—actually, he was born Giacomo Falcone, but he Americanized it before he and Rosalyn married. Their son, Zane Falcon, carried the hatchet with him during World War I, where he commanded an infantry company. As far as we know, he was the last member of the Thorne family to hold it."

"Did he die in the war?" Willis asked.

"No." Rose sounded less than certain. "What became of Captain Zane Falcon after the war is a matter of some debate. It's difficult to separate fact from fiction."

Bones immediately recognized the name. "Wait. Captain Falcon was a real dude?"

Willis now fixed Bones' with a questioning stare. "You've heard of this guy?"

"Yeah. I mean, sort of. He was a character in some of those old adventure pulp novels."

Willis just blinked at him, uncomprehending.

"You know, like Doc Savage or Brock Stone?"

Willis shook his head. "Sorry. Never heard of any of those guys. Pro wrestlers?"

"Jeez, did you grow up under a rock?" He turned to Rose. "When I was a kid, my uncle—Crazy Charlie—had a big box of them in the garage. Captain Falcon. Hurricane Hurley. The Padre... Oh, man. What a blast from the past. I devoured those things. And he was a real guy?"

Rose inclined her head slightly. "Just like Buffalo Bill Cody or Wild Bill Hickok—actual historical figures whose exploits were exaggerated and fictionalized in the dime novels. It's unlikely that any of the stories of

Captain Falcon's adventures are true, but yes… he was a real person. And this isn't the first time someone has 'found' Captain Falcon's legendary hatchet."

Bones looked at her sideways. "Rose…Rosalyn. That's not a coincidence, is it? You're family?"

"Actually, it is a coincidence. No relation, at least none that I'm aware of. Rose was my great-grandmother's middle name. That particular branch of the Thorne family tree died with Captain Falcon."

"How did he die?" Willis asked.

Rose drew in another breath. "As I said, it's always been rather difficult to separate fact from fancy when it comes to Captain Falcon. My great-grandfather wrote those stories believing it was all a fiction. It was only later that he learned the truth. Or what he believed was the truth."

"Wait, Dodge Dalton was your great-grandfather?" Bones turned to Willis. "That's the guy who wrote the Captain Falcon stories."

"Great-grandad Dodge wrote a story he claimed was a true account of his search for the real Captain Falcon." She hesitated a moment. "That book, *In the Shadow of Falcon's Wings*, ends with Falcon's death. Aboard a plane that crashed into the sea after leaving Antarctica."

"Antarctica?" Willis shook his head. "That's at least two thousand miles from where we found the wreck."

"The aircraft in the story was a prototype for a long range seaplane. Would that match your wreck?"

Before Bones could answer in the affirmative, he saw Rose's gaze suddenly shift to the door behind them. He turned, curious to see what had distracted her, just as the grenade came flying into the office.

5

The assault team leader grinned as he saw a hot white plume rising from the target vessel. The eighty-foot motor yacht, was still a good half-mile away, too far out for him to see the crew, even with his enhanced night-vision goggles, but the smoke was impossible to miss.

"Well that explains why they're slowing," he said into the throat mic of his Motorola tactical radio. "Looks like they blew an engine. Stay frosty, gents. They know we're coming, and if they're armed, we can expect a warm welcome."

The five shooters acknowledged with mumbled affirmatives. They were already hunkered down behind the gunwales of the sixty-five-foot cabin cruiser, weapons cocked, locked and ready to rock at the first sign of incoming fire.

The leader would have preferred to simply drill the boat full of holes from a distance, but his handler had promised a bonus if they recovered any useful material—computers, written notes and photographs, artifacts—and that would be a whole lot harder to do if the motor yacht was shot all to hell.

He secretly hoped the other crew would surrender without a fight. That would certainly make killing them a lot easier.

He waited until they had closed to within a hundred yards of the drifting yacht before giving the order to back off the throttles. A haze of smoke hung over the other vessel, and the salt air was tinged with the odor of burning oil, but there was no sign of activity aboard.

The assault team leader didn't like that one bit. "Anyone got eyes on?" he said, subvocalizing into the mic.

The replies came back one at a time—all negative.

His 2IC—second-in-command—who was standing beside him, manning the auxiliary helm on the flying bridge, wrapped it up succinctly. "They're either hiding below decks or they bugged out."

The leader's instincts told him the other crew was still on the target vessel, but he had to consider all the possibilities. "I don't see their dinghy. Could we have missed them taking off?"

"We would have seen the heat from an outboard on IR."

"Not if they were rowing."

The 2IC shrugged in the darkness.

"Okay, let's assume they're still there, waiting to jump out when we try to board. I want you covering the hatches from here while we go over tactically, and clear the objective top down."

"Shouldn't we fire a shot across their bow? Give 'em a chance to surrender?"

"Nah. Why waste a bullet?" The leader keyed his mic again. "Go on my signal. And if you see anything moving, shoot to kill."

The jolt that vibrated through the hull as the blacked-out pursuit boat bumped up against *Sea Foam*, was Maddock's signal to move. He gave Corey's shoulder a reassuring squeeze, then dipped his head below the black water, and began moving his legs in a powerful scissors-kick. The long diving-flippers on his feet supplied extra energy to each kick, allowing him to move through the water with a minimum of effort, and more importantly, without creating a disturbance that might be visible to anyone on the other boat looking for him.

Reasoning that the attackers would have superior numbers, Maddock had made the decision to avoid a head-on confrontation. After setting a small oil fire on the deck near the engine hatch to simulate a breakdown, he and Corey—the only member of his crew with no military experience—had gone into the water on the sheltered side of the boat. Matt Barnaby would remain aboard to 'greet' the boarding party.

Maddock kept one hand extended out before him, maintaining contact with *Sea Foam*'s hull until he reached the waterline. Although he couldn't see a thing, he knew the other boat was there, right in front of him, and that if he wasn't careful, he might smack his head against the hull. Even if the impact didn't knock him unconscious, it would almost certainly reveal his presence to the crew, taking away his one advantage: the element of surprise.

He groped forward with both hands until his fingers encountered something solid—the hull of the second boat. He rested his fingers against it, feeling faint vibrations as the vessel rocked gently in the calm seas. High above, he knew, the boarding party was crossing over to seize their prize.

He was running out of time.

He kicked forward again, swimming fast but smooth, until he reached the far side of the boat. He surfaced quietly near the bow, then worked his way down its length to the stern. Although the sky was overcast, hiding moon and stars, the darkness on the surface was by no means absolute. A stripe of faint blue-green lit up the water near the aft-end of the boat—bioluminescent plankton stirred up by the churning screws—and a silvery haze smudged the sky, marking the moon's location in the heavens. It was just enough to reveal the silhouette of the boat above him.

Moving slow and stealthy in order to avoid literally rocking the boat, he crawled up onto the swim platform where he slipped off his flippers and took his Walther from the ZipLoc bag he'd used to keep it dry. He was just about to check the luminous dial of his watch to see how much time he had left when he heard the pop and hiss of an Orion Starblazer aerial signal flare shooting five hundred feet up into the sky.

Maddock kept his head down, eyes averted from the tiny red sun that blossomed into existence high overhead.

Perfect timing, Corey. Maddock thought as he rolled over the transom.

He knew the flare would only last a few seconds, but while it burned, it would level the playing field a little and if the attackers were using some kind of night-vision tech, as he was almost certain they were, then it might just give him an advantage. Bright light could temporarily disable night observations devices—NODs—or even briefly blind a man wearing them.

Maddock swept the pistol back and forth, searching the rear deck for targets, but there was no one there. The bad guys were all evidently on *Sea Foam*.

He kept moving, running for the ladder-like steps up to the flying bridge, then bounding up them. As his head cleared the deck, he spied someone at the helm controls. The man was little more than a shadow, outlined in red.

He wore black tactical gear, his face hidden by a matching balaclava and a set of NODs, which he was evidently trying to reset. His head snapped toward Maddock and his hands dropped to the pistol holstered at his belt.

That was when the flare went out, plunging the world once more into darkness.

Maddock fired once, the muzzle flash revealing that his target had already moved, then shifted his aimpoint and fired two more shots.

The night erupted in gunfire.

Maddock leapt up onto the flying bridge and threw himself flat on the deck. He was pretty sure he'd hit the man with both shots; if he hadn't, he would know pretty soon. In any case, the shooting was all coming from *Sea Foam*; evidently, the boarding party had met a little resistance.

Keep your head down, Matt.

He groped forward until his hands encountered the unmoving form of the man he'd just shot. His fingers slid across familiar textures—Nomex and nylon webbing, similar to gear he had worn on SEAL missions. The man wore a tactical vest, festooned with pouches for magazines, grenades and other gear. Maddock kept going until his hands found what he was really after: the man's NODs.

He wrestled them off the man's head and held them up to his own eye, working the power button to turn them on.

Aside from a faint streak across the display—the after-image of the flare—the world was revealed in glorious green-tinged monochrome. The first thing he saw was the would-be attacker lying supine on the deck in front of him. The man was still alive, stirring and groaning in pain as he struggled to stay conscious. Maddock's aim had been dead-on, but his opponent's tactical vest was more than just a place to store extra gear. It had Kevlar inserts and plate hanger, both of which had stopped the rounds from the Walther cold.

The man's eyes flashed open, his pupils already dilating to adjust for the darkness. In the display of the NODs they looked like the glowing orbs of some supernatural entity.

He can't see me, Maddock thought.

Then the man's hands shot out and closed around his neck.

Maddock reflexively tried to pry the fingers loose, dropping both the NODs and his Walther in the process. That was about all he accomplished. The man's stranglehold felt like an iron band across his throat. He could feel his pulse throbbing, his blood forcibly dammed before it could deliver life-sustaining oxygen to his brain. Through the fog, he could hear the man shouting, calling out to his comrades for assistance.

Maddock knew he would not be able to break the man's grip, not in the second or two left before he lost consciousness, so he pushed back the primal impulse to struggle, and instead met the problem head-on. He reached out and grabbed the man's head in both hands and smashed his forehead into the bridge of the man's nose.

The impact sent a flash of pain through Maddock's skull, and the sound of cartilage snapping reverberated through his cranium, but mercifully, the stranglehold slackened enough for him to squirm free. He thrust the man away from him, slamming his head into the deck until the man stopped struggling.

As the fog lifted, Maddock heard answering shouts from below. At least some of the boarding party were crossing back to their vessel in response to the calls for help. He had no idea how many he would be facing, but knew that his Walther wouldn't be enough to stop them, especially if they were all wearing body armor.

He needed something a lot more powerful.

Groping in the darkness, he quickly found the stunned man's tactical vest, tore open one of the pouches and pulled out a baseball-sized object. Muscle memory took over from there. He deftly stripped off the metal safety band, slipped a finger through the split-ring dangling from the arming pin, yanked it out, and then, with an almost indifferent flick of his hand, he tossed the fragmentation grenade out onto the rear deck of the cabin cruiser.

As soon as the grenade left his hand, Maddock dove over the control console and slid down the sloped superstructure onto the foredeck. In the faint light, he could make out a human form moving right in front of him. There was a shout, and then a muzzle flash as the man started shooting. The air around Maddock sizzled with incoming rounds, the Plexiglas window cracking with multiple impacts. Maddock kept moving, rolling toward the shooter, praying the grenade would detonate before the gunman got a bead on him. He figured the superstructure would shield them both from the blast and the deadly spray of hot metal, but hopefully the explosion would distract the man long enough for him to—

There was a flash, and then he was weightless and spiraling down into the darkness.

6

The flash-bang grenade was small and cylindrical, its highly reactive magnesium core partially shielded by a heavy-duty aluminum shell that was perforated with holes like a piece of Swiss cheese. Bones instantly recognized it as it sailed through the air toward them. Before it could hit the floor, he turned away and dove across the desk, tackling Rose to the ground behind it. The desk would shield them from the one million candle-power magnesium flash, but there wasn't much he could do about the bang except tilt his head to the right, partially covering his ear with a shrugged shoulder. The standard stun grenade produced 180 decibels of sound, a noise louder than a jet engine or a shotgun blast.

In the confined space of the small office, it hit like a sledge-hammer.

Bones' bell had been rung by flash-bangs plenty of times during SEAL training exercises, and he knew how to cope with the disorienting aftermath, but that didn't make it any less unpleasant. A loud whining sound, like the noise of a hospital EKG flatlining, pierced through Bones' skull. He felt like he was on a spinning merry-go-round, unable to tell which way was up, and knew that if he tried to stand, he would immediately crash sideways.

He knew what he would not be able to do, but he also knew what he still could do.

Twisting around, he got his hands on the edges of the desktop, and then without rising, started pushing, shoving the desk across the room.

He got only a few feet before the desk struck something. The sudden jolt caused Bones to slip and fall forward, but as his face hit the floor, he glimpsed a pair of shoes protruding through the narrow gap at the bottom of the desk.

That explained the abrupt stop. He had just run into someone.

They weren't Willis' shoes, so Bones figured they had to belong to the same person who had tossed the flash-bang into the room.

Bones scrambled forward again, thrusting head and shoulders into the kneehole beneath the desk, and then stood up, erupting off the floor like a jack-in-the-box, heaving the desk forward as he did.

The desk tilted away, the top slamming the unseen attacker backward, but because Bones was still woozy from the flashbang, he reeled sideways and crashed onto the overturned desk. There was a stabbing pain in his chest as he struck its underside. That discomfort would be nothing compared to what a bullet might do if he didn't keep moving, but he allowed himself a triumphant smile as he spotted the shoes again, now protruding from under the desk like the legs of the Wicked Witch of the East sticking out from under Dorothy's house. It was too soon to declare victory though. Bad guys, like Wicked Witches, usually had back-up.

The air in the office was thick with smoke, but through the haze, Bones saw Willis darting toward him, evidently a lot more steady on his feet than Bones was. Willis knelt and scooped up a pistol, outfitted with a sound suppressor, and aimed it toward the door.

It took Bones a few seconds to register the fact that Willis was shouting at him. He still couldn't hear a thing, but when Willis pointed back at Rose, he was able to make a rough guess.

Get the girl.

Something like that anyway.

Bones rolled off the desk, but stayed on hands and knees, unsure of his equilibrium. He reached Rose a few seconds later, shaking her gently to get her attention. Her eyes met his—a good sign—and her lips moved.

"I can't hear you," he shouted.

She shook her head and pointed to her ears.

"Oh. You can't hear me either." He pointed at the door, where Willis was poised to shoot at the first sign of a threat. "We have to go."

She nodded, seeming to understand, but then reached out and grabbed something off the floor beside her.

The tomahawk head.

Bones brought himself to one knee, then cautiously rose to his feet.

So far, so good. He extended a hand to Rose, helped her to her feet, and without letting go, led her toward the door, tapping Willis' shoulder to let him know they were ready to move out.

There was a body lying just beyond the entrance, a Caucasian man wearing a hoodie, splotched with blood from a pair of entry wounds in his chest, and still holding a silenced pistol in one outstretched hand. As they stepped past, Bones bent down, planning to help himself to the weapon, but Rose squeezed his hand to get his attention and shook her head. She lashed out with a foot, kicking the pistol, sending it skittering away across the carpeted floor. Then she grabbed Willis' hand, indicating that he should leave the other gun behind as well.

He stared at her like she was crazy, and said something, possibly to that effect.

Rose shouted something that was either an obscenity or *Trust me.*

Probably the latter.

Willis frowned, but then thumbed the magazine release and racked the slide to clear the chamber, before wiping the pistol down with the edge of his T-shirt and tossing it back into the office.

"Great," Bones muttered. "Now we're unarmed."

But just a few seconds later, he realized the wisdom of her decision.

Although he couldn't hear it, a fire alarm was blaring, probably triggered by the smoke from the flash-bang. Flashing strobe lights mounted high on the walls were showing the way to the fire stairs, and people were already streaming out of the other offices on the floor, heading for the exit. He assumed that they had all heard the noise of the grenade detonating, but not the subsequent shots. As far as anyone knew, it was a fire emergency, not an active shooter event, which would have necessitated a different, more defensive response—locking down the building and sheltering in place until the SWAT team arrived. If he and Willis—who were not only physically imposing, but conspicuously not white—were spotted running through the building with guns drawn, they probably wouldn't make it past the front door. Unarmed as they were, they could simply go with the flow.

That would get them out of the building at least, but if the two goons who had just tried to kill them had brought along reinforcements, they would be up the creek.

Hang on a sec, Bones thought. *What the hell just happened?*

While he was no stranger to life-and-death situations, he usually had some idea of who the bad guys were and what they wanted. This attack had come completely out of the blue.

Suppressed weapons. Flash-bang grenades. Military-grade hardware. Whomever their enemy was, they had access to some serious firepower, and they weren't afraid to use it in a crowded public place.

But who had they been targeting? And why?

This wouldn't be the first time that he stumbled into the middle of someone else's problem. Maybe Rose had pissed somebody off with one of her lesson plans. But the timing of the attack just didn't feel like a coincidence.

The tomahawk? He shook his head. *No. That's crazy.*

Even if the hatchet had belonged to the real Captain Falcon, at best, it was a collector's item. And who else besides them even knew of the discovery?

He would have posed the questions out loud, but since he wouldn't have been able to hear the answer, what was the point? If Rose knew the answers, she would tell them when they were safe—and able to talk with their inside voices. Until then, all that mattered was staying alive.

7

Maddock's gag reflex jerked him back into reality, waking him into a nightmare of drowning. He thrashed about blindly, his body wracked with a coughing spasm as it tried to purge his lungs of the cold sea water. It took him a moment to realize that he was on the surface. It took a lot longer for him to remember where he had been before that.

He lifted his head out of the water and saw flames, scattered pools of oil and floating debris burning all around him, and realized intuitively what had happened.

The grenade he had tossed onto the rear deck had triggered a secondary explosion, probably the fuel tanks, and that had blown the cabin cruiser to smithereens. The blast had launched him out into open water.

His relief at having survived that catastrophe immediately gave way to panic. He dog-paddled in a circle, searching all around for *Sea Foam*.

"Maddock!"

The shout was faint but unmistakable. He spun around again, looking for the source of the voice, waving his arms above his head. "Corey! Here!"

A searchlight stabbed out through the gloom. Maddock oriented himself toward it and began swimming, but after a few seconds, the illuminated circle fell upon him, followed quickly by a ring lifesaver. He slipped one arm through the hole in the center and allowed his crewmate to reel him in like the catch of the day.

Corey still dressed in his bright orange survival suit

and dripping wet from his own excursion, was alone at the other end of the rope.

"Where's Matt?" Maddock said as the other man reached down to pull him aboard.

"Out cold," Corey replied, nodding over his shoulder to an unmoving form sprawled on the deck.

"Shot?"

Corey shook his head. "I think he got hit by some flying debris. I made sure he was alive and breathing. Then I started looking for you."

"Any survivors on their side?"

"I didn't see anyone else. I think all that gear they were wearing probably dragged them down. Boss, what the hell happened?"

"We got lucky." Maddock looked out over the water again. "This time."

The damage to *Sea Foam* was mostly cosmetic and all above the water-line. Matt Barnaby on the other hand probably had a concussion, but even if his injuries had not been serious enough to warrant medical attention, Maddock's decision to return to port would have remained unchanged.

Although piracy on the high seas was becoming increasingly common, Maddock was fairly certain that the men who had attacked them had not been mere brigands attempting to seize a target of opportunity. They had been speaking English, with American accents, and their weapons and equipment marked them as professionals—paramilitaries or mercenaries.

A hit squad.

But working for whom?

Until he had an answer to that question, the search for the *Waratah* would have to be put on hold.

The sat phone started ringing when they were still fifty miles from port. It was Bones.

"You're not gonna believe what happened to us."

Maddock felt his pulse quicken. "Let me guess. Someone tried to kill you."

There was a long silence on the line—the unavoidable delay of satellite transmission lag—and then he heard Bones say. "Dude, you told him?"

Willis's voice was barely audible. "When would I have done that? We've been together the whole time."

"Just tell me what happened," Maddock said.

He listened patiently as Bones recounted everything that had transpired, beginning with their meeting at the Buffalo University and ending with their narrow escape from the two gunmen.

"We had some unexpected company here, too," Maddock said when his partner finished.

"That proves it then. They're going after everyone who knows that we found Falcon's tomahawk."

Maddock frowned. "Bones you know how I feel about coincidences, but honestly, I can't see how an old axe head rates attention from an international hit team."

"The tomahawk is just the tip of the iceberg. Rose can explain it better than me. I'll let her tell you when we get there."

"Wait, you're coming here? Are you sure that's a good idea?"

"Positive," Bones said. "If she's right, that's where the answers are."

"You mean the wreck?"

The lag delay was maddening, but not as maddening

as Bones' cryptic answer. "Not exactly."

"Antarctica?" Maddock glanced over at Bones, and then back to Rose Greer. "You're serious?"

The red-haired woman nodded confidently. "That's where Captain Falcon found it."

"The Outpost?"

"That's what my great-granddad called it in his book."

They were gathered in the restaurant of the Durban hotel where Maddock and the others were checked in under assumed names. Despite a killer headache and a new scar, Matt had declared himself fit for duty, but Maddock thought it best to steer clear of *Sea Foam* for a while.

"I read the book on the flight over," Bones supplied. "It matches exactly what we found. The clipper, the second airplane and the mid-air collision. Even the hatchet was right where the book said it would be. It all fits."

Maddock made a mental note to add *In the Shadow of Falcon's Wings* to his already out of control To-Be-Read list, even though he was pretty sure Rose had already hit all the salient points.

As she told it, in 1938 or thereabouts, a young pulp fiction author named David "Dodge" Dalton had gone looking for Falcon—the man who had inspired his fictional stories—after the kidnapping of the American president. That daring crime had been committed by a gang of mercenaries using technology that, even in the present sounded like it belonged in a Buck Rogers story—exoskeletons made of an indestructible metal that imbued the wearer with, among other things, the power of flight and the ability to shoot lightning bolts. Over the course of the novel, it was revealed that the exoskeletons were actually the creation of an advanced early human civilization—artifacts discovered by the "real" Captain Falcon in an ancient outpost buried under the ice at the bottom of the world. Dodge pursued the president's kidnappers literally to the ends of the earth, and after escaping the Outpost—which actually seemed to be some kind of elaborate prison facility—chased after the kidnappers' plane—a stolen prototype for the Boeing 314—in a smaller floatplane—a bi-wing Grumman J2F "Duck." In the climax of the story, the two planes collided in mid-air, and were last seen plummeting from the sky as the heroes escaped using some of the advanced Outpost technology.

All except for Captain Falcon, who made the ultimate heroic sacrifice.

"Think about it," Bones continued, enthusiastically. "There's no way the government would have let a story like that go public. A kidnapped president. The theft of an advanced aircraft. Lightning weapons. They had to cover it up. Then and now."

Maddock raised a skeptical eyebrow. "You think our government sent those killers after us?"

"Not the whole government. You know how it works. One hand doesn't know what the other is doing. Plausible deniability. We're probably dealing with some kind of black-budget defense research agency. They've probably been exploiting the tech from the Outpost for the last eighty years."

Maddock frowned. "If any of that were true, why would they have let this Dodge Dalton write his book in the first place?"

"Because, without tangible evidence—like that plane—it reads like science fiction. You try to suppress that, it just makes people suspicious."

"Actually," Rose added, "the story was only published a few years ago. Maybe it went out before they could stop it, and they've been watching to see if anyone would take it seriously."

Bones turned to Rose. "Tell him the rest."

"There's more?" Maddock said.

Rose grinned sheepishly. "It's more conjecture than proof, but… Mr. Maddock, have you ever heard of Station 211?"

"Sounds like the name of a ska band."

"It's actually the name of a facility rumored to have been built by the Nazis in 1939, in Neuschwabenland or New Swabia, a territory in the region of Antarctica known as Queen Maud Land. It's about 2,600 miles south of here."

Maddock nodded slowly. "Nazis."

"Station 211 is just a rumor, but a Nazi expedition to Antarctica really happened in 1938. The area was officially a Norwegian territory, but that didn't stop the Nazis from moving in. The purpose of the expedition was ostensibly to create a whaling outpost for Germany. Whale oil was still an important resource at the time, but the explorers spent the better part of two years flying over the interior, surveying it and, according to some reports, finding ice free areas in the Mühlig-Hofmann Mountains, fertile green valleys fed by hot springs. In the more outlandish stories, they found technology from the ancient civilization of Atlantis."

Maddock exchanged a look with Bones.

"I know," Rose went on, misinterpreting the look. "It sounds crazy. But after the war, Admiral Richard Byrd put together a huge expedition—Operation High Jump—to explore the same area. Byrd reported finding a green valley with forests growing on the surrounding slopes. Even stranger, in an interview Byrd warned of an unspecified threat from aircraft based in the polar region."

"He actually used the words 'flying objects,'" Bones chimed in. "A lot of people believe that Operation High Jump was actually a mission to retrieve alien spaceships originally discovered by the Nazis."

Maddock knew that his partner loved a good conspiracy theory, especially when aliens were involved.

"Another popular theory was that Byrd was speculating about the possibility of a hollow earth, with entrances at the poles. That's also something the Nazis believed." Rose raised her hands in a defensive gesture. "I'm not saying I believe any of that, but it's a well-known fact that the American government scooped up a lot of Nazi scientists after the war."

"Operation Paperclip," Bones supplied.

"Admiral Byrd might have been acting on secret information about Nazi activities in Antarctica."

"So you think this Station 211 is the Outpost described in your grandfather's book."

"Great-grandfather, but yes. I mean, until you guys showed up, I didn't think any of it was real, but…" She shrugged and looked over at Bones. "Like he said. It all fits."

Maddock wondered if Bones and Rose were being a little too hasty in pinning everything on a grand conspiracy, but he was having trouble coming up with a plausible alternative. Complicating the situation was the fact that Jimmy Letson had gone off the grid. That wasn't like Jimmy, and it had Maddock more than a little worried.

If the government really was willing to kill them to cover something up, then there was only one way to take the heat off.

Expose it for everyone to see.

"Okay," he said. "Pack your long johns. We're going south."

8

Maddock had a rough idea of the challenges they would face below the Antarctic Circle, but the first major obstacle presented itself before they could even depart. Just getting to Antarctica would be a prodigious undertaking.

At her maximum sustainable cruising speed, it would take *Sea Foam* five days to reach the coast of Antarctica, a voyage that would take her through some of the most dangerous seas on the planet. But even if the yacht had been built to withstand the harsh polar environment, there was another far more compelling reason not to travel by water. *Sea Foam* had already been attacked only 200 miles from port. Maddock doubted they would survive a second attack, especially if it happened 2,000 miles from civilization. Flying in was a much better option, but unfortunately it was almost prohibitively expensive.

Almost.

For the low price of just $20,000, a Cape Town-based logistics agency provided round-trip air passage to Novolazareskaya, a Russian research base situated on the Lazarev Ice Shelf. In addition to being a hub for scientific pursuits, "Novo Base" provided a staging area for thrill-seekers and adventure tourists, the kind with more money than sense.

Maddock secured passage for himself, Bones and Rose—the rest of the crew would stay in Durban with *Sea Foam*, to hopefully leave a blind trail for the hit squad to follow—and after dropping a few more bills on polar equipment, the three of them boarded the plane, a massive Russian-made Ilyushin Il-76, painted white with a bright blue nose and a stripe running down the length of the fuselage, for the six hour flight to the end of the earth.

"This little jaunt is going to put a dent in our rainy day fund," Maddock said.

"What good is having a platinum card if you can't splurge once in a while?" Bones replied. "Besides, if we don't come up with something to get those goons off our backs permanently, all the money in the world isn't going to make much difference."

"True enough. Which brings us to the question of where we go once we get there." He turned to Rose. "Any idea where we're supposed to look for this Station 211?"

"If that was known, it wouldn't be a rumor anymore. It's generally believed that Admiral Byrd found what he was looking for in the Mühlig-Hofmann Mountains, but you won't read that in the official sources. It's the same reason why you won't see it on Google Earth."

"I see why you and Bones get along so well. How did Dodge Dalton find the Outpost?"

"The devices from the Outpost react with each other. Sort of a magnetic attraction. They're drawn to it like a homing beacon. It's something to do with the metal. A scientist my great-granddad worked with called it 'adamantine.'"

"Like in the comic books?" Bones said.

"Greek mythology, actually. It was the indestructible metal of the gods. The chains of Prometheus were forged from it."

"Unfortunately, we seem to be fresh out of ancient adamantine gizmos," Maddock said. "Unless you've been holding out on us."

"Actually, I think we do have something." She dipped into her shoulder bag and brought out the tomahawk head.

Bones folded his arms over his chest. "The aliens made that?"

"They weren't aliens, Bones," Rose replied patiently. "And no they didn't, but I think it's possible that it may have picked up some of the properties of adamantine."

"Sort of like magnetizing a piece of steel," Maddock said. "That could explain why it doesn't show any sign of corrosion. You think that will be enough to guide us?"

"I was thinking we could suspend it on a string, like a pendulum or dowsing rod. Once we get close to the mountains, we should observe some kind of effect." Rose gave a helpless shrug. "I hope. Sorry. It's the best I've got."

Maddock just nodded.

It was a balmy 31 degrees Fahrenheit on Schirmacher Oasis, the ice-free plateau where Novo Base, with its three-mile-long airstrip was situated. Rose, with her heavy parka tied around her waist, and her polar-fleece jacket liner unzipped, strolled down the plane's cargo ramp like it was a summer day—which in fact, it was. She stretched after the long flight and took in a deep breath. "Wow. Africa and Antarctica in the same day. Now I can cross them both off my bucket list."

Bones, fully-outfitted in his cold-weather clothes, was less enthusiastic. "I could have gone my whole life without coming here. Remind me again why I'm here instead of Matt? Rangers love this cold weather crap."

"You mean aside from his concussion?"

Bones made a dismissive gesture. "Pshaw. I had a flash-bang blow up in my face. I still can't hear out of my left ear."

"Okay. Then how about the fact that we might just be about to crack one of the biggest UFO mysteries in history. Admit it. You wouldn't miss this for the world."

Bones gave a non-committal grunt. "I'm just saying, I wish it was a little warmer."

"This is warmer," Rose said. "You really should peel off some of those layers until we're out on the ice. You're going to perspire in there, and believe me, you don't want your sweat freezing."

"Oh, suddenly you're the polar expert?"

"I'm from Buffalo. I know a thing or two about cold weather."

"Keep your goggles on though," Maddock added. "Snow blindness is one of the biggest dangers of being here."

It would have been more accurate to say that snow blindness—literally sunburned eyeballs—was one of the *most common* dangers. The affliction, which caused symptoms ranging from a painful sensation—some described it as a feeling like having broken glass under the eyelids—to temporary loss of vision, was just one of a long list of hazards awaiting visitors to the southern ice, but unlike those others, it took a few hours of unprotected exposure to the glare of sunlight reflecting off the ice for the symptoms to set in. It was painful, but not immediately lethal, unlike most of the other items on that list.

Although there were limited guest facilities on the plateau, it seemed prudent to spend as little time there as possible, so as soon as their gear was off the plane and loaded onto a bright yellow snowcat—another service provided by the logistics company for a small fortune—they headed out.

In keeping with their cover story, they had submitted an itinerary for their "adventure ski vacation," but it had also seemed wise to avoid stating their actual destination, which meant that the weather report and crevasse map supplied by the logistics company were pretty much useless once they left the plateau. The only way to safely negotiate the various hazards of the landscape—weak ice-bridges over geothermal heated lakes and streams, crevasses that could swallow the snowcat whole—was by moving slowly and paying attention to tell-tale clues on the surface. The Mühlig-Hofmann Mountains were only about a hundred and twenty miles from Novo Base, but traveling in a straight line was out of the question, and what should have taken them four hours took closer to fourteen, or at least it felt that way.

Maddock was used to long hours of travel on the water, but driving the snowcat was nothing like putting *Sea Foam* on a heading and letting her do all the work. He had to be wide-awake and fully alert every second, even when he wasn't at the controls. After two hours, he switched out with Bones, and then Rose demanded a turn. Since the cab was heated and they had round the clock daylight it made sense to keep driving, but by the time they finally reached the figurative end of the road, they were almost too exhausted to set up camp.

Outside, they got a taste of what Antarctica really had to offer. Maddock and Bones had to fight a steady ten-mile-an-hour polar blast and sub-zero temperatures, but once the tent was pitched and anchored, the interior immediately began warming up thanks to constant sunlight bathing the exterior panels. With the last of their energy, they stripped down to their thermal underwear and crawled into their sleeping bags.

"Yes!"

Rose's shout roused Maddock from a deep dreamless sleep. He felt like he had only just drifted off but when he glanced at his watch, he saw that more than six hours had passed.

He sat up and looked over to see the historian bent over something on the floor of the tent, but looking at him with a triumphant grin. "It works," she said. "Check it out."

Maddock squirmed out of his warm sleeping bag and crawled over to her. When he saw what she was doing, he reached over and slugged Bones until the latter stirred.

Maddock ignored his friend's warning growl. "Wake up," he said. "You need to see this."

Rose had threaded a length of paracord through the axe eye—the slot where the wooden handle, or haft, was supposed to go—and was dangling the tomahawk head like a plumb bob.

Only it wasn't dangling. Not straight down at least. Instead, the cord was stretched taut at a shallow angle, just a few degrees below horizontal. Maddock reached out and touched a cautious finger to the metal blade. It was warmer than he expected, and swayed a little. He applied more pressure, pushing it down several inches, but when he moved his hand away, it fell—or rather rose—back to its previous position.

"Holy crap," Bones muttered, now fully awake. "That's trippy."

"Like I told you," Rose said. "We can follow it like a dowsing rod. This will take us right to the Outpost."

"In case you weren't paying attention today," Bones replied, "You can't always travel in a straight line down here. And we don't know if it's a mile or a hundred miles."

"I think there's a way to narrow it down a little," Maddock said, pulling on his snow pants.

Once they were suited up, they all headed out into the biting cold. The hatchet head continued to hang askew, always pointing in the same direction no matter which way they turned. Maddock oriented his GPS unit—unlike the sat phone, which relied on communications satellites, the global positioning system was truly "global" in its coverage—and stared toward the mountain peaks in the distance.

He plotted the azimuth into the GPS, then they started off on foot, heading away from it and the shelter of their camp, at a perpendicular angle to the invisible line for a distance of about a mile, and then plotted in another vector. The two lines crossed in a valley about twenty-five miles southwest of their camp. The elevation at the site was nearly two hundred meters higher than their present location, but the hatchet head was still pointing at a slight downward angle.

"It's under the ice," Bones said. "That's not going to make this easy."

"If you're right about Base 211, someone else may have already done all the hard work," Maddock replied. "I guess we'll know when we get there."

It took three hours to find a pass through the maze

to the valley marked on the GPS. As they got closer, the "angle of the dangle" as Bones put it, increased but surprisingly even when they were squarely on the coordinates, it did not point straight down.

"I guess X doesn't mark the spot after all," Bones said.

"Maybe I was off by a couple degrees when I ran the plot," Maddock said. He doubted that was true, but couldn't think of a better answer.

"I don't think that's it," Rose said. She held the axe head out in front of her and turned her body until she was facing the same direction it was pointing. "I think we just need to keep following wherever it leads."

Maddock glanced over at Bones who was peering through the cab window. "I'm not sure we'll have to do that," he said, his enthusiasm finally breaking the grip of the cold. "I know where we need to go." He pointed toward a distant black peak protruding above the ice in the direction Rose was indicating.

"That mountain? You seeing something I'm not?"

"It's not a mountain," Bones said. "Look closer. It's a pyramid."

Maddock was not as certain about the identification as Bones. The jutting black massif did look perfectly symmetrical, with what looked about like the same angles as the Great Pyramid of Khufu on the Giza Plateau in Egypt, but he had seen plenty of similar rock formations carved by nature rather than the artifice of human engineers.

Man-made or not though, the axe head was leading them in that direction.

They drove the snowcat as close to it as the terrain would allow, and then debarked to finish the trek on foot. The slope was so steep that they had to break out the mountaineering equipment in order to keep going. The axe head continued to lead them forward even though, by climbing, they were almost certainly moving further and further away from whatever it was they were trying to find.

Then they found the cave.

9

Maddock shone his flashlight into the icy throat, but beyond about twenty yards, the beam vanished into shadow, illuminating nothing.

He glanced over at Bones. "Something's not right about this."

They had ventured only a little ways inside, just far enough to find shelter from the constant wind, so he didn't have to shout to be heard, but even without the wind, it was brutally cold. The perpetual summer sun did not reach very far beyond the threshold of the ice cave.

"What are you talking about?" Rose interjected. She held out her hand, displaying the makeshift pendulum which was still pointing ever so slightly forward, into the depths of the ice tunnel. "The hatchet brought us here. This is exactly where we're supposed to be."

"We came here looking for a secret base, built by the Nazis and taken over by the U.S. government. Or whoever it was that tried to kill us. So where is it?"

Bones nodded slowly. "He's right. It doesn't look like anyone has been here in… forever."

Behind her goggles, Rose's eyes widened in surprise and alarm as she began inspecting the immediate area. "Maybe this is a back door. I don't know. But this *is* what we came here to find."

Maddock had no argument for that. "Maybe you're right. Watch your step and stay on your toes."

They started forward, down a smooth sloping passage that seemed too perfect to have been created by natural forces, but showed absolutely no indication of having been bored out by artificial means. The tunnel curved gently but relentlessly to the right, a counter-clockwise corkscrew spiraling down into the ancient ice. The grade was so steep that, without crampons and ice axes, they probably would have been unable to walk it, but as they made their way down, the dangling tomahawk head began to lift, indicating that their descent was indeed bringing them closer to the anomaly that was affecting the axe head.

After about fifteen minutes of trekking, the passage opened into a much larger cavern in the ice. The floor of the hollow was flat and clear. The walls were curved, like the inside of an enormous air bubble frozen in the ice, but cutting through the middle of the cavern was a slanted flat wall. The thin layer of clear ice could not hide the black stone underneath.

"The pyramid!" Bones said.

"We've been circling it," Maddock confirmed. "I'd guess we're about four hundred feet down from where we started."

Rose checked the tomahawk again. It was hanging straight out in front of her. "We're almost there."

Almost where? Maddock wanted to ask, but the answer appeared as if by magic.

"That wasn't there a second ago," Bones said, pointing to a triangular opening in the stone wall.

Maddock was pretty sure it wasn't. "I guess this is where we need to go.

The tunnel, like the opening, was a perfect equilateral triangle, about nine feet high from base to apex. The black stone remained partially hidden under the ice, but the shape was unmistakable. A short ways in however, they reached a junction with a transverse passage.

"Decisions, decisions," Bones muttered. "Should we flip a coin?

"No need." Rose held out the cord attached to the axe head, but it continued to point straight forward, into the unyielding wall.

"So much for that idea. I've got a quarter in my pocket, but I can't get to it with all this stuff on. You want to reach in for me?" He winked at her.

Rose rolled her eyes. "Get Dane to do it."

"Let's try left," Maddock said, ignoring the banter.

"Why?"

"Why not? If it doesn't lead somewhere, we can always turn back and try the other way."

Bones looked at Rose and they both shrugged.

The passage extended for about thirty yards before making a right turn. As they moved, the tomahawk shifted, relative to their direction of travel, but kept pointing to a fixed point somewhere on the other side of the wall until, midway down the adjacent passage, they came to another opening. The tomahawk was pointing straight into it.

Rose laughed nervously. "Wow. It feels like something's pulling on it."

Maddock looked over. The cord trailing from her hand was stretched taut. He reached out and put his hand on the cord, feeling the tension there. "May I?"

She looked back at him suspiciously, but then nodded.

He twisted the cord around his gloved hand once, twice and then gripped it firmly before telling her to let go.

He thought he was prepared for the transfer, but the

cord almost yanked him off his feet. He allowed himself to be drawn forward, his curiosity more powerful than his caution. Just beyond the entrance, the passage opened into an enormous vaulted chamber—the hollow interior of the pyramid.

Bones looked up in awe. "I'll bet this was some kind of hangar. For the UFOs."

Maddock glanced over at Rose. "I thought this place was supposed to be some kind of prison. Wasn't that what you're great-grandfather's book said?"

Rose shook her head uncertainly. "Yes, but in his next book, the Outpost was destroyed, so I really don't know how reliable they are."

"There's a second book?"

"Actually, there was a whole series. You can buy them online."

"That would have been good to know earlier." Maddock shot an accusatory glance at Bones.

The latter shrugged. "I didn't know."

Maddock continued forward, following the tomahawk like someone being pulled along by an enormous dog straining against its leash, until it crunched into an enormous ice hummock. Although his light could not reach to the lofty apex, Maddock had no doubt he was standing almost directly beneath it, and that the goal of their search lay in the exact center of the structure.

"There's something hidden under here," he said. He let go of the cord and the tomahawk remained where it was, plastered against the hummock. He took out his mountaineering axe and began chipping away at the ice around the object, but after just a few hits, the jagged pick end broke through, revealing an empty space at the center. Even stranger, when he wrestled the pick free, a puff of warm air hit his face. He took another whack at it, and this time, a section of ice bigger than his head broke loose and vanished into the newly created hole, along with the tomahawk.

Maddock shone his light into the gap and saw, just a few feet away, a black sphere, about eighteen inches in diameter. Stuck to it like a paperclip to a magnet, was the tomahawk. The object was completely ice free, and suspended in mid-air with no apparent means of support. The small cavity inside the hummock was thick with a strange fog, like dry ice vapors, leading Maddock to believe that the object was somehow sublimating the ice—evaporating it without first melting it into water—and freeing itself after years, or perhaps even millennia, of imprisonment.

"I think we woke something up," he said, not looking back. "Bones, give me a hand with this."

The big man stepped forward and added his ice axe to the effort, and in a matter of minutes they hacked out an opening large enough to crawl through. Maddock shouldered his way into the gap. The air inside was warm, but only in comparison to the sub-zero conditions outside. Maddock felt no radiant heat from the object.

He wormed in a little further, until he was close enough to touch it, which he did after only a moment's hesitation. He knew there was a faint possibility that he would get fried to a crisp like a fly in a bug-zapper, but his instincts told him that if the object—the artifact or orb or whatever it was—was dangerous, it was probably already too late.

The object bobbed a little at his touch but that was all that happened.

He gripped the cord attached to the tomahawk, and gave it an experimental tug. The orb moved toward him like a helium balloon on a string, but as he pulled it closer, he could feel the resistance increasing, as if the black sphere was being pulled back to its original position by an invisible bungee cord. He pulled harder still, wrestling the orb out of the cavity in the hummock, and wrapped both arms around it to keep it from going anywhere.

Bones let out a low whistle. "Holy crap. What the hell is that thing?"

"I don't know, but I'm guessing it's the reason those goons tried to kill us."

"Goons, Mr. Maddock?" The unfamiliar voice echoed in the vast hall. "That's unkind."

Adrenaline dumped into Maddock's bloodstream as he whirled around, shining his light at the perimeter of the chamber, searching for the source of the voice. Bones grabbed Rose, thrusting her behind him, as if to shield her with his body, and shone his light out as well.

As if in answer, several spots of light appeared near the entrance; high-intensity LED lights, all trained on the three of them.

"I'm sure if you really got to know us," the voice went on, "You would come up with something much more colorful."

10

The lights grew brighter as the men holding them moved closer. Maddock squinted against their brilliance but did not look away. He counted six lights in all. Bones shone his own light at them, revealing what Maddock already knew in his gut: the lights were attached to the Picatinny rails of assault rifles. The weapons were wrapped in white camouflage tape, and the men carrying them wore similarly colorless winter coveralls, with matching ski masks and gloves. There was a seventh man in the center of the formation, similarly attired, but without weapon or light. They stopped about ten yards from Maddock and the others, spread out in a semi-circle with their weapons all raised and ready.

"Drop the light, Mr. Bonebrake," the unarmed man said. "And raise your hands, all of you."

It was the same voice that had addressed them from the darkness. His face was completely concealed behind a white scarf and goggles.

"Who the hell are you guys," Bones said, his voice almost a snarl. He lowered the light but did not comply with the other demands. Maddock likewise remained exactly as he was, clutching the orb in a bear hug.

The man laughed without humor. "When I said you should get to know me, I was being facetious. TBH, it would be a waste of time for both of us."

"Then why haven't you just killed us," Maddock said. "Maybe you're afraid of what I can do with this?"

He thrust the orb forward, and was pleased to see several of the gunmen flinch. It was worth the effort of manhandling the sphere, which wobbled in his grasp like a living thing, struggling to break free and return to where he had found it. Only his firm grip on the tomahawk head kept it from doing so.

The man composed himself and managed another laugh. "I could ask you the same question, but then I already know the answer. You have no idea what it is you've found. No idea of its potential. Or how to unlock it."

"Wrong," Rose said. It came out as a hoarse, fearful whisper, but she cleared her throat, straightened and took a deep breath. "You're wrong about that. My great-grandfather literally wrote the book on this place, and I've read every word. If you don't back off, I'll show you just how much I do know."

Despite the gravity of their situation, Maddock felt a swell of pride for Rose's courage in facing down their foes.

The other man cocked his head sideways to look at her. "Ah, Ms. Greer. Yes, I'm familiar with those books. Very entertaining science fiction, but hardly what I would call a user's manual. If you're clinging to the hope that you will be able to use the anomaly against us as a weapon, I fear you will know only disappointment before you die."

Maddock didn't know if Rose was bluffing, but the fact that the man was still talking told Maddock that *he* was. And just like that, the pieces fell into place.

"You didn't know how to find this place, did you?" The silence that followed confirmed Maddock's guess. He pushed forward. "All this time, we thought you were trying to cover this up, but you were looking for it, too."

"And you led us right to it," the man replied. "Bravo,

Mr. Maddock. You are as good as your reputation."

"Crap," muttered Bones, then looked up suddenly. "Wait. So are you or aren't you working for the government?"

The man ignored the question. "Cards on the table, Mr. Maddock. I don't think you know what to do with the anomaly, but I have no idea what will happen if I try to kill you while you are holding it. I'm prepared to take that chance, but all things being equal, I'd just as soon not. So, in the interest of expediting things, I'll be generous. Put it down, right now, and I will allow the three of you to leave."

"Uh, huh," Bones said. "Sure you will."

The man spread his hands in mock-apology. "I tried. Though, TBH, I would have been disappointed if you had said 'yes.'"

"TBH? Seriously, dude. WTF? Do you have any idea how stupid that sounds?" Bones turned his gaze to the other gunmen. "Have you told him how stupid that sounds?" He shook his head and added, "SMH."

The commando leader ignored him, and turned to the gunman on his immediate right. "Try not to hit the anomaly."

"Wait!" Maddock shouted.

The other man held up a hand, signaling his minions to stand fast. He cocked his head at Maddock. "You're full of surprises. Or is this where you try to lull me into complacency and then at the last second…what's the expression? Pull a fast one?"

Maddock shrugged, careful not to lose his grip on the sphere. "You've got all the guns."

"Yes, I do. You would do well to remember that, Very well, then. Put it down and walk away."

Maddock slowly, carefully, pushed the orb away from his body, holding it out in both hands. "Come and get it."

"Dude," Bones muttered in a low voice. "This isn't usually how we do things."

Maddock looked his friend in the eye. "It's the only way, Bones. Just be ready to move as soon as I hand it over." He let his gaze flick ever so slightly to the right, hoping that Bones would get the message

Bones nodded slowly.

The leader of the commando team—Maddock decided to call him "TBH"—turned to his chief lieutenant again. "If anyone of them so much as sneezes…"

The gunman nodded and squared his shoulders behind the stock of his assault rifle, making sure that the barrel was pointed straight at Maddock.

TBH advanced with slow tentative steps, until he was standing only a couple feet away. He cautiously reached out for the orb.

"Careful," Maddock warned, just before contact was made. The man flinched as if he had been stung, which was exactly the reaction Maddock had been hoping for. He grinned. "This thing has a mind of its own. You sure you really want it?"

TBH sneered through the scarf covering his face, and then closed his arms around the sphere.

Hidden from the other man's view, Maddock tightened his grip on the tomahawk head and braced himself for what he knew was coming. "All yours, then."

He let his other hand drop and stepped to the side, wrenching the tomahawk loose even as the orb yanked the other man forward toward the center of the pyramid.

Unbalanced, TBH lurched forward, stumbling as he tried to stay on his feet while being dragged along.

In the split-second that followed, as the gunmen struggled to process what they had just seen, both Bones and Maddock sprang toward them, with Bones rushing the men on the right and Maddock running at the men on the left. The high-intensity tactical lights flashed as the men tried to reacquire the moving targets, but before they could, the two former-SEALs had tackled two of the six gunmen to the icy floor.

Although the commandos had superior numbers and firepower, Maddock and Bones had just turned those advantages into liabilities. The gunmen couldn't shoot at them for fear of hitting one of their own comrades, which bought the two treasure hunters a few seconds to figure what to do next.

Bones squirmed around behind the commando he was fighting and then reached out with his long arms to grab the man's assault rifle by the stock and barrel. He pulled it up as if curling a barbell, level with where he thought the man's throat might be, and then jerked back hard, crushing the receiver assembly into the man's windpipe.

Maddock's solution was quicker and more decisive. He slammed his fist—the one holding the tomahawk—into the side of his foe's head. Although the heavy hood of the man's white parka muted the sound of the impact, it offered little protection from blunt force trauma. The man went limp, dazed, unconscious or possibly dead. Still clutching the axe head, Maddock snatched up the man's rifle and squeezed the trigger.

A deafening report filled the chamber. Maddock hadn't really taken the time to aim, and none of the rounds found their mark, but the eruption of noise and the random impact of bullets against inward sloping walls triggered a hailstorm of ice fragments. The remaining gunmen scattered, sprinting for cover behind the hummock.

"Rose!" Maddock shouted. "Run for it!"

Before she could move however, a fierce shout rose from the center of the hummock. Maddock brought his captured rifle around, shining the tac-light on the commando leader who was now standing without difficulty, gripping the orb in both hands. Even from several yards away, Maddock could tell that something was different. The air seemed to be vibrating, crackling with something like static electricity.

A cold knot of dread seized Maddock's guts. Without hesitating, he pulled the trigger, emptying the rifle's magazine at the standing figure, but instead of spattering the ice behind TBH with bloody chunks of flesh, the bullets evaporated with little blue flashes, right in front of the man.

The commando leader never even flinched.

The rifle went silent, its ammunition gone, but through the ringing memory of the thunderous reports, Maddock could hear laughter.

"Well what do you know?" the man chortled. "The anomaly creates an impenetrable energy shield, just like in the Dodge Dalton book. Let's see what else he got right?"

Then, the orb in his hands began to crackle and dance with long fingers of blue-white lightning.

11

Maddock knew he wouldn't be able to outrun the lightning, so he did the only other thing he could think to do. Tossing the empty rifle aside, he drew back his arm and hurled the tomahawk.

He didn't aim it at TBH, but instead launched it over his foe's head.

The other man, perhaps confident in his invincibility or lost in his apotheosis was oblivious to the piece of steel whirling above his head. It arced around like a boomerang, and then shot toward him like a guided missile. The energy shield might have protected him from bullets, but the adamantine-infused tomahawk passed right through, seeking out the orb.

There was a bright flash and a pop, like a light bulb burning out, and then darkness.

Half-blinded by the abrupt shift from brilliant light to gloom, Maddock blundered forward, rushing to the barely visible figure slumped on the ground in front of the hummock. TBH lay face down, his body covering the sphere. Because of his white camouflage outerwear, it was difficult to distinguish him from the surrounding ice, but the red stain between his shoulder blades was unmistakable.

Maddock knelt and rolled the man onto his side. The metal sphere shifted with him, as if pinned to his body, which was exactly what had happened. The tomahawk head, drawn by the energy field of the orb, had effortlessly passed through both the energy shield and the commando leader, killing him instantly. The spike on the back of the axe blade had penetrated clear through the man and now protruded from his chest to make contact with the orb.

There was something different about the sphere, though it took Maddock a moment to realize what had changed. The orb was no longer being drawn toward the center of the pyramid. Whatever the commando leader had done to activate it had evidently switched off its automatic homing function.

What the hell is this thing?

"Maddock!" Bones yelled from behind him. "Time to go!"

As if to underscore the urgency of the admonition, a burst of rifle fire ripped through the air in the chamber, followed by several more.

Maddock knew they would never make it to the exit, not unless he came up with a major game changer.

"Really wish I'd read that book," he muttered as he reached out for the orb. He braced himself, expecting a shock or worse, but the only unusual thing he felt was a slight warmth radiating from the metal, penetrating the thick fabric of his gloves. He tried to lift it but encountered resistance from the body of TBH, which was still pinned to the sphere. He got it free, but only after planting his feet against the man's torso and pushed with all his might until the axe head tore loose.

He turned the orb in his hands, looking for a switch or control panel, but the metal was smooth, a perfect sphere without any disruptions. "Power on," he shouted. "Shields up."

"Don't say it!" Rose called out, her voice barely audible over the din. "Think it!"

Think it? Maddock shook his head, and then did just

that, mentally uttering the same commands.

Nothing changed. *But if it did,* he thought, *would I even know it?*

He imagined an invisible barrier, a bubble of energy around him, like something from a science fiction movie, stopping the bullets cold.

He had no idea if it was really there at all.

He turned to find Rose and Bones a few steps away. The latter was firing his captured assault rifle to keep the remaining enemy pinned down, but Maddock knew he would soon run out of ammunition.

"Bones! I'll cover you. Go! Now!"

Bones gave him a sharp, doubtful look, but then grabbed Rose by the hand, and started across the icy floor toward the outer edge of the chamber. Maddock sprinted after them. The points of his crampons scraped uncertainly on the floor. The climbing spikes were designed for slow deliberate movement, not running, but he stayed on his feet. Directly ahead, searching beams of light cast a shadow-show on the walls of the chamber, accompanied a moment later by the thunderous reports of multiple assault rifles. Maddock expected at any moment to feel the hammer-punch of a bullet, or worse, to see Bones or Rose struck down, but miraculously, they all reached the triangular passage unscathed. Either the orb was truly shielding them or they were just that lucky.

Bones led the way, navigating the passages back to the exterior with uncanny precision. As they emerged out into the ice cave, they found a pair of unusual vehicles—they looked like a cross between amusement park bumper cars and fan boats—waiting just outside the entrance.

Bones shook his head. "I guess now we know how

those jokers managed to get down here so fast."

"What are those?" Rose asked.

"Hovercraft," Maddock said, approaching one of the sleek vehicles. Its white fiberglass upper hull rested on an air skirt that looked like an enormous inner tube. The open cockpit had a control console at the front, with a long padded bench running lengthwise down the middle. The controls were basic, not much different than a jet ski, with a set of handlebars, a bank of indicator dials and a key in the ignition. He grinned in satisfaction. "And it's our express ride out of here."

"You know how to drive it?"

"How hard can it be?" Maddock dropped the orb into the foot well, and then clambered over, straddling the bench behind the console. He turned the key and hit the ignition switch, and was rewarded with a faint hum as the fan assembly at the rear began spinning. The machine was a lot quieter than Maddock expected. During their time in the SEALs, he and Bones had ridden on large military air-cushioned landing craft, big enough to transport Humvees from ship-to-shore. Those sounded a little like the inside of a tornado, but this was barely louder than a lawn mower. As the rushing air pressurized the flexible skirt, the hovercraft began to drift a little. Maddock experimented with the controls and quickly figured out how to more or less make the machine do what he wanted it to.

"All aboard!"

Rose hesitated, so Bones swept her up in his arms and deposited her in the back of the idling craft, but instead of immediately following her, he moved over to the second hovercraft and used his ice axe to tear a large gash in the rubber air skirt.

"That should slow them down a few minutes," he shouted as he climbed over.

Maddock nodded and turned the nose of the craft toward the mouth of the cave, and goosed the throttle. The hovercraft slid across the ice, picking up speed as it shot into the narrow passage.

"Who were those guys?" Rose shouted.

"No clue," Maddock replied, not looking back. "But I don't think they're working for the government."

"Then who?"

"You think it could be our old pals?" Bones said.

Maddock shrugged. "Could be."

"Who are you talking about?" Rose said.

"A bunch of racist nutjobs that call themselves The Dominion," Bones explained. "We've tangled with them before. This is just their style."

Maddock knew the far-right quasi-religious terrorist group did not have an exclusive on turning ancient relics of power into weapons of destruction, but he did not contradict his friend. "As soon as we can get a call out, we're gonna drop this hot potato in Tam's lap."

"Who's Tam?"

"A lady we work for sometimes. She *does* work for the government."

"You trust her?"

Bones just laughed. He and Maddock had an unusual relationship with Tam Broderick, the leader of a CIA task force called "the Myrmidons," dedicated to squashing the Dominion permanently. Maddock and Bones occasionally freelanced for her, but when it came to trust, they knew that Tam could be trusted, first and foremost, to do whatever it took to accomplish the mission.

After a few scrapes and bumps, Maddock got the hang of driving, and opened the throttle to full, pushing the hovercraft up the slope like a rocket. It had taken them fifteen minutes to descend the corkscrewing passage, but less than five minutes after leaving the cavern at the base of the pyramid, a light appeared at the end of the tunnel. Maddock didn't slow down.

"Hang on!"

The hovercraft raced toward the opening and then shot like a bullet from the mouth of the ice cave.

Rose's screams seemed to echo across the valley, but after just a few seconds, what had been a shriek of terror changed to a whoop of exhilaration as the hovercraft slid down the side of the ice-covered pyramid like a runaway roller coaster.

Maddock allowed himself a grin of triumph, but as the valley floor rushed up at him, his sense of elation fizzled like a dud firecracker.

At first, he thought his eyes were playing tricks on him. Aside from their waiting snowcat, the landscape was a uniform white, but as they got closer, he saw that it was no mirage.

Surrounding the snowcat, barely distinguishable from the sparkling white ice, were four more camouflaged hovercraft.

12

The wind whipping through the open interior was bitterly cold, cutting through Maddock's scarf and face mask like they were made of cheesecloth., but he gritted his teeth against the frigid blast and gripped the handlebars like they were the only thing keeping him from flying off into oblivion. As the valley floor loomed closer, he could just make out the human figures crowding around the idle vehicles. He didn't need to see the men clearly to know that they were probably packing some serious firepower.

Maddock figured they had one thing going for them: the commandos below didn't know what had happened inside the ice-bound pyramid, and had no idea who was in the hovercraft racing down the slope toward them. That uncertainty would only last until the gunmen realized that the trio were wearing North Face parkas instead of white camouflage shells.

"Stay down," he called back to the others. "We're going to blow through."

He would have preferred to veer off, skirt the valley floor and keep as much distance between them and the commandos as possible, but on the steep downslope, the idea that he was in control of the hovercraft was just wishful thinking.

The slope flattened out and he felt the craft decelerating. Now he could see the other hovercraft clearly, silhouetted against the horizon ahead, and right in front of him, the snowcat, with its heater and all their gear and food, seductively close, impossibly out of reach.

He pushed the throttle to its maximum and steered away from it. In the corner of his eye he saw movement, commandos jumping out of their motionless hovercraft… Pointing… Shouting….

Shooting.

With a loud crack, the fiberglass hull to Maddock's left erupted in a spray of splinters. Almost simultaneously a second crack—the sharp report of an assault rifle—echoed across the valley.

Maddock cut right, or tried to. Steering a hovercraft was accomplished by turning the control vanes on the fan, redirecting the flow of air at an angle, but the machine had a lot of forward momentum to overcome. It behaved more like a hockey puck than an ice skate. Instead of changing direction, the craft started to spin on its axis, turning dizzying curlicues across the icefield as it continued more or less in the same direction. He quickly corrected his mistake, pointing the nose in the direction of travel.

A few more shots were fired but none of them found their mark, and after a few more seconds, they ceased altogether. A quick backward glance revealed why.

The commandos were in pursuit.

Maddock reckoned they had about a three-hundred-yard lead on the enemy hovercraft, easily within the effective range of their assault rifles. They had not started firing yet, but it was only a matter of time before the lead started flying again, and any attempt at evasive maneuvers would only shrink the distance between them. He kept the throttle maxed, but knew he would never be able to outrun a bullet.

"Rose!" he shouted without looking back. "If you know how to make that orb work for us, now would be a really good time."

"I'm trying!" she replied.

Maddock wondered if that was the explanation for how they had made it through the gauntlet relatively unscathed.

Bones leaned over his shoulder, shouting in his ear. "Hope you've got a back-up plan, dude."

"Working on it," Maddock answered. He checked the fuel gauge. The tank was three-quarters full, but he had no idea how far they could get on that. Novo Base was at least a hundred-and-fifty miles. The coast was a lot closer, but neither option would necessarily mean safe harbor if the commandos decided to chase them all the way.

And if they couldn't make it that far, it probably wouldn't matter. They would freeze to death at the bottom of the world.

It felt like a replay of the showdown on the open ocean. Outnumbered and outgunned. Nowhere to hide and no chance of outrunning their enemies. That left only one option.

Déjà vu all over again, he thought.

"I've got an idea," he said, and then added. "You're not gonna like it."

Bones clapped him on the shoulder. "As long as it's not turning around and playing chicken with these guys, count me in."

Maddock grimaced behind his scarf. "Umm…."

"Crap. You're kidding. That's your plan? What are we gonna do, throw snowballs at 'em?"

Maddock looked over his shoulder to where Rose was kneeling in the bilge space, hugging the orb. "Rose! How's that force field coming?"

She looked up and gave a helpless shrug.

Bones heaved a sigh. "Okay, let's do this."

Maddock nodded and gripped the handlebars. "Hang on!"

He cut hard to the right and, as before, the hovercraft pirouetted, turning around without immediately changing direction. Just as quickly, he straightened the control vanes, stopping the spin at the halfway point so that they were sliding backward. The machine shuddered as momentum fought a losing battle against the air being forced through the fans. The hovercraft slowed, stopped for just an instant, and then began moving forward, back into the valley.

The four enemy hovercraft seemed to be moving across the ice at warp speed, a hundred… seventy-five yards away, side-by-side in a picket line. Orange-yellow tongues of flame lanced out from the approaching vehicles. They were so close now that, even if he had wanted to, Maddock couldn't have veered off to avoid a collision.

"Hang on!" he shouted, and then there was a lurch as the hovercraft rose up beneath him and went airborne. The sensation abruptly changed to a feeling of weightlessness as the craft fell away, but that too lasted only an instant. The hovercraft crashed down, bouncing and skipping across the ice.

Maddock struggled to get upright again. The hovercraft seemed intact. He could only surmise that it had somehow—impossibly—ridden up and over the other machines.

Had Rose succeeded in using the orb to create a protective force field around them?

He glanced back, saw both Rose and Bones, hanging

on for dear life, apparently unhurt.

The valley floor ahead looked clear, but unfortunately, the only way out of it was up the steep slope of a mountain. He knew the hovercraft could make the climb—the commandos had done it when they had followed them into the ice tunnel—but it would be slow going and burn a lot of fuel.

Then something happened that sent a chill down Maddock's already freezing spine.

Appearing as if from nowhere, rising above the black pyramid, was an enormous airplane. It had the same profile as the Il-76 that had borne them across the Southern Ocean—wide fuselage, shoulder wing configuration with four engine nacelles and rear stabilizer wings mounted atop the elevated rudder, but unlike that jet, this aircraft was a dull battleship gray. The plane swooped down, filling the valley with its bulk, and then just like that, it was above them, passing so close that Maddock ducked reflexively. He glanced up quickly, saw that the plane's landing gear was fully deployed, its rear-cargo ramp already lowered.

The plane was going to land. The bad guys had called for reinforcements.

Crap. Maddock thought. *As if things weren't already bad enough.*

Bones was shouting something, but the roar of the jet's engines drowned him out.

He glanced back, ready with a shout of his own. "Rose! If you've figured out how to control that thing, now would be—"

The rest of his sentence was lost in a new eruption of noise—not the distinctive report of assault rifles but something much louder, a rapid staccato burst, like a string of firecrackers amplified ten thousand times.

Directly behind them, a second sun—a white-hot supernova—blossomed into existence.

Maddock instantly knew what had happened, and when he spun the hovercraft into another 180° to get a look, his suspicions were confirmed.

A giant plume of ice marked the spot where the giant jet aircraft had just touched down, but the space between them and it had been transformed into a battlefield of fire and ice.

Bones let out a whoop of triumph. "Holy crap, dude. Did you see that?"

Maddock nodded dumbly.

Amidst the geyser-like steam plumes rising from flash melted ice were a dozen smaller fires sending up columns of black smoke—the burning wreckage of at least one of the hovercraft, and the smoldering bodies of the gunmen who had been riding in it, scattered haphazardly across the ice.

As the jet had passed over them, its anti-missile countermeasures had been activated. The magnesium flares, which deployed in a shotgun burst, were a defensive measure, designed to fool a heat-seeking missile by providing it with a thermal target even hotter than the plane's engines, but someone onboard the aircraft had used them as a weapon against the commandos.

"That was a C-17," Bones continued. "An Air Force bird. I never thought I'd say it, but hooray for the cavalry."

Maddock scanned the terrain ahead. The plane—a C-17 Globemaster, if Bones' identification was correct—had stirred up a blizzard of swirling ice and smoke, but at the periphery of the storm, he saw something moving away at a right angle.

At least one of the commando hovercraft had survived.

"Save the celebration until we're clear," Maddock said. He opened the throttle wide and the hovercraft charged forward.

As they neared the artificial ice storm, Maddock saw the commando hovercraft turning, coming around to pursue them. In the corner of his eye, he spotted another machine on the opposite side, likewise maneuvering for another attack, and then the world dissolved into a haze of blowing ice.

The hovercraft crunched and shimmied through the flaming debris, but after a few seconds, the cloud thinned enough for him to see the C-17, its engines still blasting out roiling convection waves of heat exhaust. The ramp to the open cargo hold beckoned invitingly, as did the two figures standing on it, arms waving in a "hurry up" gesture.

Over the roar of the jet engines, he could just make out the sharp crack of rifle fire. The figures on the ramp reacted. One of them ducked back inside the plane, the other produced a handgun and began firing back.

Maddock kept the throttle maxed, closing the remaining distance in seconds to race up the ramp, past the man who was still firing his pistol at the pursuing commandos, and into the cavernous cargo bay.

It was like being swallowed by some monstrous leviathan.

He reversed the throttle, but the craft had too much momentum to simply stop. Thankfully, the cargo space was empty. He caught a glimpse of some moving in front of him, scrambling to get out of the way, but then the forward bulkhead filled his vision and he barely had time to brace for the imminent collision.

The crash wasn't as bad as he expected. The hovercraft had already given up most of its forward velocity, but the sudden stop nevertheless ejected him from the machine, hurling him into the bulkhead. His winter clothing afforded him some protection, but the impact knocked the wind out of him.

For several seconds, all he could do was lie stunned and motionless on the deck. He could hear shouting voices, and then felt a shudder rising through the deck plates as the aircraft began moving… accelerating.

The plane was taking off.

All he could do was hang on as the aircraft surged forward, the deck tilting upward as the plane climbed back into the sky. When it finally leveled off, he sat up.

Bones and Rose were gingerly climbing out of the hovercraft, the latter still holding the mysterious orb. Behind them, at the far end of the long tunnel-like cargo bay, the ramp was rising. Maddock caught a final glimpse of the ice-covered valley and the distinctive black pyramid before the door closed, sealing them inside the belly of the beast.

They had made it. They were safe.

EPILOGUE

The man who had fired the pistol from the ramp walked calmly up the length of the cargo bay toward them. The second figure, the one that had nearly been run down, was also advancing and as he approached, he pushed back his hood and removed a full-face ski mask, unleashing a long cascade of black hair.

"He" was actually a she, and Maddock recognized her instantly.

Bones spoke first, his voice evincing the same disbelief that Maddock felt. "Jade?"

Jade Ihara, the half-Japanese, half-Hawaiian archaeologist, who happened to be Dane Maddock's ex-girlfriend, offered a half-smile. "That was quite an entrance."

"Jade." Maddock pulled the scarf away from his face. "What the hell are you doing here?"

"I was in the neighborhood. Lucky for you."

"Never thought I'd say this," Bones chortled. "But damn it's good to see you." He looked past her to the other man. "Prof, is that you?"

Pete Chapman, who had earned the nickname "Professor," had served with Maddock and Bones when they were SEALs, and was currently working with Jade as a facilitator and sometimes-bodyguard, though his actual employer was the U.S. government, and specifically, Tam Broderick's Myrmidons task force.

But the man walking toward them stripped off his cold-weather covering, revealing medium-length wavy dark hair, a full beard, and an unfamiliar face.

"Actually," Jade said, "Pete's off doing a favor for Tam. So are we, I suppose. She's the one who put us on your trail."

Maddock frowned. He was starting to remember why Jade was his ex-girlfriend. "Who's 'us,' Jade? You obviously know a lot more about what's going on than I do."

"For a change," Jade shot back.

"Is there something going on between you two?" asked the bearded man.

Bones laughed. "Duh."

Maddock ignored him and faced the stranger. "Maybe you're who I should be talking to."

"Probably." The man looked past him to Rose and the black metal sphere in her arms. His eyes widened in surprise. "You found it?"

"You know what that thing is?" Bones asked.

"Not really. I know that they call it 'the anomaly,' but not much more than that."

"But you know who 'they' are?" Maddock said. "The guys that just tried to kill us…The Dominion?"

The man shook his head. "They call themselves 'Prometheus.' They're very secretive, and very powerful."

Bones snorted. "Great. Just what we needed. It's like we got put on some kind of mailing list for Villain-of-the-Month Club."

"What do they want?" Maddock pressed.

"What everyone with power wants; more power. They want to rule the world. And they want control of things like that." He pointed at the orb. "Unfortunately, that's about all I can tell you about them, and I've been hunting them for twenty-five years."

"Since kindergarten then?" Bones said. It wasn't

much of an exaggeration. Beneath his beard, the man looked like he might be in his early thirties.

"It's a long story," the man replied.

"I'm guessing you've got a few of those," Maddock said. "You got a name?"

The man stuck out his hand. "Nick Kismet."

Bones laughed again. "Is that like, your stage name?"

Jade rolled her eyes. "Way to call the kettle black, *Bonebrake*."

Kismet laughed, too. "That's another one of those long stories. Actually, I work for a UN cultural preservation agency. My job is to protect antiquities. Keep them out of the hands of people like Prometheus."

Maddock nodded in Rose's direction. "So you're here for that? The anomaly. Take it. It's all yours."

Kismet and Jade exchanged a look, then the latter spoke. "Maddock, the anomaly is just the—"

"Don't say it," Bones cut in.

"—tip of the iceberg," Jade finished.

"She said it," Bones groaned.

"It's true, Mr. Maddock," Kismet confirmed. "Prometheus has begun their endgame, and it's up to us to stop them. All of us. This is just the beginning."

The End

ARCANUM

Book Two of The Elementals

PROLOGUE

Plymouth, England 1910

The coachwork canopy of the Lanchester 16 kept the persistent drizzle at bay, but did little to banish the chill. The driver seemed impervious to both, but the young boy who sat beside him had lived most of his life in the desert and the cool, damp air cut deep into him despite his best efforts to disappear completely into a heavy wool blanket.

The boy's name was Hassan ibn Ali, though he had not been called this in many years. His master—the man who now drove the Lanchester along the muddy old carriage road—called him 'Blue Boy' or sometimes just 'Blue,' and mostly that was how he thought of himself. The master was not a cruel man, though Blue greatly feared to cause him displeasure. He had seen the man call down lightning from the heavens and that alone was enough to terrify him. Besides, he liked the color, especially the cerulean hue of a cloudless sky at noon. Whenever he saw that, which wasn't often at this latitude, he thought of home and the life he had lived before the master's arrival.

It almost felt like a dream to him now.

Their destination was a great stone house, perched atop a hill. Blue supposed that on a clear day, the house would have a spectacular view of Plymouth Sound to the east but on this dreary night, the only indication that they were near water was the relentless pulses of illumination against the dismal clouds. Two flashes every ten seconds from the Eddystone lighthouse which lay several miles offshore, at the entrance to the harbor.

The house was dark and looked deserted, but as they rolled up the drive toward it, the driver worked the klaxon, sending out a piercing note to herald their arrival. As the car pulled to a stop, a door opened revealing lamplight within. The Lanchester's engine coughed and sputtered for several seconds and then with one final harsh bang, like a gunshot, fell silent. Blue shed the blanket like the second skin it had become and with great reluctance opened the door and stepped out into the gray drizzle. As soon as he was in the open, he deployed a large umbrella and immediately found some shelter under its capacious dome, but he knew this would only be a brief reprieve. He circled around to the opposite side of the automobile and held the umbrella high above the door to protect the driver as he emerged. As the umbrella moved away from Blue, he again felt the chilly rain on the back of his neck but he endured this discomfort with gritted teeth. His duties did not require him to be warm or dry.

He had to hurry to keep up with the master's long determined strides, which posed a new set of problems. The mud was slippery underfoot and with his arm extended, it took all his concentration to keep his footing. By some miracle, they reached the front door where a man holding an oil lamp gestured for them to hurry inside.

The old house was draughty and Blue could hear the sound of water trickling against stone, indicating at least one leak in the old thatch, but it was a marginal improvement. He shook the water off the umbrella before setting it aside, and then helped the master out of his cloak and galoshes. Beneath his wet weather clothes, the master wore a long saffron colored gown, decorated with spangles, and wound about his head was a white turban, adorned with a star ruby cabochon brooch. The costume was probably meant to make him look like a holy man or mystic from the Far East, but the overall effect was a touch too theatrical, making him seem more like a stage magician or worse, a carnival mountebank.

It was a deliberate choice, more effective at altering his appearance and hiding his true identity than any magic spell.

He did not always dress like this. Only when he was with Blue… Only when he was Adam Garral. And when he was Garral, he wanted those who saw him to remember his outlandish attire, not his true face.

The man with the lamp did not speak, and with the light held before him, his face remained hidden in shadow. When they had doffed their wet weather clothes, the man turned and beckoned them to follow.

They were led to an interior room where a roaring fire at last drove the chill from Blue's bones. He unconsciously moved closer to the hearth, savoring the warmth that radiated from it. The man with the lamp—Blue now saw that he was about the same age as the master, of similar build and handsome, though heavier—set the light down on a table, and settled himself into one of the chairs arrayed around it.

Garral glanced down at the seated man for a moment. "Still playing at cards, Alick?"

Blue craned his head to get a better look and saw dozens of rectangular pieces of pasteboard spread out on the tabletop. He edged closer, curious despite his desire to stay near the fire, and saw familiar symbols sketched on some of the cards—swords, cups, pentacles—and crudely drawn figures on others. Most were blank.

The man at the table looked up, a scowl on his slightly plump face. "I hate that name."

"I know," Garral said, gravely, then burst out laughing.

The other man shook his head irritably. "Why are you here, Adam?"

"You know why," Garral replied. "The mirror. You have it. I want to look into it."

"The mirror is a bauble. A parlor game."

"Then you should have no objection to letting me have a look."

The card maker regarded him with naked suspicion. "You've learned something, haven't you? Some new insight?"

"I won't know until I've tried."

The card maker nodded slowly. "Very well, but you must share it with me."

Garral inclined his head in a gesture of surrender.

The other man leaned to the side and began rooting in a carpet bag that rested alongside his chair. When he straightened, he held in his hands something that looked to Blue like a misshapen dinner plate made of smoky glass. He placed it on the tabletop and slid it toward the visitor.

Garral sucked in his breath when he saw it but tried to hide his reaction behind another smile. He stared down at the obsidian disc for a moment, his expression only mildly curious, but Blue could sense the eagerness in him. Garral's entire body seemed to vibrate with it, like a plucked harp string. Blue took an involuntary step closer, as if drawn by his master's magnetism.

Garral abruptly pivoted, grabbed a chair and

adjusted it so that it was positioned in front of the black mirror, and then, snapping the sleeves of his ornate gown with a dramatic flourish, lowered himself into it.

He placed his hands on the table, palms down to either side of the mirror, and closed his eyes as if meditating. After a few seconds, his eyelids fluttered open and he reached up with this right hand to touch the ruby on his turban with a finger. His lips began moving, framing a silent incantation. Blue knew this was a pretense, a charade to divert their host's attention away from what Garral was doing with his left hand. Under the table, hidden from the other man's view, but not from Blue, Garral was gripping a small block of cobalt colored stone.

The object was a talisman of some sort. Blue still remembered the first time he had seen it, the night Garral had called down fire from the sky, the same night that he had entered into his master's service. The stone, unlike the ruby brooch, was a source of real power, though Garral had never succeeded in duplicating what had happened on that fateful night. Now, or so it seemed, he was trying to unlock its potential in a different way.

Garral now leaned over the flat black mirror as if to stare into it, and slowly, tentatively, reached down to touch it with his right hand.

The moment his fingers made contact, he jerked them back as if the mere touch had burned him. Blue ran to his master's side, reflexively laying a steadying hand on Garral's shoulder. In that same instant, Garral touched the mirror again.

A memory sprang unbidden into Blue's mind. He vividly recalled the first time he had seen the mirror, resting on an altar in a room made of jade, hidden at the heart of a dark pyramid temple in the jungles of New Spain—the land now known as Mexico.

But no, that couldn't be right. He had never seen this strange mirror before… Had not felt even a faint glimmer of recognition upon seeing it.

Yet his memory of its discovery was beyond vivid.

A score of men had died on the journey to reach the temple, felled by wild beasts and fever, hazards common to the emerald hell through which they had blazed a path, seeking gold and other riches. Five more had died inside the maze of passages that cut through the pyramids interior, and what had killed them was beyond Blue's comprehension. Everything about the pyramid defied reason. The walls were joined at impossible angles, like something that could only exist in a nightmare….

He remembered taking it from the altar… Picking it up with his own hands….

Now he remembered another day, many months later. He was on a ship… Not a steam-powered vessel, but a sailing ship, a massive craft with three masts stabbing up into a cloudless azure sky. The riggings hung empty, the sails lowered, the ship unmoving. The crew, swarthy, rough looking men, stood in rows on the deck, similarly motionless. A second ship lay alongside the first, the two held together with ropes and grappling hooks. Men, armed with long knives and old matchlock pistols and muskets, were crossing over.

Pirates, Blue thought, and then a name came to mind.

Drake.

Blue staggered back a step, and as he lost contact

with Garral, the flood of memories ceased with the abruptness of a door slamming shut. He shook off a sudden sensation of vertigo and returned his attention to Garral, desperate to know what he had just experienced, but afraid to ask.

Garral had not moved. He sat as still as a statue, one hand touching the obsidian mirror, the other surreptitiously gripping the lapis lazuli talisman. Blue started to reach for him again, but hesitated, remembering that they were not alone.

The card maker was staring intently, almost hungrily, at Garral.

Before Blue could do anything else, Garral jerked in his chair and then sat up straight. His head turned back and forth, eyes dancing as if trying to remember where he was.

"Adam," the awed card maker whispered. "What did you see?"

Garral stared at him mutely for a moment, then reached out across the table with both hands. His left seized one of the blank paste board cards. His right wrapped around the long shaft of a pencil. He brought both to him and then began sketching an image.

The tip of the pencil moved with preternatural swiftness and precision, and in mere seconds, an image took shape. It was a human form, and for a moment, Blue thought he was looking at the likeness of the crucified Christ. Garral continued sketching, adding details—small figures surrounding the central figure, a web of lines that reminded Blue of the riggings on the sailing vessel he had… remembered? Imagined?

Garral stopped sketching, contemplating the sketch for a moment, and then laid the pencil down beside the card.

"That?" The card maker said. "That is what you saw? What is it?"

Garral returned a cryptic smile. "Why, my dear Alick, it's everything."

McMurdo Station, Antarctica—Now

"When I got on this plane, I really thought it meant I was done freezing my balls off." Uriah "Bones" Bonebrake gazed down the lowering ramp of the US Air Force C-17A Globemaster III extended range cargo plane and out across the stark white Antarctic landscape and shook his head sadly.

"You know what happens when you assume."

Bones turned and met the smirking gaze of his tormentor. "Yes Jade, I do. I know that some *ass—you—* will give *me* a freaking spelling lesson."

"I don't often take the big guy's side," said Dane Maddock, standing right behind Bones and next to Jade. "But he's right."

Jade Ihara rolled her eyes. "You always take his side, Maddock. That's your biggest problem."

"That's because he's figured out that I'm usually right," Bones said, with a grin that was more menacing than friendly. "And you haven't. That's *your* biggest problem. As rescues go, this one kind of blows. We're still in Antarctica, we still have that orb we picked up at the Outpost, and as far as we know, this Prometheus group—whoever they really are—is still after us. And I'm still freezing my balls off. Which part of that did I get wrong, Jade?"

"The part where you actually have balls, I think."

"Play nice kids," Maddock said. "Let's not fight in front of our new friends."

"Sorry," said Rose Greer, standing just behind him. "But I'm with Bones. It's been fun, but I am so over this place."

Maddock blew out his breath in a long audible sigh. He could see the exhalation floating in front of him, a vapor cloud turning into ice crystals before his very eyes. "Well, we can't leave until we return the snowcat."

"I hate to be the bearer of bad news, but I think that ship has sailed." This came from the remaining member of their group, Nick Kismet. "We may still be in Antarctica, but we're about two thousand miles from your snowcat. I don't think I'm going to be able to convince the pilot to make another trip like that anytime soon. Especially not with what happened this time out."

Five hours earlier, Kismet and Jade had swooped in with the C-17 to pluck the rest of them from the middle of a harrowing firefight on the polar ice. The snowcat in question—a loaner—had carried Maddock, Bones and Rose from Novo Base on the part of the continent that was closest to the southern tip of Africa, to the Mühlig-Hofmann Mountains where they had discovered what appeared to be a man-made pyramid, jutting up from the ice like an enormous black tooth. Stranger still, they had discovered a tunnel in the ice which took them inside the structure, where they had found a strange spherical artifact with extraordinary, and quite possibly supernatural properties. Shortly after finding it however, they had been attacked by a group of gunmen—agents of a mysterious group that Nick Kismet had subsequently identified as *Prometheus*.

Although they had made it out of the pyramid with

the artifact, they had been outnumbered and outgunned, and the situation had looked pretty dire until the unexpected arrival of Kismet and Jade aboard the C-17. Unfortunately, they had been obliged to leave the snowcat behind. If the surviving Prometheus gunmen hadn't already helped themselves to the tracked all-terrain vehicle, it would eventually be covered over by an ever-deepening blanket of ice and swept away by the relentlessly advancing glacier.

After the rescue, the plane had flown nonstop over the frozen continent to McMurdo Station on the Ross Ice shelf, and as Kismet had pointed out, despite the fact that they were still on the same continent, the snowcat was as far away from them now as Los Angeles was from Detroit, and every inch of it was in the harshest, most unforgiving landscape on earth.

"Screw the pilots," Bones said. "You couldn't convince *me* to go back. Not for a million bucks."

Maddock wondered if a million dollars would cover the replacement cost of the snowcat and sighed again. It would be a hell of a tax write-off, at least.

The cargo ramp settled into place and with one final whine of effort, the hydraulic actuators went silent. Beyond the ramp lay the packed snow of Williams Field—one of the official runways servicing McMurdo Station.

"Actually," Bones said as he stared out at the brutally austere environment, "I'm not even sure I want to get off this plane. Can't we just hang here while they top off the tanks?"

Kismet shook his head. "I'm afraid this bird won't be heading back to civilization until we've accomplished our primary mission."

"Believe it or not," Jade chimed in, with more than a hint of sarcasm in her tone, "We didn't actually come down here just to pull your asses out of the fire."

"Oh, if only there had been a fire," Bones sighed.

"Come on, Jade." Maddock said. "Don't tell me you just happened to be in the neighborhood. You knew right where to find us. And you already said that Tam sent you here. So what's really going on?"

Jade glanced over at Kismet. "Do you want to tell them, or should I?"

Kismet shrugged. "They're your friends."

"I wouldn't go that far," Bones grumbled.

"Me either," Jade shot back acidly, but then she shifted her gaze to Maddock and her expression softened a little. She pointed out at an approaching red shape, a massive vehicle trailing a cloud of blowing snow. "There's Ivan. Come on. I'll tell you what I know on the way, and Nick can fill in the gaps."

With that, she moved past Bones and started down the ramp. Maddock knew she was being stingy with the information just to piss him off. Evidently, she was still sore about how their relationship had ended. He also knew the only way he was going to get any answers was to play along, so he followed her down to the ice.

Bones just shook his head. "Now I gotta ride with some dude named Ivan. I'll bet he smells like beets. This day just keeps getting better."

PART ONE—JADE

1

"You really should consider carrying a pistol."

Jade Ihara glanced over at the lanky, sandy-haired man who had just growled at her, and frowned. "That's what I have you for," she retorted.

Pete "Professor" Chapman shook his head wearily. "I'm not Rambo. Even I need back-up once in a while."

Jade didn't have any real objection to guns, and had used them once or twice in particularly sticky situations—situations a lot like this, actually—but there were some very good reasons why she chose not to make a habit of carrying, not the least of which was that most of the countries where she operated—Jade was an archaeologist specializing in pre-Columbian American cultures—took a dim view of visiting scholarly types walking around packing heat. It was true; Professor wasn't Rambo, and she wasn't Indy-anna Jones or Angelina what's-her-name... The *Tomb Raider* chick. Actually, if anyone was Indiana Jones, it was Professor in his Explorer fedora, a lucky charm he'd picked up in Costa Rica during one of their adventures together. But headgear or no, running around the jungle, looting temples and blasting away the bad guys wasn't her standard operating procedure.

"In case you haven't no—"

She broke off as another volley of automatic rifle fire tore into the sandstone right above her head, spraying them with chips of stone and hot lead fragments. The gunmen were shooting from multiple locations, closing in on them like a noose.

Jade ducked reflexively, even though she was already ducking just about as low as was humanly possible. Professor calmly stabbed his semi-automatic pistol in the direction from which the fire had come, squeezed off several shots in rapid succession.

Professor was actually a lot more Rambo-like than he cared to admit. Despite his nickname, he wasn't really a college teacher—not at the moment, anyway—and hadn't been when he'd earned the nickname early on in his first career as a Navy SEAL. His teammates had started calling him that because of his encyclopedic knowledge of just about any subject imaginable and because of his tendency to lecture. He was currently working for a highly-classified elite US government task force called the 'Myrmidons' and more specifically, acting as Jade's bodyguard-slash-assistant, which is why *he* had no compunction about carrying unregistered weapons wherever Jade's work took her. In truth, Jade wasn't even sure how he was able to smuggle the weapons into the various destinations they visited, but she trusted that he would always be ready to face down whatever threat presented itself.

Sometimes—this time, in fact—the threat was more than he could reasonably handle, but Jade really didn't see how the situation would be that much different if she was armed, too.

"I'll think about it," she said, but before she could say any more on the topic, Professor grabbed her arm and dragged her away from the sloping stone face, and toward the nearly impenetrable jungle. A hail of bullets tore into the rock wall, right where she had been crouching a moment before.

Another burst from a rifle raked the jungle canopy as the two of them plunged headlong into the underbrush. Roots and vines snagged Jade's feet and would have tripped her up, but the tangle of ferns and thorny branches kept her upright, even as they lashed her face and arms. Professor had traded his pistol for a machete, but with the gunmen behind them, there wasn't time to do much more than swing wildly and hope for the best. There was a perfectly good trail, not fifty yards away, but Jade knew they'd never reach it, and even if they did, it would only make it easier for the gunmen to find them.

After just a few seconds of crashing through the brush, Professor seemed to get the hang of moving through the dense rainforest, finding the path of least resistance, but Jade could hear shouts and movement in the jungle all around them. The gunmen were still close, and probably closing in.

"This way," Professor whispered, pulling her along as he ducked through a gap in the thicket that looked barely wide enough for a cat to slip through. Jade did her best to move stealthily, but the rustling noise she made as she pushed forward sounded to her like a jet taking off. Something snagged her hair and jerked her head back. Just a branch, but it was enough to stop her in her tracks. She wrapped a hand around her ponytail, gripping it like she would a length of rope to keep her hair from being torn out by the roots, and then drove forward again, hastening after Professor.

The site they were visiting, located in the remote jungles of Manu National Park, a biosphere reserve with few roads and only a handful of permanent occupants—all indigenous natives from the friendly Matsigenga tribe—was supposed to be safe; safe of course being a relative term in the jungle.

They had come here to investigate the so-called "pyramids" of Paratoari, a series of sandstone formations in the Peruvian jungle, first noticed in satellite photographs taken in 1976. Seen from space, the formations—at least eight uniformly shaped and sized objects arranged in evenly-spaced parallel rows— appeared too symmetrical to be the work of geological forces, and for at least twenty years thereafter, they were believed to be evidence of an undiscovered archaeological site, perhaps even the lost Incan city of Paititi. The first on-site investigation in 1996 however not only confirmed the alternative and boringly-plausible hypothesis that the so-called structures were in fact naturally occurring rock formations but also revealed that they were not as perfectly symmetrical as they appeared in the satellite photographs. This revelation however had not dampened the enthusiasm of fringe archaeology enthusiasts—the sort of people who believed that ancient civilizations were influenced by extraterrestrial visitors.

While Jade did not doubt the accepted truth—that the "pyramids" were just truncated ridge spurs—there was some evidence of an Inca presence in the area, including ancient paved roads, platforms, and petroglyphs, all of which raised the possibility that the Inca might have revered the naturally occurring pyramid-shaped rocks, possibly even excavating passages and interior chambers in which to hide the long-sought legendary gold of Paititi, passages which had subsequently been hidden by the dense jungle foliage. If Paititi did exist, and there were several compelling lines of evidence to suggest that it did, it was almost certainly located somewhere in the region, so why not under the "pyramids"?

It was a longshot of course, but the only way to rule it out definitively was with an on-site survey, which was why Jade and Professor had flown to Cuzco, high in the Andes mountains, and then driven a rented Land Rover down the treacherous and winding primitive roads into the Amazon Basin to a spot near the native settlement of Shintuya on the banks of the Madre de Dios River. The Paratoari site was just a few miles to the west, but getting to it required crossing the river and then bushwhacking through the dense forest. After an hour or so of hacking a path through the foliage, they had stumbled onto what they assumed was a trail cut by some previous expedition. It was only when they neared the pyramid-shaped rocks that they realized who was actually using the trail.

Jade was both physically and mentally prepared—as prepared as anyone could ever really be—for the ordinary dangers common to tropical rain forest ecosystems: animal predators, snakes, spiders and other bugs, toxic plants, mosquito- and water-borne diseases. But she had not anticipated stumbling across a camp of armed men living in the woods.

They were probably drug smugglers, shuttling cocaine from a processing plant hidden in the jungle to an illegal airfield for transport out of the country, or possibly anti-government Shining Path guerillas—or more likely some combination of the two. There weren't supposed to be any drug smugglers or guerillas in the area, but then those people didn't exactly advertise their presence in Trip Advisor.

Bottom line, there were a lot of bad guys, maybe as many as a dozen, and one more pistol between herself and Professor wasn't likely to tip the odds.

2

The green hell seemed to go on forever, but no matter how long they toiled, their pursuers were always close, never more than a few hundred yards away. The gunmen clearly didn't want word of their illicit presence to reach the authorities, and weren't likely to settle for anything less than two bullet-riddled corpses.

They were moving down a gentle slope, which was good, but the area was thick with underbrush and they had to fight for every inch. Then, without any warning, the jungle opened up, like the sea parting in some kind of Biblical miracle. Jade heard Professor shout something—a warning—but before she could fully process the significance of anything she was seeing or hearing, the ground beneath her was abruptly no longer beneath her. She pitched forward, half-sliding, half-falling down a steep embankment toward the muddy water of the Rio Madre de Dios. She barely had time to draw a breath before plunging face first into the surprisingly chilly water.

She thrashed for a moment before righting herself, and as she rubbed the water from her eyes, she could feel the current dragging her along.

"Swim for it!"

Jade craned her head around and found Professor, just a few yards further upriver, swimming with powerful strokes toward the far shore. She also spotted their Rover, a distant speck on the road just above the opposite river bank, falling further away with each passing second, and realized that she needed to be doing the same. She reached out and began clawing and kicking through the water.

Several sharp reports sounded behind her and she heard the harsh crack of bullets splitting the air above her head, sizzling into the water all around. Jade ducked under the surface, both to conceal herself from the shooters and to use the water itself as a shield. High-velocity rounds, like the kind fired by the assault rifles the gunmen were using, shattered on impact with water.

She had seen it on *Mythbusters*, so it had to be true.

She swam underwater for several strokes, feeling much more in her element here than she had in the jungle, but after several seconds, the need to breathe forced her back to the surface. She raised her head cautiously, and saw that she was now a good hundred yards further downriver and more than halfway across. She could see the gunmen behind her, semi-distinct shapes against the verdant backdrop. They had stopped shooting. Jade guessed they had lost track of her, and knew that could change at any second, so she ducked under the surface again and kept swimming until her knees began dragging against the mud in the shallows at the far river bank.

She crawled up onto shore, staying low and moving slow, like a crocodile—

Are there crocodiles here?

The thought triggered a momentary panic. No, there weren't crocodiles, but there were caimans—a smaller but no less dangerous reptilian predator—as well as snakes—and not just any snakes, but anacondas, the largest snakes on earth, some big enough to swallow a human child whole. Ravenous piranhas weren't outside the realm of possibility either, but even deadlier were the threats too small to be seen with the naked eye; insidious flesh- and brain-eating protozoans and parasites.

"Jade!" Professor's hissing voice brought her back to the moment. She turned to look for him, but saw only mud and reeds.

"Where are you?"

Something moved just a few yards away and she nearly screamed before realizing that the mud-covered creature coming toward her *was* Professor.

Totally Rambo, Jade thought.

"These guys can't shoot for crap," he whispered. "But we're not out of their range yet, so stay low until you're on solid ground. Then, when I give the signal, run like hell for the Rover."

Crawling through the mud and running like hell didn't sound like much fun to Jade, but the prospect of a quick motorized escape at the end was more than worth it. "Gotcha," she replied.

"Then move."

Jade started forward, trying to move slow and stealthy, but almost immediately sank up to her elbows in the thick mud.

"Crap," she muttered. She tried to extricate herself, fighting the muck for every inch.

"Now," Professor shouted. "Run for it!"

"Really?"

She gave up on slow and stealthy, and wrenched herself out of the mud, thrashing and stumbling forward. Professor was twenty yards ahead of her sprinting through the grass, practically floating over the mud flats.

The familiar crack of gunfire sounded again. Jade glanced back. She couldn't make out the gunmen on the bank, but she did spot three… No, four shapes splashing in the water, halfway across the river.

Jeez, these guys are persistent, she thought.

A bullet creased the air just a few feet to her right, smacking into the mud with an audible hiss. That was all the motivation Jade needed. She launched herself forward, clawing at the mud until, mercifully, she felt something almost like solid ground underfoot.

Professor was now more than fifty yards ahead of her; halfway to the road and the waiting Rover. With his head start, he would at least be able to get the vehicle started so they could take off as soon as she reached it.

Almost unconsciously, she patted her pockets, checking to make sure that she didn't have the keys.

That would suck.

But no, the keys weren't in her pockets. Professor had driven last, so he almost certainly had the keys.

Unless he lost them while crawling around in the mud. That would really suck.

Suddenly, a thunderous cracking sound filled the air. The noise hit Jade like a slap. She had no idea what had caused it but knew it couldn't be anything good, so she threw herself flat on the ground in a reflex of self-preservation. In the corner of her eye, she saw a bright pink-orange flame, like a signal flare but much faster, streaking over the tall grass at the river's edge, streaking toward the—

There was another loud crack, harsher than a rifle report or even a peal of thunder, and a flash as the Rover transformed into a pillar of smoke and fire.

3

Jade rolled into a protective fetal curl, covering her head with her arms as the hot shock wave slammed into her, and stayed in that position for several seconds afterward as pieces of flaming debris began raining down all around her. By some miracle, none of it found her, but this was little comfort. Without the Rover….

She pushed the dire thought away and raised her head. "Professor? You still with me?"

"Jade! Over here!"

She started to rise, cocking her head to home in on his voice, but he stopped her with a hiss. "Stay down."

Something rustled in the grass beside her and she flinched, half-expecting to find herself staring down the gullet of a black caiman, but it was just Professor. "Stay down," he repeated. "If they suspect we're still alive, they might shoot another RPG."

"What, because blowing up the Rover twice sends a stronger message?"

"I meant shoot it at us. RPGs aren't exactly the ideal antipersonnel weapon, but just like horseshoes, sometimes close is good enough."

"Oh. I knew that."

He looked away, searching the surrounding area as if looking for a target. Jade realized that he had his pistol out.

"I saw three or four of them swimming across," she said.

"I know," he said without turning to her.

"Have you got a plan?"

"This is it." He thumbed a lever on the side of his

pistol, caught the magazine as it fell from the grip. After a quick visual inspection, he shook his head and slid it home again. "We play possum and hope they don't trip over us."

"How are we going to—"

"Shhh!"

Jade frowned. Was Professor silencing her because the bad guys were close or was he just trying to avoid answering her questions? She wasn't sure which explanation was better, but nevertheless did as instructed, clamping her mouth shut.

At first, the only thing she could hear was the sound of her own breathing, but after a few seconds, she could hear other sounds. The crackling of the flames that were still burning in the wreckage of their Land Rover. The soft rushing sound of the river. The rustling of something or someone moving through the vegetation… Men shouting in Spanish. Not too close, but definitely too close for comfort.

And then she heard something else. The distinctive roar of a jet engine, growing louder with each passing second.

Crap! Just when I thought this day couldn't get any worse.

She jolted as several rapid-fire reports sounded nearby. Without offering a word of explanation, Professor abruptly rolled over onto her, covering her body with his own, one hand clamped over her mouth. She knew he was just trying to protect her, but it took every ounce of self-control she possessed to simply lay there and let it happen.

A moment later, she heard a scream, which was abruptly cut off by what sounded like a stampede in the tall grass. It took another second or two for the buzz saw report of the distant machine gun to reach her ears, but when it did, she put two and two together.

The approaching aircraft—a helicopter—was shooting at the men on the ground with a large caliber automatic weapon. The kind of weapon soldiers might have.

"We're saved!" she shouted, or tried to. The exclamation was almost completely muffled by Professor's hand, and what came out sounded more like "Wuh say."

"Shhh," he said again, whispering into her ear. "We don't know who that is or what they want. They'll probably shoot first and ask questions later."

She hated to admit it, but he was right. Nobody knew they were out here, which meant the helicopter wasn't there to save them. Even if it was the Peruvian military, ready to take down the smugglers or terrorist or whatever they were, they wouldn't be able to differentiate good guys from bad, not from the air at least.

Okay, so maybe we're not saved.

The noise grew louder, the helicopter beating the air and flattening the grass with its rotor wash, as it descended, setting down on the road near the burning Rover, less than a hundred yards away. There hadn't been any shooting after the initial burst, but all that meant was that the soldiers were waiting for some fool to poke his or her head up so they could shoot it off.

She heard more shouting now, which seemed unusual given the amount of ambient noise. Even more surprising however, was *what* the man was shouting.

"Jade! Jade Ihara!"

"Wuh thu feh?" Jade muttered into Professor's

hand.

As if waiting for that cue, he let go, rolling off her. "Someone here to see you," he whispered.

Jade glared at him. "What am I supposed to do?"

Professor shrugged. "Ask them what they want."

"And what if what they want is to blow my head off?"

"I don't think it is, but I'll cover you. Trust me."

"Trust you," she grumbled, but then rose up on all fours and slowly... very slowly, stood with both hands raised high in the air.

As her head came up above the surrounding foliage, she saw clearly the helicopter idling on the ground, a stone's throw from the blasted remains of the Land Rover. It was definitely a military aircraft. Its bulbous fuselage bristling with weapons and rocket pods looked like a gigantic high-tech killer wasp. Half-a-dozen men, all wearing green-gray camouflage uniforms were fanning out from it in a loose semi-circle, and as Jade appeared before them, they all shifted their assault rifles toward her.

"Don't shoot!" she cried. "It's me. I'm Jade."

She didn't know if they could hear or understand, so she reached her hands a little bit higher, and as she did, she realized that one of the men didn't look like the others. Instead of a camouflage uniform and combat gear, he wore denim jeans and a khaki bush shirt, its long sleeves rolled up above his elbows. He had a thick beard and his uncovered head was an unruly black mop, tousled by the persistent rotor wash. He was good-looking, too; not movie-star or male-model pretty-boy handsome, but rougher, more masculine. His dark eyes locked onto her, and as he started toward her, she knew that he was the one who had been calling her name. The man turned away for a moment, shouting to the nearest soldier, who in turn barked an order to the others, and just like that, the rifles were aimed elsewhere.

Okay, that's a hopeful sign, Jade thought.

The man returned his attention to her and kept moving forward until he was only a couple steps away. He cupped a hand over his mouth and in a voice that was only slightly softer than a shout, said, "Dr. Ihara, I presume?"

She grinned, strangely giddy at his use of her academic title. "That's me."

"You can put your hands down," he said, extending his own right hand.

She dropped her arms, feeling a flush of embarrassment, and quickly accepted his hand clasp. "Hi. Call me Jade."

"Nick Kismet."

Kismet? Seriously? What is this guy, a rock star or something? She decided not to say it aloud.

His gaze flitted past her just for a moment, then he added, "Tell your friend that it's safe to come out. We're the good guys."

Jade laughed nervously, then turned, searching the grass for Professor but he was nowhere to be seen. She shrugged. "He's kind of shy. I guess he'll join us when he's ready. So what are you doing here, Nick Kismet?"

"Believe it or not, I was looking for you."

"Well, here I am. But that doesn't really answer my question."

He chuckled softly. "It looks like you guys could use a ride out of here. How about we talk about it on the way?"

"On the way to where?"

His expression became a little more serious. "That's one of the things we need to talk about."

4

After climbing aboard the helicopter, Jade donned a set of earmuff style headphones that, thankfully, brought the noise level from the engines down to a dull roar. After making a futile effort to wipe some of the mud from his fedora, Professor climbed in and took the air chair next to her. The misshapen hat lay on his lap, looking miserable but not defeated. Kismet sat across the aisle, and as both men fitted their commo headsets in place, the rest of the soldiers crowded in, filling up all the other seats and whatever other space they could find. When the last man was in, the aircraft began to shake and shimmy and then Jade felt an unsettling heaviness as it lifted off. Through one of the side windows, she could see the emerald expanse of the Amazon basin falling away behind them.

Professor's voice sounded in Jade's headset. "Okay, now that we can hear ourselves think," he said, his tone even gruffer than usual, "maybe we can run through those introductions again, and then you can explain exactly how it is that you just happened to be out here. Your timing is a little suspicious."

"I'd say my timing was perfect," Kismet replied, evenly. "But you're right. As I said before, I was out here looking for…" He hesitated, glanced over at Jade. "For you."

"Right," Professor retorted, making no attempt to hide his suspicion.

Or is it jealousy? She wondered.

"Okay, introductions take two," Kismet said. "I'm Nick. You're Jade. And you're… Sorry, I don't think I actually caught your name."

"Call me Pete." Professor narrowed his gaze at Kismet. "You're American. Are you a spook?"

Kismet shook his head. "No. I work for the UN. Specifically, for the Global Heritage Commission."

For the first time since meeting him, Jade felt a twinge of doubt. Maybe this wasn't a rescue after all.

The Global Heritage Commission was the enforcement arm of UNESCO—the United Nations Education Science and Cultural Organization. Jade didn't fully understand the political or bureaucratic intricacies of either body, but she was familiar with the mission of the former. GHC liaison agents worked with local law enforcement agencies to ensure the preservation of World Heritage sites and protect other unique cultural properties, which included random inspections of archaeological digs to ensure that the practices being used conformed to established guidelines and to expose illicit backdoor sales of artifacts to collectors.

"You work for the Global Heritage Commission and you're looking for me? Why? I haven't done anything wrong," Jade said, and then silently amended the statement, *Not lately anyway.*

"It's nothing like that," Kismet said, shaking his head emphatically. "Truthfully, I need your help with something. Something that has nothing to do with archaeology."

"If we refuse, are you going to kick us out?"

"Just hear me out."

Jade shrugged. "Go on."

"I understand that you had a hand in executing the estate of Gerald Roche."

Jade exchanged a wary glance with Professor.

Until his death, about a year earlier, Gerald Roche had been a notorious conspiracy celebrity and the author of several books about a purported takeover of global human society by what he called "changelings," so-named for the faerie creatures who substituted their own offspring for human children. There was some debate about whether Roche had actually believed that the changelings were supernatural creatures or merely a metaphor for the ruling elite, but after his murder, Jade and Professor had discovered a very real—and all too human— shadow government dating back several centuries. Roche himself was an odd character, and a notorious collector of occult memorabilia and other rare curiosities, which was how Jade had first become acquainted with him.

"Not exactly," she said, guardedly. "I was working with Dr. Allenby at the British Museum to preserve the collection intact, but the actual executors had other ideas. The provenance of most of the pieces was a bit dodgy—that was the word Dr. Allenby used—so we didn't put up too much of a fight. Most of the collection was sold at auction."

Kismet pursed his lips together in disappointment. "I'm specifically interested in a manuscript that might have been in his library. A book called the *Liber Arcanum.* Does that ring any bells?"

Professor leaned forward. "You're going to have to be a lot more specific than that. *Liber Arcanum* literally translates to 'Book of Secrets.' Every alchemist and occultist worth his salt wrote his own book of secrets, and I'd be willing to bet money that Gerald Roche had about a dozen of them."

Jade saw something change in Kismet's expression. His earlier confidence was gone, replaced by something that seemed almost like embarrassment or guilt. "As you might have already guessed, this gets into stuff that's a little… weird."

"We can handle weird," Jade said.

"If it involves Roche," Professor added, "that's pretty much a given."

Kismet nodded. "In April of 1904 an Englishman named Adam Garral climbed up the Great Pyramid at Giza in Egypt and spent the night inside the King's Chamber. Exactly what happened next is unclear, but when he emerged early the following day, he had in his possession a strange amulet which he claimed to have found in a hidden room deep within the pyramid—a room that no one else has ever found. He called the talisman 'the Apex,' probably because of its shape. It's a pyramid about so big." He held up his hand, finger and thumb spaced about three inches apart. "Made from a solid block of lapis lazuli, with what looks like a small skeletal hand gripping the exterior.

"Adam Garral was a minor occult figure in his day and it would be typical behavior for someone like that to concoct a wild origin story for a supposedly enchanted knick-knack, but for reasons I'm not prepared to go into right now, I think he was telling the truth."

"And you're trying to find this Apex," Jade guessed.

Kismet shook his head. "No. I already know where it is. I'm trying to figure out what happened next. Garral wrote in his diary that the Apex enabled him to, among other things, read a book he called 'the Liber Arcanum,' which was written in Enochian script. Enochian is a ciphertext language invented by Dr. John Dee and the magician Edward Kelley in the late 16th century, though they claimed it was actually the Angelic first language that mankind spoke before God confused the languages at the Tower of Babel."

"I've heard of it," Professor said, sending a wink in Jade's direction. "Despite that fanciful story, Enochian is remarkably similar to English in its grammatical structure and syntax."

Jade suppressed a giggle. "Most Americans think Jesus spoke English, so why not?"

Kismet frowned at the interruption, but pushed ahead with his story. "I'm not looking to prove Garral's claims, but I do want to find out what happened to him. He found something in that book, and whatever it was caused him to leave England, after which his trail vanishes. The only lead I have right now is this *Liber Arcanum.*"

"Which is written in Enochian," Jade said. "Enochian means John Dee, which brought you to Gerald Roche, which in turn brought you halfway around the world to me. You're going to an awful lot of trouble to find this guy."

Kismet shrugged. "I just missed you in Cuzco. Had to pull some strings to get the army to give me a ride out here."

"Lucky for us that you did." She stared at him a moment longer. "This isn't official business, is it? It's personal."

Kismet regarded her for several seconds then nodded. "Adam Garral was my great-great-grandfather."

Professor raised an eyebrow. "You're using your official capacity to investigate a personal matter?"

"If you're that worried about it," Kismet shot back,

"I can always make this official. But that would mean billing you for the rescue."

Jade stifled a chuckle and held up her hands. "Okay, we're all friends here." She faced Kismet. "First, thank you for getting us out of there. Second… I'm sorry, I don't recall seeing anything called the Liber Arcanum at Gerald's place in London, but that doesn't mean it wasn't there. If you'd like, I'd be happy to help you—"

"Jade," Professor said, his tone disapproving.

She waved him off and kept talking. "I'll put a call in to Kelly… Dr. Allenby. If she doesn't have it, she might know where it ended up."

"I appreciate it, but really there's no need for you to go to the trouble. You've already pointed me in the right direction. I'd hate to tear you away from your work here."

Jade glanced out the window again. The jungle looked deceptively peaceful from so high up. "I could go for a change of scenery. Oh, and a shower."

5

It was late evening before Jade and Professor managed to find a hotel room, procure some fresh clothes, and otherwise get cleaned up after the misadventure in the jungle. With a five-hour time difference between Cuzco and London, Jade knew it was already too late to reach Kelly Allenby at the British Museum, but she sent off a brief email, asking Allenby to call at her earliest convenience, before hitting the shower. She lingered there longer than she had intended, letting the hot water sweep away both the mud and grime, and the weariness of her post-adrenaline letdown.

When she felt vaguely human again, she toweled off, changed into her new clothes—nothing fancy, just a pair of dark green cargo shorts and a cream-colored tee with a silk-screened likeness of the Inca creator deity, Viracocha—and was just about to head down to the hotel restaurant to have dinner with Professor and Nick Kismet, when a knock sounded at her door. She peered through the peephole and saw Professor—likewise cleaned-up—waiting outside. He was alone and looked unusually pensive, fidgeting with his fedora which Jade noticed was now clean and restored to its original shape. Jade was accustomed to his gruff, almost dour manner, but she thought he looked even grumpier than usual.

She put on her best smile and threw the door open. "Hey, I was just on my way down."

"We need to talk first." He made a "let me come in" gesture, and she stepped aside, allowing him to enter. He walked past her and sank into a chair.

Jade sat on the corner of the bed. "Why so glum,

chum?"

Professor frowned. "I called Tam."

Tam was Tamara Broderick, an operations officer with the Central Intelligence Agency and leader of the Myrmidons. She was also the person who had assigned Professor to keep Jade out of trouble, which—if Jade was being honest—was pretty much a full-time job.

"Ah. Well, that's enough to put anyone in a bad mood," Jade retorted playfully.

"I thought I'd do a little background check on our mysterious savior."

Jade nodded slowly. Now Professor's mood made a bit more sense, but she still couldn't tell exactly what was bothering him. "And?"

"And, it seems that Nick Kismet is a bona fide hero. Served in army intelligence during the first Gulf War. He was involved in some kind of highly-classified op. Above top secret stuff. Sensitive Compartmented Information. Almost everything about him is SCI, and not even Tam has the clearance to read those files. All I could really dig up is what's on the Global Heritage Commission website. He's been with them since the mid-90s."

"He doesn't look that old."

"You'll have to ask him about that," Professor said curtly, then softened a degree or two. "You're right. He doesn't look a day over thirty. I don't know, maybe he found the Fountain of Youth or something."

Jade nodded absently, thinking that Professor sounded just the teensiest bit jealous of Nick Kismet.

Her relationship with Professor was unusual to say the least. He was her bodyguard and technically her assistant though she thought of him more as both an equal and a partner, even if his name didn't appear in the credits, so to speak. As a rule, letting things go from professional to personal was always a bad idea in a situation like that, but they had gone through too much together to be anything less than close friends. While she wasn't completely closed off to the idea of taking things to the next level, there was one other complication that neither of them had quite worked out.

Many years before, Professor had served in the SEALs with Dane Maddock—Jade's ex-boyfriend. Maddock was very much an ex, though there had been a few times when she had hoped things might break differently. She wanted to believe she was over him, but the feelings were still there, and for some perverse reason, the universe kept finding ways to remind her of them. Like arranging for her to work in close collaboration with one of Maddock's old teammates.

She probably could have dealt with that, but she sensed it was a problem for Professor as well. Maybe dating a swim-buddy's ex was a violation of the "bro code" or something. and as near as she could tell, he wasn't ready to cross that line.

Sometimes that bothered her; it was like Dane Maddock was still interfering with her love life. Mostly though, she was just relieved that she didn't have to make a choice that would fundamentally alter their status quo.

Still, there was no reason for Professor to be feeling jealous or protective where Nick Kismet was concerned. It wasn't as if she was going to be working closely with the guy or anything.

"You don't trust him?"

Professor shrugged. "Oh, I trust that he's not an enemy of the United States."

He is *jealous*, she thought. "Then what's got your undies bunched?"

"Tam needs me in Washington."

Jade was taken aback. "Why?"

"Something to do with Maddock's friend Jimmy Letson. She wasn't able to go into much detail, but it sounds like he's gone off the grid and that has her spooked. She's got her hands full with something else, so she asked me to look into it."

"When do we leave?"

He shook his head. "Tam wants you to stay here and work with Kismet."

"Uh, in case you've forgotten, I don't work for Tam."

The faintest hint of a smile flickered across Professor's face, but just as quickly vanished, replaced by the same irritated frown that had first greeted her. "Well, I can't make you work with him, but you can't come with me. I *do* work for Tam, and she told me to leave you behind." He paused a beat before adding, "She made it very clear that it would be in everyone's best interests if you helped him. She would owe you a favor."

Jade wagged her head sideways in a "whatever" gesture, but she secretly was pleased at the idea of Tam Broderick owing her a favor. "So I'm just supposed to chill here until you get back?"

"Here. Or wherever the search takes you. But to answer your original question, I'm heading to the airport now."

"What? What about dinner?"

"Rain check. Besides, three's a crowd." He shrugged. "I'd tell you to take care of yourself, but you never listen anyway. But if it's any consolation, from what I've read—maybe it would be more accurate to say, from what I haven't read—I think you'll be in good hands."

He stopped abruptly as if realizing too late how awkward the comment sounded, then rose to his feet and headed for the door. "Gotta go," he muttered, shoving his hat onto his head. "Taxi's waiting."

6

The restaurant maître d' escorted Jade to the table where Nick Kismet was seated. Jade appraised him as she made her approach. He still wore the same casual attire as before, yet there was something different about him. It took her a second to realize what it was, and by that time, she was standing across from him.

He rose to greet her, retaking his chair only after she had taken hers. As he did, he turned to the waiter and gestured to the empty rocks glass on the table. "Another for me. And the lady will have…?" He glanced at Jade.

Jade couldn't decide if Kismet was trying to be a gentleman or if he was naturally pushy, nor could she decide how she felt about it. "The lady will have Dos Equis if you've got it."

The waiter gave a helpless shrug. "*Lo siento.*" Then he added in accented but passable English. "We have Budweiser."

Jade made a face. "Great. Got anything local?"

"*Si.* We have a Ayrampo Roja—red ale—on draft from Cerveceria del Valle Sagrado. It is very popular with international visitors."

Jade looked back at Kismet. "What are you drinking?"

"Twelve-year-old Macallan. But I'm willing to live dangerously if you are."

"Ha. Okay. Let's do it."

Kismet flashed what she could only describe as a roguish grin and then turned back to the waiter.

"*Tenemos dos, por favor.*"

As the waiter moved off, Kismet faced Jade. "I wouldn't have taken you for a beer drinker," he said.

In truth, she wasn't. When she drank, which wasn't often, it was usually in social situations and she would drink whatever was put in front of her, knocking back pints or shots as if to prove she could hold her own with any grad student or former Navy SEAL. She had picked up a taste for Dos Equis when she and Maddock had been an item, and she still defaulted to it for old-time's sake, which was probably a sign of weakness on her part.

Still, where did Kismet get off making assumptions about her?

"Shows what you know." She paused a moment, then said. "You got a haircut."

His mouth twitched into something that wasn't quite a smile, then he shrugged and changed the subject. "Where's your friend? Skipper, wasn't it?"

"Very funny. It's Professor, but you can call him Dr. Chapman. Or you could have, if he hadn't been called away on other business." She hesitated, feeling Professor's absence even more acutely. *God, this is like being set up on a blind date.* "He's a SEAL, you know," she added with perhaps more assertiveness than the situation called for. "And he's got friends in very high places. He checked up on you before he left,"

"Is that a fact?"

"Damn straight. I know all about you, Nick Kismet."

"And yet you're still here," he said, laughing. The waiter arrived a moment later with two pint glasses filled with amber colored liquid. Kismet regarded her across the table for a moment then looked up at the waiter.

"We'll need a few more minutes, I think."

When they were alone again, he continued. "So, if you know all about me, I guess we'll have to come up with something else to talk about. You, for instance."

Jade now regretted the hasty comment since, in fact, she knew almost nothing about him, but before she could think of a retort, her phone began buzzing. She dug it out of her pocket, hoping against hope that it would be Professor calling to let her know that his plans had changed and he was already on his way back, but it wasn't him; it was Kelly Allenby.

She hit the button to accept the call. "Kelly. What are you still doing up? It must be after midnight there."

Allenby's laughing voice filled her ear. "Jim took me to the cinema, and drinks after. I only just saw your email."

"You didn't have to get back to me right away," Jade said. "It's nothing that can't wait until morning."

"No need to wait. It's a simple request with a simple answer."

Jade didn't like the sound of that. A simple answer in this case probably meant they were out of luck. She noticed Kismet watching her intently. "Kelly, I'm here with…uh, Nick. Nick Kismet. Can I put you on speaker?"

"Certainly."

Jade set the phone on the table and tapped the touch-screen to activate speaker mode. Kismet leaned over. "Dr. Allenby, I'm Nick Kismet with the Global Heritage Commission."

"Please, call me Kelly. I've heard a lot about you, Mr. Kismet."

Kismet chuckled. "I'm getting that a lot today."

"Jade says that you're looking for a manuscript from the estate of Gerald Roche, written in Enochian script, called *Liber Arcanum*, possibly authored by John Dee or Edward Kelley. Is that right?"

"Pretty close."

"The museum wasn't able to acquire all of Mr. Roche's library, but we were able to scan everything before the collection was released for auction. We have a virtual copy of every rare book or manuscript in his collection. Now, there's good news and bad. The bad is that there's nothing explicitly identified as *Liber Arcanum*. But there are several manuscripts that haven't been identified yet, so it's possible that one of them is what you're looking for."

"That is good news," Kismet said, with a genuine smile.

"I'll email Jade the link to the online archive. You can view the scans at your leisure."

Jade could see that Kismet was eager to get started. "Thanks so much, Kelly," she said. "I thought we were going to have to travel there in person."

"Oh, I wish you would. I'd love to see you again and catch up. And I wouldn't mind a chance to meet you in person too, Mr. Kismet."

"If you ever do," Kismet replied, "You'd better call me Nick."

Jade thanked Allenby again, and then rang off to check her email. The link was there, as promised, but when Jade clicked through and began selecting files to view, she realized the limitations of the technology. The crabbed handwriting was indecipherable in normal view, and when she tried to zoom in, she had to scroll back and forth to read complete lines. Not that she could actually read the odd script, which looked a little like Greek.

"You're going to need that Apex thingy if you want to read this," she remarked.

Kismet shifted in his chair, suddenly looking a little nervous. "There are online translation tools that can help with that," he said. "And I'm good with languages. Even made up ones."

"Hmm. We're going to need a bigger screen."

"I've got a tablet computer in my room," Kismet said. "That should make it easier to view the scans." He paused a beat before adding. "You said 'we.'"

"Yeah. Why? Were you planning to kick me to the curb?"

"Not at all. I just assumed that you—"

"Yeah, well you know what happens when you assume." She took a long pull from her beer, then brought the glass down a little more forcefully than she had intended. "I vote we order room service, and move this party to your place."

She allowed herself a small smile when she noticed that, under his thick beard, Nick Kismet was blushing.

7

"**Party,**" **Jade decided,** wasn't the right word for what happened next. It was more like... Well, work. But Kismet's room was quieter than the restaurant, and so far, he had been a perfect gentleman.

Maybe a little too perfect. Jade wouldn't have minded catching him sneaking an appraising glance at her once in a while, but his attention was entirely consumed with the images from the British Museum online archive.

The larger screen on Kismet's tablet computer did make it easier to *see* the scans, but did not make them any less incomprehensible. Worse, as Kismet opened one file after another, flipping through the documents like they were pages in a retail catalog, he seemed to lose all interest in conversation.

"Are you sure you haven't got one of those Apex thingies?" she asked after a while.

He looked up, blinking several times as if trying to relieve eye strain. "What?"

"You haven't used any of those online resources you were talking about. From where I'm sitting, it looks like your sight-reading this stuff." Even as she said it aloud, she realized that was exactly what he was doing. "Oh, my God. You do have it, don't you?"

"I... It's not like that," he said, a little too quickly. "I'm not reading it, I'm just trying to get an overview."

"Bull crap," Jade fired back. "You're reading it. You've got the Apex stone, don't you?"

Kismet sighed, then reached up to the collar of his

shirt and tugged it down to reveal a pendant dangling from a rawhide strip around his neck. It was exactly as he had described it, a pyramid of dark blue lapis lazuli flecked with gold pyrite and white calcite, with ridges that looked exactly like the bones of a child's hand fused in place as if gripping it.

"Can I try it?"

Kismet didn't react visibly, but Jade could tell that the question discomfited him. She had a mental image of Smeagol from Lord of the Rings, lovingly clutching the ring and whispering "Precious," and decided not to press the issue. "How does it work? Is it automatic? Like a universal translator?"

"I'm not really sure that it's doing anything," Kismet admitted. "I told you I was good with languages. It wasn't an exaggeration. I've looked at a lot of this writing since I started looking for the *Liber Arcanum*. At first, it was hard to decipher, but now..." He shrugged. "The script looks exactly the same, but it just sort of makes sense to me."

"But you're actually reading this?"

"Skimming it. I've seen most of this stuff before in other editions, so what I'm really doing is looking for something different. Something that..."

He trailed off, prompting Jade to take another look at the screen. The image on the screen was more of the same—strange Enochian glyphs, the so-called Angelic language—but they were not broken up into words or discrete lines. Instead, the arrangement looked more like a word search puzzle, with each individual character evenly spaced in relation to the next, to form a grid— Jade's best guess was that it was a fifty-by-fifty grid. The script remained unreadable to her, but Jade thought she could see intentional patterns, as if the strange letters had been used to produce a picture. But that wasn't the really weird part.

There were words written on the page, outside the grid. English words. Comments, with little arrows drawn to underlined portions of the text. Without context, the comments themselves were just as cryptic. There were references to elements and directions, and names that sounded like Latin words, followed by numerical notations that might have been page or chapters numbers.

Kismet had not said a word for what seemed like several minutes. "Is this it? Is this the one?"

"This is the *Liber Loagaeth*," he said, speaking slowly.

"What does that mean? Is it, or isn't it the book you're looking for?"

"The name means 'Book of the Speech of God' but it's sometimes also called '*Liber Mysteriorum.*' 'Book of Mysteries.' Edward Kelley composed it based on a revelation he claimed to have received after looking into John Dee's crystal Shew Stone."

Jade coughed nervously. "Never heard of it."

"The book itself is fairly well known, but there's no definitive translation. This is a hand-written copy. It was a fairly standard practice for occult students to write one in their own hand. I think this one belonged to Adam Garral. That's his writing in the margins."

"Get out." Jade slugged him playfully in the shoulder.

Kismet grinned, but then resumed clicking through the pages with renewed enthusiasm. Each new page was a different grid, with even more elaborate—and clearly intentional—patterns, and on each were more notes. Kismet seemed to devour them all in a single glance, not even giving Jade enough time to read the scribbled comments. Then, for no apparent reason, he lingered on one page, reading it several times. Finally, he offered an explanation.

"This page…it's different than the other versions."

"Different how?"

"There's a mention here of the smoking mirror which shows the past and the future. I'm paraphrasing of course. It's widely believed that Dee and Kelley used both crystals—like the Shew Stone—and an obsidian scrying mirror obtained in the New World, but this is the first time I've seen an explicit reference to it. In this passage, the angel is recounting how the mirror was found in the temple of someone named…" He paused. "Well, that's odd. It just says the 'pyramid temple of smoking mirror.'"

"Not so odd," Jade said. "The Aztec deity of divination was named Tezcatlipoca, which literally translates to 'smoking mirror.' He was the god of, among other things, obsidian. Obsidian mirrors are a common artifact found in his temples."

"Okay, that makes sense. What's really strange is that I've never seen mention of the mirror in any of Dee's writings."

Jade nodded, recalling a conversation about the topic with Kelly Allenby at the British Museum. Although several crystal balls and other items were associated with Dee and his divination attempts, none of those objects had been reliably proven to have ever belonged to him.

"The angel talks about showing distant lands and

things to come," Kismet continued, "and promises to show the seer how to find the other elemental temples."

"What does that mean?"

Kismet shook his head and swiped his finger across the tablet to bring up the next document. Jade gasped in disbelief. The document was not written in Enochian script, nor did it appear to have ever been a part of the grimoire. It was a letter, written on a piece of stationery that bore the letterhead: "BRITISH ANTARCTIC EXPEDITION 1910, 36 & 38 VICTORIA STREET, LONDON S.W."

The missive written to a certain Capt. J.E. Grace, was both a note of thanks, for a contribution in the amount of £1,000, and of congratulations, praising Captain Grace's expertise with horses and welcoming him to the expedition. It was signed, "Your faithful servant, R. Scott."

In the blank space at the top of the page, someone—the same someone that had made notes in the margins of the occult manuscript—had written: "Poor Scott. He thinks he'll find immortality at the Pole, but I've got the map! VITRIOL!"

"One of these things is not like the other," Jade said, shaking her head as she read the letter a second time. There was an accompanying notation from the archivist, indicating that the letter had been discovered between two pages of the folio, and was included in the file exactly as it had been found. "What do you suppose that's doing there?"

Kismet just stared at the screen for several moments in silent contemplation. Finally, he shook his head. "Unbelievable."

"What's unbelievable?"

He pointed to the screen. "This letter. Do you know what it is?"

Jade shook her head uncertainly. "Antarctic expedition…1910…Scott. Kind of rings a bell."

She was acutely feeling Professor's absence now. He would have already launched into a thorough explanation of the letter's significance.

"Robert Falcon Scott was a British naval officer and polar explorer. He wanted to be the first man to reach the South Pole. That's what this expedition was all about. He made it to the pole, though another expedition led by Roald Amundsen beat him there by a month. Scott and his team all died on the return trip. This man—Captain John Edward Grace—was with him almost to the end. According to Scott's diary, Grace suffering from frostbite and scurvy, left the tent and walked out into a blizzard so that the others wouldn't waste any more resources on him. Supposedly, the last thing he said was, 'I am just going outside and may be some time.' His sacrifice ultimately didn't matter because Scott and the others only made it another twenty miles before getting stopped in their tracks by the storm. They all starved to death."

"Okay," Jade said slowly. "And this is important why?" Silently, she added, *Professor, where are you when I need you?*

Kismet took a deep breath and let it out. "I think Adam Garral and Captain Grace were one and the same."

"You think?" Jade said, enunciating the words like an accusation. "He's your great-grandfather. Don't you know? I mean, you look it up on Ancestry.com, yeah?"

Kismet's face screwed up in a look that was part-annoyance and part-reservation. "Until recently, I never had a reason to investigate the family lore. I was told that Garral was something of a wandering libertine. Even his relationship with his wife, my great-great-grandmother, was an unconventional one; something to do with an occult rite if I understand correctly. He was always off on some adventure or another, and while he would write from time to time, it wasn't like he could send GPS tagged photos from his smartphone. All she really had was his word for it. And when he disappeared in 1910, she just assumed he was off on another adventure. But aside from the oral tradition, there's really not a lot of information about him. It's not impossible… No, scratch that. It's entirely plausible that he was leading a double life."

"Okay, but this other guy, Grace, he's a known historical quantity."

"Good point." Kismet closed the browser window displaying the letter and opened a search engine, into which he typed in the name of the polar explorer.

John Edward Grace had been born in 1880 to a landed family in London. Although the family occupied the manor hall at Gestingthorpe near Sudbury, Grace spent his school years in Putney, London and then attended Eton College, though he did not complete his studies there. He only had one sibling—a sister—and his father died when Grace was just sixteen. Perhaps inspired by his uncle, a famed explorer and naturalist, Grace embarked on a military career, which took him to the far-flung corners of the empire—South Africa, India, Egypt—where he was commended for bravery and ultimately promoted to the rank of captain. In 1910, he took an interest in joining Scott's expedition, buying his way onto the competitive roster with a sizeable monetary donation, though according to Scott, it was Grace's expertise with horses that was the deciding factor. Most of Scott's team was composed of close acquaintances and polar veterans from Shackleton's expeditions, with Grace being a rare outsider.

The relationship between the two men was tense at times, with Grace complaining about Scott's leadership, but Scott nevertheless included him in the five-man team that set out on the final push to plant the Union Jack at the South Pole. Unfortunately for them, when they arrived, they found a tent left behind by Amundsen along with a letter dated thirty-five days earlier. Even worse, owing to increasingly difficult weather conditions and injuries—including a fall that killed one member of the team—the return trip took longer than expected and the dog-sled teams that were supposed to meet them never showed up. The men quickly ran out of supplies, which led to further health complications. Grace, suffering from scurvy which may have aggravated an old war injury, soon succumbed to frostbite and gangrene, and knowing that his death was looming, left the tent and vanished forever into history. His famous parting words may have been apocryphal, but embodied a bold and self-sacrificing spirit.

And yet, there was clearly more to the man than history realized. For nearly a century, it was believed that Grace had died without offspring, but a 2002 biography offered compelling evidence that Grace had fathered a child out of wedlock, with a 12-year-old Scottish girl.

"That takes sowing wild oats to a new low," Jade remarked.

"You know if he lived one secret life, maybe he had another; one that nobody knows about."

"That would be a scandalous revelation, even today. It sounds like this guy is still a national hero."

Kismet nodded slowly. "I'm not interested in rewriting the history books. I just want to know what happened to him." He paused. "Adam Garral left the Apex with his wife and infant son, and if he and Grace were really the same person, then we know where he went. But why?"

Jade snapped her fingers. "The note scribbled on that letter. It said something about immortality."

Kismet clicked back to the document and read the handwritten note aloud. "'Poor Scott. He thinks he'll find immortality at the Pole, but I've got the map! VITRIOL!'"

"Vitriol? That's some kind of acid, yeah?"

Kismet nodded. "It's an archaic term for sulfate. But it's also an acronym for the motto of medieval alchemists. *Visita Interiora Terrae Rectificando Invenies Occultum Lapidem*. 'Visit the interior of the earth and rectifying you will find the secret stone.'"

"Oooh, there's a secret stone. Interior of the earth? Does that mean a cave, or are we talking hollow earth theory?"

"For the alchemists, it was probably the latter. And the secret stone was a reference to the Philosopher's Stone which could supposedly transmute base metals into gold or even make a person immortal."

"Immortality," Jade said. "Scott was looking for the immortality of fame, but Grace—or Garral—was looking for the real deal, and the map he had led him to the South Pole."

"Most hollow earth theories held that there were openings to the interior world at the poles. Even as late as the 1950s, some of these scientific expeditions were actually looking for an entrance." Kismet tapped his fingers on the table, deep in thought. "You know what? I think the name 'Garral' is another clue?"

"How so?"

"Garral is a very uncommon surname, but it was used by Jules Verne in the novel *Eight Hundred Leagues on the Amazon*."

"And Jules Verne wrote *Journey to the Center of the Earth*," Jade said, catching on.

"Something my great-great grandfather read in the *Liber Arcanum* convinced him he could find an entrance to the interior world in Antarctica. I think he was being literal when he said he had a map."

"I guess it led him astray."

"Maybe. Or maybe he never got the chance to go looking for it on his own. Maybe that's what he was trying to do at the end."

"You think Scott was lying about his condition? Frostbite and gangrene?"

"Probably not. Maybe at that point, he was delusional. If he was, the map is probably still with his body." Kismet stared at the screen for a long time. "We need to find him. His remains, I mean."

Jade grimaced. "Umm, you're kidding, right? You're talking about finding a needle in an Antarctica-sized haystack."

"Not necessarily. Scott recorded the exact coordinates of the camp where Grace vanished. Assuming that he really was suffering from frostbite, he wouldn't have gotten far."

"Maybe not, but it's been over a hundred years. That spot is probably buried under a ton of ice."

"Probably," Kismet agreed. "But with modern technology, I think we can definitely shrink the haystack down to something a little more manageable."

"We?"

"I thought you would want to see this through. Unless you're planning to kick *me* to the curb," Kismet said, throwing her earlier words back at her.

"That was before you said anything about Antarctica." Jade shivered just thinking about it. But, she also recalled what Professor had said about sticking close to Kismet. She let out a growl of defeat, but before she could articulate the terms of her surrender, a knock came at the door, followed by a loud female voice: "Room service."

"Took them long enough," Jade muttered, though secretly she was grateful for the interruption. It would give her a few seconds to think of something better to say to Kismet. She pushed out of her chair and started for the door. "I'll get it."

She reached the door in a few quick steps and, after checking the peephole to make sure that the woman on the other side of the door was indeed wearing the attire of a hotel server and pushing a tray-laden cart, threw the door wide.

"Perfect timing," she started to say, but the cheery greeting turned to a yelp of alarm as, first one, then a pair, then four men, who had been lined up along the wall, just outside the peephole's periphery, surged toward her.

8

Kismet was on his feet in an instant, but the intruders had the initiative. They also had guns—large semi-automatic pistols—which they trained on Kismet and Jade. One of the men grabbed Jade by the arm and pushed her back into the room.

Jade's first thought was the men who had pursued her and Professor through the rain forest had somehow tracked her here, intending to finish what they had started earlier. It was a reasonable conclusion; the men were a rough-looking bunch and with their dark hair and swarthy complexions, they might have passed for locals. But when the fifth member of the group—the woman pushing the room service cart—stepped right past Jade and stalked toward Kismet, Jade realized they weren't here for her at all.

The woman was strikingly beautiful. Her long glossy black hair framed an angular face with an olive complexion and high cheekbones; Mediterranean features, Jade decided, or possibly Arabian. She now saw that the server's jacket hung loose on the woman's frame, as if several sizes too big; no doubt borrowed from an actual hotel employee. The woman strode into the room with the confidence of a runway model, stopping when she was almost face-to-face with Kismet. Jade had only an oblique view of the confrontation, but she could see the anger radiating from the woman's coal black eyes.

"You have something that belongs to me," the woman said. Her voice was about what Jade expected, smooth and melodious, and decidedly at odds with the menace that dripped from every consonant.

Kismet, who had his hands raised, regarded her with thoughtful wariness. "I think you've got the wrong room."

She stared back at him for several seconds, then gave him a cold smile. "No, Nick Kismet. I am exactly where I want to be."

Okay, Jade thought. *Definitely not here for me.*

Although her heart was pounding like crazy, she willed herself calm, took a deep breath and cleared her throat. "Well you two obviously have some catching up to do," she said, trying to inject some bravado into her tone to mask just how terrified she was. "I'll leave you to it."

And with that, she pivoted toward the exit. The move took her captor by surprise, and before he could react, she twisted out of his grip.

Jade wasn't sure what she was trying to accomplish. On one level, she thought the intruders might just let her go. Unlikely, she knew, but not impossible. High-stress situations sometimes did funny things to people. Maybe they would be so focused on Kismet that they wouldn't know how to react until she was already in the clear.

And if that happened, what then? Should she run for it? Call for help? Pull the fire alarm, maybe?

It was a moot question. The man wasn't about to let her leave the room. He twisted around and made a grab for her, which was, after all, what she had actually been expecting him to do.

From the moment the gunmen barged into the room, Jade had started mentally reviewing all the self-defense lessons she had ever received. Maddock had taught her a few moves, and Professor had built on that foundation with semi-formal instruction in grappling and basic martial arts. One thing he had said now came back to her; just two words: *Don't hesitate.*

In a potential hostage-taking scenario, Professor had told her, the longer you waited, hoping for someone to come along and save you, the more control you gave to your would-be captor. It was important to act quickly and decisively before those roles—hostage and captor—became fixed, hardening like concrete. Jade had remembered that lesson, forcing herself to act, to move, to do something…anything… before that deadly inertia could set in.

The rest was almost automatic.

She allowed the man to seize her forearm, but as he did, she sidestepped into his weak side, performing an aikido combination known as *Irimi Nage*—the entering throw. She moved in close, almost spooning him from behind, and got her free hand up onto his neck, pushing him in the direction he was already traveling. She could feel his astonishment in the tightening of his muscles, the immediate reflexive resistance. Professor had taught her to be ready for that, too. As the man shifted, trying to brace himself, she shifted too, whirling him around, unbalancing him completely.

Even as she launched into the almost choreographed routine, the rest of the intruders began reacting as well, but Jade's decisiveness had deprived them of the initiative. They still had the numbers, but for the moment, she was calling the shots. Guns swiveled around and were aimed uncertainly in her direction. What were they supposed to do now? Shoot her? That wasn't the plan. Almost in unison, they looked to their leader, the striking woman who had been in the process of confronting Kismet, only to discover that situation had undergone a similarly dramatic change.

"Guns down!" Kismet barked.

Jade finished the throw, putting the gunman on his back, hard enough to knock the wind out of him, and glanced up just in time to see Kismet whirl the woman around so that she was facing the other men. He had his left arm securely around her waist, and his right snaked up under her right armpit to press something to her throat.

It was a knife, but that description seemed inadequate. Jade was reminded of a scene from an old movie—*Crocodile Dundee*—where the Aussie hero, threatened by a mugger with a switchblade, laughingly says, "That's not a knife," and then, drawing a wicked-looking ten-inch long Bowie knife, finishes with, "*That's* a knife."

Kismet's weapon of choice wasn't a Bowie knife, but something even bigger, and perhaps just a touch more wicked-looking. It was a *kukri*, the signature weapon of the fierce Gurkha warriors from Nepal. The blade had an odd boomerang shape, with the cutting edge on the inside of the elbow-like bend. Jade had seen similar knives, variations on the same style, but the knife Kismet held looked less refined than most she had seen, rougher, more authentic somehow, and Jade couldn't help but think that it had probably spilled more than a little actual blood.

She also wondered where he had been hiding it.

"Guns down." Kismet repeated in a flat tone. "Or she dies."

The gunmen all looked to the woman—Kismet's hostage—taking their cues from her, and she evidently wasn't ready to submit. "You're outnumbered, Kismet," she hissed. "If you kill me, you will certainly die."

She had an oddly formal manner of speech and an accent that suggested English might not be her first language.

"Don't bet your life on that," Kismet said, and then directing his gaze at the gunmen, added. "Don't bet *her* life on it. Put the guns down." Then, before they could accede or refuse, he snapped. "Jade, come over here now."

Jade lurched into motion, hurrying over to stand behind Kismet before any of the gunmen could even think about trying to grab her in order to balance the terms of the standoff.

Not that she would have submitted easily.

She recognized that he was doing the same thing she had. Reacting, moving, refusing to get bogged down in inertia. She got close to him, turning so that they were back to back.

The woman started to say something, another defiant threat perhaps, but Kismet silenced her with a rough shake and growled in her ear. "Tell them to drop their guns, or you will bleed."

"Do as he says," she said, her voice tight.

One by one, the gunmen lowered their guns. They did not drop them, but aimed them at the floor, as if testing Kismet's resolve.

It was a mistake.

The woman let out a wail as the blade bit into the flesh under her throat. Almost simultaneously, the pistols began thudding on the carpet.

"That's better," Kismet said. "Now, get in the bathroom."

The men hesitated, so Kismet dug the blade of the kukri in again until the woman whimpered. "Do it!"

The men grudgingly filed into the small lavatory room and, without being told to do so, closed the door.

"Get their guns," Kismet said to Jade.

Jade hurried forward and collected the weapons, holding them with the same kind of caution she might have used holding a snake. "What should I do with them?"

He shrugged. "Think of something."

She dumped them on the room service cart, and then picked up the domed tray cover and used it to conceal them. "Cool. What now?"

"Grab my tablet. And then get ready to move. We're getting out of here in a minute. But first…" He moved his knife away from the woman's throat but did not release her. There was a two-inch long red line on the skin below her jaw, slowly oozing tears of blood. "Who are you?" he hissed. "And what the hell do you want?"

She made a noise in her throat, as if trying to gather enough saliva to spit. "You killed my husband. And I am going to kill you."

"I've killed a lot of husbands," Kismet retorted. "You'll have to do better than that."

Jade felt an ominous chill at his casual admission.

He's kidding, right?

She looked away quickly so her face would not betray her, and grabbed the tablet off the table, tucking it under one arm.

"His name was Alexander Cerulean," the woman hissed.

Kismet nodded slowly. "And you are?"

"Aliyah."

"Okay, listen to me Aliyah. I get that you think you need to avenge your beloved, but that's not going to happen. Get over it. Go home and move on with your life. If you don't, I promise you'll join your husband in hell. This is your only warning."

Then, to punctuate the ultimatum, he drew back his hand and hammered the butt end of the kukri into the back of her head.

Aliyah Cerulean crumpled to the floor.

Kismet whirled to face Jade. "Go! Get the elevator."

Jade threw the door open and raced into the hallway, with Kismet right behind her. She sprinted to the elevator foyer, punched the call button and then looked back to see if any of Aliyah's men were giving chase. There was no sign of pursuit, but Jade knew that might change at any second. She looked back at the elevators, checked the indicators above each set of doors. The hotel had only five floors, and Kismet's room was on the third, so they shouldn't have had to wait more than a few seconds, but like the proverbial watched pot, it seemed to take forever. Finally, there was a loud chime as one of the cars arrived, and a moment after that, the doors slid open.

She started to go inside, but Kismet held her back. "Not this one," he said. He leaned head and shoulders inside the car, punched a button on the panel, and then drew back before the doors could close. He then pivoted away, rounding a corner and heading down an adjacent hallway. "Come on."

"What the hell are you—?" Kismet was gone before Jade could finish the question, so she hurried to catch up to him. She caught up to him just as he was entering a door at the far end of the hallway; the placard beside it showed a graphical representation of someone descending a staircase.

Stairs, Jade thought. *What the hell is he doing?*

To her further consternation, instead of heading down toward the exit, Kismet began ascending. Jade didn't even bother to ask, but hurried after him.

When he reached the next landing, Kismet pushed through the door and headed down the corridor, moving at a fast walk, too fast for Jade to simultaneously walk and talk. She could barely contain her ire when he arrived at what appeared to be his ultimate destination: the elevator foyer.

"Are you kidding me?" She snarled. "Why didn't we just—?"

He touched a finger to his lips. "Shhh."

"Don't shush me," she shot back, though in a considerably lower voice.

Kismet just pointed to the indicator. The one above the door to the car she had summoned earlier showed that it was now in the lobby. The elevator beside it was rising, responding to someone else's call.

It stopped on the third floor.

Jade frowned. She was starting to grasp Kismet's overall intent, but that didn't mean she was prepared to forgive him for not including her.

God, he's *even more annoying than Maddock.*

Another thirty seconds passed, and then the indicator changed to "2" and kept going.

Kismet let out the breath he had been holding. "I think they took the bait. Now they can chase their tail for a while trying to figure out where we went."

"So, you never had any intention of leaving the

hotel?"

"Oh, we're leaving. But not until we're good and ready."

"'We' again? You're making a lot of assumptions, Nick Kismet."

"You're right." He inclined his head in a deferential bow. "Thanks for your help, Dr. Ihara. It's been a pleasure working with you. I'll send you a postcard from Antarctica."

"And now you're assuming that I *don't* want to go with you," she shot back. "Why don't you try asking?"

A mischievous smile formed on his lips. "Okay. Dr. Ihara, I'm going to Antarctica. Would you care to join me?"

She stared back at him, her eyes hard as diamonds. "That woman, Aliyah… Did you really kill her husband?"

His smile slipped a notch. "A few weeks ago, Alexander Cerulean stole the Apex from my father. I tracked him to Cairo, to the Great Pyramid. He…" Kismet hesitated a moment. "We struggled and he fell. It was self-defense."

"Yeah? You do that a lot?"

He uttered a short, humorless laugh. "More than I care to admit." He paused a beat, then added, "Speaking of self-defense, you handled yourself pretty well back there."

"Thanks."

"Look, I'm sorry that you got dragged into this."

"It happens." She shrugged. "So, Antarctica, huh? Gonna be cold, yeah?"

Kismet nodded. "Yeah.

PART TWO- MADDOCK

9

"Back up a second," Dane Maddock said, holding up his hands, palms out. "Jimmy's in trouble?"

Jade frowned, evidently irritated at the interruption of her narrative, and for a few seconds, the only sound was the soft murmur of Ivan's engine vibrating through the vehicle, and crunch of the heavy-duty monster-truck sized tires compressing ice crystals on the frozen road that linked the airstrip to the permanent installation of McMurdo Station.

Ivan was not "some dude" as Bones had suggested. That mystery had been cleared up as soon as the large red and white all-terrain all-weather multi-passenger vehicle had pulled up beside them. Painted in big block letters on the front fender of the enormous shuttle were the words: "'Ivan' the Terra Bus."

Jade finally glanced over at Kismet. "Maybe you should field this one."

Kismet nodded. "As near as we can put together, when you asked your friend, Mr. Letson, to look into the mystery of that plane wreck you found in South Africa, it tripped some kind of silent alarm and put both you and him on Prometheus' radar."

A few days earlier, Maddock and his crew of underwater treasure hunters had found the sunken wreckage of what appeared to be an old *Boeing 314 Clipper*—an enormous flying boat built just before World War II. What made the discovery unusual was the fact that there was neither a record of such a plane crashing there, nor of the plane's actual existence. Only a handful of planes from that line had been built, and all of them were accounted for. Jimmy had made a few discreet inquiries, none of which had really helped much, and that had seemingly been the end of that.

Except, immediately afterward, Jimmy had gone incommunicado. Then a group of mysterious killers had made, not one but several attempts on their lives as they slowly pieced together the story of the mystery clipper's final flight. The trail had led them to Antarctica where they had discovered the strange orb in the frozen pyramid their new traveling companion Rose Greer had dubbed 'the Outpost,' but until Jade and Kismet had arrived, swooping down out of the sky to scatter the attacking enemy, Maddock did not know who was behind it all. Nor had he realized that Jimmy had been caught up in the web as well.

Now he had a name to attach to the killers who had pursued him. Prometheus.

"Jimmy's safe by the way," Jade added. "He's with Professor. They're the ones who figured out that Prometheus was coming after you down here. Since we were close, Tam asked us to come bail you out. Lucky, yeah?"

Dane Maddock wasn't a big believer in luck. He faced Kismet. "You seem to be the expert on Prometheus. Who or what are they?"

Kismet took a moment to consider his answer. "Jade has told me about some of your… ah, adventures? So I know that you'll understand what I mean when I say that there are… things. Objects. Artifacts and relics, and such, that are *powerful*."

"Oh, brother," Bones said, wagging his head. "You

would not believe some of the crap we've seen."

"I think I might at that," Kismet said. "The short answer to your question is that Prometheus is a secret society dedicated to controlling those objects of power. Not just controlling them, but erasing them from history. They think they're doing us all a favor. That human society isn't ready for the truth about… Well, everything. Gods and devils, aliens…You name it, they want to keep it a secret. They chose Prometheus the Titan—the god of foresight—as their mascot, because he tried to protect mankind from the games played by the gods. That's what they think they are doing."

"Sounds very paternalistic," Maddock said. "And arrogant."

"I don't know," Bones countered. "People are pretty stupid. I mean, I don't trust our government with some of the stuff we've found, and ours is better than most."

Kismet gave an ambivalent shrug. "You're not wrong about their arrogance. They recruit only the best and brightest. The intellectual elite. Which makes them particularly formidable. And their wall of secrecy is all but impenetrable."

"You evidently penetrated it."

Kismet grimaced. "I have a… call it an inside source. But even so, I've only scratched the surface. What I do know is that in the last few years there's been a schism. One faction supports the original mission, the long game. The other side has more of a use-it-or-lose-it philosophy. The latter group is weaker but desperate enough to go for the nuclear option."

"Do you mean that literally?" Bones asked.

"Maybe. My source told me that orb you found— the anomaly—has been on their hit list for a while." He glanced at Rose, who carried the strange black sphere in a backpack slung over one shoulder. "When Mr. Letson's inquiry got flagged, the splinter faction realized somebody was looking for it and decided to make their power play."

Bones nodded slowly, and then articulated what Maddock was thinking. "Helluva coincidence that you— the expert on Prometheus—just happened to be here on unrelated business."

Kismet rubbed his bearded chin. "I'm not so sure it's unrelated after all."

"What a surprise," Bones chuckled.

Maddock reflected on the story Jade had recounted to them. "You're thinking that this relative of yours, Garral… Grace. He was looking for what we found?"

"It's certainly possible, though based on what we know of Scott's expedition, he never got anywhere close to the valley where you found the Outpost. But if there was a pre-historic civilization down here, there could well be other outposts just like it buried under the ice."

"That's consistent with the stories my great-grandad wrote," put in Rose Greer. Rose, a history professor from upstate New York, had found the solution to the mystery of the Clipper wreck in the pages of a pulp novel written by her great-grandfather, David "Dodge" Dalton. and ultimately guided Maddock and Bones to the Outpost.

"It's possible that Grace-Garral was looking for the anomaly," Kismet said. "But I think the anomaly is part of something bigger. Garral mentioned a map. I think the anomaly might be a compass, pointing the way to something else. But we'll know for sure when we find his remains and see the map for ourselves."

"About that," Maddock countered. "I've read about Scott's expedition and I remember what happened with Grace. His body wasn't found by the search parties who went looking for Scott, and that was a hundred years ago. Not only is he probably buried under fifty feet of ice, but the ice itself is constantly moving, so even if you had the exact coordinates where he died—which you don't—he wouldn't be there."

Kismet nodded. "I've retained the services of a top-notch engineering firm to help me locate and recover Garral's body. Their expert puts the ice cover closer to seventy-five feet and he estimates the ice has advanced about thirty miles closer to the Ross Sea. That gave us a ballpark to play in. After that, we plugged in survey data from Operation IceBridge to identify anomalous densities in the target zone at the estimated depth."

Operation IceBridge, Kismet explained, was a NASA program designed to produce a comprehensive database of polar ice in order to accurately gauge the effects of climate change. Survey aircraft equipped with an extensive array of remote sensing technologies made repeated flights over the ice sheets, building a detailed three-dimensional model that went all the way down to bedrock—as deep as two miles in some places—or to the sea, as was the case with the Ross Ice shelf.

Maddock was impressed, and a little jealous of the resources Kismet had at his disposal. "Your guy found something?"

Kismet shrugged. "A few somethings. Unfortunately, the radar can only tell us where the anomalies are, not what they are."

"So it might be a body," Bones muttered, "or it might just be a big pile of penguin crap."

"I'm afraid so," Kismet admitted. "We've identified more than a dozen anomalies and prioritized them based on location and size. Our best match has an 86% probability, but there's only one way to know for sure."

Bones rolled his eyes. "If it's anything like ice-fishing, count me out. Unless there's a lot of beer, that is."

"Sounds time-consuming," Maddock said. "And with Prometheus breathing down our necks, time is one thing we don't have a lot of."

"You're right," Kismet said. "If they haven't figured out where you went or that you're with me, they soon will. We'll probably only get one shot at this."

There was a lurch as Ivan came to a full stop in front of the reception building.

"You can chill here…" Kismet started to say, then stopped himself. "Uh, I mean stay here. Arrange your own transportation home. Or you can head to the work site with me. It's a couple hours by helicopter. Honestly, I don't know what the safest option is."

"I think we're all in this together," Maddock said, then glanced at Bones and Rose. The latter nodded. Bones glowered, but didn't contradict his partner, or even offer one of his typically off-color wisecracks. Maddock took that as a vote in favor.

After a brief stopover in the sprawling quasi-city that was McMurdo Station they headed to the helicopter operations center to board a waiting Bell 212 for the flight to the work site. When Kismet had mentioned an engineering firm, Maddock had expected to find a small army of roughnecks deploying industrial equipment and derricks to support vertical drills, but as they approached, all he saw was a bright yellow festival-sized tent, looking forlorn in the bleak white landscape, about two hundred yards from the designated landing pad. As the helicopter touched down, a figure in a heavy parka emerged from the tent, and pulled back a flap closure to permit a tracked vehicle, fitted with a large fuel tank, to roll out into the open. The man in the parka swung up into the cab of the refuel vehicle, after which it surged forward to meet the helicopter.

While the driver of the fuel truck set about the task of topping off the Bell's tanks, the passenger came over to meet Kismet and the others. He threw back his hood to reveal a full head of dark, shoulder length hair and a young but craggy, deeply tanned visage, partially hidden behind a pair of mirrored aviator-style sunglasses. "Didn't expect you back so soon," the man said, gripping Kismet's hand.

"Things happened fast," Kismet said, then turned to make the introductions. "Jason Quinn, this is Maddock, Rose and… uh, Bones. Jason is a senior project director at ARGO."

Maddock was familiar with ARGO—the acronym stood for Alpine Research and Geographical

Observation. The Colorado-based enterprise, originally established in 1902 by President Teddy Roosevelt as a scientific agency tasked with exploration and development in cold-weather climates, had eventually gone private, transforming into one of the world's leading civil engineering services, though they continued to work closely with the US government.

Quinn shook hands with the new arrivals one by one, but when he exchanged clasps with Bones, one of his eyebrows came up from behind a mirror lens and he grinned mischievously. "Bones, huh? And here I thought we were looking for a fully intact cadaver."

"On that subject," Kismet said. "Any progress?"

"Please say you found the frozen stiff and we can all go home," Bones said, hopefully.

The man grinned. "Come and see for yourself."

He led them on foot back to the tent. Under the voluminous yellow canopy, surrounded by huge piles of what looked like fresh powder snow, was a nine-foot wide hole, its depths hidden in shadow.

Bones' crack about ice-fishing wasn't far off the mark, but it was ice fishing with a high-tech upgrade.

Sitting alongside the hole was a strange-looking machine that looked like a cross between a robotic octopus and the shredder disc from the world's biggest Cuisinart.

"That's our baby," Quinn said, pointing to the device. "We call it the Ice Worm. It's an autonomous ice borer, equipped with radar and M-wave sensors."

Maddock thought he detected a hint of pride in Quinn's tone; it was the same pride he heard in Bones' voice whenever he employed their remote underwater vehicle, which he lovingly nicknamed Uma.

"The cutter head is studded with diamond blades," Quinn went on. "Diamond is just about the best conductor of heat, which means the cutter can turn at high RPMs without melting the ice and turning this place into a slushy nightmare. The manipulator arms are just there to hold it in place. All this…" He gestured to the mounds of snow piled up around them. "Is shaved ice—about 4,700 cubic feet worth. We use blower fans to create a negative air-pressure environment in here. Sucks the ice right out of the shaft."

"You make it sound easy," Maddock remarked.

Quinn shrugged. "There's a lot to be said for having the right tools for the job. Unfortunately, the Ice Worm can only get us to within about six inches of the target anomaly. Any deeper, and we run the risk of accidentally shredding the target." He walked over to a table near the machine and bent over a waiting laptop computer. "Take a look."

A couple mouse clicks woke the computer up and a couple more brought up a grainy monochrome image. It didn't take much imagination to see the shape of a human body, curled up as if in repose. "I think that's our guy," Quinn announced. "But you'll have to do the rest the hard way."

"Ice fishing," groaned Bones.

"'Fraid so," Quinn said. "As soon as Curtis gets done fueling the helo, we'll start rigging the lines so you can go down." He paused a beat. "I expect you'll want to handle the recovery personally."

Kismet nodded.

"I'll go down with you," Maddock said. "Two can work faster than one." At a questioning glance from Kismet, he added, "Might as well make myself useful.

What else is there to do?"

Alleviating boredom was only part of the reason why Maddock had volunteered to go into the pit. The truth of it was that Kismet's search had fired his own curiosity.

He expected to be challenged by the other members of the party. Expected to hear Jade demanding to go in his place since she had provided the clue that had brought Kismet here. Expected to hear Bones claim that *he* was the better climber. Expected Quinn to pull rank or cite some made-up safety concern.

But no one spoke up. Jade stared at him, blankly. Quinn shrugged. Bones just muttered, "Well I sure as hell ain't crawlin' into that frozen ice hole."

Kismet simply nodded. "Thanks."

Maddock gave Jade a meaningful glance then nodded toward Bones. "You two… Don't kill each other, okay?"

Jade frowned. "Don't look at me."

Maddock knew better than to ask for more, but doubted there would be any problems. The friction between his ex-girlfriend and his best friend was like the fire triangle; remove one corner from the equations—namely himself—and there would be no flames.

He turned to Rose. "One other thing…"

11

Maddock, a more experienced climber than Kismet, went first, rappelling into the borehole. Under normal circumstances, fast-roping down without a belayer would have posed no challenge to either of them, but the frigid temperatures and the requisite protective equipment brought with it a whole new set of variables. Maddock made a cautious descent, using the points of the crampons strapped to his mountaineering boots for traction, as he methodically worked his way down the smooth curving wall of the shaft. The blue-white interior of the borehole reflected and amplified the beam from his headlamp, lighting up the confined space like the old ice tunnel ride at Universal Studios. Finally, after about five tedious minutes of down climbing, he reached the bottom.

The floor of the shaft bore the marks of the Ice Worm's teeth, a pattern of concentric grooves radiating from the center, under a scattering of ice powder, but beneath the scoured translucent surface, Maddock could easily distinguish a large dark mass, pressed up against it like an insect trapped in amber. He looked away, turning his attention to the immediate task, and called up. "I'm set." His voice echoed weirdly.

After a few seconds, Kismet's voice, distant and distorted, came back. "On belay?"

Maddock held the twinned ropes in his gloved hands, ready to take up the slack in the unlikely event Kismet lost control of his descent, and shouted back, "Belay on."

"Descending!"

The rope twitched in Maddock's grip as the other man made a careful but rapid descent without incident, and ninety seconds later, Kismet was standing beside him.

"So much for the easy part," Kismet remarked, staring back up the long shaft.

Maddock nodded his agreement. Getting back to the surface would be a test of both skill and endurance. They would have to front-point their crampons into the ice and inch their way back up the rope using mechanical ascenders, but that ordeal was the last thing on Maddock's mind. As Kismet began sweeping away the powdery ice shavings, Maddock unslung the backpack he'd brought down, and took out the black orb they had recovered from the Outpost and set it down on the floor, directly above the dark shape under the ice.

The orb was about eighteen inches or so in diameter, but unusually light, like a piece of Styrofoam. When they had first discovered it at the bottom of what might or might not have been a man-made pyramid hidden under the ice, it had actually been floating a few feet off the ground, suspended in some kind of invisible force field. That same force field had sublimated the ice surrounding it, turning it from a solid into a vapor without first melting it into water and without producing any detectable heat. Maddock was hoping to make it repeat that trick now, but after a minute or so of rolling it back and forth, there was no detectable change.

He looked up at Kismet and shrugged. "Well, it seemed like a good idea at the time."

"Maybe there's a step you missed," Kismet said. "How did you get it to work back at the Outpost?"

"I don't think we did anything. It just sort of woke up all on its own." Even as he said it, he realized that wasn't quite accurate. They had done something, albeit not intentionally. "The tomahawk," he said, thinking aloud.

The sunken wreckage of the seaplane had not been the only clue to lead Maddock and the others to the Outpost. They had also found a metal hatchet head, engraved with the name of a pre-Revolutionary War soldier named Stephen Thorne. The strange history of that artifact had brought them together with Rose Greer, who had supplied the missing pieces of the puzzle, but the tomahawk had done something else, too. The blade, infused with a rare metal Rose had identified as 'adamantine' had been drawn to the orb like a magnet. Before taking the orb down into the borehole, Maddock had peeled the hatchet head away and entrusted it to Rose for safe-keeping, but now he wondered if perhaps the two objects worked together to create the phenomena he had earlier observed. Before he could explain this to Kismet however, the other man began stripping off his gloves.

"I've got an idea."

Maddock sucked in an apprehensive breath. Although the bottom of the borehole was considerably warmer than the air outside the tent, sheltered and insulated by the ice itself, like the inside of an igloo, the temperature was still well below freezing. Without the protection of his gloves, Kismet would experience frostbite in a matter of minutes. The other man seemed unconcerned however. He flexed his fingers and rubbed them together for a moment, then reached up to his neck and unfastened the collar of his heavy winter parka.

Maddock caught a glimpse of something, a block of gleaming blue stone worn like a pendant around Kismet's neck, and knew it had to be the Apex stone Jade and Kismet had talked about, the talisman that had prompted Kismet's search for John Edward Grace. Kismet closed his left fist around the Apex, and then reached out and placed his right hand on the orb.

At first, Maddock didn't think anything was happening. There was no pyrotechnic display, no discharge of electricity. But after a few seconds, he realized that the air around them was growing thick with fog. He swept his hand through the mist, trying to brush it away, but like smoke, the vapors were pulled into the vacuum created by the movement, but in that brief moment, he saw clearly the results of Kismet's experiment.

The ice was giving up its dead.

Kismet remained like that for a full two minutes before drawing his hand back away from the orb. His bare fingers were covered in a dusting of ice crystals, but he shook them off and then stuffed his hands back into his gloves. The mist began dissipating immediately, coalescing into snowflakes which settled onto the floor, still partly obscuring what the orb had revealed. Kismet brushed the snow away to reveal the body, now completely free from its frozen tomb.

The cadaver lay on its side in a fetal curl, a last futile attempt to preserve body heat. Kismet gently rolled him over. In the stillness, the sound of the still frozen body crunching on the snow was both surreal and ominous. Then Maddock got a look at the man's face.

He couldn't recall if he'd ever seen a picture of the explorer, but making the identification would have been easy for anyone who had. The face peering up from the fur-lined hood had a leathery yellow cast, except around the nose which was shriveled and black, and the man's lips had pulled back to form a wide grimace, but otherwise the body was almost perfectly preserved, even the eyes which were open in an eternal sightless stare.

"Is it him?" he asked. "Grace?"

Kismet nodded but said nothing. After a moment of silent regard, he reached out and began peeling back the stiff fur garments. He rooted around for a while and then drew out a rectangular parcel that might have been a leather pouch or book cover. As Kismet meticulously unwrapped it, allowing it to fall open in his hands, Maddock saw that it was the latter.

The cold arid environment had left the paper brittle but the writing was crisp and legible.

"His diary," Kismet said, cautiously turning the pages, only giving each a brief glance. "I think we may have solved another mystery," he said after a reading a few pages. "I think the reason he decided to leave the others was to make sure nobody ever found this."

"A secret worth dying for?" Maddock said.

"Bigger than that. This would have outed him, and not just as an occult practitioner if you get my meaning."

Maddock was pretty sure he did.

"He knew he was going to die," Kismet went on, "and he knew that if this record ever made it back to civilization, his legacy as a heroic explorer would be tainted by—"

He broke off as something slid out of the book, fluttering as it fell, and came to rest on the cadaver's chest.

It was a stiff piece of paper, like a card or

bookmark, adorned with an elaborate painted image. Maddock's first thought was that the object was a picture postcard, but the proportions weren't quite right; the card was narrow and oblong, more like an over-sized playing card. Kismet retrieved the card and held it up for closer inspection.

The picture was of a smiling nude figure. The subject was androgynous, but seemed more male than female. Rising up behind him was a familiar representation of a caduceus—a staff with wings and two entwined snakes, often used—mistakenly—as a symbol of medicine. The figure's face was turned up, as if gazing at the sun, and his arms were outstretched, one raised higher than the other, and hanging in the air around him, like falling objects caught in a freeze frame were several strange objects adorned with cryptic symbols; Maddock didn't recognize them but felt like he should. There were other esoteric designs on the painting and a strange web of lines, like cables on a suspension bridge, radiated out from behind the figure. The man's feet were crossed, left over right, as if he was being crucified on the caduceus, but something that looked almost like another pair of wings spread out from his heels, covering the lower half of the painting.

"It's Hermes," Maddock said. "Or Mercury, but they're more or less the same. See the winged sandals and the caduceus?"

Kismet nodded in agreement, then flipped the card over to reveal another image, a cross that divided into multi-colored panels, and at its center, a single red rose.

Kismet gave a thoughtful hum. "The Rose Cross. It's one of the oldest symbols of alchemy." He looked up at Maddock. "This is a tarot card."

Maddock didn't know much about occult practices so he took Kismet at his word. "So it's not the map?"

Kismet turned the card back to the image of Hermes. "I think maybe it is. Look at these symbols.

"There are four suits in the Tarot deck, just like regular playing cards. Each one is linked to one of the four elements of esoteric tradition—fire, earth, water, and air." He pointed to the object close to the god's right hand. It reminded Maddock of the Olympic torch, except entwined with the flames was an equilateral triangle. "This represents the suit of staffs or wands—or clubs. It corresponds to the element of fire. And this shape here—the triangle—that's a fire symbol. Only I don't think it's just a triangle. It's a pyramid."

"That makes sense," Maddock agreed. "The word pyramid comes from an ancient Greek term that translates as 'fire in the middle.' So that's one. What about spades, hearts and diamonds?"

"In tarot, the suits are wands, swords, cups and coins—also called disks or pentacles." He chuckled. "I really fell down the rabbit hole doing research on Adam Garral. Anyway, this black object below it definitely looks like a disk to me. And this…" His gloved fingertip shifted over to Hermes' left side, to an object that resembled a trophy or two-handed drinking cup. Directly above it was another circle, but unlike the disk, it was rendered in such a way as to suggest a three-dimensional shape—a sphere.

"Cups," Maddock said, catching on. "Water."

Kismet nodded. "Modernized into the suit of hearts. Hearts pump blood which is mostly water. This last one…" He slid his finger down to the final image which appeared to be a puffy cloud pierced by something that looked like a shard of glass or a jagged lightning bolt. "That must be swords, representing the element of air."

"Okay. I'll buy that it's a tarot card, but how is it a map?"

"I'm not sure it's a literal map, although it might be. It's more like a set of instructions for a scavenger hunt. Adam Garral found one piece of the puzzle in Egypt, in the Great Pyramid."

"The Apex."

"He was down here looking for another."

"Which one?" Even as he asked it, Maddock realized the answer. "The orb. That's what he was looking for. But which one is it?"

"If I had to guess, I'd say cups. The shape, like a drop of water. And it was sealed up in ice."

Maddock recalled how Kismet had used the Apex and the orb in concert to evaporate the ice covering the frozen remains of John Edward Grace. "So now we have two pieces. What do we win if we collect all four?"

"Immortality. The ability to transmute the elements." Kismet nodded toward the corpse on the floor. "That's what he thought anyway."

"And Prometheus? What do they want with it."

"What else? Power."

"Everybody wants to rule the world," Maddock muttered. "So I guess we better find the other two pieces first, and make sure they don't get their hands on any of them."

Kismet laughed softly. "I like the way you think, Dane Maddock."

"It's Bones. He's a bad influence. So, any idea where to look next?"

"One or two." Kismet dropped the card back into the journal then closed the leather cover and stuffed the parcel into the pocket of his parka. "But first, let's go somewhere warmer. I think we've accomplished all we can down here."

Maddock knew he wasn't just talking about the borehole. "Bones will be glad to hear it."

Kismet stood and moved back, giving Maddock room to retrieve the orb. When the black sphere was again nestled in the backpack slung over Maddock's shoulder, Kismet knelt beside the remains of the polar explorer and leaned in close. "Don't worry, old man," he whispered. "Your secret's safe forever."

12

Because air transport was a scarce resource in Antarctica, the helicopter that had brought them to the work site had returned to McMurdo Station, and wouldn't be available again for several hours. So while Quinn and his partner Curtis Johnson—a gregarious fellow with a grin as big as a Halloween jack-o-lantern— began bulldozing the ice shavings into the borehole, both to rebury Grace and at least partially return the landscape to its original condition, Kismet, following Rose's advice, went to work creating digital copies of both the journal and the strange tarot card.

Rose had immediately recognized the image on the card, confirming and clarifying Kismet's original identification.

"This is the Magus card from the Thoth deck created by Aleister Crowley," she said, enlarging the image on the screen of Kismet's tablet computer. "A version of it, anyway. There are some differences."

"Thoth was an Egyptian god, right?" Maddock said.

Rose nodded. "The god of wisdom and knowledge."

"Isn't Thoth also the Egyptian version of Hermes?"

"The ancients made that connection, though strictly speaking, the god on this card is a representation of Mercury."

"Same dif," Bones muttered.

"There are similarities, but they aren't the same," Rose insisted. "Crowley was very particular about the imagery he chose for this deck, and specifically this card. He wasn't happy with the first few attempts, much to the chagrin of his collaborator, Lady Frieda Harris. He made her paint at least four different versions before finally settling on one that looked pretty much like this. He didn't call it the Magus, though. His name for the card was the Juggler, which is more consistent with the symbolism used in earlier decks, where the magician isn't a sorcerer but more of a sleight-of-hand performer. His decision to show a divine figure instead of a human was very controversial among occultists of his time." She paused a beat and then delivered her caveat. "John Edward Grace disappeared in 1912. Crowley didn't start work on his tarot deck until 1938."

"How is that possible?" Jade asked.

Bones shrugged. "Duh. Magic."

Kismet stared at the image on the screen with renewed interest. "You said this isn't exactly the same as Crowley's card."

"If we had WiFi down here, I'd show you a side-by-side comparison."

"Is it possible that Crowley and Grace knew each other?"

"Assuming that he and Adam Garral are one and the same, I'd say it's very likely. They traveled in the same circles, and I don't just mean the occult. Crowley was a renowned mountaineer and world traveler. It's also widely believed that he was working for British intelligence. That story you told us about Garral spending a night in the Great Pyramid. Crowley claimed to have done that also. Maybe they both did, or maybe he borrowed the story from Garral. Either way, I don't think it's a coincidence."

Maddock saw where things were headed. "So maybe Garral-slash-Grace showed Crowley this card back in 19-aught-whatever, and thirty years later, Crowley tried to reproduce it from memory."

"I still say magic," Bones said. "But if the egg came before the chicken, where did iceman get the card in the first place?"

"Hand painted tarot decks have been around since the 15th Century. They would have been collector's items for occult enthusiasts in the 19th and early 20th. But like I said, the imagery on the Thoth Magus is unique."

"Whoever painted this one knew about the Apex. And the orb from the Outpost."

"John Dee!" Jade exclaimed.

"It's pronounced: 'Yahtzee,'" Bones said.

Jade ignored him. "Grace must have found the card in the Liber whatchamacallit, the same way you found it in his diary."

Kismet inclined his head toward her. "That makes sense. And if Dee really was some kind of seer, maybe he saw the Apex and the orb in one of his visions."

"Dee didn't have visions," Jade corrected. "Kelly was the one who had the visions. Dee just wrote it all down." When she realized everyone was looking at her expectantly, she grimaced. "I heard that somewhere. But the point is, he saw them." She turned to Kismet. "Remember how the manuscript talked about the elemental temples? Pyramids! Your great-grandfather found the Apex in the Great Pyramid in Egypt. Maddock found the orb in a pyramid under the ice."

"So the other two are also in pyramids," Maddock said. "Where?"

Jade shook her head. "No. Dee already had one piece. The smoking mirror from the temple of Tezcatlipoca. An Aztec pyramid!"

"Obsidian," Kismet mused. "That would represent the earth element."

"And it's shaped like a disk," Jade added.

Bones wagged his head. "Does anybody else think this is…you know, a reach? We've got an Aztec artifact that's probably… what, a few hundred years old. Then we've got something from an Egyptian pyramid that could be five thousand years old. And that orb…who even knows who put it there? And yet somehow, this kooky old mystic saw it all."

Ten years earlier, Maddock would have agreed wholeheartedly, but now he wasn't so quick to dismiss the seemingly impossible. "It's not the strangest thing we've seen," he said, and then, with a wry smile added. "Could be aliens, traveling in time and space."

Bones' skepticism immediately vanished as he latched on to the suggestion. "Aliens. Of course."

"Dee's mirror," Kismet said. "It's in the British Museum. I've seen it. And I'd be willing to bet Adam Garral saw it, too. It led him to the Apex stone, and then it led him here." He raised his eyes to the others. "There's just one piece left. Air. The sword. But where?"

Bones stroked his chin in mock-thoughtfulness. "I'm thinking it's in a pyramid. Rose? What do you think?"

She shrugged. "Don't look at me. I've read a couple books on Crowley, but I'm no expert on this occult stuff."

Jade offered a cryptic grin. "I think we need to look in the mirror."

13

Bones tilted his head back and stared up at the elaborately sculpted façade fronting the British Museum. "Have we been here before? I feel like we've been here before."

Maddock searched his memory, then shrugged. "With all our adventures, it's hard to keep track."

"No kidding. And don't even get me started on alternate timelines."

Jade wagged her head in mock despair. "Is that supposed to be funny, Bonebrake? 'Cause if so, you should go back to what you're best at—fourth-grade potty jokes."

Bones nodded as if he had just scored major points. "So you admit it. I am the best."

Kismet leaned close to Rose and in a stage whisper, asked, "Remind me again; which one did she used to date?"

Jade just rolled her eyes and headed inside.

Maddock allowed himself a chuckle. Despite two exhausting days of travel, they were all in good spirits, a fact that probably had something to do with the weather. Despite being a gray and drizzly 45° Fahrenheit, London might have been Key West after the sub-zero temperatures they had endured in Antarctica.

Jade led the way inside and went to the reception desk to check in. A few minutes later, a petite woman with cinnamon-colored hair called out to her from across the lobby. "Jade! Great to see you again!"

"Kelly!" Jade met the woman halfway, offering her hand only to get caught in an awkward hug. "Come on. Let me introduce the others."

"Others?" Allenby said, with an impish grin. "So this isn't a solo adventure?"

"Not this time," Jade said with a grin.

As Maddock shook Allenby's hand, he had a strange moment of déjà vu, as if she was already an old friend. He chalked it up to the reality bending properties of the elemental relics. With the introductions out of the way, Allenby led them to her office where the piece they had traveled halfway around the world to see sat innocuously on her desktop alongside her laptop computer.

Maddock sucked in an apprehensive breath as he laid eyes on it, and sensed a similar reaction from the others. Jade—the only one of their group who had not witnessed some kind of phenomena associated with either the orb or the Apex stone—stared at the others for a moment and then approached the obsidian mirror.

The relic was about six-inches in diameter and shaped like a teardrop, with a hole drilled through a tab-like extension on the narrow end, as if it was meant to be hung from a nail or worn like a necklace. The hard volcanic glass did provide a reflection like a mirror, but considerably darkened.

After what seemed like a few minutes, Jade said, "Well? Anything?"

Maddock glanced over at Kismet. The latter was gripping the Apex stone in his left fist, as if trying to summon its power. After a moment, he reached out with his right hand and touched the mirror, but nothing happened.

"Should we try the orb?" Rose suggested, giving her backpack a meaningful shake.

Kismet shook his head. "I don't think it would do any good. This isn't the right mirror."

"A fake?"

"Not necessarily," Allenby said from behind them. She wore a slightly perplexed expression, as if not quite sure why her visitors had been so quick to dismiss the artifact as less than genuine. "As I've told Jade, the provenance for the Dee pieces in our collection was never solidly established. We have only the word of Horace Walpole that it ever belonged to Dee, but it is an Aztec mirror. There is no question about that. Walpole received it from Lord Frederick Campbell in 1771, and claimed it had been Dee's scrying glass. That would have been more than a century and a half after Dee's death, and there's no mention of it anywhere during the intervening time period." She smiled then, as if laughing at a private joke. "Walpole *was* a novelist, so he might have made the whole thing up. They do that sometimes, you know."

Bones let out a groan of dismay.

They had all earlier discussed the possibility—the likelihood even—that the mirror in the British Museum might not be the smoking mirror described in the Dee manuscript, and what it would mean for their search if that proved to be the case, but Maddock wasn't ready to throw in the towel just yet. "When did the museum acquire this mirror?"

"I believe it was in 1966," Allenby said.

"Half a century after Adam Garral's disappearance," Kismet said. They had all agreed not to bring up the name John Edward Grace.

"Where was it in between? From 1771 to 1966? Specifically, where was it in the early 1900s?"

Allenby circled around her desk and opened her laptop. After a few keystrokes, she began reading aloud. "In 1906 it was put up for auction at Sotheby's, part of the Collection of Hollingworth Magniac, but withdrawn. Hmm. Magniac was a collector of medieval art. He died in 1867 but his son Charles maintained the collection until his death in 1891. No mention of it until the Museum acquired it from Rev. R.W. Stannard in 1966. I'll have to do some more digging to uncover how it came into his possession."

Maddock turned back to the others. "Doesn't sound like this particular mirror was making the rounds in the occult movement."

"Mirrors like this aren't exactly rare," Allenby said. "To the best of my knowledge, this is the only one actually linked to Dr. John Dee, but who's to say if that's really the case."

"And the others? Where would we start looking?"

"A year ago, I would have told you to go visit Gerald Roche. If it's not in a private collection, something like that would probably end up at the Museum of Magick in Plymouth." She rolled her eyes as she said it. "Magic spelled with a 'k'."

Bones screwed up his face in an expression of mock-confusion. "K-A-G-I-C?"

"That's a real thing?" Maddock asked, ignoring his partner. "Sounds like a tourist trap."

"They must be doing something right, because they're surprisingly well funded." Allenby looked over at Jade. "Most of the manuscripts from Roche's collection ended up there."

"If Garral's copy of the *Liber Loagaeth* went there," Jade said, "maybe the mirror did, too."

Maddock was thinking the same thing, but made an effort to temper his enthusiasm. "It's a place to start looking."

14

Plymouth, England

The Museum of Magick—with a 'k'—occupied an old stone building that looked like it might once have been a fortress or a church. The structure appeared to have been built into the side of the limestone cliff, and had a commanding view of the Plymouth Sound, where the Mayflower had begun its famous voyage, bearing the pilgrims to the New World. Not surprisingly, the area was brimming with tourist attractions, including a world-class aquarium, a historic royal citadel, an art deco public pool, and a seventy-foot-tall red and white lighthouse, which had once stood nine miles out to sea on the treacherous reef known as the Eddystone Rocks. As was the case with most seaside tourist destinations, there was little activity given the season and the blustery weather, but the shops and attractions were still open for business, including the Museum of Magick.

Plymouth was three-and-a-half hours from London by train, and nearly six by car, so they chose the former, catching a taxi from the station to the Museum's front door. Braving the rain, they hurried inside and approached the ticket counter where a young man with shoulder-length wavy blond hair, dressed all in black, greeted them with an amused if slightly surprised smile which brightened a few degrees when he saw Rose and Jade.

"Thought I was going to be able to shutter early," the young man said. "Guess it's a good thing I didn't."

"Must be our lucky day," Bones muttered.

They paid the entry fee, a modest £5 apiece, and headed directly inside, browsing the exhibits which were, contrary to Maddock's expectations, more informative than sensational. The displays began in pre-Roman times with the Druids and other pagan religions, which laid the foundation for Wicca and other modern traditions of witchcraft, then moved into the history of religious persecution of witches, to include those who were guilty of nothing more than using herbs and other traditional healing methods. At one point, Bones launched into an impromptu performance of the "witch-test" scene from Monty Python and the Holy Grail.

"So if she weighs the same as a duck," he said in terrible approximation of a British accent, pointing at Jade, who returned a withering scowl. "Then she's made of wood."

"And therefore?" said a voice from behind them with a far more convincing accent.

Everyone turned to see the young man who had taken their money at the door, entering the gallery.

"A witch!" Bones chortled.

Jade shot daggers at him. "Maybe I should turn you into a newt. Oh, wait. That would be an improvement."

"We like witches here," the young man said, beaming at Jade.

Jade managed a half-hearted smile. "I'm not a witch. But thanks."

"A goddess then," he said with a wink.

Bones gave a disgusted snort, but Maddock, sensing that Jade might be able to make use of the attention she was receiving, shot an elbow into his friend's ribs. Bones grunted, but didn't say anything more.

Message received.

"Since we're a bit slow at the moment," the young man continued, "I thought I'd check up on you lot. I'm Aramis." He stuck out his hand. "Aramis Black."

Maddock pre-emptively elbowed Bones again.

Jade shook the proffered hand and quickly introduced everyone, first names only.

"If you have any questions," Black said, "I'll do my best to answer."

"Actually," Jade said, "We heard you had one of the best collections of Dee manuscripts. We were hoping to get a look at some of those."

Black registered pleasant surprise again. "I see you didn't just come here on a lark. Yes, that's correct. We have an entire room devoted to Dee. He was the first to truly bridge the gap between the spirit realm and scientific understanding. His work is the foundation for our exploration of magic."

"Is that magic with a 'k'?" Bones asked.

Black seemed not to hear. "The Dee Room is just ahead, but I'm afraid the manuscripts you're asking about aren't on display. They're reserved for scholars."

"We *are* scholars," Jade said, then nodded toward Bones. "Except for him. He's just a cretin. I'm an archaeologist. Rose here is a history professor. Our interest in the manuscripts is academic."

"I should have chosen my words more carefully," the man said. "What I meant to say is that they are reserved for the initiated."

Sensing that the answer would test Jade's patience, Maddock stepped forward. "Then this isn't just a museum. It's a temple, as well."

"In a manner of speaking."

"And I take it you're not just the guy that works the

counter."

"No. I am an adept, and among other things, I am the historian of the Order."

"We aren't initiates," Kismet said. "But my great-grandfather was. Adam Garral."

Black raised a skeptical eyebrow. "Adam Garral was your great-grandfather?"

"Great-great actually, but yes. You've heard of him?"

"He was a great magician. One of the greatest. If he had not disappeared…" Black shook his head as if the century-old mystery was still a source of grief. "He was one of the founders. A pillar of the movement. Crowley took all the credit, but Garral was the wellspring. The true Therion. Some say he transcended this reality."

"I know that he was studying the *Liber Loagaeth* before his disappearance. I'm trying to retrace his footsteps, so to speak. Solve an old family mystery." Sensing he was on the right track, Kismet drew out the leather-bound journal and opened it, displaying the brightly-colored tarot card. "And maybe learn a little more about this."

The young man's eyes went wide as saucers.

Bones chuckled. "Not bad for a bunch of non-initiates."

Black looked up from the card, staring at Kismet with a mixture of awe and dread. "Where did you find this?"

Kismet held the journal up. "Family papers."

Black brought his fingertips together in what was either a thoughtful gesture or an attempt to enchant them. "Those would be a valuable addition to our collection. Perhaps we can come to some sort of arrangement."

Kismet appeared to consider the offer. "The papers are private, but I might be willing to make an indefinite loan of this card. Tell you what. We really came here looking for Dr. Dee's obsidian mirror."

"Dee's Speculum is in the British Museum in London," Black replied, a little too quickly.

"We've seen it. And I think we both know it's not the real deal."

"We have other mirrors in the collection," said Black, equivocally. "I don't believe any are historically linked to Dr. Dee. You're welcome to have a look at them but if you're proposing an exchange… Well, I couldn't possibly authorize anything like that."

"Maybe we should be talking to someone else," Jade suggested.

Black frowned but then inclined his head. "You're right, of course. I'll ring the director straightaway. Why don't you continue your tour? There are several scrying mirrors in the spiritualist collection, just past the Dee room." He seemed about to add something more, but then changed his mind and simply exited without another word.

When he was gone, Bones let out a snort of laughter. "Aramis Black? Seriously?"

"I feel like we've already had this conversation," Jade said.

Bones shrugged. "Fair enough. Anyway, I'd love to play poker against him."

Maddock nodded. "He definitely knows something about the mirror. Did you notice how he reacted when you mentioned Adam Garral?"

Kismet gave a thoughtful nod. "I did. And I agree

that he's not telling us everything. But it's his move."

They continued making their way through the exhibits. The Dee Room was a veritable shrine to the occult scholar. The walls were covered with photo-enlargements of pages from the Liber Loagaeth and other examples of Enochian writing, and there were a number of replica artifacts and a few that purported to be authentic. There was even a diorama of Dee and Kelley, sitting together, the former bent over an open book, writing, while the latter peered into a small crystal globe positioned above the distinctive magical diagram known as the *Sigillum Dei Aemaeth*—the symbol of the Living God—a seven-pointed star surrounding a five-pointed star, both inscribed with the names of God and several angels.

After the Dee Room came an exhibit chronicling the persecution of witches, both in England and in the American colonies. They didn't linger there, but pushed on to the exhibits concerned with the emergence of spiritualism and the occult in the late 19th and early 20th Century. Maddock was surprised to learn that both arose from serious, albeit misguided, scientific inquiry into the nature of both the universe and the human psyche. As with Dee, a Christian who believed he was in communication with angels, much of the belief system of both the spiritualists and the occultists—men like Aleister Crowley—derived from traditional religious belief systems—Christianity and Jewish mysticism. One display gave the story behind the unusual spelling of 'magick.' Crowley had added the extra letter to differentiate what he called, "the Science and Art of causing Change to occur in conformity with Will" from sleight of hand performance magic.

It was, Maddock thought, both fascinating and a little disconcerting. Those who believed in Crowley's system of Magick—also called Thelema—did so with a feverish intensity, enacting rituals that ranged from absurd to disturbing. Of course, the same could be said for the rites of most religions. What was the Eucharist if not a sympathetic ritual, eating God's flesh and blood in order to gain some special favor with the spirit realm. It was just human nature to desire power over life and death, and all religions represented a concerted effort to find it. Magick was no different.

And yet, Adam Garral had used occult knowledge to find the Apex. Had his magical studies allowed him to unlock real supernatural power? Or had he merely gotten lucky, stumbling over the discovery while looking for something else, mistaking coincidence for some sort of divine action?

Maddock did not share these musings with the others. He wasn't as interested in understanding the power of the elemental relics as he was in keeping them out of the wrong hands, and he sensed Kismet shared that mission.

Black returned, an eager smile on his youthful face. He moved in close, speaking in a conspiratorial whisper. "I couldn't tell you this before, but…" His eyes darted back and forth, a touch too dramatically. "I know why you've come. The mirror you seek… The Magna of Illusion. The first elemental. I will take you to it."

15

The gray sky had deepened by several shades during their brief tour of the museum, and Maddock knew that the full dark of night wasn't far off. A persistent drizzle that didn't quite qualify as rain continued to dampen the world, but the waves crashing against the nearby Mount Batten breakwater hinted at a storm yet to come. He studied the turbulent sea for a few seconds and then turned to appraise the boat that Black was preparing for launch. The 21-foot Zodiac Pro Open 650 rigid-hulled inflatable was an excellent platform for diving and other recreational and utilitarian activities, but not ideally suited for the current weather conditions.

"Maybe we should wait until morning," he said.

"Ordinarily, this is where I would make a comment about Maddock being a wuss," said Bones, hugging his arms close to his chest as if remembering the chill of Antarctica anew. They were all a little soggy from the short walk to the harbor, but that was nothing to the soaking they would get out on the water. "But just this once, I happen to agree with him."

Black did not look up from his task. "We only have to go a little ways," he said, and pointed out across the harbor to a land mass. "Drake's Island. Just there. It's only about half-a-mile. The weather is only going to get worse, so if we don't go now, we might have to wait days."

"Why there?" Jade asked.

"That's where the Magna of Illusion is kept. We have a…" He paused as if trying to find the appropriate word. "A secure facility there. A private place where initiates can practice without distraction." He clambered over the inflated pontoons, to the pilot's bolster situated amidships, donned an orange personal flotation collar, and then settled in behind the wheel. "I'll tell you all about it on the way."

Maddock exchanged a look with Bones, then with Kismet. Both men just shrugged. Of course, they were going; what choice did they have? Black was calling the shots and he did not seem inclined to postpone the journey. Moreover, he was right about the weather. As SEALs, Maddock and Bones had both conducted boat operations under less favorable conditions, using rigid-hulled inflatable boats nearly identical to Black's Zodiac.

When they were all aboard and wearing life preservers, Black started the outboard and cast off, motoring slowly away from the pier until he was in the channel route. Once he was in the clear, he increased the throttle until the Zodiac's V-shaped polyester hull was plowing through swells. Under sunnier skies, it would have been an exciting experience, but with the gray drizzle, it seemed merely like an ordeal to be endured.

The seas calmed a little as they approached the north side of the island, which faced back toward Plymouth, but the sky continued to darken, prompting Black to bring out a flashlight to illuminate the way ahead. The crossing took about ten minutes, during which time Black told them a little about their destination.

Named for the famed explorer and privateer, Sir Francis Drake, the island had historically served as a defensive gun emplacement to safeguard Plymouth Harbor until, following World War II, such measures were deemed unnecessary. The city had used the island, with its abandoned military barracks, as a boy's adventure camp for a while, but eventually it had been sold off to a developer who had never quite managed to develop anything there. Although Black didn't come right out and say it, Maddock got the impression the real estate developer was either an initiate in the occult movement, or at the very least, getting a pay-off to maintain the status quo.

"What was it you called the mirror?" Jade asked. "Something about an illusion?"

"The Magna of Illusion," Black said. Despite the fact that he was nearly yelling to be heard over the roar of the outboard, his tone was reverent. "Discovered by Geronimo de Aguilar and Gonzalo del Rio in the Pyramid of Tezcatlipoca in the Yucatan, in a chamber of jade, with only one way in and no way out. Captured by Sir Francis Drake and brought to England where Queen Elizabeth bestowed it to her astrologer, Dr. John Dee.

"Dee chose the name. It is a reference to St. Paul's letter to the Corinthians: 'For now we see through a glass, darkly; but then face to face: now I know in part; but then shall I know even as also I am known.' In this mirror was revealed the word of angels, a vision of things to come and places unseen, but prophecy is only an illusion of what may come to pass, a possible future glimpsed in the dark glass."

The Zodiac drew up to the long pier jutting out from the island, Bones reached out with one long arm and caught the floating dock, steadying the boat while Maddock quickly tied the mooring line to a cleat. With the boat secure, they climbed out and followed Black up to the slick concrete pier.

At the end of the pier, they entered a stairwell passage cut into the cliffside. A short flight of moss-covered steps rose to a path that led them past dilapidated structures that had once housed and fed the artillerymen manning the island's defensive stations. Black led them through the midst of the abandoned complex without stopping, following the path as it curved back into the shadowy woods that dominated the crest of the island.

Rose caught up to Maddock as they left the barracks behind. "Maddock," she whispered. "I think we're close."

He nodded in acknowledgment, but then realized that she probably couldn't see the gesture. "I just hope this isn't another dead end."

"That's what I mean," she replied. "The orb. It's reacting to something. I can feel it moving in the pack. Shifting whenever we change directions, like a compass needle. I think it senses the mirror."

Maddock recalled how they had used the adamantine-infused tomahawk head like a dowsing rod to find the orb in Antarctica.

"The Apex is doing the same thing," Kismet whispered. "I think we're definitely in the right place this time."

As if overhearing their conversation, Black announced. "It's just in here." He shone his light toward a squat concrete building which Maddock guessed was a bunker or shelter built beneath an old gun emplacement. There was no door in the doorway and no glass in the windows, but otherwise the structure appeared solid enough. Black went inside, his body briefly eclipsing the light as he passed through the doorway. Maddock and the others filed in after him.

The bare floor was littered with beer cans, food wrappers and old blankets—the detritus of urban explorers and thrill seekers looking for a place to party. Black ignored the evidence of trespassers, and moved to the far wall to stand before a metal door with peeling yellow paint. The doorknob had been removed, leaving only the escutcheon. The door itself was secured with a rusty iron crossbar and serviceable padlock. The security measures might thwart vandals and trespassers, but it was hardly the level of security one would expect to safeguard a purportedly supernatural artifact.

Black produced a key and opened the lock, and then moved his hand to the missing door knob. He gave the escutcheon a twist, as if removing the lid from a jar of pickles, and it swiveled out of the way to reveal a small numerical keypad that looked anything but dilapidated. He punched in a code, and with a faint hiss of depressurization, the metal door began to move, swinging outward, and Maddock now saw that the door was actually just a façade hiding a heavy bank vault-type door.

Black darted inside the vault and reappeared a moment later with his flashlight tucked under one arm and a velvet-lined wooden box held reverently in both hands. Nestled inside the box was something that looked like a small, perfectly round window into another dimension. Even without the confirmation from the other elemental relics, Maddock would have known it was the real deal just by looking at it. Or into it.

Kismet seemed to know it as well. He met Black's gaze. "May I touch it?"

"Please do," Black said, his voice quavering in anticipation. "You are Adam Garral's heir. This should be quite spectacular."

Kismet reached out a tentative hand, touched the black mirror… And then drew back his hand as if he'd been shocked.

He looked over at Maddock and then the others. "Did you see…?" He let the question hang. Maddock hadn't seen anything unusual, but Kismet evidently had.

"What did *you* see?"

Kismet opened his mouth to answer, but then closed it again and shook his head. He turned to look at Black, who continued to regard him with a mixture of excitement and reverence.

"Kismet?" Maddock said, and then repeated the unanswered question. "What did you see?"

"I was somewhere else." He frowned. "Only I was here, too, at the same time. Everything was jumbled together."

"Amazing," Black said. "Most initiates must meditate for hours before the mirror reveals anything. And even then, it's rarely so vivid."

The Apex is giving him an assist, Maddock thought, but kept it to himself. No sense in volunteering that information to Black.

"Try again," Jade prompted.

Kismet nodded and did so, tilting his head forward to focus his gaze on the dark glass. His forehead creased in concentration. After a moment, he raised his head again and began looking around the abandoned bunker, but when he began speaking, it became apparent what he was seeing was not in the same reality.

"Pyramids," he whispered, turning a half-circle and craning his head around for a full 360° view. "Four of them. Jungle. Ice. Desert." He hesitated. "Sky."

Bones leaned close to Maddock and whispered, "A pyramid in the sky?" Maddock expected his friend to make a joke, but instead Bones took it a different direction. "Could be describing a UFO?"

"I've seen something like this before," Kismet went on. "I think it's the Tower of Babel."

Maddock got the reference immediately. According to the Bible book of Genesis, the descendants of Noah had come together to build a city and tower so high that it would reach the heavens. Their hubris had prompted God to intervene, disrupting the project before completion by confusing the languages of the builders, which caused them to scatter across the globe.

"Of course," Black said, his voice still full of awe. "You are seeing the elemental temples. The jungle temple. That would be the pyramid temple where the Magna of Illusion was found. A symbol of earth. The desert pyramid… Is it Egyptian?"

Kismet nodded slowly.

"Fascinating," Black went on. "That would certainly represent the element of fire. The Tower of Babel, a ziggurat meant to reach the heavens, would symbolize air. And ice? Well that can only signify water. I wonder where that one is?"

Maddock shot the others an urgent look, willing them all to keep silent about their discoveries.

Kismet continued turning his head, looking around at places and things only he could see. All of a sudden, he threw his arms out to the sides as if trying to regain his balance. His upper torso tilted back and forth for a few seconds before stabilizing. "Moving now. There are lines connecting the pyramids. Like wires or… A web? I'm moving along them. Jungle… Whoa!"

"I'm inside now. It's disorienting. Like being in an Escher painting. The walls… Angles…" He trailed off for a moment then nodded. "The mirror. It's here. It was here. It was always here."

"Until it wasn't," Jade said.

Maddock nodded. "He's seeing the past."

Kismet swayed silently for several more seconds then lifted his hand away. "That's the real thing, all right." He gave Maddock a knowing look that said, *We got what we came for*, then met Black's gaze.

"Thank you." Kismet extended his right hand, offering the hand painted Magus card. "It's yours, as promised."

Black smiled, but there was neither humor nor gratitude in the expression. The indirect light rising from his flashlight gave him a ghoulish appearance. "You can't leave. Not yet."

Maddock experienced a shiver of apprehension, but then Black clarified his statement. "You've experienced a revelation. You must tell me what you beheld."

Kismet managed a patient smile of his own. "I already told you what I saw."

"I do not think you did," said another voice from behind them, a female voice that did not belong to Jade or Rose.

Maddock whirled to face the newcomer, an exotic-looking raven-haired woman who gazed at them from the door to the bunker. Behind her stood several more figures; it was impossible to tell how many, but there were at least three, all male, all dressed in black. All holding guns.

"Aliyah," Jade said, hissing the name like a curse.

Maddock recognized the name from Jade's account

of her initial meeting with Kismet. Aliyah Cerulean, the widow of Alexander Cerulean who had stolen the Apex from Kismet's father, and died in a fall from the Great Pyramid.

Aliyah took a step forward, entering the concrete bunker and clearing the doorway for the others, who immediately began swarming inside. Not three, but a dozen, all armed with pistols. Maddock and the others were surrounded in an instant, at least two guns trained on each of them. Everyone but Black who was still smiling.

Aliyah's eyes never left Kismet. "You haven't told us everything. But you will."

16

If the woman's sudden appearance surprised Kismet, he gave no indication, nor did he appear the least bit intimidated. "Poor Aliyah. Still trying to avenge your dead husband. I warned you what would happen."

Aliyah spat out a laugh like a bitter taste, then stepped closer. "You still think this is about revenge."

She reached for his throat but instead of strangling him, she tore at his collar, exposing the Apex hanging around his neck. She grasped it and then yanked it away hard enough to snap the string from which it hung.

Now Maddock understood. Aliyah was working with Black; she was probably part of his secret order of magicians, presumably the gunmen with her were also members. She was an initiate, perhaps even an adept—the word Black had used to describe himself. Her husband probably had been a senior member as well, which explained why he had stolen the Apex from Kismet's father.

Kismet inclined his head as if to concede her superior position. "I see. And now you have what you need to find the other elementals."

Aliyah did not deny it. With one hand still gripping the Apex, she turned and placed her other hand on the Magna of Illusion. She closed her eyes and remained that way for several seconds, then opened them again, unable to hide a look of disappointment.

"No reception?" Bones remarked.

Aliyah just stared at Kismet. "You know where they are. We all heard you. The four temples. Where are they? How are the elementals manifest in this world?"

When Kismet did not answer, she turned to one of her henchman—one of the men holding Jade at gunpoint—and nodded. Immediately, the man seized Jade's arm and spun her around so quickly she would have lost her balance if not for his grip. He pulled her close, stabbing the barrel of his gun into the tender flesh below her jaw.

Aliyah returned her attention to Kismet. "You will die," she said, matter-of-factly. "Honor demands it. But I have no quarrel with these others. How many of them will I have to kill to get you to cooperate? Just one?" She raised a hand, poised to deliver a chopping gesture, the signal to kill.

"No. Not even one," Kismet said in a quiet voice. "I'll tell you exactly what I saw." He glanced around, making eye contact with Black and several others. "I want your word. Swear by whatever gods you worship that you'll let them all go."

Maddock expected a contemptuous rejection, but to his astonishment, Aliyah simply nodded. "I swear it."

The promise did not ease Maddock's apprehension, but for the moment, there wasn't much he could do.

Kismet took a breath. "I saw four pyramids. You already know about two of them. The temple of Tezcatlipoca in Mexico. The Great Pyramid of Khufu in Egypt. The third temple was in a land of ice."

Aliyah let out a long hiss, the warning unmistakable.

"It's in Antarctica," Kismet said.

"Ah, so that is why you went there. Don't deny it. I know that you traveled there."

"I was there to find Adam Garral's remains. That's where I found the card and his journal. I didn't even know the rest of it until just now."

That was mostly true.

Aliyah's gaze narrowed suspiciously but after a moment she seemed to accept the logic of his answer. "Where exactly is it?"

"I'm afraid there weren't a lot of visible landmarks. I could probably find it with some help from Google."

"And the elemental? Did you see it?"

He nodded slowly, betraying nothing with his eyes. "It's a sphere. Some kind of strange black metal."

"And the fourth pyramid is the Tower of Babel?"

"I think so." He shook his head uncertainly, and Maddock sensed he was genuinely confused by whatever he had seen.

"I didn't even know that was a real thing," Bones muttered. Like Maddock, he seemed calm, unperturbable, but under the surface, poised to act.

"It was and it wasn't," Rose said. At first, her voice was a tremulous squeak, but then she straightened, as if drawing courage from the fact that they had already successfully hidden their possession of the orb from their tormentors. "There was a pyramid in Babylon, a ziggurat called the Etemenanki. It was a temple to the god Marduk. Many scholars believe it was the inspiration for the tower described in the Bible. The name literally means 'temple of the foundation of heaven and earth,' which is interesting because in the Bible, the builders' intent was to build a tower that reached the heavens. The book of Genesis says that the word 'Babel' means confusion, but it's more likely derived from *bab-el*—Gate of God."

Maddock gave her an encouraging nod. "Is it still there?"

"No. When Alexander the Great captured Babylon in 331 BCE, he wanted to repair it, but eventually decided to simply demolish it and start over. He died before the new tower could be built. The ruins are still there, though."

Aliyah, who had been listening intently, now snapped at Kismet. "The elemental? Did you see it?"

"I did, but…" Kismet's forehead creased in a frown. "I'm not exactly sure what it was. At first, it was a sword. Single edge, with a curve. Like a machete."

"A *kopis.*" Aliyah's voice was an eager whisper. "What you saw was the sword of Alexander the Great, which he used to cut apart the Gordian Knot."

Maddock knew that story well. According to legend, in the city of Gordium in Phrygia—modern-day Turkey—there was an ox-cart tied to a post with an impossibly complicated knot. Alexander's oracle told him that if he could untie the knot, he would rule all of Asia, but when his attempts to do so by conventional means failed, he took a more direct approach, slicing the knot apart with his sword.

"That makes sense," Maddock said, thinking aloud. "The fourth tarot suit is swords. Maybe Alexander got the sword from the temple in Babylon and used it to cut the knot."

"The timing isn't quite right though," Rose countered. "The incident with the Gordian Knot happened in 333 BCE. That was before he conquered Babylon."

Kismet raised a hand. "There's more. It was a sword, but then it was something else. A piece of something that looked like green glass. Flat like a slab. There were marks on it. Some kind of writing, but I didn't recognize it."

Aliyah's eyes widened and she turned to Black, sharing a look of mutual disbelief. She mouthed something and he nodded. "Could it have been emerald?" she asked aloud.

Kismet nodded. "Yes. Why? Do you know what it is?"

She regarded him with a look that was, at once, both contemplative and contemptuous. "I believe it is the Tabula Smaragdina. The Emerald Tablet."

Maddock looked to Rose then Jade but neither showed any sign of recognition.

"I've heard of that," Kismet said. "It's an alchemical manuscript, isn't it?"

"It is the original alchemical manuscript," Aliyah said. "The revelation of Hermes Trismegistus, who is also called Thoth of Egypt, carved on a tablet of indestructible emerald. It is the basis for the Hermetic tradition. The tablet was discovered and translated in the 8th Century by Balinas in the city of Tyana in Cappadocia. Like the books of the Bible, the text of the Tabula Smaragdina has been reproduced many times, but the whereabouts of the original tablet are unknown.

"Perhaps the Emerald Tablet was there, in Babel, in the Etemenanki, in the time of Alexander the Great. Perhaps that is the symbolism of the story of the Gordian Knot; knowledge as sharp as a blade. Or perhaps the tablet, like the Magna of Illusion, is itself a talisman of great power." She continued to stare at Kismet, some of her anger giving way to cool calculation. "We are meant to have it. And I believe you are meant to find it."

"So you're taking my advice?" Kismet replied evenly. "Giving up on revenge?"

Aliyah's smile was as sharp and cold as a blade. "Your friends will remain here, as a guarantee of your good conduct. They will be well cared for, provided you continue to cooperate." She conspicuously dodged his question. "Together we will find the pyramid in the ice, and when we have the third element, we will use all three to find the Emerald Tablet."

Kismet held her stare, but Maddock saw a change in the man's eyes; an unspoken message to him. *Get ready.*

"I told you what I saw." Kismet spoke slowly, his tone calm, measured, but hard as diamond. "You promised to let them go."

"And I will," Aliyah retorted. "In due time."

"That wasn't the deal. You swore an oath."

Aliyah's smile faltered, the accusation clearly troubling to her if only because she had an audience.

"But that's okay," Kismet said, smiling, "because I haven't been completely honest with you. Now!"

Kismet moved so quickly that, even though Maddock was expecting it, he was taken completely by surprise. Kismet sprang at Aliyah like a rattlesnake striking, but he did not attack her. Instead, he raked his hand across hers, stripping the Apex from her grip. As he closed his fist around the talisman, he pivoted away from her, racing instead toward Rose, arms thrown wide as if he intended to tackle her.

Which was exactly what he did.

The fraction of a second it took for him to do all of this was roughly equal to Maddock's reaction time, but he hesitated a moment longer, unsure of where to focus his attention. Jade, with a pistol still pressed against her throat, was in the most immediate danger, but trying to wrest the gun from the hands of her captor was a monumentally bad idea. And the situation wasn't much better for the rest of them. He figured he had maybe another fraction of a second—the time it would take to blink—before the shooting started.

Why did he go to Rose?

The thought barely had time to flit through his brain before the answer arrived in spectacular fashion. From one moment to the next, everything changed. The gunmen adjusted their aim, fingers tightening on triggers, and then—

blink

—they were swept off their feet, hurled backward and slammed into the perimeter walls. It was as if an enormous balloon had instantaneously inflated, like a car's airbag following a collision, filling the room with its bulk, pushing the gunmen away and pinning them against the walls. Most were still gripping their pistols and flashlights, but the hands that held them were immobilized by the invisible force. Aliyah and Black had been caught up as well. Entangled like lovers, they were plastered against the rear wall near the vault door. Yet, the heavy door was still open, undisturbed by the effect. Maddock had felt nothing. Bones and Jade were likewise untouched, gaping in disbelief as they attempted to process what had just happened.

Rose was still on the ground, with Kismet covering her, hugging her... No, it wasn't an embrace. He was reaching around her, his hands pressed against the orb in her backpack.

The orb.

Maddock recalled how, in the Antarctic Outpost, the Prometheus strike team leader had used the orb to create an impenetrable bubble of energy, a force-field that protected him from bullets. Rose had tried to use it to do the same during their subsequent escape. They had survived unscathed though whether that had anything to do with the orb or Rose's ability to master it, Maddock could not say. But Kismet *had* succeeded in tapping into the orb's power, using it together with the Apex, to melt the ice away from Grace's frozen cadaver, and now it seemed he had done it again.

Kismet bounded to his feet and then reached out a hand to help Rose stand, but in that instant, the effect began to wane. Maddock saw Aliyah peel one arm away from the wall, using it to brace herself and push her entire body away. Her henchmen were similarly breaking free of the rapidly diminishing force.

Kismet looked to Maddock. "The mirror."

Maddock did a quick visual sweep, locating the box containing the Magna of Illusion. It had fallen from Black's grasp and now lay in the center of the room. He darted forward and picked it up, verifying that the flawless obsidian disk was still inside. "Got it!"

"Then let's get the hell out of here!"

17

"**I'll just ask** the obvious question," Bones said as they hurried down the path at a near-jog, as fast as they dared move in the darkness. "Why are we in such a hurry? We've got all three magic doodads, and you obviously know how to use them. They mess with us again, just put the whammy on 'em."

Without breaking stride, Kismet looked back over his shoulder. "You ever see Wizard of Oz?"

"Who hasn't?"

"You remember how Dorothy killed the witches?"

Bones shrugged. "Sure. She dropped a house on one, and melted the other with a bucket of water."

"She got lucky. Twice. I got lucky back there. I caught them by surprise. But they know a lot more about these things than I do, and maybe I won't get lucky a second time."

Maddock thought about his answer, remembering how Aliyah had tried to use the Apex and the Magna of Illusion together—tried and failed. Kismet was wrong, he decided. When it came to tapping the power of the elementals, the magicians were as much in the dark as everyone else.

Still, probably best not to put all their eggs in that basket.

They descended the moss-slick stairs and hurried out onto the pier. The rain was coming down harder now, the seas noticeably rougher. Storm waves, rebounding off the headlands and coming in from every conceivable direction, were pounding the cliffs and throwing curtains of spray over the pier. When they reached the steps leading down to the dock, Maddock half-expected to find their boat gone, torn from its mooring, but instead there were now three Zodiacs tied to the cleats. Both the dock and the inflatable boats were rising and falling a good three feet with each swell that rolled through.

By mutual accord, Maddock and Bones hurried ahead to the nearest boat, steadying it, at least to the extent that was possible, so the others could board. Rose climbed in first and as soon as she was seated, Maddock passed the box with the Magna of Illusion over to her. She accepted it without comment, slipping it into the pack with the orb. Jade boarded next but Kismet moved past them, to the next Zodiac.

"What? You too good to ride with us?" Bones called out.

Kismet laughed. "I'm not going to ride in it."

His hand dropped to his waist and, with a noise like fingernails on a chalkboard, he drew an enormous *kukri* knife from a concealed sheath and slashed it across the bright yellow inflatable gunwale. Air rushed from the ruptured cell in a flatulent whoosh. The boat did not immediately sink, but as the buoyancy chamber emptied, the craft settled lower, and water began sloshing over the gunwale, filling the bilges.

"It leaks."

He did the same to the other boat then sheathed his knife and rejoined the others, clambering into the Zodiac with Rose and Jade. Maddock went next, immediately settling into the pilot's chair, while Bones loosened but did not release the knot around the cleat. With the raft still rising and falling crazily with the sea, their timing would have to be perfect. Cast off at the wrong moment, and they might get thrown against the pier.

After checking to make sure the shift lever was in the neutral position, Maddock hit the electric starter switch, revved the motor once, twice, and then looked out to sea, watching the swells roll in. The Zodiac dipped as one wave passed, and then just as quickly began rising with the next. When it reached the crest, Maddock shouted, "Now!"

Bones gave the rope a deft twist and then leaped into the prow. His momentum caused the front end to swing away from the dock, and as the boat tilted toward the backside of the wave, it fell away from the mooring, sliding faster down the wave. At the same instant, Maddock engaged the screws and opened up the throttle. The Zodiac shot forward but almost immediately began to nose up, into the next swell.

"Hang on!"

The boat angled up, climbing the fluid slope, but as it neared the crest, he eased off the throttle to avoid shooting off the top like a rocket. Their momentum carried them over the hump and then they were falling again.

This roller coaster ride replayed again and again as they fought clear of Drake's Island. The rain continued to lash them, but as they reached the deeper water in the channel, the ride finally smoothed out a little, so Maddock gave it more throttle and pointed the bow toward Plymouth harbor. The city lights appeared to undulate up and down as the Zodiac skipped over rough seas, a tapestry of stars waving up and down as if being shaken by a giant.

But two of the lights were different. Low on the horizon, they didn't move the same as the others. More precisely, they *were* moving, detached from the fixed cityscape which only seemed to be in motion.

Two boats, exiting the harbor, heading out into the storm-tossed sound.

Probably nothing. A couple of fisherman taking their boats out to deep water to avoid the incessant pounding of the storm surge.

But Maddock's instincts told him otherwise.

He cut back on the throttle, which eased the relentless hammering vibrations from the hull smashing through the waves, but perversely made the nausea-inducing rise and fall even more pronounced.

Bones crawled back to him. "You saw 'em, too?"

Maddock nodded. He resisted the urge to dismiss what he had seen, what he was feeling. If it was nothing, it was nothing, but if it wasn't nothing, denial would only make the situation worse.

"You think witchy-poo had some reinforcements standing by?"

"Could be."

Kismet joined them. "There's another possibility."

"Prometheus."

"They might have been hanging back, waiting for us to do the heavy lifting."

"Bastards," Bones snarled.

"Typical," Kismet said, affirming the sentiment.

Maddock nodded. "So how do we—down!"

Tiny flashes of light, barely visible beside the brighter spotlights of the approaching vessels, eliminated the first possibility.

Definitely not nothing.

18

Bullets whizzed overhead with a hiss that was audible, even over the tumult of the storm and the roar of the outboard. Multiple reports, the distinctive crack of supersonic rifle rounds.

"Anyone planning to do something about that?" Bones said. "You know, like maybe raise shields?"

Rose shrugged off the backpack and shoved it toward Kismet. "You're the expert."

Kismet shook his head, more a gesture of resignation than uncertainty and reached for it, but before he could take it, Rose snatched it back. "Crap! I forgot."

"What?"

"We can't use shields."

Another volley split the air overhead, and then something thumped against one of the gunwales. Air erupted from a ragged hole in the buoyancy tube.

Bones scrambled forward and slapped one massive hand over the leak. "Check the lockers. Should be a repair kit in one of them."

"Idiots," Jade raged as she crawled forward to check the bow locker. "If they sink us, they'll lose the elementals."

"If it's Prometheus," Kismet countered, "they won't care. They have the resources to recover them."

Determining the exact identity of their attackers was a secondary priority for Maddock. Every passing second was bringing them closer to the shooters.

He cranked the wheel, cutting hard to port, carving a tight 180° turn. The lights of Plymouth were swept away, replaced by the scattered lights of rural Cornwall. In the distance, perhaps two miles away, lay a single shining beacon, the Plymouth Breakwater Lighthouse, marking the west end of the nearly mile-long manmade barrier that guarded the entrance to the bay. Maddock pointed the bow toward it and opened up the throttle.

He glanced over at Rose, who was now hugging the backpack to her chest protectively. "Rose, why can't we use the orb?"

"I just remembered something from the Dodge Dalton books. The shield is some kind of electrical field. If it comes into contact with water—"

Maddock understood. "We're toast."

"Pretty much."

Bones glanced over his shoulder and shook his head. "What's the point of having magic gizmos if they never work when you need them to."

"I don't think it's real magic," Rose said. "Just a technology we don't understand."

"Well it's pretty freaking useless either way."

"Will a first aid kit work?" Jade asked, holding up a white plastic box embossed with a big red cross.

"Is there tape in it?"

Jade popped the case open and held up a fat white donut-shaped roll of adhesive cloth. "Will this do?"

Bones shrugged and reached out with his free hand to take it.

The dark, unlit mass of Drake's Island hove into view directly ahead. *Right back where we started,* Maddock thought as he veered away from the peer angling left to hug the eastern edge of the island. As it slid by, he wondered if Aliyah and her minions were watching from the shadowy cliffs.

A glance back showed the light of the two boats hunting them, maybe two hundred yards back, matching their pace. They were easily within rifle range, and while the turbulent seas would challenge even an experienced shooter, fickle Lady Luck could easily turn her back on them.

His intent was to follow the curve of the island toward the south shore, putting the landmass between them and the hunters, but the increasingly rough seas forced him to abandon that idea. The only way to survive the incoming waves was by taking them head on.

And how long can I keep that up? he wondered.

Bones uttered a harsh curse and flung the roll of white first aid tape out into the sea. Maddock didn't need to ask what the problem was; the surface of the buoyancy tube was too wet for the tape to adhere. The inflatable boat wouldn't sink, not right away, but as the tube continued to deflate, the hull would ride lower and the sea would find its way in.

"Not long enough," he muttered. It was time for a new plan. And a new boat.

19

With a sickening crunch, the Zodiac's rigid hull rode up onto the Plymouth Breakwater and shuddered to a halt. Even though she had braced herself for the expected impact, Jade was nearly catapulted over the increasingly flaccid buoyancy tube. She waited for the rebound, and then did the very thing the collision had failed to accomplish.

She landed badly, the rocks beneath her were slippery and uneven, but in the fraction of a second it took for her to fall face-first into them, a roiling wave rushed in, covering the surface. The suddenly knee-deep water didn't cushion her fall so much as prolong it, dragging her another six feet up onto the sloping artificial reef, pummeling and scraping her body even as the sea water rushed over her head, blinding her, nearly choking her.

"Great plan, Maddock!" she snarled.

Despite the sarcastic tone of her observation, she knew it was probably the best plan given their dire circumstance. With the pair of hunters pushing them further into the teeth of the storm, and a boat that wouldn't be seaworthy much longer, getting out of the water was imperative.

She struggled to hands and knees, the rough stone abrading her skin, but it was enough to get her head clear. The wave's energy abruptly reversed, pulling her back, threatening to carry her out to sea, but she spread-eagled on the slick rock, anchoring herself until the sucking sensation passed.

Through the blurry haze, she could just make out the dark silhouette of the breakwater, and beyond it, the night sky, briefly illuminated in the glow of a signal flash from the lighthouse.

That was where she needed to go, but Maddock's plan required one thing of her first. She turned her head searching the surf, but the light was already fading, plunging her into near total darkness. "Rose!"

"Here!" The answering voice was weak, more a sputtering cough than a shout, but a moment later, Jade felt something tugging at the hem of her shirt. She groped to find Rose's hand and took it in her grip as another wave surged in and drove them both further up onto the breakwater. Jade clung to both the rocks under her, and to Rose's outstretched hand until the wave retreated. Another bright flash from the lighthouse lit up the sky above, and indirectly, the route they would need to take to reach the elevated crest of the breakwater. It also revealed Nick Kismet, clinging to Rose's other hand.

The crest of the mile-long breakwater was a flat paved platform, about forty feet wide, and mostly above the pounding surf. Working together, the trio made it to the top, just as the signal light flashed yet again. Jade glanced back. There was no sign of Maddock or Bones, but she easily spotted the two boats, closing in on the breakwater, just a few hundred yards out. She shook her head and focused on her own survival.

Kismet urged them forward at a run. Maddock had grounded the Zodiac about a hundred yards east of the lighthouse. Not far, but up on the crest of the breakwater, they would be silhouetted against the sky, easy targets for the killers in the boats. The only thing going for them was the fact that the men would not have a stable platform from which to take that shot. She didn't hear any reports—though they might have easily been drowned out by the pounding surf—and hoped that meant the shooters had reached the same conclusion. Even so, taking cover behind the lighthouse was the number one priority.

The base of the Plymouth Breakwater lighthouse was flared like the pedestal of a floor lamp, nearly twice as wide as at the top. The entrance faced more or less in the direction from which they had just come, but it would almost certainly be locked up tight, and even if they somehow were able to get it open, being inside the automated signaling station would give them no advantage. Just the opposite, they would be cornered, with no exit. Instead, they bypassed the door and veered to the left, circling around it clockwise until the great bulk of the lighthouse was between them and the men with guns. Kismet stopped, delved into Rose's backpack—which he had been carrying since they hatched the crazy plan—and brought out the orb, while Jade and Rose moved along the base in opposite directions to keep an eye on their pursuers.

They didn't have to wait long.

From her vantage on the south side of the lighthouse, Jade could see them moving along the breakwater. She reckoned there were five or six of them, though it was hard to tell as they were bunched up and obscured by rain and shadow. As they drew closer, they split into two groups heading different directions around the light. Jade backed away and hurried back to join Kismet. Rose had arrived a few seconds ahead of her and had already given Kismet the news.

"You two better take cover," Kismet said, hugging the orb to his chest. "If this doesn't work… Hell, even if it does, you're not going to want to be anywhere close to me."

"If it doesn't work," Jade replied, "You should throw that thing into the sea."

"Let me just go on record one more time," Rose put in. "This is a really terrible idea. You're going to get yourself killed."

"Don't worry about me." He nodded in the direction of the squat concrete cube-shaped structure that stood halfway between the light and the water's edge. "Go. Now."

Jade had no idea what purpose the stout structure served but it looked bulletproof. She and Rose hastened behind the building, but Jade immediately peeked around the corner to watch the confrontation.

She heard shouts, one of the gunmen ordering Kismet to put his hands up. Kismet didn't answer, didn't move.

"Come on," Jade whispered, and then remembering Bones' earlier comment, added. "Show 'em the whammy!"

For a few seconds, nothing happened. Then, everything happened all at once.

The air around Kismet lit up with the brilliance of an arc welder, accompanied by the deafening *crack* of an electrical discharge. Jade closed her eyes and drew back, but the damage was already done. The sight of Kismet— just his silhouette really—surrounded by long tendrils of lighting, was burned into her eyes like a snapshot. The afterimage dissolved into the green blob of temporary flash blindness, but she didn't need her eyes to follow what was happening on the other side of the concrete structure.

The crackle and pop of voltage, the distinctive smell

of ozone in the air. Other sounds and smells joined the tumult. The reports of a rifle, several of them. The sulfur stink of burnt gunpowder.

Kismet!

Then she felt something, like invisible cobwebs brushing against her face, an uncomfortable tingling sensation that crept all over her body.

"Rose! Get down!"

Jade barely had time to follow her own advice before lightning struck. That was what it felt like. The flash from the other side of the concrete cube was so bright that even through the green spots in her vision, the world was lit up like daybreak. The subsequent thunderclap shook the ground and drove the breath from her lungs.

And then, silence.

20

After intentionally running the Zodiac aground on the breakwater, Maddock and Bones had also gone into the water, but unlike Jade and the others, they had stayed there, watching and waiting.

And waiting.

The plan was simple. Divide and conquer, though in this instance, they would be the ones dividing their forces. Kismet, Jade and Rose would go ashore and hopefully draw most of the killers after them, and—again hopefully—unleash the orb's power to defeat the gunmen. While the three of them were doing that, Maddock and Bones would lie low—literally—staying partially submerged in the surf, hiding under the wreckage of the Zodiac until the boats came in. Once the gunmen took the bait, the two of them would sneak aboard one or both of the boats, overpower whatever crew remained, after which they would regroup and head back to Plymouth, leaving their would-be attackers stranded on the breakwater.

Simple. And far from perfect.

The abandoned Zodiac to which Maddock and Bones clung was just so much flotsam, alternately slammed into the breakwater by the storm waves and then dragged back out into the sea. The water was a hypothermia-inducing 50° Fahrenheit, but he and Bones had trained under harsher conditions in the course of their SEAL training, and knew their limitations. Maddock figured they could last at least half an hour if they had to, maybe longer. It wouldn't be pleasant. In fact, between the pummeling, the cold, and having to listen to Bones whine about "shrinkage," it would be absolute hell.

Kismet and the others would face a different set of problems. He had already twice proven his ability to control the otherworldly talisman, and Maddock felt certain their new friend would be able to deliver once again, but there was no telling what would happen when he attempted to use the orb to create an electrical force field in the rain. There was a very real chance that the orb would short out, leaving them defenseless, or even electrocute Kismet, but he had assured them all that he could handle whatever happened.

The real problem with the plan was that everything depended on the bad guys doing exactly what Maddock wanted them to do. If they didn't take the bait, come ashore on the breakwater and chase after Kismet and the others, it would all be for nothing.

Yet, what choice did they have? The Zodiac wouldn't have lasted much longer. Better to abandon it with solid ground underfoot. Worst case scenario, it would be a stalemate, and that was better than drowning in the English Channel.

They didn't have to wait long. The boats—gray and black RIBs, military versions of the Zodiac—came in cautiously, running the screws in reverse, then forward, to hold station about twenty yards off the rocks. Maddock counted eight men—four in each boat—all wearing tactical black from head-to-toe. Either Aliyah's magicians had a special operations division, which he doubted, or these guys were working for Prometheus.

One by one, three men from each boat fearlessly took the plunge. They vanished into the water, reappearing a few seconds later in the frothy surf. They scuttled up onto the rocks, moving on all fours like crabs. The two pilots shone their spotlights onto the shoreline until all six men were accounted for, then revved their motors, backing the boats away from the breakwater, getting clear of the surf.

"If we're going to do this," Bones started.

"I know," Maddock said, fighting to keep his teeth from chattering. "I've got right. You take left."

"Sure," Bones growled. "Make me swim further."

The big man ducked his head under the surface and was gone before Maddock could point out that there was no meaningful difference in the distance to the two RIBs, respectively. Maddock shook his head, fixed the location of the boat in his mind, and then after drawing in a deep breath, submerged himself and started swimming underwater.

His sodden clothes reduced his natural buoyancy to the point where he barely had to exert himself to stay submerged, and since he could hold his breath for well over two minutes, there was no need to come to the surface until he was right where he wanted to be. There really wasn't much risk of being seen by the pilots of the two boats, not unless they happened to move their lights to shine them directly on the spot where he was going to break the surface, but Maddock was a believer in Murphy's Law—if something can go wrong, it will—and he planned accordingly. Years of real-world experience gave him an almost supernatural sense of where he was in relation to the other boat, but he allowed a generous margin of error just in case.

When he was fairly certain of his position, he allowed himself to drift back up to the surface. As soon as his head cleared the water, he spotted the silhouette of the nearest RIB, about fifteen meters away, and right between him and the breakwater.

Perfect.

He repositioned to face the vessel's stern and began pulling himself through the water using a slow breast stroke that kept just his eyes and nose above the waterline. At first, he could only make out the outline of the man sitting in the pilot's chair but as he got closer and the angle of his line of sight became sharper, the man disappeared behind the bulk of the outboard. Fortunately, that would work both ways; the man in the boat would not see him coming either.

He dog-paddled closer, one hand outstretched and resting against the engine cowling to maintain a safe distance from the boat until he was ready to make his move. The outboard was still running at idle but that could change at any moment and with no warning at all. The last thing Maddock needed was for a swell to throw him into the screws just as they began turning. Carefully, so as not to transmit any vibrations through the hull, he pulled himself in close, grasping the molded stern just to the right of the engine cowling, and then slowly, stealthily, pulled himself up onto the molded transom and—

Froze as he realized he was looking down the barrel of a gun.

Crap! Maddock thought. As careful as he had been, somehow the man had sensed his presence. *So much for the stealthy approach. I hope Bones is having better luck.*

The muzzle was just a couple inches from his face, close enough that even in the low light conditions, he could tell that it was bored for a 5.56-millimeter round—an AR-15 variant of some kind. Definitely not the same kind of hardware Aliyah's magick order had been packing. The weapon was close enough that, under any other circumstances, he would have been tempted to grab the barrel, redirect it away from his face and yank it out of the gunman's hands, but his precarious position on the stern of the RIB made that a risky proposition. Not out of the question, but risky enough that he decided to consider other options.

He raised his eyes, looking past the barrel to the face of the man who held the weapon. The man was grinning, a big, hungry grin that made Maddock think of the Big Bad Wolf from Little Red Riding Hood.

My what big teeth you have....

"Dane Maddock," the grinning man exclaimed, as if they were long-lost friends. "Well, I'd be lying if I said it was a surprise to see you. TBH, I would have been disappointed if you hadn't tried something like this."

A chill that had nothing to do with the water temperature shot through Maddock. He didn't recognize the grinning man's face, but there was no mistaking the voice. Or his bizarre insistence on using "text-ese" abbreviations in everyday speech.

TBH.

That was the name he had given to the faceless leader of the Prometheus strike team that tried to capture the orb in the Outpost in Antarctica.

"No," he gasped. "No way. You're dead!"

Maddock was certain of that. TBH had been impaled on the adamantine-infused blade of the tomahawk that had led them to the orb and awakened its power. The hatchet head had gone clean through his chest. It was a mortal injury. Unsurvivable even under the best of circumstances with immediate medical attention.

TBH grinned again. "It didn't take."

A swell rocked the boat under them and water sloshed over Maddock's head but the weapon aimed at him did not waver.

"How?"

TBH laughed. "Ask my brother. Oh, wait. I guess you're not going to get a chance to do that." He paused a second and then added, "You know, because you'll be dead."

Maddock barely registered the threat—

Brother?

—but at the other end of the rifle, the Prometheus leader squared his shoulders and curled his finger around the trigger.

21

A flash, not of superheated gas driving a bullet down the barrel of the rifle and into Maddock's face, but of a lightning bolt striking somewhere just past the lighthouse on the breakwater, lit up the world. TBH's eyes shifted to the side, his attention diverted just for an instant.

Maddock was similarly distracted by the flash, but knew better than to let this momentary reprieve slip away. He put all thought of his foe's seemingly miraculous recovery out of his head, along with the man's cryptic pronouncement—*ask my brother*—and jerked his head to the side, just enough to removed himself from the direct line of fire. In the same motion, he reached up with his right hand to grasp the barrel, shoving it in the opposite direction.

The metal was suddenly hot in his grip and he felt the concussive force of an impact slam into his palm as the weapon discharged, sending a 5.56 round sizzling harmlessly past him, into the sea. Maddock felt like his hand had been slapped with Thor's hammer, but he did not let go of the barrel. Instead, he twisted his body sideways, pulling the rifle toward him. TBH, with his hand still curled around the pistol grip did not let go either, and because he had nothing to brace himself against, toppled forward, over the transom and into the water.

Maddock, still hanging onto the rifle, let go of the boat and threw his left arm around the Prometheus leader in a hug that pinned the man's arms to his side, even as both of them plunged beneath the surface. Maddock felt the other man's struggles growing more frantic and squeezed even tighter.

Weighed down by his heavy tactical gear, spare magazines and the seven-pound rifle, TBH sank like a stone, taking Maddock with him. As they descended, Maddock began counting the seconds. He could gauge their depth by the growing pressure against his eardrums. At ten feet, it was merely uncomfortable. At twenty it was actually painful. He began working his jaw and blowing through his nose to pop his ears and equalize the pressure. That brought only a few seconds of comfort, a few more vertical feet of descent.

Ten Mississippi… Eleven Mississippi….

TBH was thrashing now, desperately trying to squirm free, but Maddock did not let go. Abruptly, the descent stopped. With all the squirming, Maddock had not even felt the soft touch of the seafloor beneath him.

Sometime after his fortieth Mississippi, TBH's spasms became even more violent. He went as rigid as a flagpole, and then stopped moving completely. Maddock's own lungs were starting to burn with the need to breathe, but he held on a little longer just to be sure. He was pretty sure the man was dead, but he had thought that after their encounter at the Outpost as well.

You're dead… It didn't take… Ask my brother.

My brother.

When he got to sixty, Maddock disentangled, shoved the unmoving form of his would-be killer away, and began swimming for the surface. He hoped Bones had been luckier than he, hoped also that Jade, Rose and Kismet had survived their encounter with the rest of the Prometheus strike team. The strange electrical discharge might have just been a lightning strike, but Maddock's gut told him it was nothing so mundane.

The climb back to the surface took another thirty seconds, taxing the limits of even Maddock's extraordinary lung capacity, and by the time he finally broke through, the only thing he cared about was breathing fresh air. He gasped in several breaths, coughing out the seawater that had insinuated itself into his mouth and nose, and began searching for the RIB.

A light flashed in his eyes. He blinked and looked away, just as something struck him in the head. The blow wasn't hard enough to cause real pain; it felt almost like a jab from someone wearing boxing gloves. A moment later, he felt the object bump into him again, and realized what it was: A ring-shaped foam life preserver.

"You going to grab that?" Bones called out to him. "Just pretend it's your junk, because I'm not coming in after you."

22

Maddock grinned as the light moved away from him. He threaded one arm through the ring and hugged it to his chest as Bones began reeling him in. He could just make out the outline of the RIB, maybe twenty feet away, and his friend hauling him in like a prize catch.

"Always gotta do things the hard way," said Bones as he leaned out and pulled Maddock up and over the gunwale.

"Believe me, it wasn't by choice." Maddock decided not to share the news about the identity of the man he had just fought with. That could wait until later. "Any sign of the others?"

"Not really. Just that big flash and then nothing. Did you see it?"

Maddock nodded but did not articulate his fears about what it signified. He struggled to a sitting position. "Get me ashore. I'll go check it out."

"Thought you might want to do that. Here. I found this—well, inherited it would be more accurate. Might come in handy." Bones passed over an assault weapon— an M4 carbine if Maddock was not mistaken—and then turned to take his place at the console. The RIB lurched as Bones engaged the screws and a few seconds later, Maddock was in the water again, splashing up onto the storm barrier.

Once he was above the surf, he brought the carbine to the low ready and made his way up the sloping breakwater. He paused just below the crest, scanning the path before him for any sign of activity, hostile or otherwise. Every few seconds, a flash from the lighthouse obliquely illumed the foreground but aside from the crashing sea and the persistent rain splattering on the paving stones, all was still.

He brought the weapon up, staring through its attached EOTech holographic sight, finger poised alongside the trigger, and started toward the towering structure. He moved quickly, with short strides, rolling his feet heel-to-toe to maintain traction and avoid stumbling over unseen obstacles, and reached the base of the lighthouse in less than a minute. He turned left, intending to make a clockwise circle, but after only a few degrees of the arc, he heard something over the din of the storm.

Jade's voice. She was counting. And cursing.

"Five… Six… Seven… Eight… Breathe, damn it."

Maddock hastened in the direction of the sound, lowering the weapon, but remaining poised to revert to a more aggressive stance at the first sign of danger.

There was no need however. As he came around to the south side of the tower, he spotted them in the intermittent flash of the beacon. Rose stood by helplessly as a kneeling Jade pumped Kismet's chest with her crossed hands, and counted and cursed. When she reached fifteen, she bent over and breathed into his mouth.

The orb lay a few feet away from them, looking about as deadly as a concrete lawn ornament.

Maddock ran to them, shouting. "What happened?"

Rose started at the sound of his approach, but then fell into his arms, openly weeping. "The rain. When he tried to use it…" She faltered, words failing her, but Maddock had already figured it out. As Rose had feared, Kismet's attempt to use the orb to create an electrical force field had backfired. Evidently, it had not been a complete failure. The Prometheus gunmen had been swept away, probably blasted into the ocean, but Kismet had paid the ultimate price for that victory. The current had ripped through him, blasting him like an actual bolt of lightning, stopping his heart.

Maddock shook himself into action. Jade had done the right thing in starting CPR, but that alone wouldn't save Kismet's life. Despite what happened in movies, chest compressions could not start a stopped heart. Even the ubiquitous flatline on the EKG monitor was a complete fiction; the heart beat its life-sustaining rhythm because of electrical impulses from the brain, impulses that continued in some form even after death. The EKG was a representation of the electrical signals that kept the heart beating, not the actual activity of the heart muscle. Cardio-pulmonary resuscitation primarily served to forestall brain death by sustaining the flow of oxygenated blood to the brain and organs, but the only way to restore the heart's normal rhythm was with a jolt from a defibrillator, and the nearest one of those was back in Plymouth harbor.

He turned to Rose. "The orb did this, right? Maybe we can use it to jump start his heart again."

Rose gaped at him, horrified. "And end up just like him?"

Maddock wasn't so sure. Kismet had some kind of affinity for the orb and the other elemental artifacts, an affinity nobody else seemed to have. Except for TBH, of course.

Ask my brother....

Maddock didn't know how to put that into words, so he chose instead to simply act. He stepped forward and, bracing himself for the possibility that he was about to make a fatal mistake, scooped up the orb

Nothing. Not even a tingle of current.

"So far, so good." He turned, faced Jade and Kismet. "Get clear," he warned.

Jade looked up, her lips moving as she continued counting, and shook her head.

Rose ran forward, putting herself in between him and the others. "Maddock, don't."

Maddock was about to attempt an explanation, but just then, Kismet's entire body spasmed, like someone waking from a dream of falling, and he gasped loudly.

Jade backpedaled away, as if uncertain whether this was a miraculous recovery, or some kind of zombie-like reanimation. Maddock was similarly wary, but Kismet merely sat up, looking bewildered. He met Maddock's gaze and raised a hopeful eyebrow. "Did it work?"

You were dead… It didn't take… Ask my brother.

Maddock extended a hand and helped Kismet to his feet. The latter bounded up, as if his near-death experience was nothing but a refreshing nap. Maddock maintained the handclasp pulling Kismet even closer.

"I ran into your brother," he said, his voice low, almost a whisper. "We need to talk."

EPILOGUE
The Final Element

During the train ride back to London that night, Kismet told them the whole story, beginning with his first encounter with Prometheus and the man he now knew to be his estranged brother. The first glimpse behind what he called "the shroud of heaven" had set him on a path of discovery—not only about the true nature of reality and spirituality, but also of a mystery that began the day of his own birth.

He revealed that his father, Christian Garral, was not his true biological father. The man had adopted him shortly after his birth and subsequent abandonment. He had known that much even as a young boy, but it was only much later that he learned the unusual circumstances of his birth and parentage. Adam Garral was not, so far as Kismet knew, a blood relative.

The man Maddock called TBH, and who had identified himself to Kismet as Ulrich Hauser, was actually Kismet's fraternal twin, and while Kismet had grown up as the son of a globe-trotting adventurer and yacht racer, his brother had been groomed to lead Prometheus, an education overseen by the mother Kismet had never met.

"Your contact on the inside," Maddock realized aloud.

Kismet just nodded.

It was not merely inevitable that the two men would cross paths again, but foreordained.

Kismet also told them of his other adventures, such

as his descent into the Black Sea to find the Golden Fleece of Greek legend, or his battle against a diabolical monk to control the Judas rope.

"Wait," Bones interrupted. "Judas, as in Jesus's bro?"

Kismet nodded. "According to the story, it was the rope Judas Iscariot used to hang himself with after the betrayal. I don't know if it's true, but sometimes it's easier just to go with the devil you know."

Bones and Maddock exchanged knowing looks, but kept their silence.

Kismet's final confrontation with his brother— though now it seemed not-quite-so-final after all—had involved a search for the secret of immortality itself. Though he had been a skeptic at the outset, subsequent events had made him a believer.

Bones shook his head in disbelief. "You're immortal?"

"I honestly don't know," replied Kismet. "The effects may wear off someday, but right now… Yeah, I guess 'immortal' sums it up. I look about twenty years younger than what is says on my driver's license."

"If I ever settle down with a hot, young number, maybe you can give her a bit of what you've got," Bones said.

"You'll be settling down with your left hand," Jade said.

"I heal quickly," Kismet went on. Even from very serious injuries." He nodded in Jade's direction. "And if I don't get a haircut at least once a week, or I start looking like Cousin It."

Bones wagged his head again. "Kismet, means luck, right?"

"Luck. Fate. Serendipity. Take your pick."

"Well, I think you must be the luckiest son-of-a-bitch on the planet."

"Fortune favors the bold," said Jade.

Kismet gave a mirthless chuckle. "Believe me, I don't feel particularly lucky."

"And your brother got a dose of it, too?" said Maddock.

Kismet shrugged. "I didn't think so at the time, but based on what you've told me, that's about the only conclusion I can draw."

"So he's just going to keep coming?" Bones said. "Like Arnie?" He dropped his voice and affected a comically thick Austrian accent. "I'll be bah-ck."

"Until he gets what he wants. The Philosopher's Stone."

"So we get it first, yeah?" said Jade. "Use it against him. If it can give immortality, maybe it can take it away, too." A guilty look came over her and she quickly glanced over at Kismet. "We'd be careful with it, of course."

Maddock looked over at Rose, who held the backpack containing the orb and mirror on her lap. "First we have to find the fourth elemental. The Emerald Tablet."

Kismet stared at Maddock. "You don't have to, you know. This is my fight. And, not to put too fine a point on it, but I've got nine lives. You don't."

Bones laughed. "Not to put too fine a point on it, but you'd be nowhere without us. Stopping bad guys from taking over the world is kind of our thing."

Kismet glanced at him and then the others. "Does he speak for all of you?"

Jade gave a derisive snort and shook her head. "God forbid. But I was on board before he showed up, so I've already got dibs."

"I don't want to think about what will happen if Prometheus wins this fight," said Maddock, "but I know we'll stand a better chance if we stick together."

Kismet nodded slowly. "All right. Then let's do this."

The End

MAGUS

Book Three of The Elementals

PART ONE: HELL WEEK

Prologue

It is a perfect storm.

Hour after hour, a total assault on the senses. Artillery simulators and machine guns firing blanks nonstop, the noise crackling through my nerves like lightning. Smoke grenades spewing out a putrid fume. The stink of body odor. The scrape of sand on skin already rubbed raw and bloody. Running down to the tideline where the cold waves wash over me, sapping my strength until I've got nothing left to give.

The worst part though is that voice. A low flat monotone, barely distinguishable from the pounding surf. I wouldn't be able to hear it at all if not for the amplification of the bullhorn, but it resonates through me, dragging me molecule by molecule into a black pit of despair, sucking away what's left of my resolve.

"You don't have to keep doing this," the voice drones.

And I know he's right.

"You can go get in my truck right now. I've got some hot cocoa for you. That sounds good, doesn't it? Come ring my bell and you can have some."

There are a few defiant shouts. "Hell no, chief."

My voice is not among them. Even if I wanted to, I don't think I could get the words past my chattering teeth.

The voice drones on for a while, alternately elaborating on the effects of hypothermia and then, with something that sounds almost like sympathy, offering absolution. "Not everyone is cut out for this. This is what we do, every day… Is this what you really want? To be miserable all the time? Hot cocoa in the truck... All you have to do is ring my bell."

Is this what I really want? I can't remember why I ever thought it was.

"Boat crews," the voice says abruptly. "Line up."

I look left then right, seeing the others. Our arms are linked but we might as well be on different planets. As another wave crashes over my head, I see some of the others responding. Thrashing in the surf, struggling to rise. Struggling to help each other.

Then I'm moving, too.

We all stumble up onto the beach, assembling into our six-man boat crews, only none of the boat crews are complete. How many are left? I can't tell. There had been seventy-two of us at the start, but more than a dozen folded in the first hour.

How long ago was that? I can't remember.

"You look tired," drones the instructor as he paces up and down the line. Viewed in profile, the bullhorn looks like a part of him, a strange deformed animal muzzle, braying constantly. "Maybe you should all lie down."

A groan ripples through the rank; we all know what's coming.

I drop to my back with everyone else and immediately begin kicking. Flutter kicks. God, I hate flutter kicks. My abdominal muscles scream in protest.

The instructor counts out the rhythm for a while—"One, two, three…" We are expected to keep the count, sounding off at the top of our lungs, but the only sound I can make is a mewling grunt. Then the instructor breaks off to ask, "How was the water? Did you enjoy your swim?"

A ragged chorus of "Hooyah, chief," goes up.

"I'll bet you'd really like to get back out there, wouldn't you?"

"Hooyah, chief."

"On your feet."

I'm supposed to bound up, but it feels like I'm trapped in quicksand. Every muscle screams in protest.

"What's this?" the instructor says, his voice rising ever so slightly, a mockery of sincere interest. "I thought there were supposed to be six men to a boat crew." He looks over to one of the other instructors, who nods, right on cue. The chief shakes his head. "Some of these boat crews are light. Looks like we're going to have to change things up a little." He paces up and down the line for a few minutes. "Well this is a little awkward. I count fifty-six maggots lined up in front of me."

The instructor stops abruptly—

No. Not me. Don't look at me. Keep going.

—and looks right at me. "Maggot, how many times does six go into fifty-six?"

My teeth are chattering involuntarily, but some part of my brain has already done the math. "Nine, chief. Remainder of two."

I've always been good at math. I'm good at almost everything.

Except this.

Another voice, one that I've come to despise over the last two weeks, snarls from somewhere off to my right. "Teacher's pet."

It's the big Indian, though in this moment, I can't

remember his name. I can barely remember my own.

"Remainder of two," croons the instructor. "Well that makes this easy. As soon as two of you maggots ring my bell, we can move on with the next activity."

He pauses, allowing this to sink in. "You already know that you're not going to make it," he continues, easing back into the monotone. "You know that you're going to quit. Why put yourself through this?"

I know that some of them are already considering it because I am, but none of us break ranks.

"No one?" The instructor feigns disappointment. "All right then. Go for a swim and think it over."

I groan. I think about stumbling out into the surf again, and I think about doing that over and over and over... And then I think about what it would be like to just take that step in the other direction. End the nightmare. It would be so simple....

"Jimmy, don't!"

The shout snaps me back into the moment. I look around and see a young man from one of the other boat crews shambling forward. Until this moment, I didn't know his name—he's maggot, just like me, just like everyone else—but I know his face to the extent that I know any of them.

But in a minute or two, he'll be gone like he never even existed.

The same voice of protest sounds again. "Jimmy! Come on, buddy. We're in this together, remember? We promised each other we'd finish it together."

Jimmy's friend I do recognize. It's the young junior lieutenant, the one the Indian calls... What was it, again?

Pope.

Pope Maddock.

Jimmy just shakes his head. "I can't, Dane… Can't do it."

I see the hollow look on Jimmy's face as he turns away, and I know that, no matter what promises he made, he's done.

"I quit," Jimmy mumbles, and staggers toward the chief.

I quit.

The words strike against something in my core, like steel striking flint, and then I'm moving, heading down toward the surf again.

Because I won't quit, no matter what. And whenever I think about ringing the bell, I see his face, and it reminds me that I'm not him….

1

Annapolis, Maryland

Pete "Professor" Chapman blinked and let the memory slip away, bringing his attention fully into the present as James "Jimmy" Letson, walked right by him, showing not even a hint of recognition, and exited the hotel lobby. Professor, seated at a corner table in the continental breakfast dining room and pretending to read the morning edition of the Washington Post, watched him for a few seconds longer, before tucking the newspaper under one arm and rising to follow.

The face Professor remembered so well looked different now. Older, the cheeks fuller, rounder. Softened by too much junk food and booze, and not enough exercise. He supposed that was to be expected. They had all been young men back then, some not even old enough to drink legally.

That face—the face of the quitter—had been an anchor for him. A lifeline that had gotten him through what he thought would be the worst four days of his life.

The Navy called it BUD/S—Basic Underwater Demolition/SEAL training—phase one. Unofficially, it was just called Hell Week. It was the final exercise of the three-week introductory evolution of BUD/S in which candidates were subjected to a rigorous ordeal of physical exertion and sleep deprivation with just one goal: to identify those with the physical and mental toughness to become Navy SEALs. Four days in which candidates were put through the grinder—pushed to exhaustion, denied sleep, subjected to constant harassment. The attrition rate for the exercise was always high—typically in the neighborhood of eighty percent—and Professor's class had been no different.

There was no secret to surviving Hell Week. The purpose of the exercise was to strip away the ego completely, revealing whatever lay underneath. You either had that toughness or you didn't. Professor had found it that morning when he'd watched Jimmy Letson drop out. Over the course of the next three days, whenever he felt like he had nothing left to give, he would mutter, like a mantra, "I'm not Jimmy."

After it was over, after he survived and advanced to the next phase of SEAL training, he had let all memory of that face slip away, and would have forgotten Jimmy completely if not for the fact that his platoon leader, Lt. Dane Maddock, had remained friends with Jimmy Letson.

Now, seeing that face again after nearly twenty-five years, Professor felt the old emotions rising unbidden.

Jimmy, the quitter.

He was surprised and a little dismayed at the vehemence he felt. Lots of guys washed out. For every sailor who earned his Budweiser—the distinctive eagle-trident-pistol badge of the SEALs—there were four or more hopefuls who rang the bell during Hell Week. They weren't inherently weak or flawed. Every single one of them was still among that brave minority who had taken an oath to defend America. It was profoundly unfair to call any of them quitters, and in truth, Professor never had.

Except for Jimmy.

Twenty-two hours earlier, when Tam Broderick gave him this assignment, the only context in which he thought of Jimmy was as Dane's friend. The reporter. The researcher. The hacker.

After washing out of BUDS, Letson had taken an assignment with Navy public affairs, finishing his term of service as a Navy journalist, after which he had gone back to school to become a journalist, and had gone on to have a very successful career as an investigative reporter, thanks in no small part to his online prowess. A true child of the digital age, Jimmy Letson had been a computer hacker before there was even a word for it. A lifelong tech geek, he built his own hardware and wrote his own code. As far as Professor knew, Jimmy wasn't a Black Hat, using his skills to defraud or sow the seeds of anarchy. Instead, he was a sort of cyber-muckraker and champion of the fifth estate, while sometimes moonlighting as a researcher for Dane Maddock, who was now a private citizen and a professional treasure hunter.

It was this latter association that had brought him once more into Professor's orbit. Maddock and his crew had occasionally done some freelance work of their own for Tam Broderick as part of her task force dedicated to battling the quasi-religious far-right criminal conspiracy known as "the Dominion." Jimmy Letson had not been a part of that arrangement—indeed, while they were aware of each other, to the best of Professor's knowledge, Tam and Jimmy had never met, but nonetheless shared a deep mutual distrust.

Evidently, Tam's distrust extended to maintaining surreptitious electronic surveillance on Jimmy, which was how she came to notice that something was very much amiss in Letson's world. Without any warning, Jimmy Letson had vanished, disappearing both from his physical life and from his considerable online presence.

The disappearance was alarming enough to prompt Tam to pull Professor off his current long-term assignment, as bodyguard for archaeologist Jade Ihara, who just happened to be a former paramour of Dane Maddock. Professor had left her in Cuzco, Peru, where she was running down some kind of mystery related to an old occult manuscript, and embarked on the fourteen-hour flight to Washington D.C. where it had taken him all of four hours to locate Jimmy Letson, who was currently using the alias Ryan Duarte, and staying in a hotel in Annapolis, Maryland.

Letson went straight to his rental car—a red Hyundai Sonata—in the parking lot. Professor loitered near the hotel entrance waiting until Jimmy had pulled out onto the street, before hurrying to his own rental—a silver Toyota Prius—to take up the pursuit. He didn't need to worry about losing Jimmy in traffic; he'd tagged the Sonata with an RFID tracking chip.

Professor had tracked Jimmy down without much difficulty, which frankly surprised him. Given the man's reputation as a hacker-extraordinaire, he had expected Jimmy to do a much better job covering his tracks. It was enough to make Professor wonder if he wasn't being played. Maybe Jimmy was on a fishing expedition, trying to lure him or someone like him into the open.

But the reporter-cum-hacker was exhibiting none of the tells of a seasoned professional; no casual glances to check for surveillance as he left the hotel, no sudden turns on the road to check for a tail. Jimmy drove like any other commuter, moving along with the flow of traffic for a couple miles before turning onto Maryland Route 178—Generals Highway—heading west. He continued on for several miles before merging onto the I-97, still heading west, but instead of following the Interstate north toward Baltimore, or turning south toward D.C. he kept going west.

Tam's assumption was that Jimmy had stirred up some kind of hornet's nest and gone into hiding. Professor wasn't so sure. His sense was that Jimmy was neither running nor hiding, but chasing something. Or more likely someone. A government whistleblower, perhaps, someone living in the sprawling suburban hinterland surrounding the nation's capital.

Perplexed, and more than a little alarmed, Professor sped up, closing with his quarry until only a couple cars separated them. As Jimmy continued down the freeway skirting the southern edge of Fort George Meade, Professor became even more certain, not only of his read on Jimmy's general intention but also the reporter's current destination. He wasn't at all surprised when the Sonata turned off at the Canine Road exit, just south of Annapolis Junction, and drove into the visitor's parking lot at the entrance to the sprawling campus of the National Security Agency.

"What are you up to, Letson?" Professor muttered.

2

The man calling himself Ryan Duarte presented a government-issued CAC—Common Access Card—to the guard at the visitor control center, and waited patiently for the computerized card reader to confirm that he was authorized to continue beyond the checkpoint. That authorization was given only to government employees and private contractors who had passed an extensive background check, including at least one polygraph screening, and subsequently received additional training in the handling of materials with the designation SCI—Sensitive Compartmentalized Information. According to the information contained in the chip of the "smart" card, Ryan Duarte, a computer information specialist employed by Booz Allen Hamilton, had completed the requisite vetting process and was so authorized.

After about a minute, the card reader beeped and the guard removed the card and handed it back, along with a holographic facility-specific visitor's identification badge.

"Make sure this is visible at all times," the guard said.

Jimmy Letson thanked the guard and clipped the badge to his shirt front, before heading through to the waiting area for the on-campus shuttle. He waited until he was out of the guard's line of sight to let out the breath he had been holding.

"One down," he muttered. "Ninety-nine to go."

It was a joke, of course. While there were in fact well over a hundred security checkpoints on the campus, he would only have to go through about a dozen or so. He would be searched and questioned, required to leave all his possessions in a secure locker, and then searched and questioned some more.

The card, along with the Ryan Duarte persona, was something he had created years before with the help of a confidential source inside the NSA. He had used it from time to time in his investigations to discreetly confirm claims from other sources, but always remotely, spoofing the login with his own computer equipment. With his computer compromised, that was no longer an option, which meant it was time for his alter-ego to make his debut public appearance.

He wasn't worried about giving himself away. As a reporter, he'd bluffed his way into places with even tighter security. His real concern was that the Duarte alias might also be compromised. If that was the case, they wouldn't arrest him at the front gate; no, they'd wait until he did something really illegal.

Like using his bogus credentials to log into a computer terminal to access and delete server logs.

He still had no idea what was going on or who was stalking him. All he knew for certain was that, a few days earlier while conducting some seemingly innocuous research for his friend Dane Maddock someone had initiated a back-trace on him, systematically preventing him from erasing the logs of the proxy servers he routinely employed to mask his IP address. What was really unusual, not to mention alarming, was the speed with which the back-trace had been executed. There were few agencies in the world with the resources to do that. The NSA was definitely one of them.

Yet, he didn't think the American government was

behind this action. For one thing, the servers he used as proxies were all in foreign countries—countries which did not cooperate with American law enforcement in the investigation of cyber-crimes. For another, he had not actually done anything illegal. And to the best of his knowledge, there was nothing sensitive about the research subject.

Maddock and his crew had discovered an old plane wreck off the coast of South Africa. The discovery of the plane—a Boeing 314 Clippership, manufactured in the 1930s—was unusual because only twelve such aircraft had ever been produced, and all twelve were accounted for. Jimmy had poked around in some historical archives and found nothing. Maddock had also recovered an artifact, a steel hatchet head engraved with a name and a presentation date—Steven Thorne. April 28, 1758—and apparently infused with some kind of metal that resisted corrosion. His research into that had similarly ended with no results. That should have been the end of the matter, but when he went to erase his digital footprints from the server logs, he discovered that he had already been frozen out.

Jimmy had gone to great lengths to safeguard himself, but there was no way to know for sure if those measures had worked. Panicking, he had severed the connection, shut his network down, and walked away.

Yet, he knew that running was no solution. It was not an exaggeration to say that computers were his life. He had spent more than two decades building his virtual existence, networking, mapping systems, finding backdoors and shortcuts. His pride and joy, NAILS—a heuristic deep-web search engine for prowling the deepest reaches of the dark net—represented an investment of thousands of hours and was, as far as he was concerned, completely irreplaceable. Starting over with a new identity simply wasn't an option. Which left him only one course of action: He had to get his life back.

At a minimum, that would involve erasing the evidence of his search for the plane crash and the hatchet. From the NSA, he would be able to override whatever security measures had been used to block his access to the server logs. With a little luck, he might also be able to identify the entity responsible for that action, which would be of paramount importance in determining his next course of action.

Once he was inside, he went to one of the workstations designated for use by visiting personnel, and began the login process. As nerve-wracking as the multiple redundant security checks had been, logging into the workstation was even worse. What if the NSA was the agency that had blocked him? What if they knew about the Duarte alias, and were waiting for him to commit himself? What if—

The seal of the National Security Agency—a bald eagle, standing behind a shield with the color-scheme of an American flag, gripping an old-fashioned skeleton key in its talons—appeared on the screen, along with a simple welcome message.

Jimmy blew out his breath, and immediately began navigating to the first of several IP addresses he had earlier used as proxies to spoof his location. He was pleased to see that the system administrator login information had not changed, which would have been the first thing a real sysadmin would do following an intrusion, but his relief was short-lived. When he brought up the logs for the relevant time period, he found that the information had already been deleted. He checked another IP address in the proxy chain with the same result. Someone had beaten him to the punch.

He dug deeper into the maintenance logs, trying to find the identity of the person or agency who had made those alterations, but that information also appeared to have been scrubbed clean.

A cold lump of disappointment began to form in Jimmy's gut. He checked the next proxy server in the chain, then another and yet another, but with the same result each time.

He checked the session timer. Almost ten minutes had elapsed since his login. In the age of high-speed data transfer, that was an eternity. Had the entity responsible for scrubbing the logs noticed him sniffing around? If so, it was already too late to do anything about it, but he felt an almost overwhelming urge to get moving. The longer he stayed, the greater his chances of being found out.

But as he was about to log out, inspiration struck. He went back to the logs, and one by one, examined each one, but this time, he opened the figurative window a little wider. He scrolled down the list of IP addresses for other users who had accessed the server within half an hour either way of his original search, and then did the same with each of the other servers looking for repeats.

It was a longshot, he knew, since any hacker worth his or her salt would almost certainly have spoofed a different IP address for each intrusion, but sometimes even the best made stupid little mistakes. Like re-using a spoofed server.

There it was.

The same IP address appeared on two different

server logs.

It might have been a coincidence, but Jimmy felt certain it was not.

A trail of multiple proxies eventually led him to the SvalSat data hub in Norway and no further. Jimmy's gut told him it probably wasn't the original location of the hacker, but it was the end of the proxy chain.

And the end of what he could accomplish here.

He memorized the information and then, after doing what he could to cover his own tracks, logged off.

For a while after that, he just sat there, staring at the blank monitor, wondering what to do next. He was reasonably certain that no US government agency was responsible; they would not have erased the evidence of his intrusion….

Unless….

It occurred to him that he might have misread the situation completely. He had been working under the assumption that the entity in question was trying to track him down, either to arrest him or make him disappear, but what if they were simply trying to cover something up?

Instead of trying to figure out who's responsible, he thought, *I should be trying to figure out what's so important about that old plane wreck.*

But was it safe for him to go back home, return to his life—his computer—and carry on as if nothing had happened?

He pondered this a few seconds longer, and then realized that was the wrong question, too. Maybe it wasn't safe, but he was done running. He had skills, after all.

He took a deep breath, found his center and stood

up from the workstation. Some part of him still half-expected a squad of agents to materialize and surround him, but nobody in the building seemed to pay him any special attention. The guards searched him perfunctorily to make sure he wasn't trying to leave with any classified data, and then returned his checked belongings to him and bade him good day. His fellow passengers on the shuttle back to the visitors' welcome center didn't even look his way, and when he handed back his temporary ID badge, the guard actually smiled at him.

As he started the rental car and pulled out of his parking spot, Jimmy shifted his mental gears to his next task. With the illicit foray into the nation's premier intelligence gathering service behind him, he would now return to where it had all started—the mysterious plane wreck. Maybe there wasn't a digital record, but there had to be a paper trail.

He steered out of the parking lot and onto Canine Road, following the signs to the onramp for the southbound lanes of the freeway.

He wondered if Maddock had discovered anything more about it, and made a mental note to contact the treasure hunter as soon—

The car abruptly jolted forward, and Jimmy's head snapped back a little, though not enough to cause any pain. The accompanying noise—like a car door slamming—left little doubt as to what had just occurred.

"What the hell?" he snarled, more irritated than angry. He glanced in the rearview mirror and saw the silver car that had just bumped him, still tailgating but backing away slowly.

A faint tingle of fear went through him. What if this was more than just a simple bumper-thumper? What if this was the enemy action he had been expecting all along?

The silver car's emergency flashers came on and then the vehicle pulled over into the breakdown lane and kept rolling forward slowly, subtly indicating that he should do the same. Jimmy slowed but did not pull over.

If this was just an ordinary traffic accident, he would need to stop, need to get the other driver's insurance information. He doubted there was any damage, but didn't want to be on the hook with the rental company for even minor repairs.

He looked around. There wasn't a lot of traffic on the road, but enough that if this was more than it seemed to be, he could start waving his arms frantically for help, or simply take off running. The NSA headquarters building was only about two hundred feet away, and he wouldn't have to even reach the building to get the attention of the security guards.

Unless of course they're the ones behind this, he thought. *But then why let me leave the building?* "You're just being paranoid, Jimmy," he muttered to himself.

He flipped on his turn signal and pulled to the side, but left the engine on, the automatic transmission still in gear, his foot on the brake. If this went sideways, or if he just got a funny feeling, all he would have to do is stomp on the gas pedal.

The silver car stopped a couple lengths behind him and the driver—a tall lanky man, dressed in jeans with a button-up work shirt and wearing a brown Indiana Jones-style fedora—got out and began advancing toward Jimmy's door. The brim of the hat mostly hid the man's face; other than his race—Caucasian—Jimmy couldn't determine much else about the man. He surreptitiously checked to make sure his door was locked and then cracked the window a few inches.

The man tipped his hat back, exposing a face that, while smiling, appeared taciturn. He looked to be about the same age as Jimmy, and there was something vaguely familiar about him, but Jimmy couldn't put his finger on it.

The man placed one hand on the roof of the car and leaned down, putting his face close to the gap in the window, and as he did, the smile slipped completely away. "Hello, Letson. Been a while, huh?"

3

Professor felt the car start to move. He'd thought he detected a hint of recognition when he'd approached, but now Jimmy was freaking out.

"Letson, it's me. Pete Chapman. We did Phase One together. I was in the teams. I served with Dane and Bones."

The car lurched as Jimmy stomped down on the brake again. "Professor?"

The nasally voice was like nails on a chalkboard, transporting Professor back in time.

Can't do it. I quit.

Professor managed a nod. "That's me."

Jimmy's face registered a range of expressions. Surprise, dismay… Embarrassment? Professor could almost see the gears turning behind the other man's eyes, and imagined him being sucked into the same remembrance of their brief acquaintance.

But he wasn't interested in taking Jimmy for a walk down memory lane. "Let's exchange our info, just like this was a real accident."

"It felt pretty real to me," Jimmy remarked sourly, then he cocked his head to the side. "Wait a sec. You hit me on purpose. What's going on? What do you want?" A pause, and then, "Who are you working for?"

Professor ignored the question. "Letson, you need to tell me what you were doing in there. Whatever it is, whatever laws you've broken, I can't help you if you don't tell me the truth."

"What makes you think I want your help?" Jimmy

shot back.

Professor sighed.

"You're working for Tam Broderick's outfit, aren't you?" Jimmy pressed. "Yeah, I know all about that. Dane told me some of it, and I figured out the rest."

"That's great, Letson. So, you know I'm one of the good guys. My question is, are you?"

"Oh, so working for the government automatically equals good guys. I'll have to remember that."

"Knock it off, Letson," Professor snapped. "You just walked out of a Secure Compartmented Information Facility, and we both know that you don't have a security clearance, which tells me that, at the very least, you presented falsified credentials. That's a crime. Fortunately for you, I'm not a cop or I'd have to arrest you right now. But you've got about thirty seconds to convince me that *you* are one of the good guys, before I *do* call the cops, so don't waste it… Twenty-nine… Twenty-eight…"

Jimmy glowered for about three more seconds, then looked down just long enough to move the gearshift lever into park, and roll the window the rest of the way down. That gave him about twenty seconds, but Professor figured the point was made, so he stopped counting. As Jimmy launched into an explanation of the events that had prompted him to go off the grid, Professor raised a hand to stop him.

"Give me the Cliff's Notes version." What he really wanted was to confirm that Jimmy wasn't knowingly or unknowingly carrying out state-sponsored espionage.

"Maddock asked me to research an old plane wreck," Jimmy said. "When I tried, somebody came after me. I have no idea who or why, but they're good."

Professor blew out his cheeks. He wanted more details, but there was a time and place and this wasn't either. "All right, Dane trusts you. So does Tam in a weird grudging sort of way—"

Jimmy snorted with derisive laughter. "I'll have to add that to my CV."

"We can finish this conversation somewhere else," Professor went on. "But before we move an inch, I need your word that you aren't trying to remove classified materials from this site. We don't need the NSA coming after us."

"Trust me," Jimmy replied. "I know better than to…"

He trailed off as a car—a silver Ford Taurus—rushed past in the outside lane. Most of the vehicles that had gone by during their brief encounter had observed the courtesy of changing lanes to give them a wide berth, but the Ford passed close enough that Professor had to lean in to avoid being struck. As soon as the vehicle cleared the front end of Jimmy's rental, the driver cut to the right and slammed on the brakes, screeching to a stop diagonally in front of Jimmy's car.

"Crap!" Professor snarled. From the corner of his eye, he saw another car—same make but white—swerve off the road behind them, pulling in close behind his rental, blocking them in. There were two men in the car to the front, and probably at least as many in the car behind. He didn't need to know anything more than that to know that he and Jimmy were in serious trouble.

He reached for the door handle, already mentally choreographing how he would shove Jimmy into the passenger seat, take his place behind the wheel, bump his way out of the trap—

The door handle didn't move.

He pounded his fist on the roof. "Letson, open the—"

The doors of the blocking vehicles were thrown open in unison, the occupants emerging. The men seemed to have been turned out of the same mold—big, muscular frames covered in loose-fitting jackets; short, utilitarian haircuts. They were heavies. Mercs. Hired guns. Probably former military though probably not SEALs or Special Forces—operators knew the importance of blending in. These men weren't displaying weapons, but their strong-side hands were conspicuously under their jacket flaps, clearly signaling both possession and intent.

There was no time to explain himself to Jimmy, so instead Professor reached in through the open window, stabbing his finger down on the electronic lock button. All four doors unlocked with a mechanical click, but instead of opening the driver's door, Professor side-stepped to the rear-left passenger door, opened it, and climbed in.

"Punch it!"

Jimmy craned his head around, staring at Professor in disbelief. "What—?"

Outside, the four men were just moments away from reaching the car, at which point, if he and Jimmy were lucky, they would only be ordered out at gunpoint.

"Go! Drive!"

"We're blocked in."

"So?"

Jimmy's head snapped around to face front and without further questions, he put the still-idling car in gear. There was a grinding sound as he cranked the wheel, and then the car lurched into motion. The front end of the rented Hyundai swung to the left, forcing one of the heavies to dance out of the way, and then came to a jarring stop as it crunched into the rear end of the blocking vehicle.

Jimmy shifted into reverse, cranked the wheel the opposite way, and stomped the gas again. With a jolt, the Hyundai shot backward, its rear tires rolling off the pavement, bumping onto the soft gravel beyond. Just as quickly, Jimmy switched directions and the red sedan jumped back up onto the pavement and shot past the car and onto the roadway.

Professor kept watch on the four heavies and wasn't at all surprised to see them drawing their weapons.

"Head down!" he warned.

But the men did not fire, or if they did, the weapons were fitted with suppressors and none of the shots found their mark. Jimmy accelerated, drove under the overpass and into the turn that would bring them around in a rising circle to join the southbound freeway.

Professor risked a quick peek out the rear window and saw that the four men were returning to their vehicles, no doubt planning to give chase.

And probably calling in reinforcements, he thought. He brought his gaze forward just as the curve in the road eclipsed his view of the men.

"Any idea who those guys are?" he asked.

"I was going to ask you," Jimmy replied. "I don't think they were NSA."

Professor shook his head. "No. Definitely private sector."

Jimmy offered no comment, appearing instead to focus on the approach to the freeway. He maintained acceleration, merging into the light traffic. Professor didn't need to look back to know that the other two cars would soon close with them. Getting on the freeway had probably been a bad move, though realistically, there weren't a whole lot of other places they could have gone.

He shifted forward, leaning into the gap between the front seats to get a better look at the road ahead. Jimmy was now moving with the flow of traffic—the speedometer showed them doing about seventy even though the posted speed limit was fifty-five miles per hour.

"Floor it," Professor advised. "We need to put some space between us and them. And we need to get onto surface streets, find somewhere to ditch this car."

"What if we get pulled over?"

"I doubt we will, but even if that happens, those guys won't try anything with a state trooper standing here."

Jimmy cocked his head to the side in a shrug of resignation and then pressed down on the accelerator, adding another five miles per hour to their speed, and as soon as he was clear, swung the car into the faster moving inside lane. A green sign over the left lane announced the next exit—Exit 9—NSA Employees Only.

"Crap again," Professor muttered. It would be at least another mile before they would get another opportunity to leave the freeway and hopefully ditch their pursuers, but going back to the National Security Agency headquarters wasn't an option. "Keep going. Take the next exit."

Jimmy nodded and continued weaving in and out of traffic, accelerating the whole time. The speedometer ticked up to eighty. Eighty-five. Yet Jimmy seemed cool as a cucumber.

"Pretty fancy driving there, Letson," Professor

admitted, grudgingly.

"It's just Jimmy. And thanks. I play a lot of GTA."

"GTA?"

"Grand Theft Auto. PlayStation. You know, video games?"

"Ah," Professor said, now a little less impressed. "Well maybe dial it down a little. There's no reset button for this game."

"Reset button." Jimmy snorted, wagging his head. "Okay, Dad, whatever you say."

"Dad? We're the same age."

"Could've fooled me."

"This isn't a game, Letson. Whatever you were running from just caught up with you. And I just happen to have a bit more experience dealing with the real world life and death stuff."

"Is that a fact? You know, I was doing just fine before you decided to rear-end me, so maybe you're not the best person to be giving me advice about the real world."

Professor shuffled through his deck of scathing retorts but decided he had better things to do. "Take the next exit, whatever it is."

"Exit eight," Jimmy said, answering the unasked question. "Fort Mead and Laurel."

"You know the area?"

"Pretty well. There's an airport just off the exit."

"Airport?" Professor sat up a little straighter.

"A small one. Three-thousand-foot runway. Mostly services single-engine planes. A few helicopters."

The seed of a plan began to take root in Professor's mind. "Perfect. Go there."

"Awesome," Jimmy said, with more than a hint of

sarcasm. "Are we going to charter a plane, or just steal one?"

"I don't know. Did Grand Theft Auto teach you how to fly, too?"

"Actually, yeah. Though I prefer Flight Simulator. More realistic."

Professor shook his head wearily. "Just get us to the airport. I'll take care of the rest."

A few seconds later, another sign heralded Tipton Airport, and Professor spotted the exit lane veering off to the right. Jimmy waited until the last second to cut across both lanes and steered onto the upward sloping ramp, slowing a little as he neared the crest and entered the traffic circle at the top. As he did, Professor looked back again and saw several cars coming up the ramp behind them; he recognized two of them—the silver and white Ford sedans that had tried to block them earlier.

"Damn it," he muttered. His plan had been to ditch the car at the airport and then hoof it into the woods, hoping the men chasing them would assume they had boarded a plane, but to make it convincing, they would need a little more lead time. "Okay, forget the airport for now. Blow past and just try to lose these guys."

Jimmy feathered the brakes as he went into the soft right at the traffic circle, curling back around, but halfway through the turn, he began accelerating again. The tires squealed a little as G-forces pulled them to the left, but Jimmy deftly steered out of the slide and maintained pressure on the gas pedal as they shot down the country road.

The turn-off to the airport flashed by, and then the road narrowed to an ordinary two-lane country road. Off to the right, on the far side of a wetland, Professor could see the freeway running parallel to their current course, but then the road curved to the left leaving both the marsh and the freeway behind.

Though he was loath to admit it, Professor thought Jimmy was handling the situation pretty well. Maybe video games were good for something more than just mindless entertainment. But as capable as he seemed, Jimmy's virtual driving practice was no match for the kind of tactical driving instruction Professor had received in the SEALs, and judging by the quickness with which they were closing the gap, the men in the chase cars had taken the same course.

The silver car rocketed down the straightaway and was just a hundred yards—and maybe five seconds—behind them as they entered the turn. Professor could make out the hard visages of the two heavies in the front seats. They weren't showing guns which meant they were probably going to try to force the Hyundai off the road.

Probably.

"Letson—"

"Jimmy!"

"Fine, Jimmy. Do exactly as I tell you, when I tell you. No questions. Got it?"

He expected questions, but Jimmy just said, "Yeah."

Behind them, the lead car abruptly swung into the left lane and shot forward again—the driver had to be pushing over the century mark—and blew past them like they were standing still. Professor tracked them for a second, then glanced back and saw the second Ford closing from the rear.

"They're trying to box us in," he said.

Right on cue, the silver Ford pulled back into the right lane a hundred yards or more ahead of them, brake lights flaring red as the driver started shedding speed. Jimmy reflexively tapped his brakes, too, even though the other car was still several lengths ahead.

"No," Professor shouted. "Floor it."

"But—" Jimmy started to say, but then cut himself off and did as instructed, depressing the accelerator. The Hyundai shot forward, rapidly closing with the lead car, which was still slowing. The driver of the silver Ford, still following the playbook, turned diagonally, cutting the road and coming to a full stop right on top of the center line, blocking both lanes.

"Go left," Professor urged. "Pass him on the shoulder."

"Left? But what if—" Jimmy caught himself again, and after waiting a beat, cranked the wheel over, aiming for the shoulder on the far side of the road.

Professor knew why Jimmy had almost balked. The Taurus was blocking their view of the oncoming lane, and if anyone was trying to pass the Ford on the shoulder, the Hyundai would hit them head-on. But it was the last thing the men in the Ford would expect them to do, and therefore was exactly what had to be done. Hopefully, the shoulder would be clear.

It wasn't.

A pickup, still partially shrouded behind a cloud of rubber smoke after slamming on its brakes to avoid hitting the Ford, was just beginning to pull onto the shoulder in order to pass. Jimmy, to his credit, did not put on the brakes, but pushed the throttle harder, whipping the Hyundai hard to the right, threading the gap between the front end of the pickup and the silver car.

He almost made it.

The right front corner of the Taurus caught the Hyundai's right side with an ugly crunching sound. The impact pushed the Ford sideways, which caused the left corner to swing into the Hyundai's flanks but then with a torturous squeal, Jimmy's car broke free and rocketed ahead as he stomped the gas pedal to the floor.

"Yeah," he chortled. "That's what I'm talking about."

"Better than video games, right?" Professor said, unable to hide a grin.

"Yeah. Except I'll be on the hook for the damage."

"Should have signed the waiver," Professor replied, still grinning. He checked behind them and saw the Ford just starting to move again, then returned his gaze to the road ahead. They were approaching some commercial buildings. A gas station and a general store on the right, a restaurant or tavern on the left. He almost told Jimmy to pull off and park the car, lie low and hope their pursuers would pass them by, but the trailing cars were still within easy visual range, and the parking lots were small and sparsely occupied.

He looked further down the road to where the trees returned and spotted a sign and a turn lane that seemed to plunge straight into the woods. "Think you can make that right turn up there?"

Jimmy leaned forward a little as if to get a better look. "You mean without slowing down? I can try."

"Do it."

The Hyundai surged a little as Jimmy revved the gas, but then he eased up, letting the car coast the rest of the way to the exit. "Hang on!" he shouted, though the warning wasn't necessary, and then hauled the wheel sharply to the right. The tires screeched on the pavement. Professor could feel the right side of the vehicle growing lighter, trying to take off—or flip over—but gravity won out. The car skidded into the turn and Jimmy accelerated again, and just like that they were shooting down the narrow tree-lined lane. The road curved a little to the left, then continued straight for a couple hundred yards before turning left again.

Perfect, Professor thought, and then added aloud, "Get around that bend as soon as you can, then find a place to pull off. Left side would be best, but just get us into the woods."

He kept watch out the rear window while Jimmy raced the Hyundai to the turn. The road behind them remained empty, at least until the turn blocked his view of it. He craned his head forward again, scanning the road ahead until he saw what he was looking for. "There," he shouted, stabbing a finger over Jimmy's shoulder. "Hard left."

Jimmy cranked the wheel and the Hyundai squealed across the road and into a paved turnout—a parking area for the welcome center on the opposite side of the road.

"Turn it around," Professor said. "And back into the woods. Hurry."

Jimmy complied without comment, executing a surprisingly close approximation of a bootlegger's turn—surprising since the rental had an automatic transmission, front-wheel drive and anti-lock brakes. The Hyundai whipped around one-hundred-and-eighty degrees to face the road. There was a slight jolt as the rear wheels skidded off the edge of the pavement and onto the soft grassy earth beyond, and then another as Jimmy powered forward, bringing the car up close to the woods at the edge of the parking area.

"Head down," Professor instructed. "But be ready to

take off."

"I got it," Jimmy said, a little irritably. "We're going to fake them out and then head back the other way. I'm not as stupid as you seem to think."

Professor frowned but let the comment pass. He hunched over, staying low behind Jimmy's seat, watching the road.

The wait was interminable. "Think we lost them?" Jimmy asked.

"Not yet." It felt like they had been waiting for several minutes, but Professor had been watching the sweep second hand of his Omega wristwatch and knew that just thirty seconds had passed.

Fifteen more seconds ticked by and then without any warning whatsoever, the silver Taurus burst from behind the trees, racing past. The white Ford was only a few car lengths behind. Neither one slowed, the drivers evidently hyper-focused on the road and catching up to their elusive prey.

"Wait for it," Professor warned.

The two vehicles continued down the road, passing out of view.

"Now. Get us back to the road."

Jimmy had the car moving before the command was finished. He steered back onto the road and accelerated away. Professor kept a constant vigil to their rear, watching for any sign that the pursuers had grown wise to the deception. It occurred to him that they, like himself, might have tagged Jimmy's car, but that seemed unlikely. If the heavies had been tracking Jimmy all along, they wouldn't have made their move when and where they had, nor would they have waited until he was done at the NSA. The more plausible explanation was that they had come in response to something Jimmy had done—another silent alarm triggered by his investigation.

Jimmy had definitely kicked a hornet's nest.

The road behind them stayed clear all the way to the bend leading back to the road, and for the first time since the chase began, Professor allowed himself a small sigh of relief.

"Where to?" Jimmy asked as they rounded the last bend, slowing to pull back onto the main road. "Should I go back to the airport?"

"Let's head back to the freeway," Professor turned around. "I'll take you to a safe house—Look out!"

It came from out of nowhere, an ominous black shape—an SUV or pickup—rushing at them from their right. There was no time to react, barely time to brace for the collision.

Not that it did any good.

4

Professor awoke with a start, and for a few sublime seconds, felt nothing more than mild confusion at the unfamiliarity of his surroundings.

Then the pain arrived like a cartoon anvil dropping from the sky on his head.

The total-body muscle pain triggered a memory—the black truck coming from out of nowhere to T-bone Jimmy's rental car.

"Jimmy!" he said, almost shouting.

To his utter astonishment, he heard the other man's voice. "Hey, he's awake!"

Professor sat up, gritting his teeth against the pain. He felt woozy, and for a moment wondered if he had sustained a concussion, but dismissed that explanation; this felt more like a narcotic fog.

Another memory percolated up. He was back in the car, covered in broken glass and partially pinned by a collapsed segment of the frame… A man in a blue uniform—a paramedic?—leaning over him, urging him to remain calm, promising that they would have him out in a few seconds… And then the man had reached in with a hypodermic syringe, a drop of fluid glistening at the needle's tip.

This will help calm you down.

He looked around, his brain finally processing the visual stimuli. He wasn't in a hospital, nor was he in anything that resembled a prison cell. Rather, he appeared to be in a library, or perhaps a private museum. Three walls of the elegantly appointed room were lined with floor to ceiling bookshelves, but only about half of the shelves sported leather and cloth bound books. The rest held an eclectic display of artifacts—souvenirs from cultures around the globe and across history, along with several pieces of nautical memorabilia. It was the kind of place, Professor thought, where Dane Maddock would feel right at home.

The hardwood floor was covered by a beautiful Persian carpet. The remaining wall was mostly windows and a set of French doors with glass panels that looked out over a somber landscape of trees denuded with the onset of winter.

"Toto, I've a feeling we're not in Maryland anymore," he muttered, struggling to sit up.

"You got that right," Jimmy said, stepping into view.

Professor blinked to bring the other man into focus. Jimmy had changed clothes. There was an abrasion on his left cheek, but he appeared otherwise uninjured. He definitely didn't look like a prisoner or a hostage.

"Where are we?"

"New York," intoned another voice—masculine and booming, but friendly enough. "Long Island to be precise. Welcome to my home... Professor is it?"

Long Island? That meant he'd been unconscious for several hours.

Professor turned slowly, not trusting that his equilibrium was fully restored, and located Jimmy and the other man. The latter—their host—was about the same height as Jimmy, but considerably older, early seventies, Professor guessed, with tousled hair that was more salt than pepper and a full beard that was all white. His skin was deeply tanned, his high forehead creased with a map of wrinkles, but his blue eyes were clear and twinkled like sapphires. He was smiling, and his body language showed no hint of aggression, nor did Jimmy seem the least bit on his guard in the man's presence, but Professor remained wary.

"My friends call me that," he said.

The man laughed. "Fair enough, Dr. Chapman. My name is Christian Garral. You may call me Christian. As you like."

"Garral? You're Nick Kismet's father." Professor immediately regretted blurting the revelation.

The man's bushy white eyebrows arched in surprise. "You know my son?"

He had recognized the name from his earlier reading of the files of the man who had helped Jade and he out of a sticky situation in Peru. Nick Kismet worked for the Global Heritage Commission—a United Nations agency tasked with monitoring World Heritage sites and protecting international antiquities. Kismet had actually been in South America looking for them, or rather for Jade, on personal business. He was seeking information about a manuscript that had belonged to famed British occultist Dr. John Dee, and thought Jade, who had dealt with a notorious collector of Dee memorabilia a couple years earlier, might have some special insight on the matter. Kismet's arrival had been both serendipitous and suspicious, but a cursory check of his bona fides had impressed Tam Broderick enough to recommend that Jade stay with Kismet and help him out while Professor looked into the matter of Jimmy's disappearance.

But now the trail had circled back to a connection with Nick Kismet. Professor didn't believe in coincidences, and this was a hell of a big one.

And he had just tipped his hand.

Nothing to do about it now, he thought. *Might as well call.*

"Evidently, not very well," he replied. "I bumped into him in South America a couple days ago. He was looking for information and thought my partner Jade Ihara could help him."

Garral nodded. "Ah, yes. The *Liber Arcanum.* My boy does get around."

Professor searched the craggy face for any sign of duplicity, but saw none at all. Garral clapped his hands together. "I'm sorry, you must be full of questions about what has happened. But first, how are you feeling? Do you require additional medical attention?"

"I was drugged," Professor accused. "Was that your doing?"

"It was. My men didn't know who you were or what your intentions were, respecting Mr. Letson here." He paused and then corrected. "Jimmy, rather."

It was a small detail, but telling. Jimmy's insistence on the use of the familiar indicated that he had been won over by their host.

"My intentions were to keep him out of trouble."

"Yes, he explained it to us. We didn't realize—"

"Who's we?" Professor snapped.

For the first time since entering the room, Garral appeared discomfited, but what Professor first took for irritation was soon revealed as something else altogether.

"Go on," Jimmy urged. "Tell him what you told me."

"This will sound a bit like the stuff of conspiracy theories, but Jimmy assures me you have some experience with such things." Garral took a deep breath, let it out with a sigh. "There is a very powerful, and very old, organization—a secret society, if you like—that is secretly manipulating the destiny of humankind."

"The Dominion."

Garral shook his head. "No. At least, I don't believe they are one and the same, though in the shadowy world where these groups operate, it is difficult to say. They call themselves Prometheus, named for the Titan of Greek mythology."

Professor nodded. "Prometheus was especially fond of humans. He stole fire from the gods and gave it to men. And he put hope in Pandora's box."

"You are correct. Prometheus is often associated with the gift of foresight. A thoughtful figure who anticipates trouble and takes pre-emptive action, unlike his brother Epimetheus."

"Prometheus is also the name of a high IQ society which restricts membership to those who score in the ninety-ninth percentile. I don't suppose that's who you're talking about."

Garral chuckled. "That group takes its name and inspiration from the group of which I speak, but to the best of my knowledge, there is no direct relationship. The real Prometheus organization has roots that go much deeper. It has existed in many forms, going back perhaps as far as the Athenians in the Greek classical period, but its current incarnation began during the Enlightenment. As men began expanding their knowledge of the cosmos…" He paused a beat. "Pardon me. That is a Western conceit. I should say, as Europeans began broadening their horizons, moving forward toward the Renaissance, there were some who believed that humans were on the verge of opening up another sort of Pandora's box. A trap, left behind, perhaps unintentionally, by an ancient forgotten race of beings."

Professor ignored the obvious question, focusing instead on something else. "What do you mean by 'unintentionally'?"

"Imagine that this knowledge is a box of matches, left on a shelf. Fire is what sets us apart from other animals. It is what made civilization possible, and yet in the hands of a child, it can be very dangerous. The knowledge and power of this ancient race is beyond even our current comprehension of the universe. We are children, and this is a kind of fire we're not ready for." He paused. "That's what Prometheus believes, at any rate.

"The knowledge is hidden—encoded, if you will—in the lore and traditions of all the world's religions. Tales of gods and fallen angels who walked among humans, even interbred with them. Stories of powerful devices—technology mistaken for magic. I'm sure you're familiar with many of the myths. The men of Prometheus have, for many centuries, dedicated themselves to finding these devices and hiding them away so that humanity will not be tempted toward self-annihilation. Prometheus invites only the best and brightest into its ranks. Intelligence and vision are essential, but candidates must also exhibit the wisdom and forethought of Prometheus himself. The location of their vault is a secret known only to the innermost circle."

Professor raised a hand. "You keep saying *they*. '*They* call themselves "Prometheus."' You're not part of it?"

Garral looked chagrined. "Not exactly, but that's a long story and a detour which will take me even further from answering your original question.

"The short explanation is that there is currently a

power struggle for control of Prometheus. One faction—the radicals, for want of a better name—believes it is their destiny to use the knowledge and power which they have accumulated to take control of humanity's destiny. The other side favors the original mission. They are the traditionalists. Whichever side prevails will have control of their vast trove of knowledge and ancient technology." He hesitated, scrutinizing Professor for a moment, then went on. "My son—my adopted son—is very important to Prometheus. Particularly to the traditionalists. I'm not at liberty to go into detail about that, but suffice it to say, I was brought into their confidence."

"Okay," Professor said, nodding. He wasn't sure he believed the story about Prometheus, but he was satisfied that Garral believed it. "Let me see if I've got this right. Prometheus is in the business of tracking down and hiding artifacts purported to have supernatural power."

"Like Warehouse 13," Jimmy put in.

Professor frowned, but only partly because of the interruption. He had no idea what that reference meant, which surprised him. Probably something from a video game. He pushed ahead. "And something about that old plane wreck that Dane Maddock discovered was a loose thread that might have led back to Prometheus and their treasure trove. When Jimmy went poking around looking into it, it tripped an alarm and Prometheus went after him."

"That's mostly accurate," Garral said. "That plane and its occupants discovered an important site in Antarctica. They weren't a part of Prometheus, but when the organization learned of it, they took steps to erase the incident from the public record."

"And they're still trying to cover it up today. That's

why they went after Jimmy."

"No," Garral said slowly. "It's a bit more complicated than that. You see, the radicals are weak. They're outsiders, and without direct access to the collection of artifacts, their only hope for victory is to find something new. Something that isn't in the collection yet."

"Like something from that site at Antarctica," Professor said.

Garral nodded. "There is something there—an ancient power source. Prometheus calls it 'the anomaly.' They've known of its existence for decades, but did not have its exact location, despite numerous expeditions to find it. So they placed trigger-alerts on search topics related to the original discovery."

"That old plane was at the top of the list," Jimmy added.

"And then waited for someone else to do the heavy lifting," Professor finished.

"The radicals desperately need to find the anomaly."

"And that's why they came after Jimmy?"

Garral shook his head. "No. I'm afraid nobody 'came after' him, at least nobody I'm aware of. The men you encountered were working for me, keeping an eye on Jimmy. My... Ah, contact inside Prometheus—one of the traditionalists—warned me that they might. When you accosted Jimmy outside the National Security Agency headquarters, they thought you might be working for the radicals, and intervened. I apologize for the misunderstanding."

"You could have made contact with Jimmy any time. Brought him up to speed. You didn't. You were dangling him out there as bait."

Garral spread his hands in an apologetic gesture. "A

mistake on my part," he admitted. "I realize that now. I should have brought Jimmy into my confidence. But you'll be safe here, provided you stay below the radar."

"What about Dane Maddock?" Professor asked. "The radicals might go after him as well."

"Way ahead of you, dude… er… Professor. I tried to call him first thing. Believe it or not, he's already looking for the anomaly doohickey. Although, I'm not sure he knows it. I talked to Willis."

Willis was Willis Sanders, another former SEAL swim buddy, currently crewing on Dane Maddock's boat, *Sea Foam.*

"Maddock and Bones headed for Antarctica a few hours ago. They're pretty much incommunicado down there."

"So there's no way to warn them." Professor glanced at Garral. "I don't suppose you've got the resources to get us down there."

Jimmy threw his hands up in protest. "Whoa, what's with this 'us' stuff? And in case you've forgotten, Antarctica is a big place. We don't even know where to start looking."

"Maddock had to have left a paper trail. You can track that down. And I can have Tam task a satellite in polar orbit to look for him."

Garral spread his hands helplessly. "Time is the resource in shortest supply. There aren't exactly direct flights into Antarctica. It would take several days just to get you to an airport with service to the continent. By then, it may be too late."

Professor pondered this for a moment. Garral was right. It had taken him nearly two days just to travel from Peru to Maryland.

He broke into a grin as an idea dawned. "There are flights from Argentina to Antarctica, right? If we had somebody already on the ground in South America, that would cut a couple days off our response time."

Garral nodded, thoughtfully. "You're referring to your friend Jade Ihara?"

"And your son."

"They may have already left."

Professor shrugged. "Can't hurt to ask."

Jimmy let out a low whistle. "You want to send Jade off to rescue Maddock. I can't imagine how that might go horribly wrong."

PART TWO: WISDOM OF THE AGES

5

Kemerhisar, Turkey—one week later

"I knew this would go horribly wrong," Uriah "Bones" Bonebrake muttered, shaking his head in disgust.

"Silence," hissed the young blond-haired man who held a pistol pressed to the side of Jade Ihara's neck.

"What do you want, Black?" Dane Maddock asked.

"You know what I want," sneered Aramis Black. "Give them to me now, or she dies."

Aramis Black—that was the name the man had given them a few days earlier when they had first met but probably not the name on his birth certificate—was a magician. Not a sleight-of-hand illusionist, but an honest to goodness sorcerer, a student of the dark arts which, Maddock thought, might explain how he had been able to sneak up on them, seemingly materializing out of thin air, to grab Jade and put a gun to her throat.

Black belonged to an occult society based in Plymouth, England, presently led by an exotic raven-haired beauty named Aliyah Cerulean. Aliyah and Black, along with the other members of their order, had until recently been the guardians of a purportedly magical talisman which they called "the Magna of Illusion," an obsidian mirror found in a temple ruin in Central America in the Sixteenth Century and allegedly owned by famed occultist Dr. John Dee, who had used it for divination and prophecy.

Maddock had no idea if any of that was true, but the mirror was real enough. He knew this for a fact because he—along with Jade and Bones, and their new companions, Rose Greer and Nick Kismet—had stolen the Magna of Illusion from the order's treasure vault on Drake Island in Plymouth Harbor.

Maybe "stolen" wasn't the right word.

Aliyah, had drawn them into a trap so that she could seize two relics which were in their possession: The Apex, an amulet of blue stone in the shape of a pyramid, discovered more than a century earlier by an ancestor of Kismet's adopted father; and a black metallic sphere, which they had dubbed "the orb" but which Kismet sometimes called "the anomaly," discovered in an ice-bound pyramid in Antarctica just a week before.

The three objects—the Apex, the orb and the mirror—were part of a set, it seemed; three of four, each representing a different alchemical element—fire, earth, water, and air—and each linked to a suit in the mystical Tarot deck—wands, disks, cups, and swords. The search for the fourth relic was what had brought Maddock and his friends to the ruins of ancient Tyana, on the Anatolian Plateau of central Turkey.

Aliyah desired all four relics, believing that they would imbue her with immortality and other supernatural gifts. She had also expressed a desire to kill Nick Kismet, in revenge for the death of her husband, who had perished while attempting to steal the Apex from Kismet. The five of them had turned the tables on Aliyah and her magicians, escaping with all three artifacts, which seemed to Maddock like fair restitution for the trouble she had put them through. Evidently, Aliyah Cerulean had a different definition of "fair."

Bones shrugged in response to the threat. "Kill her. It's no skin off my handsomely aquiline Cherokee nose."

Jade glowered at him. "Maybe we should trade

places, *Uriah*."

"She will only be the first to die," Black hissed, shaking her for effect. "And lest you think you can repeat that little trick you used against us on Drake's Island, know that there are sniper rifles trained on you at this very moment."

"'Lest'?" Bones said, giving Maddock a sidelong glance. "Who talks like that?"

Maddock ignored his friend. The quips were just Bones' way of dealing with stressful situations. And pretty much every other kind of situation, too.

"How did you find us?" he asked.

His curiosity was genuine, since they had taken great pains to disguise their movements from England to Turkey, but he didn't really need an answer to the question. What he was really doing was stalling. The sniper threat felt like a bluff. On the flat plain where the ruins were situated, there weren't a lot of places with a good line of sight, though there was a stand of trees to the northwest where, conceivably, a gunman might be able to reach sufficient elevation to draw a bead on them. Maddock wasn't ready to call that bluff just yet.

Another familiar voice spoke from behind them, answering the question. "You seek the Tabula Smaragdina," said Aliyah Cerulean. "Where else would you go?"

The Tabula Smaragdina—the Emerald Tablet—was an alchemical, or more accurately, hermetical text which purported to contain the secret for creating *prima materia*—the key ingredient in the so-called Philosopher's Stone—which could be used to create an elixir of eternal life or transmute base metals into gold.

The text was well known, handed down through the centuries, translated and studied by great thinkers such as Roger Bacon, Albert Magnus, Sir Isaac Newton and even Carl Jung. The text included one of the key principles of alchemy, "As above, so below," but also hinted at a relationship between matter and energy which would not be understood until the dawn of the nuclear age. The origin of the short text—just fourteen lines—was uncertain, but the oldest documentable source of the text was found in an Eighth Century Persian manuscript called *Kitāb sirr al-ḥalīqa*—the Book of the Secret of Creation and the Art of Nature— attributed to a man named Balinas. Balinas, also called Pseudo-Apollonius of Tyana—claimed to have copied it from a tablet made of emerald—thus the name—which he had discovered in a vault below a statue of Hermes in the city of Tyana.

Maddock would have dismissed the story as fanciful if not for the fact that Nick Kismet had seen something that looked remarkably like an emerald tablet in a vision supplied by the Magna of Illusion. There seemed little doubt that the Emerald Tablet—not the text, but the original tablet itself—was the fourth elemental relic.

Maddock turned his head in the direction of the voice and saw Aliyah, flanked by two men with guns, presumably other members of her occult order.

"You obviously already have the sphere from the ice pyramid," Aliyah went on. "That's the only explanation for the power you used to defeat us at Plymouth. Only the sword remains—the elemental talisman representing air. The Smaragdine Tablet."

Maddock shrugged. "The legend says that Balinas found the Emerald Tablet in a vault under the statue of Hermes in Tyana. It seemed like the place to start looking."

Aliyah gave a cold laugh. "And it did not occur to you that others would have searched this place before you?" She shook her head. "Your ignorance amply demonstrates that you are not worthy to possess the elemental talismans."

"What's that supposed to mean?" asked Bones.

Aliyah waved a hand. "There is no statue of Hermes here. No temple."

That was something Maddock and the others had learned even before boarding the flight to Ankara, Turkey. The ruins of Tyana consisted mainly of some arches supporting a Roman aqueduct and a public bath. The rest of the city, which had once been an important settlement in the region going back to the time of the Hittite Empire in the Second Millennium B.C.E., was gone—buried under the sands of time.

"Maybe not anymore," Maddock conceded.

Aliyah laughed again. "And you imagined that, if you could find the place where it once stood, the vault would magically open to you, as it did for Balinas."

"Stranger things have happened," Maddock said, shrugging.

In truth, that was exactly what they had been hoping for. The four elemental relics were linked somehow, reacting visibly when in close proximity with each other, and they had hoped to use the three relics they possessed like a compass to lead them to the fourth.

"Is it really so hard to believe?" Bones added. "Come

on. I thought you guys believed in magic." He drew out the last consonant and then added, "With a 'k'."

Magick, as they had learned, was the preferred spelling for the occultists, a way of differentiating their 'serious' magical practices from the trickery of stage magicians.

"Give me the elemental talismans," Aliyah said, her tone as cold and hard as a glacier, "and I will let you walk away."

"Joke's on you," Bones said. "We don't have them. Kismet and Rose took them. They didn't tell us where."

"Somewhere where they'll be safe from you," Maddock confirmed with a nod. "You didn't really think we'd just wander around with them in a backpack, did you?"

Aliyah's eyes narrowed, as if focusing laser beams of pure hate energy at them. "Then there's no reason to bother with you any longer, is there?"

"Right?" Bones said. "See ya."

Aliyah turned to one of the men beside her. "Kill them."

Maddock sucked in his breath. "Are you sure you want to do that? Out here in the open?"

Aliyah's lips curled into a malevolent smile. "Do you see anyone else here?"

"Let me guess. You bribed the local police to keep everyone away so there wouldn't be any witnesses."

Aliyah inclined her head. "Like I said, I knew you would come here." She looked away and made a cutting gesture, signaling her desire to end the conversation. Permanently.

"Wait," Bones said, quickly. "I lied."

"What a surprise." Aliyah did not look at him, but

the two gunmen with her did. They raised their pistols and took aim.

Bones pressed on. "When I said I didn't know where Kismet was going to take those magical doohickeys… That was a fib. I do know."

Aliyah shrugged. "I think this is the lie. But it does not matter. I found you. I will find him."

The gunmen circled around behind Maddock and Bones, maintaining a stand-off distance of several feet. "Kneel," one of them said. "Hands behind your head. Fingers laced."

"You saw that in a movie, right?" Bones retorted. "Trust me, it's a whole lot different in real life." He didn't sound even a little bit fearful, which was more than Maddock could say for himself.

Where is Kismet, he wondered.

A foot struck him in the back of the knee and his leg folded under him, dropping him into a kneeling position.

"Wait!" cried out a new voice. A woman's voice.

Maddock looked up and saw Rose Greer approaching, her hands raised. The straps of her backpack were visible, crossing over the top of her shoulders, looping around her arms. Maddock's heart sank a little lower. The backpack contained two of the relics—the orb and the mirror.

Aliyah faced Rose. "Ah, what a surprise. Now we're just missing one. Where is Nick Kismet?"

"He's out there. Watching." Rose kept her head high, defiant, but there was still a faint quaver of fear in her voice. She locked stares with Maddock. "He told me to tell you that he took care of the sniper. He also said you should look for the laser dot."

The effect of these words on Aliyah's magicians was immediate and dramatic. The men began looking around, checking themselves to see if they were being painted with the red dot of a laser aiming device, and as they did, their attention was diverted from the three captives, which was probably exactly what Kismet intended with the message.

Contrary to popular belief, laser aiming devices were rarely used for long distance shooting, and when they were, they were almost always in infrared wavelengths, invisible without the aid of night vision goggles. The visible red dot lasers so common in movies and television shows were typically used only with handguns, and had an effective range of only about twenty-five yards, with the "dot" increasing in size as the beam dispersed over distance. At distances of more than a hundred yards, the illuminated area might be several feet across.

Maddock still wasn't convinced that there actually was a sniper, but in that moment, all that mattered to the magicians—Black and Aliyah included—was making sure that they weren't being targeted. It was just the distraction Maddock and Bones needed to seize the upper hand.

Both men exploded from their kneeling positions, easily overpowering and disarming the two would-be executioners. In a flash, both gunmen were on the ground, their pistols now pointed back at them. Jade surprised Black—and Maddock, as well—by deftly ducking away from the gun at her neck, and then twisting around in Black's grasp to ram her knee into his crotch so hard that even Bones let out a yelp of sympathetic pain.

Aliyah, unarmed and now outgunned, made an abortive attempt to flee, but only got as far as the nearest arch before a hand shot out to seize hold of her.

It was Nick Kismet, armed, not with a sniper rifle, but with his wicked-looking *kukri* knife, which he held in a saber grip, the tip just inches from Aliyah's eye.

"I warned you what would happen," he said, his voice low and menacing.

Aliyah tried to pull away, and when she failed at that, spat at him. "Go on. Kill me. Just as you killed my husband."

Kismet's expression changed, softened. He sighed and lowered the knife a few inches. "All right, you got me. I was bluffing. I never meant for your husband to die. He attacked me, I fought back, he fell. Call it self-defense or an accident. I didn't want to kill him, and don't want to kill you."

"Do you think I want your mercy?"

Kismet shook his head. "I don't care what you want. But if you keep this up, somebody is going to get hurt, and I guarantee it won't be me."

"Better believe him," advised Bones, with a chuckle. "You think you know magick? Trust me, you don't know diddly-squat."

"You have no idea what I know," Aliyah retorted.

Maddock wondered if the woman suspected the true meaning of Kismet's statement. Several years earlier, Kismet had been drawn into a quest for the secret of immortality—and he had found it. Now, not only did he look ten years younger than his actual age, but he could recover from even mortal injuries, healing completely in a matter of minutes. Maddock would not have believed it if he hadn't witnessed Kismet recover from a lethal jolt of electricity a few days earlier.

But even though Kismet was invulnerable, the rest of them weren't which was why the continued harassment from Aliyah's magicians was becoming a serious problem, particularly as they seemed all too eager to indulge in cold-blooded murder.

"Well," Kismet said lowering the knife further but keeping an unbreakable grip on the woman's arm. "It's a stalemate then. I can't allow you to keep coming after us, and since I'm not going to just kill you outright, that seems to leave only one option. You'll have to come with us."

"Now just hold on a second." Maddock's voice joined a chorus of protest. Everyone—from Jade and Rose to Black and the other magicians—had something to say about the suggestion.

Aliyah just eyed Kismet, warily. "You would do that? Knowing that I have sworn to destroy you."

Kismet shrugged. "I've been told I have a weakness for bad girls."

Aliyah's face twisted with revulsion. "In your dreams."

Maddock cleared his throat. "Nick, we can't trust her. First chance she gets, she'll turn on us. And even if she doesn't get that chance, we're not going to be able to travel with a hostage."

Kismet continued staring at Aliyah. "You don't have to be our hostage. Look, we both want to find the Emerald Tablet. We've already got three of the four elementals. That gives us an edge. But you know more about it than any of us. So, let's work together."

"And when we find it?"

"We cross that bridge when we come to it. Your best

chance of ever seeing it is with us."

Maddock exchanged a look with Bones, who just shook his head. "Put a snake in your pocket, you're gonna get bit," he said, with an expansive air, as if reciting some bit of tribal lore.

"It's painful for me to say this," Jade said, keeping her eyes on Black, along with the business end of the pistol she'd taken from him, "but I agree with Bones. She's poison. We can't trust her."

Maddock shook his head. "No, Nick's right. We're not cold-blooded killers." He turned to Aliyah. "And we're not the only ones looking for it. It makes sense to work together."

"If you refuse," Kismet said, still staring at the woman, "or if they convince me that you can't be trusted, we'll drop you off somewhere. Probably out in the middle of nowhere, far from telephones and roads."

Aliyah's eyes narrowed again, but her expression lost some of its venom. "When you put it like that, how can I say no?"

6

After depriving the magicians of the keys to their vehicles, along with all weapons and mobile communications devices, the team of five plus one, piled into their rented Toyota Land Cruiser and began the four-hour-long drive back to Ankara. Aliyah offered no resistance and showed no overt signs of treacherous intent; she even went as far as to instruct her men to return to Plymouth and await further instructions, though whether that was a sincere request or part of a pre-arranged ruse was anyone's guess. She seemed resigned to her situation, though Maddock wondered how much of that was due to the fact that she had at least two guns pointed at her the whole time.

An hour into the journey, while driving along the surprisingly modern D750 highway, which cut across the Anatolian Plateau and offered a spectacular view of the distant volcanic peak of Mount Hasan, Bones who was driving, glanced over his shoulder. "This seems as good a place as any. I'll slow down a little if you want to toss her out."

"Bones!" cried Rose from the shotgun seat. "That's not funny."

"I wasn't joking," Bones said, dead-pan. Then he reached up and tilted the rear-view mirror to adjust his view. "Or did you think I was talking about Jade?"

Jade, who had the middle row seats all to herself, pretended to scratch her nose with just her middle finger extended.

Ever the peacemaker, Rose unbuckled her seat belt and threaded her way back to the middle row. Kneeling on the seat next to Jade, she peered over the backrest at Aliyah, who sat in the rear seating area, bracketed by Maddock and Kismet. "You knew we weren't going to find the Emerald Tablet at Tyana."

Aliyah shrugged, not meeting Rose's stare. "Many have looked for it. If it was there to find, someone would have. But I wonder if it was ever there at all."

"You mean after Balinas originally found it?"

Aliyah now raised her head to look back at Rose, regarding her thoughtfully, as if trying to decide whether to trust her. "It may be that the story in the *Kitāb sirr al-ḥalīqa* is not a literal account of the discovery of the tablet."

The Persian name seemed to flow naturally off her lips, a gift of her exotic ancestry.

"An allegory?"

Aliyah shifted in her seat, ignoring the guns held by Maddock and Kismet. "Or a riddle."

Maddock now took an interest. "I like riddles."

Aliyah glanced over at him, then looked forward again. "Balinas, is also known by the name Pseudo-Apollonius of Tyana. This is the first part of the riddle."

Rose nodded. "The real Apollonius of Tyana lived in the First Century. He was a famous neo-Pythagorean philosopher and writer, though none of his original writings survive."

"He was more than that," Aliyah said firmly. "He was a magus. A semi-divine figure, traveling the world, teaching and performing miracles. Some believe his story was the inspiration for the Gospels."

"*The* Gospels?" Bones called out. "The Bible stories about Jesus?"

"Yes. There are many similarities. In fact, in the

Second Century, those who followed the teachings of Apollonius believed that Jesus was a pale imitation of the sage. In any event, Balinas lived many centuries later, and may have chosen that appellation to give his own writings more import and broaden his reach.

"That was a common practice among Classical philosophers, riding the coattails of more famous men."

Bones nodded sagely. "Like all those guys who write novels and let James Patterson slap his name on the cover."

Aliyah made a sour face. "No, nothing like that. In this instance, I believe Balinas' alter-ego was offering a clue to the true origin of the Emerald Tablet."

"The real Apollonius?"

"Let's set that aside for a moment. Balinas claimed the true author of the Emerald Tablet was Hermes Trismegistus—Hermes the Thrice-Great."

Maddock was becoming interested despite himself. "Rose told us about this. As Hellenistic culture spread across Egypt, the gods of both cultures blended together to form distinct new god-forms. Just as the Roman Jupiter is based on the Greek Zeus, Hermes Trismegistus was based on the Greek Hermes and the Egyptian god Thoth, but some of the Egyptian deities might have been men who were deified after death. It is generally believed that Thoth might have originally been the priest Imhotep—"

"The bad guy in The Mummy," Bones supplied.

"And the architect of the Step Pyramid," Rose said, with a roll of her eyes. "Thoth might also have been based on Amenhotep, son of Hapu. Hermes Trismegistus might have been an Egyptian magician and priest. A real person, not an abstract god."

Maddock snapped his fingers as inspiration dawned. "The Magus card!"

The Magus was the name assigned to a card in the Thoth Tarot deck designed by Aleister Crowley. Maddock and Kismet had found an early version of the card with the remains of Adam Garral, the occultist who had first discovered the Apex and an ancestor of Kismet's adoptive father. The card was itself another riddle, and an anachronism, as Crowley's Tarot deck had not been produced until more than thirty years after Garral's disappearance and death in the frozen wilderness of Antarctica.

Maddock leaned forward to look past Aliyah to Kismet. "The card has the figure of Mercury—the Roman version of Hermes. And Hermes is also Thoth. Three faces of Hermes—thrice-great—and all called the Magus, or Magician."

"The point," Aliyah said, her voice edged with irritation, "Is that Hermes and Hermes Trismegistus were never considered to be the same entity in the eyes of the Greeks, so it is unlikely that the Emerald Tablet written by one would have been concealed in a temple dedicated to the other."

"So we should be looking for a temple to Thoth?"

Aliyah appraised Maddock again for a moment, then seemed to relax a little. She turned to look at Kismet. "Do you recall your vision of the Emerald Tablet? You first saw it as an Egyptian sword—a *kopis*—the sword of Alexander the Great—concealed within the tower of Babel."

Kismet nodded. "It seemed that way."

"Alexander the Great spread Hellenistic culture across the world of his day—here, in what was once called Asia Minor and across the Persian world, but this influence was felt most strongly in one place. Egypt. And particularly in the city that bears his name to this day."

"Alexandria," Rose said, almost breathless. "The Library!"

She turned to look at Maddock. "Hermes and Thoth were both patron gods of the written word. Thoth in particular was the god of wisdom. And libraries. And what better place to keep the Emerald Tablet than the Library of Alexandria."

"Balinas lived in the Eighth Century," Kismet countered. "The library was completely destroyed long before that."

"Contrary to popular belief," Rose said, slipping into history-professor mode, "the Library was not sacked and burned in a single event, but rather suffered numerous episodes of destruction, some intentional, others the result of accidents and natural disasters. Earthquakes and tsunamis did a lot of damage. Nobody knows exactly where the Library once stood. It was customary for ancient civilizations to salvage the stone and other material for use in other building projects, not to mention repurposing the real estate. There's a modern city where ancient Alexandria once stood, and as you can imagine, the current Arab populace isn't keen on having the streets of their city dug up for the sake of satisfying curiosity about the Western world."

"So how are we going to find it?" Bones asked.

"Well, we do have a few clues from history. For one thing, most of the historical accounts of the Library indicate that it was part of the royal palace complex. Now, we don't know exactly where that was either, but there have been a few hopeful discoveries. In 1992, a

French archaeologist discovered the sunken remains of the royal quarters of Cleopatra VII—"

"Seven?" Bones interrupted. "There was more than one? Were they all babes?"

Rose laughed. "There were actually seven women named Cleopatra, but Cleo Seven was the famous one—the one that Julius Caesar and Mark Anthony were so enthralled with. I leave it to you to decide if the word 'babe' is accurate, but if the artwork from the time is any indication, she most definitely didn't look anything like Elizabeth Taylor in her prime. Plutarch says she was beautiful, but not extraordinarily so, and then goes on to praise her wit and charm. And especially her voice."

"Ah," Bones said, sounding a little disappointed. "A great personality and a face for radio."

Maddock tried to get the conversation back on track. "Her quarters would probably have been in the palace complex. You said its underwater?"

"About sixteen feet under," Rose said. "In the harbor, a couple hundred yards offshore."

"Well that's no problem then," Bones said, quickly getting over his disillusionment. "Underwater is where we do our best work."

"The bay is toxic," Aliyah said, calm and confident. "Poisoned with petroleum and industrial waste. But by all means, search underwater to your heart's content."

Maddock eyed her. "It's not underwater?"

"If I told you where to look, you would have no further use for me."

"Just knowing it's in Alexandria may be enough, as long as we've got the relics to guide us."

Aliyah shrugged. "I can tell you exactly where to look. Or you can take your chances. It's your choice."

"I say we take our chances," Bones said.

"Hold on a second," Jade said. "If you've known all along that it was there, why didn't you get it yourself?"

Aliyah kept looking at Kismet. "Until you saw the vision of the four elementals, we did not know what we were looking for. If we had suspected, we would have brought the Magna of Illusion here and opened the vault ourselves. Perhaps if you had not killed him, my husband would have been the one to behold the vision."

Anger had darkened her features as she spoke, but after a pause, her expression softened. "I told you in Plymouth, Nick Kismet. I believe you are meant to find it."

Kismet just stared back, stone-faced.

Maddock understood his wariness. Aliyah had set a trap for them in Tyana. Was she now trying to lead them into another?

7

Like many other cities Maddock had visited in his travels, Alexandria was a collision of past and present. The ancient past, what little of it remained, was like a granite bluff extending out into the ocean, slowly but inevitably eroding away under the relentless assault of progress.

There was plenty to remind visitors of the city's history, and indeed, tourism remained a major industry, despite recent political turmoil in the Arab world. But even though the ancient monuments, such as the misnamed Pompey's Pillar and the Catacombs of Kom El-Shouqafa, and more recent but no less historic structures—such as the Citadel of Qaitbay, which occupied the ground where the famed Pharos Lighthouse once stood, or the magnificent Mosque of Abu al-Abbas al-Mursi—continued to generate interest in the city, tourists now came as much for modern pleasures such as sunbathing and gambling, as for a deep interest in history. For many, the ancient ruins were a curiosity, on par with a modern theme park. Even the ancient Library of antiquity had been reimagined as a fantastic modern structure of glass and steel, surrounded by gardens and reflecting pools, perched at the eastern tip of the harbor. Although its collection, which included not only millions of books but also film, video archives, and over 100 terabytes of data, was greater by several orders of magnitude than its namesake from antiquity, the Bibliotheca Alexandrina seemed like just another tourist attraction.

Their flight, from Cairo—a short hop after the longer trip across the Mediterranean—landed just as the sun was settling below the western horizon. Since the end of the road trip in Ankara, where they had been obliged to dump their captured weapons, Aliyah had ceased to be their prisoner and was now a traveling companion, evidently a willing one, though Bones continued to vocally register his suspicions about her. Maddock harbored the same doubts, but was a little surprised by his friend's unrelenting antipathy toward her. It wasn't like Bones to pass up a chance to make a fool of himself in front of an attractive woman, and by any standard, Aliyah was that.

They traveled by minibus to their hotel just a couple blocks from the harbor, but stayed in their rooms just long enough to offload their luggage, such as it was, and grab a quick meal in the hotel restaurant.

As they finished their supper over cups of coffee, Aliyah began revealing the knowledge she had earlier withheld, doling the information out like a tour guide. "The Library of Alexandria was originally part of a larger institution of learning and research on subjects ranging from philosophy to astronomy to anatomy. In addition to the enormous wealth of wisdom and knowledge contained on scrolls, the institution included laboratories, observatories, and even a zoo. It was dedicated to the nine Muses of Greek mythology—the deities who inspired the creative arts—from which it derived its name: Musaeum."

"And from which we get, museum," Maddock said.

"It's described as a campus with several buildings, connected by covered walkways, gardens, dining halls and dormitories, even a theatre. Oddly enough, the one thing that original museum didn't have was an art collection, but it was the start of the Library. By 145 BCE though, the center of learning in Alexandria shifted to another building, called the Serapeum—the temple of the Greco-Egyptian god Serapis, the protector deity of Alexandria."

"Greco-Egyptian," Maddock mused. "Like Hermes Trismegistus."

"Serapis was a syncretic deity—a joining of beliefs from different religions. The name derives from a combination of the Egyptian deities Osiris and Apis, but he seems to have a lot more in common with Dionysus. Interestingly, the *Anabasis Alexandri*, generally considered to be the best source for information about Alexander the Great, says that as Alexander lay dying of fever, his companions asked Serapis—which I would take to mean a statue of the god—whether to bring him into the temple to be cured. The account says that the god spoke and told them to leave Alexander where he was. Mind you, this was in Babylon, not Alexandria.

"In any case though, the Serapeum of Alexandria was the most famous temple to the god, not to mention being the most impressive temple in the whole city. As the Musaeum declined, the Serapeum not only grew in prominence, but housed at least part of the Library Collection—the part that survived the longest. There were however statues to all the Greek gods, including Hermes, in the Serapeum. Balinas might have lived in the Eighth Century, but Apollonius of Tyana lived in the First, so it stands to reason that if he visited Alexandria, he would have gone to the Serapeum."

"So what happened to the Serapeum?"

"When Emperor Constantine converted to Christianity in 325 C.E., he ordered the Serapeum closed, along with all other temples to pagan gods. The Alexandrians held out for a while, but in 391, the Serapeum was sacked. That's generally considered to be the end of the Library of Alexandria, though it's likely that at least some of the collection was preserved elsewhere. There's even one legend that part of it was loaded aboard a Roman galley which eventually wound up in Texas."

"Really?" Bones was now definitely paying attention.

"Probably not," Aliyah went on. "Arab sources attribute the final destruction to the order of the ruling Caliph, after Muslim forces captured the city in 642 C.E. but given the subsequent Golden Age of Islam, in which science and mathematics continued to evolve throughout the period known in Europe as 'the Dark Ages,' it is likely they preserved the knowledge, rather than destroying it. After the Library of Alexandria, the greatest library in history was in the Persian fortress of Alamut."

"The seat of power for the famed Hashashin—the Assassins cult," Rose said, nodding. "My great grandad wrote about it one of the Dodge Dalton novels."

Aliyah gave a disdainful sniff, then continued, "The Serapeum is gone but we know where it once stood.

"In 297 C.E., Emperor Diocletian erected a triumphal column at the Serapeum. A granite monolith carved from a single stone, rather than stacked drums, over sixty feet high, and it's still standing today. If you read the tourist brochures, you know it as 'Pompey's Pillar' though in fact it has nothing to do with Pompey the Great who once ruled Rome alongside Julius Caesar.

The foundation of the Serapeum lies nearby, along with the entrance to the Catacombs of Kom El-Shouqafa. I believe we will find the vault with the Tabula Smaragdina within those ancient tunnels."

"Unless someone took it when they relocated the rest of the Library."

"I do not believe that happened." Aliyah turned to Kismet. "Do you recall the story of how Adam Garral found the Apex in the Great Pyramid?"

Kismet had been unusually subdued since their arrival. During the taxi ride, Maddock had observed him looking around warily, as if checking to see if they were being tailed. When he had asked Kismet about it, the man had simply replied. "I don't like the desert." Now, he straightened in his chair and nodded. "He claimed it appeared to him after some kind of out-of-body experience."

"In which he found a secret passage inside the pyramid. A passage that not only led to a secret room, but transported him through time as well. Balinas describes a similar journey into the vault under the statue of Hermes to find the Emerald Tablet. And unlike your ancestor, he did not remove what he found."

"It could still be there," said Maddock.

"With the relics you now carry, we will find that vault. It will open to us, even as it did for Apollonius of Tyana, and inside we will find the tomb of Alexander the Great and in his hand, the Emerald Tablet of Hermes Trismegistus." She pushed her empty coffee cup away. "Are you ready?"

"You mean right now?" Maddock glanced around the table and saw his look of concern mirrored in the faces of the others. "It's dark out."

"Meaning we will not be disturbed by other visitors." Aliyah folded her arms across her chest. "I expected a little more enthusiasm."

"I don't like to rush into things," Maddock said. He half-expected Bones to make a joke at his expense, but the big Cherokee just nodded.

"Well, she's got a point about not being bothered by the tourists," Jade said, though she sounded almost like she was trying to convince herself. "We can at least check the place out."

Rose seconded the suggestion. "Judging by the reaction we got in Antarctica and on Drake Island, we should be able to tell if it's there just by walking by."

Aliyah stared at the other women intently but said nothing. Maddock shot a look at Kismet, who simply shrugged. "I guess it wouldn't hurt to do a walk-by."

Although it was not required by local custom, Aliyah suggested the women wear *hijab* headscarves to avoid attracting unnecessary attention. As Jade and Rose donned their scarves, Aliyah glanced at Bones and added, "I'm afraid there's not much we can do to cover him up."

"What the hell is that supposed to mean?"

"Only that you stand out in a crowd," she replied with a coy smile.

That mollified Bones somewhat. "It's true. I am outstanding."

"Well since you've got the best view," Maddock said, "keep that head on a swivel."

He glanced over at Kismet who returned a nod of confirmation. This all felt too rushed, like a trap, but even if it was, there was no way around it. They could either go through, or go home.

As promised, the former site of the Serapeum was only a few blocks from the hotel. The surrounding neighborhood was quiet and poorly lit. All six of them stood out, though Bones perhaps more than the others, attracting the notice of more than a few *jellabiya*-clad local men, all of whom looked away quickly when Bones gave them the stink-eye.

Aliyah took them along the edge of a rocky plateau occupying several acres where no modern construction had taken place. "This is the old Bab Sidra cemetery," she explained, and pointed forward to the column, a dark silhouette thrust up into the night sky, perhaps a quarter of a mile distant. "That is where we must go."

Maddock maintained his 360-degree awareness as they moved along the edge of the cemetery, occasionally checking with Bones and Kismet to see if they had noticed anything of concern. Maddock was pleased to see that Jade also remained alert. She had, he realized, come a long way from the hapless, trouble-prone archaeologist he had rescued from a submerged ruin in Argentina all those years before. *Probably Professor's influence*, he thought. *Definitely not the girl I fell out of love with.*

The thought went through his head—and the rest of him—before he knew what was happening.

Cut it out, Maddock. He told himself, forcefully. *You've got Angel, and she's all the woman you'll ever need.*

He forced his gaze forward again as they came to the gate that blocked access to the ruins. It was closed and secured with a padlock.

"Guess we'll have to come back tomorrow," Bones said. "Oh, well. We tried."

Although the fabric of her *hijab* hid her hair, Aliyah's exposed eyebrows went up in an expression of surprise, or perhaps dismay. "I would not have thought men such as yourselves would be stopped by something so primitive."

Bones glanced over at Maddock in a "what do you think?" look. Maddock could only shrug.

Bones let out a sigh. "Challenge accepted," he said, and reached into a pocket for his lockpicking tools. "My misspent youth pays off again."

With one hand cupped over the screen of his mobile phone for light, Bones went to work on the lock. Rose moved closer to Maddock. "Dane, I'm not getting anything."

She had whispered it, but Aliyah overheard nonetheless. "The relics are not reacting?" There was no hint of coy playfulness now; her surprise was real. "I don't understand."

"Same with the Apex," Kismet said, absently fingering the talisman which hung from a rawhide cord around his neck. "Nada."

"Maybe we aren't close enough," Maddock suggested.

"We got a reaction from the orb from miles away," Rose countered.

"You have three relics now, correct?" Aliyah said. "Perhaps they are setting up an interference pattern. Canceling each other out."

The suggestion felt sincere, but Maddock couldn't help but wonder if this was the prelude to a betrayal. Was Aliyah trying to get them to separate? Isolate the relics and divide their forces?

"That didn't happen on Drake Island," Rose said.

Nevertheless, she unslung the backpack, opening it to begin rooting around inside.

"Got it," Bones said as he removed the lock from the hasp. He started to pull the gate open but stopped himself. "Or should I lock it back up?"

"At least walk around," Aliyah pleaded. "It has to be here. Maybe you just need to be closer."

Maddock looked to Kismet for some hint of what to do. The latter shook his head. "I think this is another dead end. But we're here. We might as well try it." He fixed Aliyah with a cold stare. "It's not like we're completely defenseless."

Aliyah tilted her head in a gesture that indicated she understood the implicit threat, and then reached for the gate. She swung it open and went through without waiting for them.

There was just enough ambient light for them to make out the path winding through the ruins. They passed excavations and mounds, eventually reaching the crest of the hill where Pompey's Pillar stood, its enormous base flanked by a pair of sphinx statues, each the size of a bull elephant. Aliyah led them past the column, following a route that she seemed to have memorized, and brought them to a large hole in the ground.

Maddock activated the flashlight on his phone but kept one hand over it to mute the light and mask their presence. He shone it into the hole, revealing a staircase of cut stone that descended into the gloom. Round shapes, like black ping-pong ball halves, skittered away from the touch of his light.

"Scarab beetles," Bones murmured. "Don't let them get under your skin."

"This is the entrance to the old tunnel system that once connected the temples of the Serapeum," Aliyah explained. After a momentary pause, she turned to Rose. "Has there been any reaction from the elemental relics?"

Rose shook her head.

"I don't understand," Aliyah said, her voice becoming increasingly taut. "It has to be here. You must be doing something wrong."

"I'm not *doing* anything," Rose protested. "And neither is the orb. There's nothing—"

Before Rose could finish, Aliyah sprang into motion, seizing Rose's backpack strap. Maddock started to react, but Aliyah was already moving, dragging Rose into the dark hole.

8

Maddock unhooded his light and shone it down the steps, catching just a glimpse of Rose as she stumbled along behind Aliyah. Then he was moving, too, pounding down the steps in pursuit. He felt more than heard the crunch of beetle bodies underfoot and some part of him recalled Bones' warning about the scarabs getting under his skin. That was a silly notion, he knew, a nightmare fantasy straight out of a B-movie. The Egyptian scarab was actually a dung-beetle, not a flesh eater at all. But telling himself that and believing it were two very different things, especially here, on the cusp of an ancient Egyptian catacomb. He could feel tiny insect legs crawling on his skin, mandibles clicking… Burrowing.

Crunch. Crunch.

The steps fed into a narrow tunnel and again he spied something moving in the darkness ahead. He did not stop, but in that moment of transition, he realized that the others were with him. Kismet was right beside him, and Jade and Bones weren't far behind.

Maddock skidded to a stop as his light fell upon a familiar form, lying sprawled on the passage floor, one hand raised to provide shade from the glare of the light. It was Rose. She looked a little disoriented but did not appear to be injured. There was no sign of Aliyah, though Maddock thought he heard the crunching sound of footsteps from further down the passage.

"She took my pack," Rose gasped. "She has the orb. And the mirror."

"We'll get them back," Maddock promised, helping her to her feet. He tried to inject a little confidence into his tone, though deep down, he wasn't feeling it. Aliyah now possessed two of the four elemental relics, and if she was right and the last remaining one lay somewhere in the catacombs beneath the Serapeum, then odds were good that she would soon have three.

Then Bones gave them all something else to worry about. "Holy crap. Scorpion."

Maddock followed Bones' pointing finger and saw something crawling up the outside of Rose's thigh. It was three inches in length, with a greenish-yellow segmented body, yellow legs, and a curled bobbing tail.

"A deathstalker," Kismet warned, unsheathing his *kukri.* "Don't move, Rose."

He extended the tip toward Rose's leg, placing the flat of the blade in the scorpion's path. It stopped moving, its forelegs resting a fraction of an inch from the edge, as if somehow sensing the potential lethality of the metal.

"Get it off me," Rose wailed.

"Don't move," Kismet repeated, and then with a snap of his wrist, flicked the creature away. "Dane, check her for more."

Rose was already moving, retreating back toward the stairs, her limbs twitching with the involuntary reflex known colloquially as the heebie-jeebies.

"Hold still, Rose." Maddock played his light up and down her body, and when he was satisfied that there were no other scorpions or any other creepy crawlies on her, turned and shone the light on the walls and ceiling of the passage. He saw more of the scarabs, roving aimlessly across the floor, but there were also several lighter-colored shapes.

"Deathstalker," Jade said. "Cute name." There was a faint quaver in her voice that might have been merely the result of the sprint down the stairs, but probably wasn't. She was also backing slowly toward the stairs.

Maddock had heard of the deathstalker scorpion. Despite the ominous name, its venom wasn't automatically fatal, particularly to a healthy adult and in the amount that might be delivered by a single creature, but a sting would be immediately painful, much like a bee sting, and as with bee stings, there was always the risk of a potentially fatal allergic reaction.

Unfortunately, there wasn't just one of the creatures, but dozens. Perhaps even hundreds of them, just in the area revealed by the light.

"Did I mention that I hate the desert?" Kismet said, more resigned than fearful. He continued to hold his *kukri* in his right hand.

"Right?" Bones said. "First scarabs, and now scorpions. It's like someone took all the worst parts of the Mummy movies and dumped them down here. I don't even want to think about what other horrible things might be waiting for us down there."

"Like Brendan Fraser," Jade said.

"Hey, I like Brendan Fraser," Bones shot back. "Though, I like young Rachel Weisz even more."

"Tom Cruise then?"

"We do not speak of that," Bones said, flatly.

"We need to keep moving," Maddock said, taking a step forward. He kept moving the light back and forth, up and down, making sure to avoid walking directly under any of the scorpions, or letting any of them get close enough to crawl onto his boots. After a few steps he glanced back and was relieved to see that the others were following.

Aliyah had left a clear trail for them to follow—crushed beetle carapaces and smeared bug guts stamped on the floor of the passage in distinctive footprint shapes. Not that there were a lot of places she could have gone. The tunnel continued forward for a ways before making a right turn and then another, but there were no branching passages. A hundred strides brought them to another descending staircase.

Maddock paused at the top, cocking an ear toward the unplumbed depths below and listened. The soft thud of footsteps echoed up from below. Aliyah was still on the move. Maddock started down after her.

After just a few steps, the wall to his right fell away to reveal an open space beyond, a yawning emptiness into which the scant illumination of his flashlight vanished entirely. Thankfully, there were no more creepy-crawly denizens in evidence. Maddock shied away from the edge, hugging the left wall, which he absently noted slanted as it rose toward the ever-diminishing ceiling. The wall appeared to be constructed of stacked stone blocks or bricks, all of them adorned in some way, either with relief carvings of Egyptian hieroglyphs or some kind of alphabetic writing that Maddock guessed was probably Greek. He didn't take the time to stop and look.

"Dane!" Kismet called out to him in a stage whisper. "We're in a pyramid."

The significance of this was not immediately apparent to Maddock, or it seemed, to Bones, who shot back, "So?"

"So, there aren't any pyramids in Alexandria."

"He's right," Rose said. "At least none that have been

discovered."

Maddock faltered a step as he processed this, then started moving again. "So, this is some kind of secret chamber?"

"One that Aliyah opened," Kismet replied. "Using the relics. I don't know if she did it consciously, or if the entrance simply reacted to their presence."

"Then she was right. The Emerald Tablet is here." Maddock quickened his pace.

"If it is, then it's not behaving like the other relics. I'm not getting any kind of reaction from the Apex."

The stairwell flattened onto a corner landing where the slanted wall met another just like it, apparently confirming Kismet's assessment. The stairs continued downward to the right, the number of steps half-again as many as the first flight and then turned right again, describing a square clockwise spiral down the interior walls of the hollow pyramid.

And then, the steps ended, depositing them on a broad stone pavement. The space was empty, devoid of even dust, but Maddock could just make out a trail of faint footprints leading out toward what he guessed to be the center. Holding his light high, he sprinted out across the flat, featureless floor in pursuit of Aliyah. Fifty yards or so later, he spotted her.

Whether by accident or design Maddock could not say, but Aliyah had somehow managed to find the only object contained within the pyramid—a block of stone, shaped like a rectangular prism, about four feet high and six feet long, and positioned, if Maddock was not mistaken, directly in the center of the chamber. A funerary bier, Maddock guessed, where a coffin—perhaps the golden coffin of Alexander the Great himself—had once lain. But the only thing on the bier now was Aliyah Cerulean. She had fallen across it, and now lay face down with her arms outflung, hugging the stone. She looked like a grieving widow who had thrown herself upon the coffin of her deceased beloved, only there was no coffin. Rose's backpack lay on the floor beside her, unopened. Forgotten.

"Not here," she said, her voice hollow, desolate. "It's not here."

Maddock hastened forward to remove the backpack from her vicinity, though it was apparent that Aliyah either had no intention of using the relics or lacked the ability. Only then did he acknowledge what she had said.

"It's not here?"

Kismet and Bones were already there with him, and Rose and Jade arrived seconds later, spreading out in a loose circle around the stone block. Bones asked the obvious question. "What happened to it?"

"Someone else got here first," Kismet said, a hint of bitterness in his tone. "It was foolish of us to think that it would still be here."

"Who?"

"Who do you think?" The voice, a sardonic almost-shout, echoed and rebounded from the inwardly slanting walls. It had not come from anyone in their group, but despite the weird acoustical distortion, Maddock recognized it instantly. A chill of dread shot through him.

The voice belonged to the man he had dubbed TBH, owing to the latter's annoying habit of utilizing text-shorthand in everyday speech. Maddock had tangled with the man on at least two previous occasions—first, in the Antarctic Outpost where they had discovered the orb, and then again in Plymouth Harbor, shortly after capturing the Magna of Illusion from Aliyah's brotherhood of magicians—and both encounters had ended the same way. Both times, Maddock had killed TBH.

It was only after the second encounter that Maddock had learned the truth about TBH—also known as Ulrich Hauser. The man was the leader of a radical splinter faction inside the secretive group known as Prometheus.

He was also Nick Kismet's brother, and like Kismet, Ulrich Hauser was, for all intents and purposes, immortal.

9

Every head but Aliyah's whirled around to face back toward the stairs and the source of the voice. Something was moving there, a lot of somethings.

It might have been only his imagination, but Maddock thought he could see dozens of shadowy forms spreading out in either direction, just beyond the faint reach of their combined lights. Hauser, he knew, never went anywhere without a coterie of hired killers and this time would be no exception.

"Nobody move," Maddock whispered, unnecessarily. His friends were all still as statues.

The man himself materialized a moment later, stepping into the light. His face was partly concealed behind a set of night vision goggles, but after just a few steps toward the group, he flipped the low-light device up out of the way to completely reveal his grinning visage.

"Curious advice, Mr. Maddock. Moving targets are so much harder to hit."

Maddock shrugged. "I've killed you twice already. Maybe the third time is the charm."

It wasn't completely false bravado. He and Bones had been in stickier situations, although at that moment, he was hard-pressed to remember any, but the one thing experience had taught him was that there was absolutely no value to treating any situation as hopeless.

Hauser gave a short humorless laugh. Despite his strong handsome proportions, the man looked cruel and predatory—part-Adonis, part-werewolf. He closed to within ten feet of them, and then stopped with his hands resting on his hips. He regarded them all for a moment, one by one, his stare sharpening into daggers of hate as he met Maddock's stare, then he brought his gaze back to Kismet. "Surprised to see me, brother?"

"Not really." He thrust his chin at Hauser. "Frankly, I'm a little surprised it took you this long to bounce back after getting your ass handed to you back at Plymouth."

Bones gave a snort of laughter. "Nice."

Hauser shrugged. "I was otherwise occupied. I knew you'd end up here eventually." He paused a beat. "Well? Have you figured it out yet?"

Kismet's expression twitched a little. "I'm not really in the mood for guessing games."

Hauser's grin deepened. "Oh, but this one is the best. Maybe your new friends can help." He glanced at Maddock, his nostrils flaring angrily. "Interesting company you're keeping, BTW."

Bones let out an audible groan. "This again? Oh, wait. I've got one. FWIW, you're a dick."

Hauser ignored the jibe and returned his attention to Kismet. "A hint then." He made an expansive gesture. "The lost tomb of Alexander the Great, hidden away for at least two thousand years. Locked up tight, and the only keys that can open it are the four anomalies one of which was sealed within. What does that tell you?"

Maddock, curious despite himself, considered Hauser's question, but Kismet merely shrugged. "That someone else got here first. We already knew that."

"Ah, but how? Look around you. This place has been cleaned out, and yet there are no tunnels. This wasn't the work of tomb robbers. Whoever did this knew how to unlock the door and then seal it up again."

"They didn't use the orb," Rose said. There was a

quiet defiance in her tone.

"I'd say the mirror is out, too," Jade added, jerking a thumb in Aliyah's direction. "Her magicians had the mirror this whole time and didn't even know there was anything here."

Hauser nodded, still looking at Kismet. "Which just leaves your little bauble. The Garral family heirloom."

Kismet cocked his head sideways. "You think Adam Garral took it?"

"That makes sense," Maddock said, thinking out loud. "Garral had the Apex and he probably had access to the mirror. We know he was looking for the orb. Maybe he came here first."

"But what did he do with it?" countered Rose. "Where is it now?"

Hauser continued smiling. "I like the way you think," he said, sounding like some kind of nightmarish motivational speaker. "But you jumped to the wrong conclusion. If Adam Garral had found Alexander's tomb, believe me, the world would know about it."

Kismet looked up sharply. "Prometheus."

Hauser nodded. "Did you never think to ask, of all the people in the world, why our dear mother chose to leave you with Christian Garral."

Kismet just stared back, dumbfounded. Maddock suddenly felt like an intruder in the other man's family drama. If not for the guns he knew were pointed at them at all, he would have excused himself. But like it or not, he was already caught in the conflict.

"Prometheus wanted the Apex," he said, still trying to work it out for himself. "And they knew Christian Garral had it."

Hauser bobbed his head from side to side in a vague

nod but kept his eyes on Kismet. "They wanted what it would unlock. This. The tomb of Alexander and all its secrets. The fourth anomaly was only a very small part of what was once kept here. Once the door was open and the treasures removed, our mother returned the heirloom to your adoptive father."

He paused a beat. "It's always the long game with the old guard. Always an experiment. If they had wanted the Apex anomaly, they would simply have taken it, but they were content to let Garral keep it. I suspect they wanted to observe how you would interact with it."

Kismet kept staring a few seconds longer then shook his head as if waking up. "If you already had the Emerald Tablet, why come after—"

"But I don't have it," Hauser hissed, cutting him off. "Those fools buried it away, just like they bury everything. The power to reshape the world… Reshape reality itself, and what do they do with it? Put it on a shelf where no one can reach."

"That's why you want the elementals," Rose said. "You're going to war with Prometheus."

For the first time since stepping into the light, Hauser's smile became genuine. "The Antarctic anomaly would have sufficed to accomplish my plan, but with three anomalies, nothing will stand in my way."

"Just one little problem with that," Kismet said, straightening a little. "You don't have three anomalies. In fact, by my count, you don't have any."

"Threats, brother?" Hauser shook his head sadly. "Are you sure that's how you want this to go?"

"Violence seems to be the only language you speak."

"That, and textese," Bones added.

"And yet," Hauser countered, "You are all still very

much alive."

"No thanks to you," Jade put in.

"Oh, but it is entirely thanks to me," Hauser retorted. "At this moment there are a half-dozen assault rifles trained on you—on all of you—"

"This seems familiar somehow," Bones muttered.

"I underestimated you and your friends in the past. I won't make that mistake again. If you show even the slightest hint of resistance, my men will open fire. That won't pose much of a problem for you and I, dear brother, but I think your friends will not fare so well. If I wanted you dead, we wouldn't be talking right now."

"So why are we still talking?" Kismet asked, sounding genuinely curious rather than defiant.

"Understand this, brother. I am going to take the three anomalies in your possession. There's nothing you can do to stop me. Whether I take them over the dead bodies of your friends is up to you."

"Me?"

Hauser took a step closer and then reached out to clasp Kismet's shoulder. "We're brothers, Nick. They took that from us. *She* took that from us. Kept us apart and in the dark, all for the sake of their great experiment. Doesn't that gall you?"

"So, this is about revenge? Against our mother? Against Prometheus?"

"Not revenge. It's about taking what is ours. Our birthright, brother." He gave Kismet's shoulder and emphatic shake. "They set us against each other from the beginning, cast us as rivals in their little drama. Cain and Abel. Jacob and Esau. Romulus and Remus. When all the while, we ought to have been Castor and Pollux. Brothers, fighting side by side, seizing control of our destiny and taking what we are owed. That is what I'm offering you brother."

"Offering me?"

Hauser let go and took a step back. "Come with me, and I'll let them live."

Before Kismet could answer, Aliyah raised her head and let out a wail of dismay. "No. You must not." She pushed away from the bier and threw herself at Maddock, grasping the strap of Rose's pack in another attempt to tear it away. Despite her ferocity and the swiftness with which she had acted, Maddock's fingers curled tight on the straps, refusing to give it up.

"No!" Aliyah shouted again, giving the pack a futile shake. Then, still holding on with her left hand, she raised her eyes and her right hand, index and middle fingers extended, and spoke again in a low voice that seemed to vibrate in the still air.

"*A'teh!*"

Her hand came down quickly in a straight line to point at the pavement. "*Mal'kut!*"

Maddock didn't recognize the strange language, but he intuitively grasped that Aliyah was attempting some kind of magickal ritual, perhaps trying to unleash the power of the relics.

Can she do that?

Her hand came up until it was level with her heart and then moved out to her right shoulder. "*Ve Gev—*"

The incantation was silenced by a thunderous report. Maddock felt another hard yank on the pack strap as Aliyah Cerulean jerked backward, almost lifted off her feet by the impact of a bullet. A spray of blood misted the bier behind her and then she crashed down atop it once more, this time on her back in a supine position, like an offering on an altar.

Maddock tore his gaze from her and looked back at Hauser, who now held a smoking semi-automatic pistol in his extended right arm. The fierce predatory grin was back. "We'll have none of that," he said, and then swung the muzzle toward Maddock, reaching out his left hand, palm open. "Give me that pack. Now."

Before Maddock could even think about what his response would be, Kismet stepped in front of the gun, hands raised in a show of surrender. "Don't," he said, imploring. "I'll go with you."

He turned back to face Maddock and reached out for the pack.

"Stop!" Hauser barked. He moved around Kismet, keeping the gun trained on Maddock. "Sorry, brother, but you're already too close for my comfort. Back up now, or my men will open fire."

Kismet held his ground a moment longer. "Give me your word. No one else dies."

Hauser inclined his head. "If that's what it takes."

Kismet took a step back. "Give them up, Dane."

"He's going to kill us all anyway," Jade hissed.

Kismet held Hauser's stare. "No, he's not."

Maddock hesitated. His gut told him that Jade was right and that giving up the relics would only seal their death warrant, but at the same time, what choice did they have? Or was this some bold gambit on Kismet's part?

"Trust me, Dane," Kismet said. "This is the only way."

Maddock looked over at Bones, saw the mixture of disbelief and anger in his friend's eyes, read the unasked question there. *Are we really doing this?*

But Kismet was right. They were out of options. With no better alternative, Maddock knelt and placed the pack on the floor.

Hauser moved in quickly, snatching the pack up off the floor, and then darted back out of Maddock's reach. "That's better," he said, hefting the pack onto one shoulder. He waggled the gun at Maddock. "All right. All of you, move closer."

Kismet spoke quickly. "I swear, if you hurt them—"

"They are as insignificant to me as insects on the sidewalk." Hauser gave the pack a meaningful shake. "Especially now that I have these. But I won't tolerate further interference. Or delay. Maddock, do yourself a favor and make sure I never see your face again." He turned back to Kismet and gestured into the darkness. "It's time to go, brother. We have business elsewhere."

10

As Kismet and Hauser melted into the shadows, Maddock shook off the paralysis of defeat and moved to the bier. He knew, even without checking for a pulse, that Aliyah was dead, but he checked anyway and then raised his eyes to the others and shook his head.

Bones nostrils flared in a feral snarl. "And I was actually starting to like that guy."

"Who?" Rose asked.

"Kismet. I didn't think he'd cut and run at the first sign of trouble."

"He didn't exactly have much of a choice," Jade said, defensively.

"Please." Bones waved a dismissive hand. "He could have used the relics, put the whammy on 'em. He didn't."

"Because he knew Hauser would probably kill us all before he could. He did the only thing he could. He bought us time. And a chance." She turned to Maddock. "We are going after them, right?"

Maddock just blinked.

"Dane?"

He finally allowed his eyes to focus. "And do what, Jade?"

Jade's eyebrows creased in a frown. "Stop Hauser," she said, as if the answer was obvious. "Get those relics back."

"How? The relics were the only thing that gave us an edge. Without them…" He shrugged. "Like he said, we're bugs on the sidewalk."

Jade had no answer to that, but Rose did. "Then we

make our own luck, just like my great-grandad did when he first went to the Outpost."

Maddock managed a tight smile. "I guess I'll have to read those Dodge Dalton books when we get out of here."

"Getting out of here might be a good place to start," Bones remarked.

Maddock gazed out into the darkness. There was no sign of Hauser or his gunmen, no way of knowing if they were still there or already long gone. Hauser's final warning still echoed in his ears, but they couldn't remain where they were indefinitely. "All right. But let's take it slow. I don't want to give Hauser any reason to change his mind."

One day, you will understand....

Twenty-six years later, the words still haunted Nick Kismet. The words, and the horror that had preceded them.

One day, you will understand what we have done, and why it had to be done.

Nearly three decades of searching, had brought him no closer to understanding.

Despite the appearance of filial familiarity, Kismet and Hauser had only crossed paths on two previous occasions. That first meeting was the one that stuck in his memory.

In the early hours of what history now called the first Gulf War—a U.S. led coalition to turn back Saddam Hussein's invasion of Kuwait—Kismet, at the time, an Army Intelligence officer, had been sent behind enemy lines, accompanied by a squad of Ghurkas, purportedly to rescue a highly-placed Iraqi defector—a defector who had managed to steal one of the most famous artifacts in history from the secret vaults of the Iraqi national museum. And that was when Ulrich Hauser and Prometheus had stepped into his life, and everything had changed.

Yet, while he had spent the subsequent years trying to learn the truth about Prometheus, it was the memory of what Hauser had done in the moments before making that promise—

One day….

—that filled Kismet with dread.

Hauser had brutally, cold-bloodedly, murdered the Iraqi defector and his entire family.

One day, you will understand what we have done, and why it had to be done.

Kismet didn't understand, and didn't think he ever really would, but he did know what Hauser was capable of. Dane Maddock probably had no idea how narrowly he and the others had avoided the same fate.

As he trudged up the stairs behind Hauser, the way ahead dimly illuminated by the pale green glow of the chem-lights that dangled from tactical vests worn by Hauser and his men his only goal was to put some distance between Hauser and his new friends. He didn't dare lift a finger against his brother until he knew that Maddock and the others were safe.

Shortly after leaving the stairwell and re-entering the maze of passages outside the pyramid, Kismet heard a dull rumbling sound coming from behind them. He turned around, glimpsed something moving, but only for a moment. Then all was still. He squinted into the darkness but all he could see was a featureless stone wall.

The entrance to the passage had just closed.

He whirled around and shouted into the gloom. "Sealing them in wasn't part of the deal. If you want my help, you better leave the door open."

Hauser's reply drifted back to him from further up the tunnel. "It was nothing I did, brother. If I had to guess, I'd say the passage reacts when one of the anomalies is brought into close proximity. Or when they're removed. I can't very well leave any of them here and time is fleeting. But don't worry. Your new friends will be safe down there for at least a day or two. Long enough for us to finish our business."

Kismet knew any further pleas would be futile. And there was a silver lining; although they had only met a few days previously, Dane Maddock didn't seem like the sort of person to just give up and go home. Given the chance, he would come after Hauser.

And probably get himself killed.

He stalked ahead, catching up to Hauser just as the latter ascended the last set of steps back to the surface. "And what exactly is your plan?"

Without breaking stride, Hauser pulled off his night vision goggles and stashed them in the backpack with the elemental relics. The Apex had been added to the collection, along with Kismet's *kukri*. Hauser's men hastened ahead, presumably to make sure the way was clear. "Oh, it's quite simple. We're going to storm heaven and cast the gods down from their thrones."

"Is that supposed to mean something to me?"

Hauser chuckled. "I forget sometimes how little they've allowed you to know. The vault where the collection is kept is code-named Olympus. Where the gods reside." He resumed walking, following the path through the ruins toward the entrance gate. "Once we're in control of Olympus, nobody will be able to oppose us."

"Where is it?"

Hauser chuckled. "It's embarrassing but, TBH, I don't actually know. That's something I was hoping you could help me with."

"Me?" Kismet couldn't help but shake his head. "You're the insider."

"Alas, the location of the vault was the one secret I was never made privy to. I think they were afraid of what I might do if I had direct access to it. Which, I suppose, was wisdom on their part."

"Well they sure as hell didn't tell me."

Hauser said nothing until they reached the open gate. Through it, Kismet saw a line of waiting luxury full-sized sport utility vehicles, surrounded by even more armed commandos deployed in a strategic perimeter.

"While you and Maddock were spinning your wheels in Turkey," Hauser said, "I was busy finding the one person who can tell us where to find the vault. She hasn't told me where it is yet, but eventually she will." He strode to the closest vehicle and gripped the door handle. "I can afford to be patient, but your friends in Alexander's tomb won't have that luxury. I seem to recall that you were an interrogator, once upon a time. Maybe you can get her to talk."

He opened the door, revealing the lone passenger in the spacious interior of the SUV. A woman, late-middle-aged, long straight black hair shot through with gray, framing an olive complexion that, despite a tracery of wrinkles, remained beautiful by almost any standard. Kismet had never seen the woman before, but knew her instantly.

His mother.

"Crap," Bones snarled, kicking the wall that now blocked the stairwell. "Dead end."

Maddock moved closer and shone the light from his phone onto the wall which slanted toward his head, another interior wall of the hollow pyramid. There was no sign of the passage through which they had entered; it seemed to have been erased from the very fabric of reality. "I was afraid something like this might happen," he admitted.

Bones cast an irritated frown at him. "'Let's take it slow,'" he said in a mocking falsetto which Maddock could only assume was meant to be an attempt at mimicking his own voice.

A poor attempt.

"Sorry," Maddock said, disingenuously. "I thought dealing with a potential closed door would be easier than surviving a hail of bullets. Clearly, I wasn't thinking straight."

"Whoa." Bones threw up his hands in an overly-dramatic defensive gesture. "Be careful where you point that sarcasm. You haven't been properly schooled in its use."

Jade laughed, probably enjoying the rare moment of discord between the two friends, but Rose was quick to intervene. "Can we save the recriminations for later? Like when we're out of here?"

"Why wait?" Bones countered. "We're probably gonna be here a while."

"There's got to be a way through," Maddock said,

trying to take Rose's admonition to heart as he continued searching. "If there's a way to move this wall, I don't know what it is. But it looks like it's made of stacked stone blocks. If we can knock one loose, we should be able to break through. We just need something to use as a battering ram."

"We could use Bones' head," Jade suggested. "It's hard enough to smash stone."

"If you think my head is hard—"

"Bones!" Rose said, almost shrieking. "Enough." She stepped closer to Maddock and held something out to him. "Will this help?"

Maddock looked down at the wedge-shaped object she was holding and felt a glimmer of hope. It was the adamantine-infused hatchet head they had recovered from the plane wreck off the South Africa coast. "How did you manage to hang onto that?"

She grinned and shrugged a little. "When Aliyah mentioned that the relics might be causing an interference pattern, I took it out to see if it was still affected. Then I shoved it in my back pocket."

"Has it got any magic power left?" Bones asked, looking over Maddock's shoulder.

Rose waved the axe head back and forth in front of the wall, then brought it forward until metal and stone were in contact. Nothing happened.

"It was worth a shot," Bones muttered. "Now what?"

"Magic or not, it's still a metal tool," Maddock said, reaching out for the tomahawk. He took it from Rose and started tracing the seams with the spike on the back end.

"You actually think you can dig us out with that?" Jade asked, skeptically.

"If you've got a better idea, I'm all ears."

"Hey, if guys can tunnel out of Alcatraz using a spoon," Bones said, "I think we can manage this."

"I feel like you just made that up," Jade retorted, then added a little wistfully, "I wish Professor was here. He'd know."

Maddock exerted a little more pressure on the blade as he dragged it along the seam, and the resulting noise silenced further debate. He was surprised and heartened to see a long groove trailing out behind the point. The metal had scored the old stone as if it were as soft as chalk. Encouraged by this result, he shifted his grip on the tomahawk, holding it like an icepick, and drove the point forward in a hammer blow.

It was a mistake, or at least it seemed that way to him for a few seconds.

There was a bright flash on impact—friction sparks, he guessed—and a throb of pain that shot up his arm all the way to the shoulder. He felt as if he had just touched a live wire. The sensation quickly dulled to a tingle of pins and needles as his overloaded nerves went into shut down mode. The axe head fell from his numb fingers and clattered on the floor, lost from his view in the subsequent eruption of fine rock dust the strike had caused. It was only when the dust began to settle that he saw the need to revise his opinion of the experiment.

A large pockmark—deep enough for Maddock to put both his fists in—marred the stone wall where he had struck it. There were a few large pieces of rock on the floor below but not nearly enough to fill the divot. The rest of it had been pulverized.

"Holy crap," Bones said. "Do that again."

Maddock coughed and tried to blink away some of

the grit that now stung his eyes. "I'm not sure I can," he said. "That nearly took my hand off."

"Don't be such a wuss." Bones knelt to retrieve the hatchet. "Here, let the expert take over."

With his free hand, he tugged his T-shirt up and over his head, baring his upper torso. As he wrapped the fabric around the blade he looked over at Rose, and with a mischievous grin, began flexing his pectoral muscles. "Hey, my eyes are up here."

Jade gave a snort of derision.

"I'm not sure that's going to be enough insulation," Maddock warned.

Bones shook his head disparagingly and muttered, "Wuss." Then with the wrapped blade gripped in both hands, he faced the wall. "Better stand back."

"Bones, seriously, maybe you should—"

Bones raised the tomahawk over his head, and then with an impressive rendition of a Cherokee war whoop, brought it down.

Maddock grimaced and looked away, bracing himself in anticipation of another eruption, but even so, the blast caught him flatfooted. There was another flash, as bright as a camera strobe, and then he was engulfed by a cloud of dust and grit, driven by an expanding bubble of uncomfortably warm air—the shockwave of a small detonation.

As some of the dust settled, Maddock spotted Bones, silhouetted in front of the wall. The big man was protectively hugging both of his hands close to his body, even as he let fly an almost incoherent torrent of invective.

Maddock only caught a few words. "Mother… God… Son of a … Mother." The rest was lost in the din—a grinding sound, like boulders being crushed together, that seemed to be getting louder with each passing second.

"Bones," Jade shouted. "What the hell did you just do?"

Bones fell silent for a moment, then he uncurled one of his arms to point at the wall behind him.

"I did that," Bones said, with more than a trace of pride. "You're welcome."

Through the haze, Maddock could just make out an area that was darker than the surrounding stone. It took him a moment to realize that he was actually looking at nothing—a rectangular void where one of the stone blocks forming the wall had been a moment before. The hole was big enough for even Bones to crawl through.

But the grinding sound was getting louder.

"I think we should—"

Before Maddock could complete his thought, the shape of the neatly defined rectangle of emptiness began to change. The top edge of the hole bowed down, sagging in the middle. Jagged fracture lines began radiating out from the opening like black spiderwebs, and then the entire wall crumbled, unleashing a cascade of rubble that poured down onto the steps and swept toward them like an avalanche.

11

Maddock scrambled back, sidestepping a few larger chunks of debris and ignoring the smaller pieces that brushed against his feet. Bones, closer to the collapse, was knocked backward. He twisted as he fell, throwing his arms wide in a desperate attempt to keep from being swept all the way down. The slide quickly overtook him, partially engulfing him as he slid past Maddock and continued down. Jade, closer to the wall, managed to dance out of the way, but Rose's attempt to dodge the slide took her dangerously close to the edge of the steps.

Fearing that she was about to go over, Maddock threw caution to the wind and, braving the onslaught, charged back up the steps to pull her back. He caught hold of one outflung arm and drew her away from the precipice, but as he did, a large block of stone crashed painfully into his left shin. He pitched forward as his legs were cut out from under him, taking Rose down with him in the fall, and then they were both sliding, caught in the relentless current of crushed stone.

"It's not stopping!"

Jade's shout was barely audible over the ongoing tumult, but Maddock had already realized the truth of her words. The destruction of the stone block had triggered a runaway collapse. Each block that fell out of place dislodged one or two more above it.

The side of the pyramid was collapsing. Worse, the impacts were fracturing the stairwell, obliterating the steps that they would have to ascend in order to reach the surface.

"Keep climbing," he shouted. The admonition was as much for himself as for the others. If they didn't get through that opening quickly, they would be cut off, and in all likelihood, carried down into the depths of the pyramid, entombed forever. "Push through!"

He caught a glimpse of Jade shaking her head, and then she was moving, head ducked low and covered with one upraised arm as she scrambled over the rubble. A moment later, she was gone, vanishing into the dust cloud that still swirled around the opening.

Maddock winced as another rock struck him in the shoulder, but pushed himself up into an awkward kneeling position and crawled forward, putting himself in front of Rose, using his body to shield her. He glanced down the stairs and saw movement in the rockpile. "Bones! You coming?"

A dust-streaked figure emerged from the rubble. "I ain't even breathing heavy, yet."

Maddock just shook his head. Humor—the raunchier the better—was Bones' defensive shield against the universe, but Maddock didn't think it would protect him against the avalanche. He swung his gaze forward again and measured the distance to the now gaping hole in the pyramid's wall.

The damage was spreading out in both directions, collapsing portions of the wall ahead as well as the one to their immediate right, and as they crumbled, everything above fell inward. The buried pyramid was transforming into a sinkhole.

He leaned close to Rose, shouting to be heard over the din. "Keep moving. Don't stop for anything." Then he started forward, crawling on all fours up the rubble pile. As he neared the top, he could see the opening more distinctly. Jade was crouched just inside, still warding off falling rock with one hand, urging him on with the other.

Unfortunately, between him and it was a whole lot of nothing. The last few steps to the opening were gone, fallen into a fissure. It was only about two feet across, but growing wider with each passing second.

Maddock brought his feet up under him in a crouch and then launched himself across the gap. He landed easily, but when Jade reached out with a steadying hand, he did not refuse it. After a moment to catch his balance, he turned and reached out to do the same for Rose.

But in that brief instant, the spot from which he had leaped crumbled away into the fissure, doubling the width of the gap, forcing Rose to retreat.

"Jump!" Jade shouted.

Maddock didn't like Rose's odds of making it across, but seeing no alternatives, he seconded Jade's suggestion and added, "We'll catch you."

Rose's face went slack with trepidation, but she took a deep breath, bent her knees and swung her arms back, gathering momentum for her leap of faith.

Then, seemingly from out of nowhere, Bones appeared beside her. His bare chest and face streaked with dust, he looked more like a giant golem—a creature of living rock—than a man. Without preamble or explanation, he scooped Rose up in his arms, and then propelled her out across the gap.

Maddock caught her easily, pulling her into the relative shelter of the opening. As soon as she was clear, Maddock returned to the edge, "Bones! Jump!"

But Bones was gone.

The woman said nothing; she merely regarded Kismet with a bland, unreadable expression as he climbed into the vehicle, followed by Hauser. Kismet, too, remained silent. One thing he had learned early on in his brief first career as a military intelligence officer was that interrogation was a two-way exchange, with every question, every microexpression, revealing information to the subject.

Yet, even in silence, he knew his reaction had betrayed him.

In truth, he did not think of her as "mother." The circumstances surrounding his birth were shrouded in conjecture and family lore. He was reasonably certain that she was his actual biological parent, but if his suspicions were true, she had served merely as a surrogate—a womb in which he and Ulrich Hauser had gestated. Subsequent events amply demonstrated that she felt no sense of motherly affection or duty toward him. He was simply a variable in some bizarre, secretive experiment. A pawn in the Promethean chess game.

It was true that she had watched over him, shielded him from mortal danger. Hauser had admitted as much in that first encounter. But had she done this because of her feelings for him, or because it advanced her agenda? He suspected the latter.

Even her recent overtures to him, backchanneled through his adoptive father, seemed driven more by her needs—or rather the needs of the traditionalist faction of Prometheus—than by a desire for reconciliation.

The old wisdom about the enemy of his enemy being his friend did not necessarily hold true where Prometheus—or this woman—was concerned. He wasn't yet sure what he wanted her to know about his motives or his loyalties.

Hauser ordered the driver to depart, and as the

convoy pulled away, he made a show of adjusting his position, as if trying to get comfortable in preparation for a long trip. After a few seconds of this, he raised his eyes to the woman. "Mother, look who turned up." A glance to Kismet, then back to the woman. "Wait, have you two actually met?" He laughed. "It's funny, Nick. I got to have her as a mother, but you got to keep her name. I'm not sure which one of us got the better end of that deal."

Kismet once more fought a losing battle to hide his reaction. His unusual surname was one more piece of family lore he had largely taken for granted. Now, at least, he had one answer.

The woman flashed an irritated look at Hauser, but said nothing.

"Mother," Hauser went on. "I brought Nick here in the hopes that he could convince you to tell me how to find Olympus."

She stared at Hauser a moment longer, her eyes narrowing contemptuously. Then she turned to Kismet. "I know what he wants," she said. "What do you want?"

He weighed all his possible answers. Did hedare tell her the truth? Reveal that the lives of Maddock and the others hung in the balance? Would she understand that he was just biding his time, waiting for an opportunity to turn the tables on Hauser? Would she believe that the last thing he wanted was for his psychotic twin brother to gain possession of the elemental artifacts and all the other secrets in the Prometheus vault?

He decided to answer with a different truth. "I want answers."

The corners of her mouth twitched and began to curl upward. "So, my boys are finally getting along. It's about damn time."

"Bones!"

Maddock leaned out of the tunnel opening, searching the dust-shrouded steps for any sign of his friend, but as he did, he felt the edge of the opening giving way beneath him. He scrambled back a fraction of a second ahead of the collapse. The passage filled with dust. The tumult reached a deafening climax, the floor under him shaking in a sustained tremor.

And then all was still.

Maddock crawled forward into the settling dust cloud until he reached the edge. "Bones!"

He waved his hand, trying to swat the cloud away. Somehow, he had managed to hang onto his phone and now shone its light into the emptiness beyond. The motes swirled away, affected more by gravity than anything he was doing, but after a few seconds, it cleared enough for him to see what lay beyond.

There wasn't enough left of the hollow pyramid to recognize what it had once been. The stone blocks that had formed its walls and the long descending staircase now lay mostly in a jumble on the floor of an enormous cavern—or rather a sinkhole. Without the pyramid to support it, the roof had collapsed in. Looking up, Maddock could see starlight.

Movement from below caught his eye, drawing his attention back to the ruin of the cavern. A hand had appeared from just beyond the edge of the passage opening, fingers splayed out, trying to find purchase on the rough surface.

"Bones!" Maddock cried again, his earlier

desperation washed away with a flood of relief. Though he couldn't fathom how Bones had managed to accomplish it, the big man had evidently leaped across the spreading fissure and onto the exposed cavern wall where he had clung to the bare rock, riding out the violent collapse of the pyramid.

Maddock gripped his friend's wrist in both hands and leaned back, giving the big man an assist. Bones' other hand came up and then with a dynamic heave, his upper torso rose into view, allowing him to wriggle forward onto the floor of the passage where he collapsed and lay motionless for several seconds. But despite his obvious exhaustion, behind his mask of dust and grime, Bones was grinning.

"Well," he said, "I think that finally settles the question of who's the best climber."

Maddock gaped at him in disbelief. "Seriously?" He shook his head. "Don't you mean luckiest?"

"Aw, you're just jealous, 'cause you couldn't have solved that problem."

"Bones, you *caused* the problem."

"You know, that's always been your problem. You see a silver lining and you start looking for the dark cloud. We made it out of there." He straightened, evidently remembering something. "Oh, speaking of silver linings…"

He reached to his back pocket and produced the hatchet head. The metal gleamed brightly, without a single scratch to mar its surface. He handed it to Rose. "I think this belongs to you."

"And speaking of dark clouds," Jade put in, "What are we going to do now?"

"Do?" asked Bones. "You mean aside from crawling

out of this hell hole and heading back to the hotel for beer, a shower and a bed?"

"We have to help Nick."

"Help him?" Bones snorted. "After what he did? Not a chance."

"Bones, even you can't be that thick. He did that to save us."

"If you call leaving us buried alive 'saving us'?"

Maddock jumped in. "She's right. And there's an even better reason to go after them. We need to stop Hauser from getting his hands on that fourth relic."

"How are we supposed to do that? We don't have a clue where it is."

Maddock considered this question for a moment. "I think I know someone who might be able to help with that."

12

Long Island, New York

Professor accelerated, shooting straight across three lanes of oncoming traffic, before hooking left and joining the flow of traffic heading the other direction. The car fishtailed back and forth, confounding his efforts to regain control.

"Look out," Jimmy warned, pointing a finger at a gray van directly ahead and coming up fast.

Professor swerved over into the inside lane, almost sideswiping the van, and then they were past.

Ahead, the red sports car he was pursuing took a hard-right turn.

"Turn right," Jimmy cried. "Stay with him!"

"I know," Professor snapped, and then muttered under his breath. "This is impossible."

He steered hard, realizing only as the front end swung around that the turn wasn't merely a hard right—it was a hairpin, curving almost completely around to ascend up the hillside that ran parallel to the highway. Even so, Professor mistimed the turn. The front end bounced up onto the sidewalk, narrowly missing a group of people who were standing on the corner, evidently waiting for a bus. Suddenly, the hillside was right in front of him. He tried to simultaneously brake and cut to the right, but failed to do either one. The car slammed into the hill, ejecting him into the air like a rag doll, tumbling in slow motion.

The wall-mounted 120-inch plasma screen went gray, the image frozen, and then a single word appeared slashed across its middle. "Wasted."

Jimmy sat back laughing. "Oh, dude. That was epic."

Professor resisted the urge to hurl the wireless computer-game controller against the wall. "I don't know why I let you talk me into this."

"Right, because there are so many other things we could be doing right now," Jimmy countered, still chuckling.

Professor sighed resignedly and settled back to wait for his character to respawn. Jimmy wasn't wrong. With the Prometheus situation still unresolved, Jimmy didn't dare venture out into the world, much less return to his life, and until Tam Broderick said otherwise, babysitting Jimmy was his top priority, which meant he wasn't going anywhere either.

There were far worse places to spend a week. Christian Garral's home was, by most definitions, a mansion, which meant there was plenty to keep them occupied. Garral himself was both hospitable and garrulous, which meant plenty of good food and drink, and even better conversation. Still, after a few days, Professor felt he had exhausted the list of intellectual diversions, which was why he had decided to join Jimmy in the game room. The journalist had hardly left the room during the course of their stay. Evidently, Garral's Alienware computer provided a transcendent gaming experience. For his part, Professor was astonished at the cinematic quality of the games, many of which had storylines as complex as some novels, with gameplay that required lightning reflexes and eye-hand coordination. After a few hours of watching as a spectator, Jimmy had offered him a turn.

It had been a long time since he had felt so

completely inept. Learning to use the controls was like learning how to type in a foreign language or play an unfamiliar musical instrument. The in-game tutorial had helped. A little. But now he was on his own and failing spectacularly at tasks that, in real life, he could have accomplished with ease. The worst part was, he felt compelled to keep playing.

A gentle knock on the game room door distracted him. He looked up to see Garral enter the room, phone in hand. "Excuse the interruption gentleman, but I think you'll want to join me for this call."

He placed the phone on the coffee table in front of the couch where Professor and Jimmy sat. "You're on speaker, Mr. Maddock."

"Dane?" Jimmy sat up. So did Professor.

There was a brief lag and then Maddock's voice issued from the device. "Hey, Jimmy. Professor, you're there, too?"

"I am, Dane."

"Great. I think we're going to need all hands on deck for this one." Maddock then launched into a narrative describing everything that had happened subsequent to their discovery of the plane wreck.

Professor was astonished to learn that Jade and Kismet had gotten embroiled in the adventure. While he had been babysitting Jimmy, they, along with Dane and Bones, had traveled to the literal ends of the earth, facing danger and making incredible discoveries. He was also surprisingly relieved to hear that Jade had come through it all without serious injury. Looking out for her was, after all, still his primary responsibility.

But as Maddock related the events that had just transpired in Egypt, he realized that Jade's continued safety was far from guaranteed. Prometheus—or rather, Ulrich Hauser, the apparent leader of the radical faction—was close to unlocking some kind of supernatural power that would fundamentally change the shape of the world, and Jade, along with Maddock and Bones, were intent on stopping them.

Even if it cost them their lives.

"We know that Hauser is going after the fourth elemental relic," Maddock concluded, "And it sounds like Prometheus has it. We've got to beat him to it. Unfortunately, we don't have a clue about its location."

Garral's already grave frown deepened. "I'm sorry, but I don't have that information. The location of the vault is a secret known only by a handful of Prometheus' leaders. And their identities are secret as well."

"You know someone though," Professor put in. "You've got an inside source."

Garral nodded slowly, clearly conflicted at the position he had been put in. "Yes. If anyone would know, she would. And since this concerns Nick, I believe she will help."

"She?" asked Maddock. "You're talking about Nick's mom, aren't you?"

Garral's chagrined look was answer enough. "Unfortunately, making contact with her is equally problematic. She's always been the one to initiate our conversations."

"How do you usually communicate?" asked Jimmy.

"Mostly burner phones, delivered by couriers. Sometimes SMS chat, but she always uses a throwaway account."

Jimmy's eyes narrowed in concentration. "If you'd be willing to let me poke around in your files, I might be able to get a line on her."

Garral nodded. Jimmy immediately picked up the wireless keyboard, closed out the video game, and went to work.

"That sounds like it's going to take some time," intoned Maddock. "And we don't have a lot of that to spare right now. Hauser's already on the move."

"I can definitely help with that," Jimmy replied. "He'll probably fly out. Private jet or chartered flight, right? He'll have to file a flight plan."

"I'm sure he'll cover his tracks," Professor countered.

"I'm sure he will, too. But I've got mad skills." Jimmy entered a few keystrokes, and a new window opened on the plasma screen. Under a blue header which bore the logo of the International Civil Aviation Organization, a table displayed all the flights departing Alexandria, Egypt.

"He also doesn't know that we made it out of that tomb," Maddock added. "He might not be as careful as he ordinarily would. My guess is, he's got just one thing on his mind. He'll probably go straight to wherever it is he's going."

Jimmy just nodded absently and continued navigating the site, changing back and forth between screens faster than Professor could follow, and after a few seconds he stopped trying. "Dane, you should probably head for Cairo immediately. From there, you'll have a lot more travel options, and hopefully by the time you get there, we'll have a better idea of where they're headed."

"Beat you to it," Jimmy announced before Maddock could reply. "I know where they're going."

Professor glanced up at the screen and saw displayed

the information for a charter flight that was scheduled to depart Alexandria in a matter of minutes. He blinked. "How do you know it's that one?"

"Well, for starters, the flight plan was just amended thirty minutes ago. The original destination was Paris, but now there's an addendum. Longyearben, Norway. My backtrace on the hacker that locked me out of my proxy network ended at the SvalSat facility just outside Longyearben. At the time, I thought they had outsmarted me. Roped me down a rabbit hole, but I think maybe I outsmarted myself."

Maddock's voice sounded after the requisite delay. "But that could just be a coincidence, right? We can't afford to run down that rabbit hole after you."

"Sure, it's possible. But Longyearben is remote. It's not the kind of place you just decide to visit on a whim."

A new and familiar voice issued from the speaker—"Bones" Bonebrake. "When you say 'remote'…?"

"Longyearben is in the Svalbard Archipelago," Professor supplied. "It's north of the Arctic Circle, the closest city to the North Pole."

"Svalbard," Maddock said. "Isn't that where the Doomsday Vault is?"

"The technical name for it is the Svalbard Global Seed Vault, but yes, it's a man-made cave carved into a mountain, containing frozen samples of diverse flora, against the possibility of a catastrophic event."

"You're shitting me," Bones said with a groan. "Another frozen wasteland? Why can't they ever put these things somewhere nice? Like Maui?"

"The surrounding permafrost helps keep the vault at a constant temperature of zero degrees Fahrenheit." He paused a beat, then added. "The Seed Vault would be the perfect cover for a Prometheus treasure vault. I think Jimmy's right. That's where they're going."

"Then that's where we have to go," Maddock said. "Mr. Garral, I hate to ask but—"

Garral cut him off. "You don't need to. There will be a jet waiting for you in Cairo. And I'll be waiting for you in Oslo."

"We all will," Professor said. He glanced at Garral and got a nod of confirmation.

After ending the call, Garral gave a heavy sigh. "People talk about being willing to go to the ends of the earth for their children. It seems I'll be doing that quite literally."

Professor had no doubt that Garral was capable of enduring whatever hardships lay ahead, and Kismet was his son, after all.

Jimmy cleared his throat. "Umm, I need some clarification on something. When you said we would all be there—?"

"I meant all of us. You heard Dane. All hands on deck."

"I think I'd be a lot more use to everyone if I stayed right here."

Professor fixed Jimmy with a hard stare. "The Svalbard Seed Vault is one of the most secure facilities on earth. If anyone can beat their security system, it's you."

"I can walk you through remotely—"

Professor shook his head. "That's not going to cut it. We'll need your expertise on the ground."

Jimmy blanched.

"This shouldn't be hard for you," Professor went on. "I've seen you in action. You walked into the NSA, for

God's sake. Just think of it as a real-life video game."

"A video game where I could get killed."

Professor gripped the other man's shoulder. "Jimmy, do you remember ringing the bell?"

For a moment, Jimmy appeared confused by the non-sequitur, but then his expression tightened and he jerked away from Professor. "How dare you—"

"For a long time, I thought of you as just another quitter. Big dreams and a little heart. But I was wrong about you. You just had a bad day."

Jimmy glowered at him for several seconds, then spoke through clenched teeth. "You gotta point, coach?"

"You promised Dane that you and he would finish BUD/S together. You remember that?"

"I've done more for Maddock than you can possibly imagine."

"This isn't about Maddock. It's about you. Finishing what you started. Proving it to yourself."

Jimmy's eyes danced. He glanced over at Garral, who looked on in stony silence, and then back to Professor. "You can't make me go, you know."

"Actually, I could." He paused a beat, letting that sink in, then added. "But I'm not going to because you're not going to ring the bell this time."

He didn't give Jimmy a chance to respond but turned to Garral.

"We'd better get moving."

PART THREE: HEAVEN KNOWS

13

Svalbard Territory, Norway

From a distance, the Svalbard Global Seed Vault resembled nothing less than a charcoal gray shark fin, inexplicably tipped with an enormous glittering diamond, knifing through an endless sapphire sea. The sea of course was frozen, a white snowscape that so perfectly reflected the night sky—at this time of year and so far north, there was only night sky—it was impossible to tell where one began and the other ended.

The diamond was an illuminated art piece entitled *Perpetual Repercussion*, a flat pane of glass behind which mirrors and prisms redirected and amplified natural light when available, and artificial light, delivered by fiber optic cables, during the long winter to give the piece its glow. It now shone like a beacon guiding the riders on their snowmobiles to the vault's doorstep.

Kismet drove his snowmobile—a SkiDoo MXZ 800 rented from an adventure tour outfitter in Longyearbyen—with one of Hauser's men seated directly behind him in the one-up position. The passenger was armed, the driver was not. Hauser's trust only went so far, it seemed. Two more SkiDoos carried four more of Hauser's security team. Hauser drove the fourth, with their mother seated behind him.

"I don't even know what to call you," Kismet had told the woman, the previous night during the drive to the airport in Alexandria, even before she had revealed the location of Olympus.

"I don't suppose I could convince you to call me 'mom,'" she had said with a wry smile. When he didn't respond, she went on. "Call me Leda."

"Leda," Kismet echoed. In Greek mythology, Leda had been the mortal mother of Castor and Pollux—twins sired by different fathers, one mortal—Tyndareus, king of Sparta—and one immortal—Zeus, king of the gods. Kismet doubted it was her real name, but chose not to press the issue.

"I'm sure you must be full of questions," she said. "I've wanted to answer them for so long."

"Why didn't you?"

He had an idea what her answer would be. During their second encounter, Hauser had told him about Prometheus' grand experiment, the two of them, products of some kind of engineered union, separated at birth, one—Kismet—sent out into the world with no knowledge of his heritage, watched over and occasionally protected by Prometheus, but never told the truth.

She smiled ruefully. "It wasn't the right time."

"And now it is?"

"Now it is."

When they were in the air aboard Hauser's chartered jet, winging north to a planned refueling stop in Paris before heading on to Longyearbyen, she told the story from the beginning over a bottle of Bordeaux. Hauser shared the bottle with her, saying nothing. Kismet declined.

"Much of what I am about to tell you is conjecture," Leda began, "but it is, we believe, an accurate approximation of the true prehistory of our world.

"There are common threads woven through the various mythologies of creation. One of these is a story of gods or god-like beings, putting on corporeal bodies, walking among men, taking mortal women for mates. In most stories, the offspring of the union is a demi-god— Gilgamesh, Perseus, Herakles. There are demigods in Hindu mythology. Norse. Celtic… As I said, it is a constant thread. In the religions of the Abrahamic tradition, they are called Nephilim—the mighty ones, and are said to be the children of fallen angels." Leda paused to take a sip of wine and perhaps also let the gravity of her story sink in.

"These stories are all true," she said, and then quickly amended. "After a fashion."

"Let me guess. You don't want to say it's aliens, but…"

Leda did not smile. "We call them 'the Ancients.' Rather prosaic, I suppose, but it suffices. We do not speculate on their origins, but we do believe that they were non-corporeal entities. They constructed artificial organic bodies to use as vessels—"

"Artificial organic? That sounds like an oxymoron."

"Artificial because they were created," Leda clarified. "The product of artifice. Organic because they were made to perfectly simulate the organic functions of a human body, right down to procreation.

"What happened after that is not known with certainty. Some believe the Flood myths—another nearly universal thread—are evidence of some kind of upheaval that prompted their departure, as described in early Jewish and Christian documents. Others they simply grew tired of their existence here and moved on. Returned whence they came. Whatever the explanation, they left those magnificent bodies behind. We know this because we have several of them at Olympus."

Despite the lead-in, the revelation caught Kismet off guard. "You have the... The god-bodies?"

"God-bodies," Hauser said with a chuckle. "I like that."

Leda smiled. "They appear as statues of gold, and indeed, many were discovered in temple ruins. The gold exhibits an unusual chemical signature—a stable anion that can store electrical current."

"Like the Golden Fleece," Kismet murmured.

Leda gave a satisfied nod. "You hear the truth of it, I can tell." She paused, took another sip. "You may recall in the legend that Jason encountered a metal giant named Talos. In some versions, he is a god, in others, an automaton created by Hephaestus. Regardless, Jason defeated him by removing a nail from Talos' heel, which allowed his blood—a molten substance called *ichor*, the blood of the gods—to drain out.

"About fifty years ago, Prometheus scientists made careful examinations of the god-bodies and discovered traces of a liquid metal that reacted to a strong electrical current. And when these traces were reintroduced into the god-bodies, they began to show signs of activity.

"Not life," she added quickly. "Something more akin to neuro-muscular activity. Like a postmortem muscle spasm. It is possible that ancient priests with a rudimentary understanding of electricity might have elicited a similar response, seemingly animating the statues of their gods. In any event, the effect was short-lived and the sample of charged *ichor* evaporated, but it was enough to inform our theory of the Ancients. And to begin designing other experiments."

Kismet suddenly felt nauseated, his head spinning with vertigo that had nothing to do with motion sickness from the flight. "Experiments," he rasped.

It wasn't a question. He already knew the answer.

The party dismounted their snowmobiles in front of a wide metal ramp that rose to the double doors at the entrance. From this perspective, the entrance to the seed vault looked like an ominous rectangular monolith—three stories high. The doors occupied the lower third of the towering edifice. A louvered ventilation screen, part of the refrigeration system, filled the middle, and the top was dominated by the glittering illuminated *Perpetual Repercussion.*

The entrance to the seed vault was only a short ride by snowmobile, though it seemed to take much longer. The desolate landscape had a haunted aura about it, which their arrival did not dispel.

Kismet glanced up at the video camera mounted above the door. There was no permanent staff at the Global Seed Vault—it was a repository, not a research facility. The only reason for anyone to visit, aside from occasional maintenance, was to add to the collection of seeds.

It was, Kismet thought, the perfect cover for the Prometheus operation—a repository of a different sort.

Leda had briefly explained that there was an "arrangement" between the Norwegian government and Prometheus, which was why their unscheduled visit would raise no alarms.

She advanced to the doors, producing the ring of keys she had retrieved from a vacant guest apartment in

Longyearbyen. Kismet surmised the dwelling was intended to provide temporary housing for visiting members of Prometheus' inner circle. In the sparsely populated city, where turnover was high, what was one more empty apartment?

Kismet recalled reading that no one person had all the keys and access codes necessary to enter the vault. Evidently, the "arrangement" included an exception for the senior leadership of Prometheus.

Leda used three different keys to open deadbolt locks and then pulled the door open. Hauser pushed past her, though in fact there was little to see beyond the doors. The entrance was unremarkable; a long corridor of unpainted concrete illuminated by hanging fluorescent lights. Though shielded somewhat from the elements, there was no relief from the bitter Arctic chill, so the party remained bundled up against the cold. Enveloped in heavy parkas, faces hidden behind neoprene masks, the only way for Kismet to differentiate the members of the group was by seeing who was armed and who was not. His mother and he were the only ones in the latter category. That commonality however did not make them allies.

Leda had not given Kismet time to process the revelation. "When it became apparent that two viable embryos had been cultivated, the decision was made to separate the two of you. In the old stories, demigods who were unaware of their parentage were often noble, heroic, while those who grew up knowing the truth were cruel and oppressive. Entitled."

She glanced sidelong at Hauser who laughed loudly.

"And why not?" he said, deflecting the implicit criticism. "They were superior."

Leda ignored the comment. "In every experiment, there is a control. We found a suitable father to raise you, give you a good life… A full life. Every choice that you made was yours and yours alone."

Kismet drew in a deep breath. "The mission in Iraq. Was that a mistake?"

Leda and Hauser shared a look, an unspoken conversation, then she answered. "In a word, yes. The defector was a recent initiate into Prometheus. He knew of you, knew just enough to believe that you would be able to give him and his family safe passage out of Iraq."

"So why didn't you let me?" Kismet turned his stare on Hauser. "Why did you have to kill his whole family?"

Hauser merely shrugged, but Leda was not so dismissive. "There was a disagreement about how to proceed. You know how that argument ended. The consequences of that decision nearly destroyed us. It was the genesis of the schism that still divides us. More importantly however, it set you on the path to discovery. Every demigod must one day awaken to his true nature. The time for experimentation is over. It's time for you to embrace who and what you are." She glanced at Hauser again. "Both of you."

Kismet shook his head. The revelations had left him numb. *This can't be true. Ancient alien visitors. Demigods. This is just another one of their head games.*

Yet, he knew it was true. Every word of it.

He straightened, took a deep breath. "I thought you two were at each other's throats. You're with the traditionalists. He's leading the radicals. Now we're all one big happy family?"

"He's right, you know," Hauser said, answering quickly as if the question had been weighing on him. "This is so like you, mother. Manipulative and duplicitous. I'm sorry, but I don't trust you."

She shook her head. "You were always a foolish boy, Rick. Headstrong. Refusing to wait your turn. This was always going to be your destiny."

Hauser's eyes narrowed. "You're lying. You opposed me at every turn."

"Because it wasn't time," Leda hissed.

"I decide when it's time."

"No," she said, flatly. "I made that decision when I told you where to find Olympus."

Hauser regarded her for several seconds, then without looking away, addressed Kismet. "What do you think, brother? Sending us to the end of the earth like this… Is she telling the truth, or leading us into a trap?" He shrugged. "I can handle whatever she throws at me, but the clock is ticking for your friends."

For the first time since their introduction, a look of alarm came over Leda's features. She had not been aware of the leverage Hauser had used to convince Kismet to join him. She stared at Kismet, brows furrowing in apprehension, but just as quickly, relaxed again.

"Whatever else I am," she said, "I am your mother. You have a destiny. Both of you. And I want you to succeed. Prometheus was only ever the means to that end. Olympus holds the key to your ascendance… Your apotheosis. You will become gods among men, and I… Well, I will be the mother of gods."

That, Kismet believed.

There was another double door at the end of the corridor, this one secured with an electronic lock. Leda tapped the access code into the keypad and the lock disengaged. Beyond it lay a long descending tunnel with curved sides covered in ice. As soon as they were through the doors, Leda pulled them shut again, locking them inside.

Despite his polar garments, Kismet felt colder here, as if the dry air was sucking the life out of him. They were deep inside the mountain now, surrounded by permafrost, though in reality the temperature in the vault was artificially maintained by refrigeration units. The electricity that powered the so-called Doomsday Vault was supplied by Norway's only coal-fired power plant, located in Longyearbyen.

They passed by a few unmarked doors, coming to a T-junction. The ice accumulation here was even thicker, a couple inches at least, glittering white in contrast to the gray concrete floor. Leda steered them to the right, down a short hall that dead-ended. On the left, almost completely hidden by the ice scrim was another set of double doors.

Leda brushed the ice away from the door level with one gloved hand, and then slotted in a key from her ring. The door opened, revealing a small room with another set of doors against the far wall. When they were all inside the room, she pulled the door shut, sealing them in. Kismet could feel a subtle change in both temperature and air pressure. This was an airlock, though not a hermetically sealed one. With the outer door closed, the electronic lock on the inner door released automatically. Beyond was a room that looked like an enormous warehouse, with long rows of metal rack shelving, but every single one completely empty.

Hauser swore angrily. "There's nothing here, mother."

"As far as the public is concerned," Leda explained patiently, "there are three vaults here. Currently, only vault two is in use and it is not yet at full capacity. There is, however, another vault of which the public has no knowledge."

She advanced to the open cage gate and started down the middle row. Curious despite himself, Kismet hurried after her, with Hauser and his men trailing behind.

Even up close, the back wall appeared to be covered in ice like everything else, but as she approached a spot near the corner, Leda stripped off her right glove and reached out to touch the white crystals bare-handed. A chunk of ice the size of a dinner plate separated from the wall, swinging away on hidden hinges to reveal a square of black glass. She pressed her hand flat against it, and after a few seconds, a light flashed behind the glass. A biometric palm reader, Kismet realized.

As soon as Leda removed her hand from the glass, a loud hiss echoed in the still air, and then the entire wall began to move, separating into halves which swiveled inward to create a passage into another vault, considerably larger than the space they currently occupied. In fact, Kismet could not see to the far end. There were no racks of shelves here, but the vault was by no means empty. Arrayed on the bare floor, lined up like gigantic chess pieces awaiting the beginning of a game, were dozens of sculpted human figures, each one at least eight feet in height—some much larger than that—and each one gleaming brightly with light reflecting from their polished golden skin.

Leda calmly replaced her glove. When the walls stopped moving, she gestured forward. "Well boys, would you like to meet your father?"

Not really, Kismet thought sourly, but before he could voice his revulsion at the idea, Hauser spoke up.

"Sorry mother, but the family reunion will have to wait." He held up the backpack he'd taken from Rose in Alexandria, but there was something unusual about it now. The straps were pulled taut, but instead of dangling straight down, gravity tugging the contents toward the center of the earth, the bag was hanging sideways. The elemental relics inside were being drawn toward something inside the vault. Hauser grinned hungrily. "I have more pressing business."

14

Dane Maddock peered through the lenses of his Nikon Aculon A211 binoculars and studied the area around the dark wedge protruding from the mountainside below. The surrounding snow was glowing a brighter shade of blue in the reflected light of the illuminated art piece, and he was easily able to distinguish four snowmobiles parked nearby. They had arrived just a few minutes earlier, the riders dismounting and heading into that imposing structure with the ominous nickname—the Doomsday Vault. Maddock kept scanning the area, ensuring that none of the recently arrived party was remaining outside to guard the snowmobiles. When he was satisfied that this was the case, he lowered the binoculars and unclipped a Motorola T600 Talkabout radio from the tactical gear vest he wore over his North Face parka. He keyed the mic and spoke. "Bones, you copy?"

"Only when I don't know the answer," came the reply.

Maddock rolled his eyes. It was a terrible joke, but at least Bones had stopped griping about the cold. "I think this is the place," Maddock continued. "Those snowmobiles that passed us went straight to the seed vault and stopped. Four machines, eight riders."

There was a momentary pause, probably just long enough for Bones to relay the information to the rest of the group, and then he spoke again. "You sure they aren't just there to shovel the walk?"

"Pretty sure," Maddock said.

Christian Garral had been unable to reach his contact inside Prometheus, which meant there had been no way to confirm the supposition that the secret facility was located at or near the Global Seed Vault, but given the timing, there was little doubt as to the real identity of the group that had just entered it.

There had been another plane parked on the runway of the Svalbard Longyear airport, and a check of the tail numbers confirmed it was the same plane that had left Alexandria almost twelve hours earlier. A discreet inquiry revealed that the first plane had landed a little over an hour before them—two arrivals in such a short time span was a noteworthy event on the remote island—and while they had not been able to confirm the identity of the passengers, they at least knew how many of them had deplaned. Seven men and one woman.

That news had plainly startled Christian Garral. The woman, he told them, was in all likelihood his contact inside Prometheus—Leda Hauser nee Kismet. Nick Kismet's mother.

During the flight to Oslo, Maddock and Bones had teleconferenced with Professor, and done extensive map reconnaissance of Spitzbergen Island, where the Seed Vault was situated. The vault was only about half-a-mile from the airport, so rather than traveling into Longyearbyen to rent snowmobiles, the decision was made to depart directly from the plane, traveling overland on foot using snowshoes. Bones had grumbled about the cold until Professor pointed out that the exertion of hiking through the snow would generate so much body heat that freezing to death would be the least of his concerns. After that, Bones had complained about overheating.

A half-mile snowshoe trek would be no picnic, so Maddock had given everyone the option of remaining behind at the plane. He wasn't actually that worried about their physical ability; Rose and Jade were certainly capable. Garral had been a professional mountaineer and explorer in his younger days, and still appeared to be in prime condition. Maddock's real concern was what would happen when they finally confronted Hauser. He saw no outcome that did not end in violence, and in such a situation, he would need people trained for combat like himself—Bones and Professor had that training. Everyone else would be a liability.

On the other hand, a few extra guns might make all the difference, and while the others weren't former SEALs, they all had some experience. In any event, no one had taken him up on the offer, though Jimmy had shifted nervously in his seat, shooting glances at Professor. Maddock had no idea what the latter had said to convince Jimmy to tag along, and Jimmy wasn't talking.

Maybe later, when this was over, he'd have to ply Jimmy with some Wild Turkey.

Jimmy, Professor, and Garral had been waiting for them in Oslo, along with snowshoes, cold weather gear, and even weapons—hunting rifles, which Garral explained were necessary for travel to the Svalbard territory where polar bears outnumbered people. Garral had also discreetly supplied Maddock and Bones each with a not-strictly-legal Glock 20 10-millimeter semi-automatic pistol.

While Bones and Professor led the main party up a poorly marked road from the airport, Maddock scouted ahead. His intention was to climb partway up the side of the mountain into which the seed vault had been carved in order to get a top-down look at the site, but shortly after beginning his ascent, he'd heard the noise of snowmobiles coming down the road from Longyearbyen.

The riders had blazed past, taking no note of his tracks, and continued on to the Seed Vault.

Hauser had won the race to reach the secret Prometheus facility, but not by much.

Maddock keyed his radio mic again. "Come on up. I'll meet you at the entrance."

Bones said something—it might have been something off-color or simply an acknowledgment, but Maddock had already returned the walkie-talkie to his vest and brought his rifle—a Remington 700, bolt action with a wooden stock—to the low ready. He started down the hill, backtracking down to the road below. Polar bears were a real concern, but avalanche was an even greater danger, especially here on the side of a mountain, so he moved slowly, careful to avoid triggering a slide.

As he neared the road, he spotted a line of human figures trudging toward him from the east. They were still a good hundred yards away, moving slower than his average walking pace, hampered somewhat by fatigue and unfamiliarity with snowshoes, but they were moving. Rather than wait for them, he turned toward their destination and continued to the entrance to the seed vault, moving easily in the trail of packed snow left by the snowmobiles.

Maddock stopped at the metal walkway and unclipped his bindings and stepped out of his snowshoes, stabbing the paddle-shaped aluminum frames into a snowbank, tail-end down. He glanced back and saw the rest of his party approaching. The towering figure in the lead—almost certainly Bones—was advancing at a jog, his rifle at the ready, but the rest were spaced out unevenly behind him, with some clearly struggling to stay on their feet, using their ski poles for balance.

"Come on," he muttered, knowing that his exhortation would go unheard. "We're running out of time."

He couldn't wait any longer. As soon as Bones reached him, he gestured to the door. "Cover me. I'm going to try the door."

Bones nodded and, without pausing to remove his snowshoes, took a knee and aimed his rifle at the door. Maddock let his rifle hang from its sling and reached inside his parka for the Glock pistol. Extreme cold could play havoc with semi-automatic weapons, freezing ordinary gun lubricants and deforming plastic and metal components, so he had kept the weapon inside the coat, close to his body to minimize exposure to the sub-zero temperatures, even though doing so meant that it wouldn't be within easy reach. He held the pistol in his extended right hand, and reached for the door handle with his left.

A nasally voice cried out. "Wait!"

Maddock grimaced, and turned back to see one of the figures—it had to be Jimmy—stumbling forward, waving his arms. He made it a few steps before the front of his snowshoe snagged the snow and his attempt to run ended with him going face down, half-buried in white powder. He struggled back up and started forward again.

As impressed as he was at his friend's tenacity, Maddock shook his head. "Jimmy, we have to go in.

Now. Get behind some cover."

Jimmy kept advancing coming up right behind Bones. To his credit, he made it the rest of the way without falling. "Just wait," he said again, panting to catch his breath. "Wait. I didn't let you guys drag me all the way out here so I could just sit in the rear with the gear."

Maddock wasn't sure what Jimmy was trying to say. Did he want to be part of the assault?

Jimmy wasn't reaching for his gun however. Instead, he unslung his backpack and pulled out a laptop computer. He tromped across the bridge to join Maddock in the lee of the entrance, and knelt beside him, balancing the computer on one knee.

"Jimmy, I don't think you're going to get WiFi out here," Bones said. He still had his rifle up, ready to fire at anyone who might come through the door.

"And that's why you don't get paid to think," Jimmy shot back without looking up. As the screen lit up, he stripped off his gloves and began tapping at the keyboard. After a few seconds of this, he let out a whoop of triumph. "Yes!" He pumped his fist, but then thrust the bare hand into the depths of his parka for warmth. "As I suspected, the security system here transmits data by secure satellite connection."

Understanding dawned for Maddock. "So you can hack into it?"

"I can hack into it," Jimmy confirmed, resuming his keystrokes. "It's a secure transmission, like a sat-phone. Give me a minute."

Maddock pursed his lips. Even a minute seemed like an indulgence. And even if Jimmy succeeded, it wouldn't change the fact that they would, in all likelihood, have to fight their way in. "Just keep at it," he told Jimmy. He glanced back and saw that the rest of the group had arrived. "Professor. Come back me up. We'll go in—"

"Got it!" Jimmy announced. He turned the laptop so Maddock could see the screen, which was divided into several smaller screens displaying what appeared to be nondescript hallways and empty warehouses.

"This is real time?"

"Live from the Doomsday Vault," Jimmy confirmed. He pointed to the screen, his finger moving from one static image to the next. "This is the entrance. These are different angles of the tunnel. These cover the vault doors. And here's vault two, the only one currently in use."

The indicated image showed what looked like the aisles of a big box store, but instead of bulk groceries, the rack shelves held gray tote boxes.

"Not much to look at," Jimmy said, almost apologetically.

"There's no one there."

Jimmy just shrugged. "Sorry. Maybe they're standing somewhere the cameras can't see."

Maddock shook off his disappointment. "Good work, Jimmy. At least we know what's on the other side of this door." He reached out for it again and tugged on the handle.

The door swung open. Unlocked.

Leading with his pistol, Maddock moved inside, but the interior was empty, just as the video feed indicated. At the far end of a short hallway was another door with a numeric keypad mounted on the wall beside it. He hurried forward and tried the door handle.

Locked.

He looked at the keypad then back at the open door behind him. The others were already filing in. "Jimmy, can you open this?"

The other man started to shake his head, but then stopped and came forward to take a closer look at it. "Maybe."

He said it slowly, pausing between the syllables so that it sounded like two separate words. "May. Be." Maddock took that as a good sign.

Jimmy dipped into his pack and brought out a black cable with plugs on either end. He inserted one into his laptop and then found a port on the underside of the keypad into which he plugged the other end.

Maddock took a step back, letting the other man do his magic. Then he felt a tugging on his arm. It was Rose. "Dane, look."

She was holding a piece of parachute cord, from which dangled the adamantine-infused tomahawk head. But it wasn't hanging down. Instead, it was pulling straight ahead, pointing right at the door.

"Definitely the right place," she said with a grin of triumph.

15

The fourth elemental relic was not a tablet upon which the secrets of alchemy had been inscribed, nor was it a sword in the conventional sense, but it was a large green crystal, shining with a brilliant glow that seemed too bright to merely be a reflection of the overhead fluorescent bulbs. Kismet could see how it might easily be described as a sword. The crystal was flat and broad—about four inches across—and long, at least twenty-four inches, tapering to points at either end.

One other detail made it appear sword-like. It was held in a two-handed grip over the chest of a figure lying in repose on a bier near the center of the vault, a remarkably life-like image of an athletic looking man. Like the giant statues they had passed on the way in, it appeared to be made entirely of gold.

There was a strange energy radiating from the golden figure—not the light from the emerald, but something else. Something invisible, a hum of potential energy. The crystal itself seemed to be vibrating imperceptibly, straining against the fixed grip, no doubt attracted to the elemental relics Hauser carried in the backpack. The hum was either above or below the threshold of human hearing, but Kismet felt it in every cell of his body—a vague but growing sense of unease. He swallowed, his mouth dry.

"Alexander the Great," Leda explained, though Kismet had already guessed as much.

"Was he one of your Ancients?" he asked.

"No. Just a man who thought he was a demi-god. When he died, his body was placed in a golden coffin cast from his form. According to some historical accounts, the golden coffin was replaced by one made of glass by Ptolemy X, so the gold could be melted down in order to pay debts incurred in his war to hold the throne he'd taken from his older brother. The act so outraged the citizens of Alexandria that he was deposed, exiled and eventually killed. In actuality, the priests of Hermes arranged a deception. They gave Ptolemy gold out of their own treasury, and created a sculpted facsimile of Alexander for display in the glass coffin. This golden sheath containing Alexander's physical remains was hidden away in a secret tomb beneath the Serapeum where it remained undisturbed and was eventually forgotten." She looked over at him. "Until we found it and brought it here."

"Why the subterfuge?"

"An obvious explanation is that the priests revered Alexander and saw the emperor's actions as a desecration. However, our research has yielded a different explanation. Alexander's body is radioactive."

Kismet resisted the urge to recoil. Was that the energy he had been sensing? He knew he could almost instantly recover from most injuries, but radiation wasn't like a knife blade or a bullet. In fact, just the opposite, because his seeming immortality was the result of rapid cellular regeneration, and since gamma rays could wreak havoc on cellular nuclei, triggering potentially deadly mutations, his rapid-healing might actually promote an explosion of cancerous growths in him.

"Barely above the level of background radiation," Leda added. "Though two thousand years ago, it might have been cause for concern, if not for the shielding provided by this layer of gold." She paused a beat. "You are familiar, I take it, with the story of Alexander's death?"

"I know that he died young. In his thirties. From typhoid fever, if I recall correctly. Although some think he may have been poisoned."

"He was poisoned, but not by his rivals or enemies."

"Radiation poisoning."

Leda nodded. "He found the anomaly in Babylon, in the Esagila. The door to the secret chamber opened to him. It may be that he was indeed a descendant of the Ancients. There are many alive today who carry a trace of their DNA. Your father—your adoptive father, Christian Garral—for instance. And his grandfather, Adam Garral.

"Whether through experimentation or some arcane knowledge passed down through the ages, we cannot say, but Alexander recognized that the anomaly—this emerald—was a source of incredible power. He believed he could use it to produce an elixir which would not only give him immortality, but transform him into the god he already believed he was. Unfortunately for him, the process of creating the elixir released a lethal dose of radiation. History records his slow death of fever, but it does not record that those who ministered to him during that time also sickened and died. The priests however understood what was happening. That is why they refused to bring him into the temple. They knew he would not recover, and that anyone who came into contact with him would also be afflicted. They also knew that encasing Alexander's body in gold would protect them."

"His mistake was in attempting to create the elixir

with only one of the anomalies in his possession," said Hauser, speaking for the first time since entering the vault. He still gripped the backpack by its straps, holding it suspended a few feet away from the golden figure.

"You're after the elixir?" Kismet shook his head. "Why? You're already immortal."

Hauser grinned. "You think that's all this is about? Tell me brother, have you read the text of the Tabula Smaragdina?"

Kismet had in fact read several different translations of the text.

Hauser went on. "It purports to contain the secret formula for creating *prima materia*—the First Matter, from which all other material in the universe was created."

"You mean hydrogen?" Kismet shot back, with more than a little sarcasm.

"Ah, very good. You didn't sleep through your physics classes after all. In their own unique way, the Hermetical scholars of the past understood a rudimentary form of nuclear physics. The point of the formula was not to identify *prima materia*, but to create it out of nothingness, and subsequently to shape it into anything they desired—gold, healing medicines, what have you. That is what Alexander attempted to do, and it's what killed him."

"How did he manage that with just one of the elemental relics?" Kismet asked.

"Who knows? Maybe he tried using actual fire, earth and water." Hauser waved a dismissive hand. "What is certain is that the Emerald Tablet—not that crystal there, but the ancient Hermetic text, is the key to understanding how this may be done.

"'And, as all things have been and arose from one by the mediation of one; so all things have their birth from this one thing... The sun is its father, the moon its mother, the wind hath carried it in its belly, the earth is its nurse. The father of all perfection in the whole world is here. Its force or power is entire if it be converted into earth.' The original treatise on nuclear physics, translated by Sir Isaac Newton. But also, precise instructions for harnessing the power of creation itself, using the four anomalies.

"As you know, each of them represents an elemental force. What you call 'the Apex' symbolizes fire. Also, the sun or the Father. The orb I found in Antarctica is water, but is also the moon, the Mother."

Kismet knew that Maddock and Rose had actually been the ones to discover the orb, but he let Hauser have the credit. "I thought Earth was supposed to be our mother?"

"In the most ancient traditions, the moon was a goddess, and since the moon creates the tides which primarily affect the oceans, it seems clear that sun and moon represent fire and water respectively. Of course, the rest of the passage makes it clear. Wind and earth are plainly identified. The obsidian mirror is a symbol of earth, and that—" He pointed at the green crystal. "—is the symbol of air. The womb from which *prima materia* is born."

"Newton's translation gives precise instructions: 'Separate thou the earth from the fire, the subtle from the gross sweetly with great industry. It ascends from the earth to the heaven and again it descends to the earth and receives the force of things superior and inferior. By this means you shall have the glory of the whole world.'"

Kismet tried to parse the instructions. "Separating earth from fire sounds like nuclear fission."

"You're not thinking literally enough," Hauser countered. "Newton was describing the physical arrangement of the anomalies."

The image of the Magus tarot card, which he had found in Adam Garral's journal, now flashed in Kismet's mind's eye—a divine magician, originally identified as the Roman god Mercury, but possibly a representation of Hermes Trismegistus, surrounded by elemental symbols, manipulating them like a juggler. "Earth and fire... The Apex and the Magna of Illusion. They have to be kept apart?"

"Not just kept apart. Newton's translation gives us a riddle. Separate the 'subtle' from the 'gross.' Of the two that remain, air and water, which would you describe as subtle?"

"Air?"

"I agree. Now the next part. 'It ascends from the earth to the heaven.' Logically, earth would be below fire and sky, so we would arrange the four elements vertically, with your Apex stone at the top. The emerald below it. Then the mirror, and lastly, the orb. 'By this means you shall have the glory of the whole world.' What do you say, brother? Give it a try?" He flashed a wolfish grin, and then swung the pack toward Kismet who caught it reflexively.

Kismet immediately felt the magnetic attraction between the relics and had to lean back a little to keep from being pulled off balance. As he stood there, fighting it, his earlier unease intensified into a feeling of wooziness, like vertigo. He shook his head. "This is your fantasy, not mine."

He adjusted his grip on the pack, preparing to heave it back, but Hauser raised his hands in a halting gesture. "Oh, but I insist."

Suddenly Kismet understood the real reason Hauser had brought him along. "What's the matter, brother? Worried that maybe you aren't as immortal as you think you are?"

Hauser shrugged. "Why take the chance when I've got you here to do the heavy lifting for me?"

"Aren't you afraid of what I might do with this much power?" Kismet shot back.

Hauser grinned as if amused by the suggestion. "So much for the myth of the good son, eh, mother?" He kept his gaze focused on Kismet. "Really, brother, give me some credit. I left some of my men in Alexandria with instructions concerning your friends in Alexander's Tomb. If they don't hear from me in…" He made a show of checking his wristwatch, and then laughed. "Well, let's just say if they don't hear from me in the next half hour or so, they will detonate a rather large bomb at the entrance to the ruin. Help me and help your friends. Oppose me, and I guarantee, they will all die. Tick, tock, brother."

Kismet glanced over at their mother. Leda was watching with undisguised eagerness—her offspring, solving the secrets of creation in preparation to seize heaven itself. There was not a trace of concern in her expression. "Do it, Nick. You have the blood of titans in you. You will not be harmed."

Kismet sagged in defeat. He didn't expect Hauser to keep his word with respect to freeing Maddock and the others, but until this moment, he had hoped to find a way to liberate one or all of the relics and escape. With this new threat, he was out of options. "I guess you've thought of everything," he muttered.

He curled one of the straps around his left forearm and then carefully unzipped the pack with his right hand.

Inside, the three relics were stuck together by the same magnetic attraction that was pulling them toward the emerald. The base of the Apex was perfectly centered on the obsidian mirror, which was in turn pressed flat against the sphere so that the peak of the blue pyramid talisman was pointing away from the emerald. The arrangement was too exact to be random or haphazard. The elemental relics were trying to align themselves, exactly as Hauser had described, but one was missing. The Apex—representing fire—was in contact with the Magna of Illusion—representing earth.

He reached in and tried to separate the two, but the attraction was too strong.

He recalled the instructions from the Emerald Tablet: Separate earth from the fire, the subtle from the gross sweetly with great industry.

Sweetly with great industry, he thought. *What the hell is that supposed to mean?*

"Hard work, I guess," he muttered. But how? He couldn't get enough leverage to do more than wiggle it.

But the answer was obvious.

In legend, Alexander had used his sword to cut the Gordian Knot, solving a complex problem with direct action—brute force. And in both the tarot deck and Kismet's vision of the Emerald Tablet, he had also seen Alexander's sword. Whether the story of the Gordian Knot was literal or allegorical, he could not say, but he understood that in order to separate earth from fire "sweetly with great industry" he was going to need the emerald.

He let the relics pull him closer to the golden coffin, feeling weaker with each step. He was no Superman, but the green crystal was affecting him like Kryptonite. And as he advanced, the attraction intensified, overpowering him, yanking him forward until the bag made contact with the emerald. As it did, the gem was ripped free of the sculpted hands, twisting away to shoot across the remaining distance. There was a distinctive clink as it pierced the fabric of the pack and made contact with the orb, sticking straight out like an arrow piercing an apple. As it did, the pack twisted around and dropped to the vault floor with the emerald pointing straight down. The backpack slid down the length of the emerald and settled into a shapeless heap around it, revealing all four elemental relics, joined together for possibly the first time ever. They remained upright, just barely touching the floor, perfectly balanced like a top or gyroscope, but without any spinning.

Kismet could feel energy radiating out from it— invisible, inaudible, but nevertheless palpable. It was sucking the life out of him. And he knew why. The relics were not aligned correctly. He would need to pry them apart, reassemble them in the correct order.

And if I do? What happens then?

He moved in closer, wrapping his left arm around the orb for leverage, and then gripped the Apex, pulling it with an effort that seemed to take the last of his waning strength. It resisted stolidly, as if the two relics had already fused together at the atomic level, but then, just when he was about to give up, it broke loose and came away in his hand.

He could feel it tugging against him, straining to be reunited with the others, like a powerful magnet, but the simple act of separating one piece of the puzzle seemed to reduce the weakening effect of the joined artifact. Without letting go, he reached down with the hand that held the Apex, and took hold of the emerald.

The green crystal refused to break contact, but he did manage to rotate it away from the floor.

Separate earth from fire... The emerald goes between the mirror and the Apex.

He slid the pyramid down the length of the crystal and placed it at the point opposite the orb. The Apex seemed to jump out of his hand, positioning itself with the point of the emerald exactly at the center.

He allowed himself a relieved sigh. He'd gotten that part right at least.

With one hand gripping the emerald and the other on the mirror, he began pulling, bringing the two objects together, scraping them across the outer surface of the orb until at last, they made contact. He maintained the pressure, lifting one edge of the mirror so that the other edge, the one closest to the tip of the emerald tilted down, and pushed the crystal up, onto the mirror—

The relic jolted in his hands, the emerald sliding to the center of the mirror as if suddenly realizing that was where it was meant to be. Immediately, the combined object flipped upright again, rotating in Kismet's grasp until the Apex was pointing straight up. Light began pulsing along the emerald, traveling down from the Apex and vanishing into the inky darkness of the Magna of Illusion, but after a moment, something like beads of mercury began appearing on the surface of the obsidian mirror, pooling together and running off the edge to drip down onto the orb. But instead of rolling down the curved surface of the large sphere, the beads vanished as if sucked up by a sponge. A few seconds later, the orb itself began to glow, like an enormous black light bulb. It was not a carbon-tungsten filament that was producing the illumination however, but rather a pool of shining quicksilver accumulating at the bottom of the sphere's interior.

There was one other significant change. Kismet could still feel invisible energy radiating out from the newly created object, but the timbre of it was different. No longer did he feel like it was draining the life out of him. Just the opposite, he felt an infusion of energy. Literal warmth, spread through his body, tingling in his extremities, growing unpleasantly hot inside his thermal winter garments.

Yet, the physical discomfort was the least of his concerns. He understood now what Hauser had hoped to accomplish.

By this means you shall have the glory of the whole world.

The elemental relics were creating *prima materia*—First Matter—the stuff from which the universe had been created.

The scientists of Prometheus had given it a different name however.

Ichor. The blood of the gods.

Fuel for an army of god-bodies.

16

"**I told you** he went along with this just to save us," Jade whispered in Maddock's ear.

He shot her an angry look, a finger pressed to his lips, signaling her to silence, though it was plainly evident that nobody outside their little group had heard her.

Once past the electronic lock inside the entrance, they moved quickly into the vault. Most of the doors had been left open, as if Hauser's team could not be bothered to shut them.

A check of the security cameras still showed no sign of Hauser's group, but Rose's hatchet head, continued to point the way like a compass needle, and when the inner airlock door opened, the mystery was solved. Although positioned in such a way as to be uncovered by the security cameras, the entire back wall of the vault had swung open to reveal another chamber. And in that vault they found wonders beyond comprehension. There were display cases containing objects of incredible beauty and obvious wealth—crowns and amulets, scepters and swords, but the most impressive part of the collection were the statues. There were at least two dozen of them, assembled in ranks like the terracotta armies found in the tomb of Chinese emperor Qin Shi Huang, except these were each eight to ten feet in height, towering over Maddock, and appeared to be made of solid gold. The statues were remarkably lifelike, depicting well-muscled male and voluptuous female figures, all of them exuding power and sensuality. They reminded Maddock of sculpted Greek gods.

The biggest surprise however had been the voices that drifted through the forest of towering metal figures. Maddock and the others had crept forward, close enough to observe what was happening without being noticed, though in fact, the group huddled around the golden coffin were so completely focused on the powerful elemental relics, and the task of arranging them according to ancient Hermetic wisdom, that Maddock and the others might as well have been in an alternate universe.

Jade was correct, though. Kismet was going along with Hauser's plan because he believed their safety was at stake.

They had to let him know that Hauser's threat was a bluff, but how?

A few well-placed shots would thin out the opposition, but once the shooting started, there was no telling what would happen. Then there was the fact that Hauser had control of the relics and knew how to use them. He might easily deflect their attack with a force field or roast them all with lightning bolts.

Then fate decided to give them a break. Hauser handed the backpack with the relics to Kismet.

"What's he doing?" Bones muttered.

"Maybe he's worried about radiation poisoning," suggested Rose. "Maybe that's the one thing that can kill him."

"Good to know," Bones said.

"Then it can kill Nick, too," Christian Garral said, his voice betraying his anxiety. "And us if we get too close."

Maddock studied the group gathered around Alexander's coffin. There was no question regarding the loyalties of the five gunmen but what about Leda? Whose side was she on?

Judging by her interactions with her two sons, the answer was her own.

"We need to break this party up." He turned his head to Bones. "Think you could create some kind of distraction? Something that might draw a few of those guys away?"

"Divide and conquer?" Bones eyes narrowed in thought then a broad grin spread across his face. "I know exactly what to do."

"Professor, you go with him. When you're in position, break squelch on the radio. I'll signal back when we're ready for you to go, and then I'll send you the number of targets headed your way. Voice if I can, but if not, I'll key the mic with the number."

Bones nodded and then turned to Professor. "You're gonna love this."

As the two men moved off, Maddock returned his attention to what was happening below. Kismet had neared the golden coffin and was struggling to align the relics. That they were having a harmful effect on him was plainly evident.

"What's your plan?" asked Garral.

Maddock quickly outlined what he needed Garral and the others to do, and then waited with the Motorola pressed to his ear, the volume just barely loud enough for him to hear the scratch of static when Bones signaled that he was in position.

Maddock gave a hand-signal to the others to get ready, and then clicked the push-to-talk and whispered, "Do it!"

For several seconds, nothing happened at all.

Directly ahead, Kismet had succeeded in rearranging the elemental artifacts, and the subsequent change almost caused Maddock to forget about the plan.

The orb had turned semi-transparent and appeared to be filling up with a substance that looked like liquid light.

Suddenly, a crashing sound—like a bus hitting a brick wall—reverberated through the vault. A fraction of a second later, there was another crash, and then another, each one progressively louder. Hauser's group were visibly startled by the noises. So was Maddock.

Bones, what the hell did you just do?

He got the answer a couple crashes later when he spied movement among the statues off to his left. They were toppling over like bowling pins, with each one striking one or two more as it fell in a chain reaction. Maddock wasn't sure how Bones had managed to start the domino effect—each of the statues must have weighed tons—but once begun, there was no stopping it.

The coffin at the center was a few yards removed from the impact zone, but the gunmen nevertheless retreated a few steps. Each impact released a shockwave that vibrated through the floor and buffeted the air. Even after the last affected statue fell, the echoes of the crashes continued to reverberate in the large vault in a deafening cacophony.

Yet, through it all, Nick Kismet did not move. He stood frozen, statue-still, as if in a trance, while beads of glowing energy perspired from the obsidian mirror and were absorbed into the orb.

Hauser was gesturing to his men, shouting words that were inaudible over the ongoing tumult, and three of them moved off, presumably to investigate the disturbance. They approached the statues cautiously,

As the three gunmen disappeared behind the statues, moving warily as if fearing another round of collapses, Maddock broke squelch three times, hoping Bones would get the message. He waited a few more seconds, and then raised his hand. "Now!"

In unison, Maddock and the others emerged from their hiding places, each one of them aiming a weapon at a designated target. Maddock took aim at Hauser and shouted, "Guns down! Nobody move!"

Maddock had instructed his companions to fire at the first sign of aggression, but hoped a display of force would suffice to win the battle without a shot fired. It wasn't that he was squeamish about bloodshed, but rather because there was no telling what might happen if bullets started flying. Garral seemed to know how to handle firearms, but Rose, Jade and Jimmy looked far less comfortable with their weapons, and if they missed or merely hesitated, their slight numerical advantage would evaporate.

Hauser whirled around, surprise quickly giving way to anger. "Maddock!"

The two remaining gunmen had tensed but wisely had not attempted to raise their weapons.

"I mean it," Maddock said, holding the weapon steady, Hauser's face visible just above the luminous Trijicon dot on the front sight. "Make the wrong move and you're dead. That may not mean anything to you, Hauser, but I'm betting your men might feel differently. Now, get those hands up. All of you."

As the two gunmen grudgingly complied, Maddock took another step forward and risked a quick glance past Hauser to where Kismet was standing. "Nick, you all right?"

Kismet did not answer right away, prompting Maddock to repeat the question. This time, he got a reply. "Stay back," Kismet rasped. "It's not safe."

No kidding, Maddock thought. Aloud, he said, "We need to get out of here."

"It's not that simple. This thing is making *ichor.*"

Maddock knew the word from Greek mythology. *Ichor* was the blood that flowed through the veins of the gods. He wasn't sure what it meant in this context, but it was obviously something bad. "You've got the relics, so you're calling the shots."

"Get everyone out of here. Now that I know you're all safe—"

The crack of rifle fire cut him off. It hadn't come from nearby but from somewhere out in the vault—several shots in quick succession, and not all from the same kind of weapon. Bones and Professor had engaged with the three gunmen who had gone to investigate the toppling of the statues.

The remaining two men flinched and began looking around anxiously, as if weighing their chances at attempting some kind of offensive action, but it was Hauser who ultimately seized the moment. Maddock squeezed the trigger, knowing that his shot would only temporarily take Hauser out of action, but he was a fraction of a second too slow. Hauser ducked under the bullet and sprang at Kismet. In the same instant, the two gunmen broke in opposite directions, seeking cover behind the fallen statues, firing their assault rifles on the move.

Pandemonium erupted in the vault. Bullets were sizzling through the air, sparking off solid surfaces or whizzing harmlessly away into nothingness. Maddock dropped low, quickly assessing his options. There weren't many. He tackled Leda to the floor, drawing her behind the relative cover of the bier containing Alexander's coffin. He didn't know whose side she was on, but figured she was more valuable alive than dead.

He came up on one knee searching for a target, and from the corner of his eye, saw Kismet and Hauser struggling, with the combined elemental relic caught between them. The object wasn't affixed to anything, yet it remained upright and immobile, as solid as a flagpole, while the two men wrestled for control.

He felt Kismet's eyes on him and glanced over. The man was shouting something, barely audible over the thunder of battle.

"Get out of here!"

Maddock didn't know what Kismet was planning, but the advice was sound. He gripped Leda's hand and pulled her after him, making a break for the edge of the circle of statues where the others were waiting. He was faintly aware of a shift in fire, Jimmy and Garral trying to suppress any action from the shooters as best they could with their bolt-action rifles. He made it just halfway before a brilliant flash—light and heat—from behind him filled the vault, followed almost immediately by a shockwave that slapped him flat, sending him and Leda sprawling.

He thought it had to be an explosion, maybe a hand grenade, but there had been no sound. In fact, even the gunfire close in had ceased. Shaking off the effects of the blast, he scrambled back to his feet. Leda was still down, dazed, but as Maddock reached for her, he saw her gaze flash back to where they had just been. Where her sons were battling for control of the elemental talisman.

Maddock looked as well, and instantly saw what had caused the flash.

At first glance, it appeared that Kismet had ceded control of the relic to Hauser. The latter had both arms wrapped around the relic while Kismet had not only let go but had retreated a few steps.

But there was something different about the relic. It was no longer vibrating at the same frequency as before, nor was *ichor* pooling on the surface of the mirror. In fact, the Magna of Illusion was no longer in contact with the emerald. Instead, it seemed as if the orb and mirror had rotated upside down so that the emerald, still topped with the Apex, was protruding directly from the top of the sphere, while the mirror was now at its bottom.

Maddock immediately realized what had happened. Kismet had pried the emerald away from the obsidian mirror, breaking whatever kind of circuit had been created. That had been the source of the eruption that had flattened Maddock. The relic had then reassembled itself in a different order.

Hauser's hands were moving frantically, trying to separate the relics and undo what Kismet had done, but he was already too late. The orb was expelling the fiery substance that had been accumulating inside it. Glowing ichor was oozing from the mirror, accumulating into a fat molten globule underneath the elemental relic.

Kismet snatched something off the ground—Rose's backpack—and thrust a hand inside. When he withdrew it, he was holding his *kukri*. Without a moment's hesitation, he leaped at his brother, swiping the knife in a broad lateral arc. Hauser's eyes went wide and he ducked away. Instead of taking his head off, only the tip of the blade made contact, gouging a line of red across the man's cheek. As Hauser let go of his prize, dancing away to avoid another slash of the *kukri,* the growing blob of *ichor* fell away, but it did not hit the floor. Instead, it burst like a bubble, evaporating into a glittering cloud that rose into the air and then, as if caught in a vacuum, dispersed in all directions.

Maddock's attention was still fixed on Kismet and Hauser, so he only caught a glimpse of the *ichor* mist settling onto the statues, briefly condensing into droplets on their metal surface before being absorbed. But when he spotted motion from the corner of his eye, he turned his head for a better look.

It was no mere optical illusion, no trick of the light. All around him, the giant golden figures were beginning to stir.

17

The statues moved slowly at first, like sleepers dragging themselves up to consciousness. Their golden exterior was as supple as actual skin, allowing smooth, unrestricted motion, such that the only sound was of heavy hands thudding against the solid concrete floor as the fallen statues began struggling to right themselves. Those that had survived Bones' diversion without being toppled simply straightened and began milling about.

Watching them, Maddock searched for some indication that they were truly alive, but saw none. They seemed more like animatronic figures than living beings.

Animatronic figures as big as elephants and evidently, completely independent.

His observation was cut short by a burst from an assault rifle. He swung his eyes in the direction of the muzzle flash, and saw one of Hauser's men, surrounded by the shuffling figures. Bullets stitched one of the statues, but instead of cratering the soft metal, the rounds vanished into it like a pebble thrown into a pond. There were even ripples of energy spreading out from the points of impact, meeting and canceling one another out.

Yet, as impotent as the attack proved to be, it got the attention of the animated statues. Those nearest the gunman immediately swung to face him. Perhaps sensing his imminent peril, the man tried to flee the circle, but a golden hand shot out from his blind side and plucked him off the ground. The statue—a male figure with curly hair and beard—lifted the gunman like a doll and dashed him to the floor. Maddock heard the crunch of the man's bones breaking. Immediately, the other statues raised their fists above the shattered form, and then with what seemed like mechanical efficiency, proceeded to pound the man into a bloody pulp.

Another flurry of motion distracted Maddock. He glanced toward it and saw Hauser's retreating back disappear into the midst of another cluster of statues. Kismet was close on his brother's heels, his *kukri* still bared and ready for action. Only then did Maddock realize that the elemental relic was gone, taken presumably by Hauser as he fled. Kismet reached the statues a moment later, and then he too disappeared as the statues turned to follow, ponderous but relentless.

Maddock grabbed Leda's wrist and began moving away from the vault's center, and away from the unfolding carnage. He could feel the eyes of some of the statues turning toward him, following his movements, shifting toward him as if drawn to any motion, but he did not stop. Off to his left, he heard another burst of gunfire—the other gunman—which was just as quickly cut off. The swift reprisal seemed to confirm his working theory that the statues were at their most lethal when attacked.

"Don't shoot at them!" he shouted, straining to make himself heard over the thud and crunch of another pulverization-in-progress. Still gripping his pistol, he awkwardly unclipped his radio and squeezed the push-to-talk. "Bones! Do not engage those things. Get out of the vault."

He didn't wait for a response, but kept moving, heading for the spot where he'd left the others. He spotted Garral and Rose. The two were poised like running backs on a football field, watching for the opening that would allow them to make a break for the end zone. He found Jade and Jimmy nearby, similarly dodging the giant automatons as they shifted this way and that, moving far slower than those that had killed the gunmen.

"Get to the exit!" he shouted as he got near the others. "And whatever you do, don't attack them!"

"Which way?" asked Jade, ducking to avoid a slow swipe from a tall Aphrodite.

The question confounded Maddock. In the confusion, he had become disoriented, and with the statues now in motion, milling about and blocking his view of the vault's edges, he had no idea which direction to go.

Leda chose that moment to pull free of his grip, but she did not flee. Instead, she just stood there at arm's length, massaging her wrist where Maddock had held it. She met his gaze and then looked to his left. "That way."

Maddock was about to thank her, but just then something struck his cheek. It was cold and hard, like a hailstone.

No, not like. It *was* hail. Tiny pellets of ice were falling all around him, bouncing off his parka, rattling tinnily on the statues, or just splattering wetly on the floor.

Wet? He looked down and saw that this impression was indeed correct. The little hailstones were melting on the floor, leaving big damp splotches on the concrete.

"What's happening?" Rose shouted over the increasing patter.

"The *ichor* is raising the temperature in here," Leda said. There was no urgency in her tone. She might simply have been commenting on the weather. "It's thawing the permafrost."

The air was still cold enough to freeze the meltwater as it dripped down from the ceiling, but judging by the swiftness with which it melted again on the floor, the temperature was continuing to rise. The hail was now more like wet sleet, and coming down harder.

As if they didn't have enough to worry about.

"We've got to move," Maddock said. "If we get soaked, we'll freeze solid when we get outside."

"Maddock! Bring your ass!" Bones' voice reached out to him—not a radio transmission, but a shout. Through the haze of falling precipitation, Maddock could just make out his friend's towering form, one arm raised and waving him on.

Maddock saw something else, too. Something that Bones had missed. He pointed, frantic. "Bones! Behind you!"

Bones turned just in time to see a towering Zeus-like figure, one lazy hand reaching toward him. Bones started to pivot away, but before he could, something slammed down onto the statue, crushing it to the floor. A boulder, as big as a car, had fallen onto the golden automaton, flattening it. The impact jolted the floor and sent Bones sprawling toward Maddock, but he scrambled back to his feet as more mud and debris began to pour down from the melting permafrost ceiling.

Kismet ducked under a reaching hand, narrowly avoiding it, then dropped to his knees and slid between the legs of the titanic figure. Ice pellets were falling from the ceiling, melting into a slushy mess underfoot, which made the slide easy but recovering from it a lot trickier.

The vault was definitely warming up, the permafrost thawing, but that situation, like the rampage of the reanimated statues, had to take a back seat to his pursuit of Hauser. He popped back up just as Hauser cut to the right, disappearing behind another pillar-like leg. He was weaving through the god-bodies like a pinball, trying to shake his pursuer. Encumbered as he was by the elemental relic, the best he could do was to stay a few steps ahead, but with the statues running interference, a few steps was all he needed.

The golden giants were moving faster, reacting to them as they had to the attack by the gunmen. Their rampage was mindless. The *ichor* energized their bodies, but without the consciousness of the entities that had once occupied them, they were simply reacting according to some kind of primitive default behavior written into whatever they had that passed for a brain. Their actions reminded Kismet of warrior ants, swarming in response to a threat. But what was driving them to attack him? He wondered if it was the close proximity of the relic. Were they drawn to it, recognizing it as the source of their potent lifeblood? Or was Hauser using it to control them somehow? Either way, Kismet knew that getting the relic back, separating the pieces and scattering them once more to the four winds was of paramount importance. If Hauser escaped the vault with the relic, there was no telling what kind of hell he might unleash on the world.

Kismet spotted the open vault door through a forest of legs as tall as he was. If he could get there before Hauser….

Too late. His brother was already there, his silhouette starkly visible against the whiteness of the seed vault beyond. Hauser seemed to hesitate there, just for a second, then he was gone, disappearing down the aisle between the empty racks.

As he reached the opening a moment later, Kismet saw the reason for his brother's pause. The false walls that served as a secret entrance to the Prometheus vault were swinging closed. They were moving too slow to prevent him from slipping through, but even as he did, he realized the true reason Hauser had done this.

Kismet might be able to make it out, but his companions would be imprisoned inside, trapped with an army of mindlessly destructive automatons.

He looked back, searching for some sign of Maddock and the others, but all he saw through the blur of precipitation were gigantic golden figures stalking relentlessly toward him.

"Damn it," he muttered. This was why he preferred operating solo.

He returned his attention to Hauser, who was now more than halfway to the airlock door, and knew what he had to do. He took off down the aisle at a full sprint.

The only way to help the others was to stop his brother, get the relic back. If he didn't he would almost certainly have a lot more deaths on his conscience. Besides, he wasn't even sure he would be able to stop the door from closing, or get it open again once it was shut. His mother might know, and she was in there, too.

That realization only added to his growing sense of guilt.

Even though it was the right choice, the only choice, it felt like he was abandoning them all to an uncertain fate. Alexandria all over again, only worse.

Fifty feet ahead, Hauser was past the steel safety

cage. He slammed the gate shut behind him with such force that it rebounded halfway open again, but he was already gone, shooting toward the airlock doors.

Kismet blasted through the gate just as Hauser entered the airlock and pulled the door shut, practically slamming it in his brother's face. Kismet had too much momentum to stop and crashed into the doors. The impact rattled his teeth and he bounded back, spilling painfully onto the floor, but he was up again in a heartbeat, reaching for the lever.

Locked.

He rattled it repeatedly, knowing that it would disengage as soon as the outer door was closed again. *Unless Hauser wedged it open,* he thought.

Unwilling to wait and see, he jammed the point of his *kukri* into the gap between the doors and attempted to pry them apart. The thick blade was more than tough enough to serve double-duty as a crowbar, but he wasn't just fighting the lock. The rising temperatures had increased the already slightly higher air pressure in the vault, forcing them to remain shut. He tried to drive the knife in deeper, but his gloved hand slipped off the hilt, sliding along the length of the blade. He winced as the edge slice through Gore-tex and skin alike, and snatched his hand back in an instinctive protective reflex. Blood was already seeping through the gash in the glove, dripping down to stain the floor in dark red blotches.

He bit down on the finger of the glove and yanked it off. Blood was streaming from the gash, but he wiped it on the front of his parka. His hand was throbbing all the way up to his elbow. Rapid healing abilities did not grant him any immunity from pain, but he gritted his teeth and did his best to ignore it as he resumed trying to force the doors open.

A loud crash filled the vault, shaking the floor and dislodging a shower of ice chunks from the ceiling above. The accompanying shock wave buffeted Kismet, shoving him forward and nearly knocking him down again.

A glance over his shoulder confirmed what he already knew had happened. Through the parallel rows of shelves, he could see an uneven gap in the back wall. The god-bodies were smashing through it. If the walls of the vault would not contain them, nothing would. Before he could turn back to his task, there was another resounding crash and one of the golden forms stumbled forward into the empty seed vault where it immediately began shoving shelving racks out of the way, intent on clearing a path for the exit.

Kismet whipped his head back around, desperate to get the airlock doors open. To his astonishment, he discovered this had already been accomplished. The tremors had shaken the doors off their hinges. He bolted through, and kept going, past the still-open exterior doors. He made the turn and headed back to the long tunnel leading up to the surface where he finally caught sight of his brother, just for a moment as the latter slipped through the door at the far end.

He sprinted ahead, crossing the full distance in about thirty seconds. He was surprised at how winded the effort left him. His brief exposure to the relic in its correct alignment had not, it seemed, completely recharged his batteries. Nevertheless, he dug deep and poured everything into catching his brother.

As he burst through the last set of doors, emerging into the darkness of the Arctic at midday, he heard the diminishing whine of a snowmobile engine. A white plume trailed out behind a dark speck shooting away, straight down the hill, toward the not-so-distant lights of the airport and the plane that would carry Hauser away, along with a power that might reshape the world.

Or destroy it.

Without a moment's hesitation, Kismet jumped on one of the remaining snowmobiles, started it, and took off after his brother.

18

It was quickly apparent that the golden giants had lost all interest in Maddock and the others. That was the good news. The bad news was that the animated statues were now clustered around the only exit from the vault—a breach they had forced in the false walls separating the Prometheus vault from the empty seed vault.

The even worse news was that the permafrost overhead was melting fast and coming down even faster.

Maddock had one arm raised overhead to ward off falling rocks and mud. It was a symbolic effort but at least it kept the mud out of his eyes.

"When I heard this place was called the Doomsday Vault, I thought it meant something else," Bones said, shouting to be heard over the din. He looked past Maddock to the line of stragglers behind him. "Where's Kismet?"

"He took off," Maddock said. He knew there was more to the story, but once again, their new *friend* had made a unilateral decision and abandoned them all.

Bones evidently felt the same way. "Again? Screw that guy. He's off the team." He glanced over at Christian Garral and Leda Hauser and shrugged. "Sorry, but you're kid's a dick."

Garral grimaced, apologetically, but Leda's face was an emotionless mask.

"There's Professor," Jade shouted, pointing in the direction the logjam at the exit, and to a figure huddling in the relative shelter of the wall nearby.

Bones nodded. "I hope he can figure out how we're gonna get through that mess 'cause I got nothing."

As if to mock his hopelessness, the mass of statues surged again and then, like a shower of champagne behind a loosened cork, exploded through the hole. beyond the opening, Maddock could see the statues continuing their destructive rampage, trashing the shelves in the empty vault. The giants were still between them and freedom, but at least the way out of the Prometheus vault was clear.

Behind them, huge chunks of the ceiling continued to crash down, obliterating what little remained of the collection and splattering the fleeing group with cold mud, but as they cautiously started through into the seed vault, something changed.

The statues' movements were growing sluggish. Some were squatting on their haunches or kneeling amidst the ruin of the seed vault as if uncertain what to do next. One of them—a male figure—took a tentative step toward the exit, but then froze in place.

"The *ichor* is depleting," Leda said, pushing forward.

Beside Maddock, Bones muttered. "Translation: Dead batteries."

"Not dead enough," Maddock said. "We need to get past them."

Easier said than done. The giants had transformed the seed vault into a nightmarish obstacle course. The neat orderly rows of shelving were broken and scattered across the floor, and the steel posts that had supported them were bent and twisted around the slow-moving statues like tentacles. Worse, the warming effect had followed the giants, and despite the refrigeration system, ice and chunks of melting permafrost were starting to fall from the ceiling.

Maddock glanced back to make sure everyone else was still with him. "Watch your step," he advised, "And keep your head on a swivel."

With that admonition, he started forward, picking his way over the tangled metal and ducking slow swipes from the giants. He guessed their dwindling power supply would be completely exhausted in another two or three minutes, but they couldn't afford to wait and see. Not only was the vault still coming down around them, there was an even bigger problem. Hauser had possession of the elemental relics. Despite his irritation with Kismet's decision to leave them all behind, he knew why the man had done it. It was bad enough that Hauser seemed to be unkillable. They couldn't afford to let him add "omnipotent" to his resume.

He reached the far end of the vault without mishap, noting the drops of blood that were freezing on the floor, and kept going. There were more bloodstains on the floor, a trail leading all the way back to the front door and beyond. Someone had been injured during the escape from the vault, and the dark drops showed exactly where they had gone.

The air outside, cooler than in the vault room, quickly froze the mud on his coat and snow pants into a crust that crackled as he ran. Thankfully, the waterproof outer shell of the garments had resisted saturation.

Although the snowmobiles were too far away for him to hear them, their headlamps showed their location and progress. The lead vehicle—almost certainly Hauser—was halfway to the airport, the second machine—Kismet—trailing by about a hundred yards.

Maddock ran to one of the two remaining

snowmobiles. Bones landed in the saddle of the other. He knew there was almost no chance of either of them catching Hauser, but Kismet was almost close enough. Almost.

Maddock searched the line of figures emerging from the seed vault until he identified Professor. "Prof! Can you do something with that rifle?"

The other man squinted into the distance. "I doubt I can hit him."

Jimmy piped in. "Let me take a crack at it. I'm pretty good with a sniper rifle."

Maddock gaped at him. "Since when?"

Professor rolled his eyes. "Video games."

Maddock shook his head, more an expression of disbelief than denial. "Whatever. You don't need to hit him. Just give him something to think about. Keep him away from the airport. Buy us some time."

Maddock hit the starter and the snowmobile roared to life. He goosed the throttle until the skis fell into the trail left by the other two machines, and then opened it wide.

The wind chilled his unprotected face, pelting him with ice crystals that stung his cheeks. He had to squint to keep from being blinded. His only consolation was that the ordeal would not last long. It would only take a few minutes to cover the distance to the airport.

Hauser was already almost there.

The rifle report cracked overhead, loud enough for him to hear it over the engine noise and the rush of air. Another followed quickly. Then another. Jimmy and Professor were alternating their shots, setting up a constant, if slow-tempo, barrage of suppressive fire. He couldn't tell where the bullets were hitting, but evidently they were close enough. Further down the hill, the headlights of the lead snowmobile abruptly veered to the right.

Maddock risked opening his eyes a little wider, tracking the course correction. Hauser was zigzagging, carving a wavy line in the snow, but with each left turn, he pushed closer to the illuminated runway. Up on the hill, Jimmy and Professor seemed to realize what the other man intended; not only did they intensify the rate of fire whenever Hauser shifted back to the left, they also appeared to be directing their shots closer, adjusting their aim and dialing in on the moving target. Accurate or not, the constant fire was having the desired effect. Hauser's evasive maneuvers had cut his lead on Kismet by half, and Maddock and Bones were closing quickly as well.

Without letting go of the throttle, Maddock reached up, unclipped his walkie-talkie and held it against his ear. "Bones, you still with me?"

Bones' voice crackled back a moment later. "Right on your ass. Gotta say, the view sucks."

Maddock suppressed a chuckle. "Then let's change it up a little? I'm gonna sweep wide-right. Try to push him back toward you."

"Gotcha," was all Bones said.

Maddock immediately veered off the blazed trail, plunging into the untrammeled snow. It was like floating on a cloud. Over the top of the waist-high accumulation, he could just make out Bones' snowmobile, charging straight down the hill, and further out, two pinpoints of light—the headlights of Hauser's and Kismet's machines—drifting across the horizon in front of him, getting closer as he moved to intercept.

Hauser must have realized what he was attempting. After a few seconds, he veered back in the other direction, but his window of opportunity had already closed. He was past the airport and running headlong toward the open water of the fjord beyond.

Maddock stood up for a better look and saw Kismet, closing fast on Hauser, driving him relentlessly forward. Bones had swept to the left, cutting off any escape in that direction. Directly ahead, the white snowscape ended abruptly, marking the transition from ice to water.

"We got this bastard," Bones shouted over the radio. "He's got nowhere to go."

Maddock felt a twinge of apprehension. Hauser was like a cornered rat; with no avenues left for escape, his only option would be to fight, and with all four of the elemental relics in his possession, he would be more than a match for all of them.

Hauser had evidently reached the same conclusion. His snowmobile slowed and came to a full stop less than twenty yards from the water's edge, but he did not dismount. Instead, he remained in his seat, wrestling with the burden he had carried out of the Prometheus vault, fighting to pry the individual relics apart in order to assemble them in the correct order so he could use it to blast them all to oblivion.

Something flashed into Maddock's view. It was Kismet on his snowmobile, still running at full speed in pursuit of his brother.

He's not going to stop, Maddock realized.

Kismet didn't stop, but he launched himself off the snowmobile at the last instant, rolling away as the riderless machine kamikazed into Hauser's vehicle.

From his vantage a hundred yards away and closing,

Maddock saw the two snowmobiles come apart in an eruption of shattered fiberglass, metal and smoke, and then a second later, heard and felt the impact.

Maddock kept the throttle wide-open, charging toward the smoldering wreckage. The snow around the site of the collision was dark with oil stains and pieces of debris, but despite the violence of the crash, he knew better than to count Hauser out of the fight. He spotted Kismet, evidently unhurt, shaking off the effects of his tumble in the snow, then he saw something that caused him to let go of the throttle and slam on the brakes.

A dark hole had opened up under one of the broken snowmobiles, swallowing it completely.

He saw Bones approaching from the other direction and started waving frantically to get the other man's attention. Remembering the radio, he keyed the mic and shouted, "Back off. There's thin ice here. We're over water."

Bones must have gotten the message because he immediately turned away, heading back toward the lights of the airport.

Maddock knew he should probably do the same. Most of the fjord was ice free but evidently land ice had crept out over the water to form a shelf along the coastline. The mass was thick enough to support the weight of the snowmobiles, or rather it had been until the crash. Now there was no telling how much longer it would remain solid beneath him. Reasoning that he'd have a better chance of making it off the ice shelf on foot, he dismounted and cautiously started toward the wreck site. He found Kismet again and waved his arms. "Nick. Over here."

Kismet's head turned toward him but before he

could reply, a grinning form materialized out of the darkness behind him. It was Hauser, and in his hands, the elemental relic—re-configured as it had been in the Prometheus vault—was beginning to glow.

Maddock threw out both hands in a plaintive gesture. "Stop. You'll melt the—"

An ear-splitting crack cut him off, and then the entire section of ice under all three of them came apart.

19

Maddock threw himself flat, spread-eagling to distribute his weight. Hauser had vanished completely, dropping through the newly created fissure like a stone. Kismet, thrown off balance by the upset, tried to crawl away from the edge, but the ice beneath him gave out, plunging him into the frigid water as well. He thrashed on the surface for a moment, struggling to pull himself back onto the newly created floe. As he clawed for a purchase, his bare right hand left dark splotches on the white ice—fresh blood from an open wound—but the frozen surface crumbled at his touch, and as the water infiltrated his clothes he was dragged under.

"Crap!" Maddock snarled, knowing what he had to do.

Without leaving his prone position, he shrugged out of his parka and kicked off his boots. After the exertion of the escape from the vault and the subsequent snowmobile chase, the rush of cool air was refreshing for a second or two, but then the bitter edge seeped through his thermal undershirt and his muscles began clenching, drawing in against his torso, an automatic reaction to preserve body heat.

"Crap," he muttered again. "This is gonna suck."

The worst part was, he knew exactly how bad it would suck, but he nevertheless planted his palms on the icy surface and propelled himself ahead, sliding on his belly like a penguin. As he neared the edge, the ice floe tilted down with his weight, dropping him into the frigid sea.

The effects of immersion in nearly-freezing water on

the human body were well understood by medical science. Many of the immediate reactions were involuntary, but some were not. Survival depended on knowing the difference and acting accordingly. Initial exposure—cold shock—was the most dangerous part. Cold receptors in the skin would trigger immediate physiological responses, beginning with a "gasp" reflex.

Maddock made sure to keep his head up, his face clear of the water as he went in to avoid drowning as the cold water washed over him, triggering that sudden inhalation.

Next came uncontrollable hyperventilation, a heart rate increase, and a spike in blood pressure—all of it, a natural response to hostile temperature, but potentially fatal, especially to those with a weak constitution. After the initial gasp, one of the next big dangers was giving in to panic, which in tandem with the involuntary urge to hyperventilate, could severely limit the oxygen supply, causing a person to black out.

Maddock knew that the effects would subside quickly, usually peaking with the first minute of exposure, but he also knew that Kismet, who was experiencing the same symptoms, but already underwater, did not have a minute.

He forced himself to hyperventilate even faster for a moment, trying to override the involuntary response, and then stopped and drew in as deep a breath as his chest would allow. Then, he rolled forward and dove into the water, aiming for the spot where he thought Kismet had gone down.

He knew that if he couldn't find Kismet on that first breath, he wouldn't get another chance, so he threw his arms wide, sweeping them back and forth, kicking to propel himself deeper. He had expected everything to be pitch black under the ice, and so it took a few seconds for his chill-addled brain to process the fact that there was a pale glow rising up from the depths.

It was the relic, still generating *ichor* despite being totally submerged.

In the instant that he realized it, the glow intensified to near solar brilliance, the lighting up the world beneath the ice like daylight. Maddock couldn't bear to look directly at it, but as he turned away, he spotted a blurry silhouette drifting nearby.

Maddock kicked toward the shape, hooked it with an arm. He could tell by the feel that it was a body—Kismet's body—still twitching, fighting to survive the double-punch of cold shock and drowning. Maddock reversed his position in the water, turning away from the radiance below, and began kicking hard to reach the surface. Before he'd gone even a few feet, the light abruptly went out.

Maddock didn't know what to make of the development, and in truth, he barely retained the mental capacity to care. His arms and legs felt oddly detached. He could only tell that he was still holding on to Kismet by the amount of drag he was experiencing in trying to reach the surface. A moment later, he broke through and was welcomed by an icy chill that froze the water on his skin into stinging ice crystals. He kept kicking until Kismet emerged beside him, gasping and still struggling to stay afloat.

It took him a few seconds to orient toward shore, seconds in which he slid ever closer to the threshold of hypothermia. Simply getting out of the water wasn't going to be enough to save them. If anything, the water temperature—just above freezing—was warmer than the air above, so getting to shelter, somewhere warm, was imperative.

"Maddock!" Bones' shout rolled across the dark water. The big man was crouched at the edge of the broken ice shelf, waving frantically. "Over here."

Maddock began kicking toward him, paddling with his free hand, but Kismet was like an anchor. "Swim, damn it!" he gasped. "Swim or I'll leave you behind."

"Do it," Kismet coughed. "Leave me."

So much for the motivational speech, Maddock thought. "Forget it. Just swim."

Kismet broke free of his hold, pushing away, and immediately sank again, but Maddock snared the other man's wrist and kept swimming. Bones was just a couple yards away, then a few feet. A few inches.

Bones reached out and snagged him under the arm, dragging him up onto the ice, and Kismet with him. The cold air left him almost completely paralyzed, barely able to breathe, but he remained fully conscious, fully aware, as Bones dragged him and Kismet back to the snowmobile

"You know it's a good thing you managed to fish yourself out," Bones grumbled as he slung both of them across the passenger seat. "Because no way in hell was I gonna go in there after you."

He stripped off his parka and covered them with it, then rubbed his arms vigorously. "Brrr. You know what, next time a job takes us anywhere that requires long johns, you just count me out."

"Bones," Maddock said, struggling to get the words past his chattering teeth. "Just drive."

20

When the fog of cold finally receded, allowing him to think more or less coherently, Maddock sat up and looked around. He immediately recognized his surroundings—the sleeping cabin of Garral's chartered jet. He was in one of the small beds, stripped naked but concealed under several layers of blankets.

He sat up and looked around, spotted Nick Kismet, similarly covered up, but otherwise looking no worse for wear, thanks, no doubt, to his extraordinary regenerative abilities.

"Welcome back to the land of the living warm," Kismet said, smiling.

Maddock chuckled. "Still hate the desert?"

Kismet inclined his head. "Maybe I'm hating it a little less." He rolled a coffee mug between his palms, one of which, Maddock noted, was wrapped in a thick gauze bandage. He recalled the blood trail in the vault, and the red stain on the crumbling ice just before Kismet had gone in. Kismet's immortality appeared to be wearing off.

Maddock also remembered Hauser's reluctance to manipulate the elemental relics personally. Perhaps he had known, or at least suspected, that the radiation from the combined artifact might have exactly such an effect.

If so, then maybe Hauser had lost his invincibility as well.

Maybe he was truly dead, this time.

One can hope, Maddock thought.

He sat up a little higher. "So what did I miss?

Where's everyone else?"

"Sleeping I think. We've been in the air for a few hours. Dad thought it would be better for us to get out of town before the local authorities got involved. Leda…" He hesitated. "My mother stayed behind to run interference for us. At least, that's what she said. She's probably doing damage control for Prometheus, hiding the existence of the secret vault and recovering whatever she can."

There was a note of bitterness in his tone, as if, despite their evident success in thwarting Hauser, they had been handed a defeat.

"What about the relics?"

Kismet was silent for a long time. When he finally spoke, it was with a weary resigned voice. "I'm sure she'll take care of them."

Epilogue

The woman stood at the bow deck rail of the Norwegian coast guard vessel, statue-still and seemingly impervious to the cold as she stared out across the emptiness of the frozen white landscape. She did not dwell on the events which had transpired nearby just a few days earlier. Things had gone badly, but she did not consider it a failure. That was the thing about experiments; the goal wasn't necessarily to produce a set of desired outcomes, but rather to gather data with which to refine the experiment in the next iteration.

And she felt confident the next iteration would be the last.

Although his actions had very nearly cost her control of the organization, her eldest son's actions were consistent with his psychological profile. In the next phase, she would funnel his reckless ambition, focusing his supernova bright energy into a laser that would cut through the barrier between heaven and earth.

Her thoughts were already on that not-too-distant day.

It would take a few weeks to move the golden god-bodies from the wreckage of the seed vault, but that would be easy enough to do. The local authorities had already circulated the story that global warming in tandem with a power failure, had caused the permafrost inside the vault to melt, assuring the public that Vault Two, which contained almost a million seed samples had escaped unscathed. The repair effort would provide the perfect cover for recovery and removal of the contents of the Prometheus vault, and while she knew that many items had probably been damaged beyond repair, she only needed one viable god-body for completion of the grand design.

Once the anomalies—what her youngest had taken to calling "the elemental relics"—were recovered, she would have Ulrich use them to produce a supply of *ichor*, albeit in a more controlled fashion than before, which would permit Prometheus' scientists to begin harvesting genetic material.

And then?

Then she would be more than just the mother of a pair of demigods.

A voice intruded on her musings. "Ma'am?"

She turned and found one of the ship's officers, bundled up against the cold, standing beside her at the rail. The man had a pinched expression, as if he was the bearer of dire news.

They must have found him, she thought, hiding a smile.

She had told them what to expect, that this was a recovery operation. Ulrich would appear as dead to them, a drowning victim. She would have to move quickly to hide his resurrection from the crew. Keeping her face expressionless, she faced the officer. "Have you found something?"

She was actually surprised it had taken them so long. The crew had been running search lanes using an array of instruments—towed sonar, magnetometers, even a remotely-operated undersea vehicle—for several hours already. The incident had occurred in shallow water, and she had expected quick results.

"No ma'am," the man said, and now she realized the real reason for his apprehension. "There's nothing here.

Nothing at all."

"That's impossible. I saw him go into the ice right here. I saw with my own eyes."

The officer nodded patiently. "All the same, there's no trace of him. The captain requests that we expand the search area."

The woman frowned. She could understand how the body might have been carried away by currents and tides, but the relic should not have been affected by those forces.

Her mind raced with possibilities. Had Ulrich recovered on his own, escaping a watery grave with the relics in hand? It seemed unlikely, especially since she had placed the entire archipelago under intense surveillance almost from the moment she had witnessed her sons falling through the ice, but what other explanation could there be?

This iteration of the experiment was still ongoing, it seemed.

"Ma'am?" the officer asked again.

She blinked still pondering the significance of this development, then faced the officer. "Perhaps I did not see what I thought I saw," she said. "Tell the captain to call off the search and return to port. I have business elsewhere."

The End

ABOUT THE AUTHORS

David Wood is the USA Today bestselling author of the action-adventure series, The Dane Maddock Adventures, and many other works. He also writes fantasy under his David Debord pen name. When not writing, he hosts the Wood on Words podcast. David and his family live in Santa Fe, New Mexico. Visit him online at davidwoodweb.com.

Sean Ellis has authored and co-authored more than two dozen action-adventure novels, including the Nick Kismet adventures, the Jack Sigler/Chess Team series with Jeremy Robinson, and the Jade Ihara adventures with David Wood. He served with the Army National Guard in Afghanistan, and has a Bachelor of Science degree in Natural Resources Policy from Oregon State University. Sean is also a member of the International Thriller Writers organization. He currently resides in Arizona, where he divides his time between writing, adventure sports, and trying to figure out how to save the world. Learn more about Sean at seanellisauthor.com.

Printed in Great Britain
by Amazon